Carol Marinelli recently filled in a form asking for her job title. Thrilled to be able to put down her answer, she put 'writer'. Then it asked what Carol did for relaxation, and she put down the truth—'writing'. The third question asked for her hobbies. Well, not wanting to look obsessed, she crossed her fingers and answered 'swimming'—but, given that the chlorine in the pool does terrible things to her highlights, I'm sure you can guess the real answer!

USA TODAY bestselling and RITA® Award–nominated author **Caitlin Crews** loves writing romance. She teaches her favourite romance novels in creative writing classes at places like UCLA Extension's prestigious Writers' Programme, where she finally gets to utilise the MA and PhD in English Literature she received from the University of York in England. She currently lives in the Pacific Northwest, with her very own hero and too many pets. Visit her at caitlincrews.com.

THE ITALIAN'S FORBIDDEN VIRGIN

CAROL MARINELLI

THE SECRET THAT CAN'T BE HIDDEN

CAITLIN CREWS

MILLS & BOON

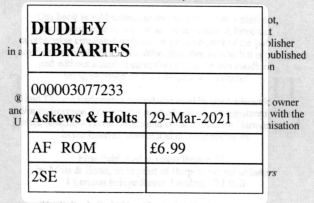

The Italian's Forbidden Virgin © 2021 Carol Marinelli

The Secret That Can't Be Hidden © 2021 Caitlin Crews

ISBN: 978-0-263-28239-9

MIX
Paper from
responsible sources
FSC® C007454

This book is produced from independently certified FSC™ paper
to ensure responsible forest management.
For more information visit www.harpercollins.co.uk/green.

Printed and bound in Spain
by CPI, Barcelona

THE ITALIAN'S FORBIDDEN VIRGIN

CAROL MARINELLI

CHAPTER ONE

GIAN DE LUCA WAS the Duke of Luctano, yet he chose not to use his title. Others, though, could not quite bring themselves to let it go.

And as he finished up the working week in his sumptuous office suite, on the ground floor of his flagship hotel La Fiordelise, in Rome, his PA informed him that his date—for want of a better word—had arrived.

'I was supposed to meet her at the theatre,' Gian said, barely looking up as he signed off on some paperwork.

'Yes,' Luna agreed, for she was more than aware of his heavy schedule and that he kept his private life and work as separate as was possible, 'and a driver was ordered, but it would seem she wanted…'

Luna paused for slight effect, which told Gian she was about to quote directly.

'"To save the Duke the trouble."'

His pen paused and then Gian's final signature of the day appeared darkly on the page as the nib of his pen pressed in firmly. 'I see.'

'She also asked not to be treated as a hotel guest and made to wait in Reception. Given that pre-theatre dining is about to commence, she suggested meeting you in the restaurant.'

Gian held in a weary sigh. His restaurant was not a personal dining room for entertaining lovers. As soon as his dates started throwing around his title like confetti, or attempting to pull rank with his staff, or trying to get too familiar, it signalled the end for Gian. 'Tell her I'll be out shortly.'

'Except you have Ariana Romano in Reception waiting to see you.'

This time Gian could not hold in his sigh. His slate-grey eyes briefly shuttered as he braced himself for a mini-tornado, because it was always drama whenever she suddenly arrived.

If Ariana felt it, she said it.

'What does she want now?'

'A private matter, apparently.'

He kept his door open to her, given he was friends with her father Rafael and older brother Dante, in as much as Gian was friends with anyone. Growing up, he had been sent to Luctano each summer to stay with some distant aunt and her husband who, like his parents, hadn't much wanted him around. Those summers had often been spent hanging out with the Romanos.

Aside from the family ties, there were business connections too. Ariana was on the committee for the Romano Foundation Ball, which was held here at La Fiordelise each year. In small doses Gian chose to tolerate her, yet she was somewhat of an irritant. Rather like heavily scented jasmine in the flower arrangement in the foyer, or when lilies were left out just a little too long. Ariana had clung and irritated long after she had left and now, on a Friday evening, he had to deal with her in person.

'Bring her through then,' Gian said. 'Oh, and then take Svetlana through to the Pianoforte Bar to wait for me there...'

And there he would end their...*liaison*.

At thirty-five, Gian was considered one of Italy's most eligible bachelors.

His wealth and dark brooding looks were certainly a factor, but Gian was no fool and was aware that his title was coveted. He was the Duke of Luctano, even though his family had left the Tuscan hillsides generations ago and he had been born and raised in Rome. Or, rather, Gian had raised himself, for his hedonistic parents had had no time or inclination for their son.

Gian was, in fact, Italy's most *ineligible* bachelor for he had no interest in marriage or settling down and always stated up front with women that, apart from a handful of lavish dates, they would go no further than bed.

Gian had long ago decided that the De Luca lineage *would* end with him.

His sex life—Gian had never so much as contemplated the word 'love'—was rather like the stunning brass revolving doors at the entrance to La Fiordelise—wealth and beauty came in, was spoiled and pampered for the duration, but all too soon was ejected back out into the real world. Svetlana's behaviour was nothing unexpected: she had shown her true colours to his PA, and that was that.

They all did in the end.

Gian was jaded rather than bitter, and more than ready to get through this meeting with Ariana and then deal swiftly with Svetlana. So much so that he didn't bother to step into the luxury suite behind his office to freshen up for a night at Teatro dell'Opera; the gorgeous box with its pink-lined walls would remain empty tonight.

As would the luxurious suite behind his office.

His lovers never got so much as a toe in the door of his private apartment at La Fiordelise, for Gian was intensely private.

He sat drumming his fingers silently on his large black walnut desk, waiting for Ariana to arrive. But then, on a wintry and gloomy January evening, it was as if a vertical sunrise stepped into his office. Ariana's long black hair was slicked back into a low bun and she wore a suit and high heels. Except it was no ordinary suit. It was orange. The skirt sat just above the knee and the no doubt bespoke stockings were in exactly the same shade, as were the velvet stilettoes and large bag she carried over her shoulder. On most people the outfit would look ridiculous, but on pencil-thin Ariana it looked tasteful and bright…like a streak of burnt gold on the horizon heralding a new day.

Gian refused to be dazzled and reminded himself of the absolute diva she was. Ariana was the one who should be performing at Teatro dell'Opera tonight!

'Gian,' she purred, and gave him her signature red-lipped smile. It was the same smile that set the cameras flashing on the red carpets in Rome, but Gian remained steadfastly unimpressed—not that he showed it, for he was more than used to dealing with the most pampered guests.

'Ariana.' He pushed back his chair to stand and greet her. 'You look amazing as always.' He said all the right things, though could not help but add, 'Very orange.'

'Cinnamon, Gian,' she wryly corrected as her heart did the oddest thing.

It stopped.

Gian *should* be familiar. After all, she had known him all her life, yet she was suddenly reminded of his height and the deep tone of his voice. He wore a subtly checked suit in grey with a waistcoat, though his height meant that he wore the check rather than the check wearing him.

Of course her heart had started again—had it not she would have dropped to the floor—but it was jumping around in some ungainly trot as he walked towards her.

Pure nerves, Ariana decided. After all, she did have a huge favour to ask!

'I apologise for not coming out to greet you,' Gian said

as he came around the desk and kissed her on both cheeks. 'I was just finishing up some work.'

'That's fine. Luna took good care of me.'

Except she felt far from fine. Ariana rather wished that the nerves in her chest would abate, yet they fluttered like butterflies—or perhaps fireflies would be a more apt description because there was a flash of heat creeping up her neck and searing her cheeks, but then Gian was, to say the least, rather commanding.

Cold, people called him.

Especially back home in Luctano, where gossip and rumour abounded. The history of the De Lucas was often whispered about and discussed in her home town—at times even by her family. Though a child at the time, Ariana could well remember the shock and horror in the village as news of the fire aboard their luxury yacht had hit in the early hours of a Sunday morning. And, of course, she still remembered the funeral held in Luctano for the Duke, the Duchess and the heir apparent...

People whispered about the fact that Luca hadn't attended the renewal of his parents' vows, and his lack of visible emotion at the funeral.

Yet, as Ariana sometimes pointed out, the fact that he hadn't attended had saved his life.

And, the villagers would add, happy to twist the truth, *his brother's death made him a duke*. As if Gian had swum out into the ocean and torched the boat himself!

'Basta!' Ariana would tell them.

Enough!

Ariana actually *liked* his steely reserve.

Her own self was so volatile that when life spun too fast, it was to Gian she turned for his distant, measured ways.

While rumour had it he melted women in the bedroom and endeared both staff and guests with his calm assertiveness, it was the general consensus that behind his polished façade there was no heart or emotion, just a wall of solid black ice. Ariana needed that wall of black ice on side so she kept her smile bright. 'Thank you for agreeing to see me.'

'Of course.' Gian gestured for her to take a seat as he did the same. 'Can I offer you some refreshments?'

'No, thank you.' Gosh, small talk was difficult when you had a huge favour to ask! 'How was your Christmas?'

'Busy,' Gian responded, then politely enquired, 'Yours?'

Ariana lifted her hand and made a wavering gesture, to show it had not been the best, though she did not bore Gian with the details, like how, in the manner of a tennis ball in an extended rally, she'd bounced between Florence and Rome. Gian already knew all about her parents' divorce and her father's subsequent marriage to the much younger Mia. After all the marriage had taken place here!

And he knew too that her father wasn't at home in Luctano but in a private hospital in Florence and so she gave him a brief update. 'Dante is hoping to have Papà moved here to Rome,' Ariana said, but left out the *hospice* word. 'That should make things a bit easier.'

'Easier for whom?' Gian enquired.

'For his family,' Ariana responded tartly, but then squirmed inwardly, for it was the very question she had been asking herself since her brothers had suggested the move. 'His children are all here, his Rome office...' Her voice trailed off. Though the impressive Romano Holdings offices were in the EUR business district of Rome, Dante had taken over the running of the company when their father had remarried.

Gian's question was a pertinent one—and confirmed for Ariana that she needed to speak with her father and find out exactly what it was *he* wanted for the final months of his life. 'It is not all decided,' she admitted to Gian. 'We are just testing ideas.'

'Good,' Gian said, and she blinked at the gentler edge to his tone. 'I visited him yesterday.'

'You visited him in Florence?'

'Of course. You know I have a sister hotel opening there in May?' Gian checked, and Ariana nodded. 'I always try and drop in on Rafael when I am there.'

For some reason that brought the threat of tears to her eyes, but she hastily blinked them back. Ariana was not one for tears—well, not real ones; crocodile tears she excelled at—but at times Florence, where her father was in hospital, felt so far away. It was an hour or so by plane and she visited as much as she could. So did her brothers, and of course Mia was there and the family home in Luctano was nearby...but at night, when she couldn't sleep, Ariana always thought of her father alone.

There was a break in the conversation that Gian did absolutely nothing to fill. A pregnant pause was something Ariana was incapable of. If there was a gap she felt duty-bound to speak. Any lull in proceedings and she felt it her place to perform. Gian, she felt, would let this silence stretch for ever and so of course it was she who ended it. 'Gian, there is a reason I am here...'

Of course there was!

Her slender hands twisted in her lap. She was nervous, Gian realised. This was most unlike Ariana, who was usually supremely confident—arrogant, in fact. It dawned on him then what this urgent appointment might be about. Did she want to bring her latest lover here, without it being billed to the Romano guest folio so as to avoid her father or brothers finding out?

It was often the case with family accounts, but if that was what Ariana was about to ask him...

No way!

There was no question he would facilitate her bringing

her latest lover to stay here! 'What is it you want?' Gian asked, and she blinked at the edge to his tone.

'I have decided that I want a career.'

'A career?' His features relaxed and there was even a shadow of a smile that he did not put down to relief that she wasn't intending to bring her lover here. It was typical of Ariana to say she wanted a career, rather than a job. 'Really?'

'Yes.' She nodded. 'I've given it a great deal of thought.'

'And your career of choice?'

'I would like to be Guest Services Manager here at La Fiordelise. Or rather I would like to be Guest Services Manager for your VIPs.'

'All of my guests are VIPs, Ariana.'

'You *know* what I mean.'

He had to consciously resist rolling his eyes. 'Why would I simply hand you such a position when you have no experience? Why would I let you near my VIPs?'

'Because I am one!' Ariana retorted, but then rather hurriedly checked herself. 'What I am trying to say is that I know their ways. Please, Gian. I really want this.'

Gian knew very well that whatever Ariana wanted, Ariana got—until she grew bored and dismissed it. Ariana should have been put over her father's knee many years ago and learned the meaning of the word 'no'. There was no way on God's earth that she was going to *play* careers at his hotel. So, rather than go through the motions, he shook his head. 'Ariana, let me stop you right there. While I appreciate—'

'Actually,' she cut in swiftly, 'I *would* like some refreshments after all. Perhaps, given the hour, some champagne is in order.' Her pussycat smile was triumphant as she prevented him ending their conversation.

Ever the consummate host, Gian nodded politely. *'Nat-*

uralmente.' He pressed the intercom. 'Luna, would you please bring in champagne for myself and Ariana.'

Ariana's smile remained. No doubt, Gian assumed, she was thinking she had won, but what she did not quite understand was that Gian was always and absolutely one step ahead. Luna had worked at La Fiordelise even before his family had died and knew his nuances well. It was often what was *not* said that counted, and right at this moment Vincenzo, the bar manager, would be pouring two *glasses* of French champagne.

A bottle and ice bucket would *not* be arriving.

This was no tête-à-tête.

'I have brought my résumé,' Ariana said, digging in her suede designer *cinnamon* bag and producing a document, which she handed to him. He took it without a word and as he read through it, Gian found again that he fought an incredulous smile.

For someone who had practically never worked a day in her life, Ariana Romano had an impressive résumé indeed.

At least, it *read* well. She had studied hospitality and tourism management, although he knew that already. Naturally, she was on the Romano Board, and on the Romano Foundation Board too.

As well as that were listed all the luncheons, balls and functions which Ariana claimed to have planned and organised singlehandedly. Except—

'Ariana, you do not "create, design and implement the theme for the annual Romano Foundation Ball",' Gian said, and used his fingers to quote directly from her résumé. 'My staff do.'

'Well, I have major input.'

'No, Ariana, you don't. In fact, you barely show up for the meetings.'

'I always attend.'

'I can have Luna retrieve the minutes of them if you

like. You rarely show up and you don't even bother to send an apology. The fact is you consistently let people down.'

'Excuse me!' Ariana reared, unused to him speaking so harshly, for, though cold, Gian was always polite.

Except here, today, they had entered unknown territory.

Usually when they discussed the Romano Ball, given the fact she was Rafael's daughter, Ariana's suggestions were tolerated, lauded even. Now, though, Gian refused to play the usual game of applauding her inaction, or nodding as she reeled off one of her less-than-well-thought-out ideas. He picked last year's ball as an example. 'You said you were thinking "along the lines of silver" and no doubt went off to plan your gown.'

He watched her lips press tightly together. Even clamped shut, Ariana had a very pretty mouth, but he quickly dragged his attention away from that thought and back to the point he was trying to make. 'Following your suggestion, my staff created a silver world, whereas you did nothing more than turn up on the night...' he held her angry gaze '...in a silver gown.'

'How nice that you remember what I was wearing,' Ariana retorted.

'Call it an educated guess.'

Ouch!

Suddenly, under his withering gaze, in this private meeting she had demanded, Ariana felt as gauche and naive as the virgin she was, rather than the temptress she portrayed. 'Well, I was the one who came up with a forest theme for this year,' Ariana reminded him.

'Tell me,' Gian pushed, 'what have you done to help implement the forest theme, apart from choose the fabric for your gown?'

Ariana opened her mouth to answer and then closed it. He watched her shoulders briefly slump in defeat, but then she rallied. 'I suggested ivy around the pillars in the ballroom.'

He looked as unimpressed with her suggestion as he had at the board meeting, Ariana thought. But, then, Gian considered decorations and themes and such somewhat vulgar.

'And berries,' Ariana hurriedly. 'I suggested a berry dessert. Fruits of the forest...'

Gian did not so much as blink; he just stared at her pretty, empty head.

Only...that wasn't right, and he knew it.

Ariana, when she so chose, was perceptive and clever, but he refused to relent. 'What about last month, December, the hotel's busiest time, and you reserved the Pianoforte Bar for yourself and your friends' exclusive use, yet forgot to let Reservations know that it was no longer required.'

'You were paid,' Ariana interrupted. 'My father—'

'Precisely.' It was Gian who now interrupted. '*Your father* took care of things. It is so very typical of you, Ariana. If something better comes along, then that is where your attention goes.'

'No!' Ariana shook her head, angrily at first but then in sudden bewilderment because he was usually so polite. 'Why are you speaking to me like this, Gian?'

'So that you understand completely why my answer to your request is no.'

It sounded as if he meant it, and Ariana wasn't particularly used to that so she tried another tack. 'I studied hospitality and—'

'I know you did.' Again, Gian cut her off. 'You might remember that it was necessary for you to do three months' work experience to pass your course and so I spoke to your father and offered for you to do your placement here.' His eyes never left her face. 'You failed to show up on your starting day.'

Ariana flushed. 'Because I decided to do my placement at the family hotel in Luctano.'

'And you didn't even think to let me know?'

'I thought my father's staff had contacted you.'

But Gian shook his head. 'The fact is, Ariana, you chose the easier option.'

'I wanted to work here, Gian,' Ariana insisted. 'But my parents wanted me at the family hotel.'

'No.' Gian shook his head, refusing to accept her twisted truth. 'You declined when I explained that your placement would consist of *working* in all areas of the hotel. You were to spend a week in the kitchen, a week as a chambermaid, a week—'

It was Ariana who interrupted now, her voice fighting not to rise as she cut in. 'I felt I would get more experience in Luctano.'

'Really?' Gian checked. 'You thought you would get more experience at a small boutique resort in the Tuscan hills than at an award-winning, five-star hotel in the heart of Rome?'

'Yes,' she attempted. 'Well, perhaps not as extensive as I would have had here but...' Her voice trailed off because her excuse was as pathetic as it sounded, but there was another reason entirely that his offer to work at La Fiordelise had been declined all those years ago. 'That wasn't the only reason I said no, Gian. The fact is, my mother didn't want me working here.'

'Why ever not?'

Even as she opened her mouth to speak, even as the words tumbled out, Ariana knew she should never be saying them. 'Because of your reputation with women.'

CHAPTER TWO

'PARDON?'

Gian was supremely polite as he asked her to repeat her accusation, but far from backtracking or apologising, Ariana clarified her words.

'My mother didn't want me working here because of your reputation with women.' She didn't even blush as she said it. If anything, she was defiant.

Still, such was the sudden tension that it was a relief when there was a knock on the door and soon Luna was placing down little white coasters decorated with La Fiordelise's swirling rose gold insignia and two long, pale flutes of champagne, as well as a little silver dish of nibbles.

The dish in itself was beautiful, heavy silver with three little heart-shaped trays, individually filled with nuts, slivers of fruit and chocolates.

It was easier to focus on incidentals because, despite her cool demeanour, Ariana could feel the crackle in the air that denoted thunder, and as the door closed on Luna, she stared at the pretty dish as she re-crossed her legs at the ankles.

'Ariana.' Gian's voice was seemingly smooth but there was a barbed edge to his tone that tempted her to retrieve her bag and simply run. Gian carried on, 'Before we continue this conversation, can I make one thing supremely clear?'

'Of course,' Ariana said. Unable to look at him any longer, she reached for a glass.

'Your mother had no right to imply or suggest that I would be anything other than professional with the work experience girl—or, in fact, any of my staff!'

'Well, you do have a formidable reputation...' Ariana started and raised the glass to her lips.

'With *women*,' Gian interrupted and then tartly added, 'Not teenage girls, which you were back *then*.'

Ariana nodded, the glass still hovering by her mouth. Even as he told her off, even as he scolded her for going too far, there was something else that had been said there— that she was different now compared to then.

She was a woman.

And Gian De Luca was a very good-looking man.

She had known that, of course. His undoubtedly handsome looks had always been there—something she had registered, but only at a surface level. Yet today it had felt as if she'd been handed a pair of magical eyeglasses and she wanted to weep as she saw colour for the first time.

He was beautiful.

Exquisitely so.

His jet-black hair framed a haughty face, and his mouth, though unsmiling, was plump in contrast to the razor-sharp cheekbones and straight nose.

She could not be in lust with Gian *and* work for him— that would never ever do!

She wanted to pull off those imaginary glasses, to be plunged back into a monotone world, where Gian De Luca was just, well...

Gian.

Not a name she wanted to roll on her tongue.

Not a mouth she now wanted to taste.

He was just Gian, she reminded herself.

The person she ran to when trouble loomed large.

She put her glass down on the small coaster as she attempted to push her inappropriate thoughts aside and rescue the interview. 'Mamma didn't mean it, Gian. You know what she can be like…'

'Yes.' Gian held in a pained sigh. 'I do.'

Too well he recalled joining the Romanos at their dinner table as a small boy. *'Straccione,'* Angela would say, ruffling his hair as he took a seat at the table. It had sounded like an affectionate tease; after all, how could the son of a duke and duchess be a ragamuffin and a beggar?

Except Angela had found the cruellest knife to dig into his heart, and she knew how to twist it, for Gian had always felt like a beggar for company.

Gian wasn't quite sure why Angela rattled him so much.

Ariana did too, albeit it in an increasingly different way.

He did not want Ariana working here. And not just because of her precious ways but because of this…this pull, this awareness, this attraction that did not sit well with him. 'Let's just leave things there, shall we?' he suggested. 'While we're still able to be civil. I could put you in touch with the director at Hotel Rav—' He went to name his closest rival but Ariana cut in even before he had finished.

'I was already offered a job there, and in several other hotels as well, but each time it was in return for some media coverage. I really don't want cameras following me on my first day.'

'Fair enough.' While he understood that, the rest he didn't get. 'What *are* you hoping to achieve by this, Ariana?'

'More than I am right now,' she said, and gave a hollow laugh.

He looked at her then.

Properly looked.

Ariana was, of course, exquisitely beautiful, with a delicate bone structure, but he suddenly noticed that rather than the trademark black eyes of her father and brothers, or the icy blue ones of her mother, Ariana's eyes were a deep navy-violet, almost as if they'd tried to get from blue to black, but had surrendered just shy of arrival.

Gian rather wished he hadn't noticed the beguiling colour of them and rapidly diverted his gaze back to her résumé.

'Why don't you formally interview me?' Ariana suggested. 'As if we don't know each other. Surely you can do that?'

'Of course, but if you want an honest interview, what happens if you are not successful?' She wouldn't be, he knew, but as he looked up she held his gaze as she answered.

'Then I shall walk away, knowing I tried.'

Walk away, Gian wanted to warn her, for there was a sudden energy between them that could never end well.

He scanned through her supposed work experience and attempted to wipe out a lifetime of history so they could face each other as two strangers. In the end, he reverted to his usual interview technique. 'Tell me about a recent time when you had to deal with a difficult client or contact…'

She wouldn't be able to, Gian was certain.

'Well…' Ariana thought for a moment. 'I wanted an interview with the owner of a very prestigious hotel, but I did not want to utilise my family contacts as I felt that would do me no favours.'

Gian felt his lips tighten when it became clear that she was speaking about trying to get in contact with him. 'Ariana,' he cut in, 'may I suggest that you don't make the person interviewing you the *difficult contact*.'

'But he was difficult. My goal was to get a full audience,' Ariana continued, 'and so I sent in my résumé, but when I heard nothing back…'

'You sent in an application?' Gian started scrolling through his computer, *almost* apologetic now, because an application from Ariana Romano *should* have been flagged—at the very least so he could personally reject her. 'Vanda has been on leave over the festive period…' He paused, for he could find nothing. 'When did you send it?'

'This morning,' Ariana replied, and then took a sip of her champagne.

'This morning.' Gian sighed, and leaned back in his chair. He looked upon the epitome of instant gratification. When Ariana wanted something she wanted it now!

'So, when I heard nothing back, I printed off my résumé and took it to him personally.'

'And what was the result?'

'I made him smile,' Ariana said.

'No,' Gian corrected, 'you didn't.'

'Almost.'

'Not even close.' He let out a breath as he tried to hold onto patience. 'Ariana, you asked for a proper interview, so treat it as if we've never met. Now, tell me about a time you were able to deal successfully with another person even when you may not have liked them.'

'Okay…' She chewed her bottom lip and thought for less than a moment. 'My father was recently given a terminal diagnosis. He still has months to live,' she added rather urgently, 'but…' She swallowed, for Ariana could not bear to think of a time months from now and dragged her mind back to the present. 'I am not a fan of his new wife.'

'Ariana, I am asking about professional—'

'However,' she cut in, 'I spoke calmly to her and said that I would like to be part of all interviews with the doctors and that for his sake, we should at least be polite.'

Curiosity got the better of him. 'How is that working out?'

She gave a snooty sniff and re-crossed her legs. 'We've both kept our sides of the agreement.'

Gian rather doubted it. Ariana and Mia were a toxic mix indeed! 'I was actually hoping you could give me examples that involve work, Ariana.'

'Oh, believe me,' she countered. 'Mia is work.'

Gian just wanted this charade over and done with. Both their glasses were nearly empty so he would ask one more question and then send her on her precocious way. 'Tell me about a time where you did something for someone else, not to earn favour, and without letting them know.'

'That would defeat the purpose,' Ariana deftly answered, 'if I later use it in an interview to show how benevolent I am.'

He liked her answer. In fact, were it a real interview, it might score her points, except he wasn't sure that Ariana wasn't simply being evasive. 'It's an important question, Ariana,' he told her. 'The role of Guest Services is to make a stay at La Fiordelise appear seamlessly unique. The aim is that our guests never know the work that goes on behind the scenes. So,' he added, 'I would like an honest answer.'

'Very well.' She was hesitant, though, for to tell him revealed more than she cared to. 'My brother...' She tried to remember that this was an interview and she should treat Gian as if he were a stranger. 'My twin brother, Stefano, is to marry soon—at the end of May.'

'And?'

'I have been somewhat excluded from the wedding plans.'

'Despite your extensive planning experience,' he added rather drily.

'Despite that!' Ariana answered crisply. 'They have decided that they don't need my help.'

He saw the jut of her chin and that her hands were rigid in her lap, and suddenly Gian did not like the question he had asked, for he could see it was hurting her to answer.

'Eloa,' Ariana continued, 'Stefano's fiancée, had her heart set on the wedding being held at Palazzo Pamphili…'

'Where the Brazilian Embassy is housed.' Gian nodded. He knew it well, for the superb building was across the square from the hotel, and even with his connections he knew how hard it would be to arrange a wedding there.

'I sorted it,' Ariana said.

'How?' Gian frowned, quietly impressed.

'That is for me to know,' Ariana responded. 'However, to this day, Eloa and Stefano think that they arranged the reception venue by themselves.'

'You haven't told them that you were behind it?'

'No. They have made it clear they don't want my help and it might sour things for them to know I had a hand in it.'

She watched as he put down her résumé and she continued to watch his long fingers join and arch into a steeple. He slowly drew a breath and Ariana felt certain that he had not been persuaded, and that she was about to be told that his answer was still no. 'I really do want to work, Gian.' There was a slightly frantic note to her voice, which she fought to quash, but there was also desperation in her eyes that she could not hide. 'I love the hotel industry and, you're right, I should have done my placement here…' It wasn't just that, though. 'I want some real independence. I'm tired of—' She stopped herself, sure that Gian did not need to hear it.

Yet he found that he wanted to. 'Go on,' Gian invited, casting his more regular interview technique aside.

'I'm tired of living in an apartment my family owns, tired of being on call when my mother decides I can drop everything for her. After all,' she mimicked a derisive tone, 'I couldn't *possibly* be busy.' She screwed her eyes closed in frustration, unable to properly explain the claustrophobic feeling of her privileged world.

Oh, many might say that life had been handed to Ariana Romano on a plate.

The trouble was, it wasn't necessarily a feast of her choosing.

While she had a family who seemingly adored her, even as a child Ariana had always been told to take her toys and play somewhere else.

To this day it persisted.

While she had access to wealth most people could only dream of, there was a perpetual feeling of emptiness. For Ariana, the golden cup she drank from was so shot through with holes that no gifts—no trust-funded central Rome apartment, no wild party, no designer outfit or A-list appearance—filled her soul.

'I want a career,' Ariana insisted.

'Why now?' Gian pushed.

'It's a new year, a time when everyone takes stock…' She suddenly looked beyond Gian to the window behind him and saw white flakes dance in the darkness. 'It is starting to snow.'

'Don't change the subject,' Gian said, without so much as turning his head to take in the weather. It was Ariana he was more interested in. 'Why now, Ariana?'

Because I'm lonely, she wanted to say.

Because before Mia came along, I thought I had something of a career at Romano Holdings.

Because my days are increasingly empty and there surely has to be more to life than this?

Of course, she could not answer with that, and so she took a breath and attempted a more dignified response. 'I want to make something of myself, by myself. I want, for a few hours a day, to take off the Romano name. Look, I know what I'm asking is a favour, but—'

'Let me stop you right there,' he cut in. 'I don't do favours.'

There was from Ariana a slight, almost inaudible laugh, yet Gian understood its wry gist and conceded. 'Perhaps I make concessions for your father, but he was very good to me when…'

Gian didn't finish but Ariana knew he was referring to when his brother and parents had died and, to her nosy shame, Ariana hoped to hear more. 'When what?' she asked, as if she didn't know.

Nobody did silence better than Gian.

Surely, not a soul on this earth was as comfortable with silence as he, for he just stared right back at her and refused to elaborate.

It was Ariana who filled the long gap. 'I didn't get my father to lean on you, Gian,' she pointed out. 'I'm trying my best to do this by myself.'

'I know that,' Gian admitted, for if she had asked her father to call in a favour, then Rafael would have had a quiet word with him when he'd visited yesterday.

'I won't let you down, Gian.'

But even with Ariana's assurances, Gian was hesitant. He did not want Ariana to be his problem. He did not need the complication of hiring and, no doubt, having to fire her. And yet, *and yet*, he grudgingly admired her attempt to make something of herself, aside from the family name she'd been born into.

She broke into his thoughts then. 'Perhaps you could show me around?'

'I do not give guided tours to potential staff, that is Vanda's domain…'

'Ah, so I'm "potential staff" now?'

'I did not say that.'

'Then, as a family friend, you can show me around.'

Gian took a breath, and looked into navy violet eyes and better understood the predicament her parents must find themselves in at times. How the hell did you say no to that?

CHAPTER THREE

To the surprise of both of them, Gian agreed to the tour of La Fiordelise.

Ariana's clear interest in the hotel pleased him, and if it had been a real interview, her request would have impressed him indeed.

'Just a short tour…' he nodded '…given you are my final appointment for the day.'

Perhaps it was the single glass of champagne on a nervously empty stomach, but Ariana was giddy with excitement as she stood up. There was even a heady thought that perhaps they might conclude the tour in the restaurant, and then dinner, of course.

And there Gian would offer her the role of VIP Guest Services Manager!

Oh, she could just picture herself in the bespoke blush tartan suits and pearls that the guest services managers wore!

It felt very different walking through the foyer with Gian at her side. Ariana was more than used to turning heads, but there was a certain deference that Gian commanded. Staff straightened at his approach, and guests nudged each other when he passed. There was a certain *something* about Gian that was impossible to define. Something more than elegance, more than command.

Ariana would like to name it.

To bottle it.

To dab her wrists with the essence he emanated.

Soon they had passed Reception and the Pianoforte Bar where, unbeknownst to Ariana, Svetlana sat drumming her fingers on the table, her silver platter of nuts empty, as was her glass. Vincenzo was taking care of that, though, and shaking another cocktail for her, yet Gian barely gave her a glance. He was working after all.

'You know the Pianoforte Bar…' Gian said rather drily, thinking of the array of colour Ariana and her friends made as they breezed in on a Friday night for cocktails to get the weekend underway. 'No doubt your friend Nicki shall be here soon.'

'She shan't be,' Ariana said. 'Nicki is away, skiing with friends.'

'Don't you usually go?'

'Yes, but I didn't want to be stuck on a mountain with Papà so unwell so I told them to go ahead without me.'

'They're staying at the Romano chalet?'

'Of course.' Ariana gave a tight shrug. 'Just because I can't go it doesn't mean I should let everyone down. It's our annual trip.'

That took place on her dime, Gian thought.

He loathed her hangers-on, and all too often had to hold his tongue when her entitled, self-important friends arrived at La Fiordelise courtesy of her name.

He could not hold his tongue now. 'Your partner was asked to leave here the other week.'

'My partner?' Ariana frowned, wondering who he meant. 'Oh, you mean Paulo…'

'I don't know his name,' Gian lied.

Absolutely he knew his name, and those of her so-called friends who added their drinks to the Romano tab, even when Ariana was not here. Gian had even spoken to Rafael about it and had been disappointed with his response: 'Any friend of Ariana's...'

Could Rafael not see his daughter was being used? No, because in his declining years it was easier for Rafael not to see!

'Paulo was never my partner,' Ariana cut in. 'He and I, well...' She shrugged, uncertain how to describe them. 'It's just business, I guess.'

'Business?' Gian checked.

'The business of being seen.'

Oh, Ariana...

Still, she was not here for life advice, so Gian brushed his fleeting sympathy aside and got on with the tour.

'This is the Terazza Suite. It caters for up to thirty and is used for smaller, very exclusive functions...'

'Is this where my father married *her*?' Ariana asked, refusing to use Mia's name. She had been invited to the wedding, but of course neither she nor her brothers had chosen to attend.

'Yes,' Gian said, without elaborating about the wedding. 'It opens out to a terrace adjacent to the square, though it is too cold to go out there now.'

'I would like to see it.'

The Terazza Suite was empty, but it took little imagination to see that the gold stencilled walls and high ceilings would make a romantic venue indeed.

One wall was lined with French windows and when she pushed down on a handle Ariana found that of course it was locked. *'Per favore?'* she asked. She sensed his reluctance, but Gian first pressed a discreet alarm on the wall then took out his master key and unlocked a door.

As she stepped out it was not the frigid air that caught her breath, more the beauty of the surroundings. There was the chatter and laughter from the square, which was visible through an ornate fence.

'In spring and summer there is a curtain of wisteria that blocks the noise,' Gian explained, looking up at the naked vines, 'but it can be dressed for privacy in winter.' He told her about a recent Christmas wedding with boxed firs for privacy, only Ariana wasn't really listening.

Instead, her silence was borne of regret for not being here to support her father…

'Certainly,' Gian continued, 'it is perfect for more intimate gatherings…'

'You mean weddings that no one wants to attend,' Ariana said, shame and regret making her suddenly defensive.

'You are showing your age, Ariana,' Gian said.

'My age?' Ariana frowned as they stepped back into the warmth and he locked up behind them. 'I'm twenty-five.'

'I meant in brat years,' Gian said, and left her standing there, mouth gaping in indignation as he marched on, just wanting this tour to be over. 'You already know the ballroom…' He waved in its general direction as she caught up, but Ariana had more than a ballroom on her mind.

'Did you just call me a brat?' She couldn't quite believe what he had said.

'Yes,' he said. 'I did.'

'You can't talk to me like that.'

'You're almost right. Once I employ you I can't tell you what an insufferable, spoilt little madam you are…'

But though most people would have burst into tears at his tone, Gian knew Ariana better than that. Instead he watched her red lips part into a smile as realisation hit. 'You're going to take me on, then?'

'I haven't quite decided yet,' Gian said. 'Come on.'

'But I want to see the ballroom.'

'They are in the final preparations for a function tonight.'

'I would so love to see how others do it,' she said, ignoring Gian and opening one of the heavy, ornate doors and gasping when she peeked in. 'Oh, it looks so beautiful.'

'It is a fortieth wedding anniversary celebration,' Gian told her.

'Ruby,' Ariana sighed, for the tables were dressed with deep red roses and they were in the middle of a final test of the lighting so that even the heavy chandeliers cast rubies of light around the room with stunning effect. 'I know I get angry about my parents' divorce,' she admitted—although as she gazed into the ballroom it was almost as if she was speaking to herself— 'and it is not all Mia's fault, I accept that, but I was always so proud of their marriage. Of course, it was not *my* achievement, but I was so proud of them for still being together when so many marriages fail...'

She gave him pause. Gian looked at her as she spoke, and could almost see the stars in her eyes as she gazed at the gorgeous ballroom.

'I should have gone to Papà's wedding,' Ariana said, for the first time voicing her private remorse. 'I deeply regret that I stayed away.'

Gian was rarely torn to break a confidence. The truth was, Rafael had been relieved that his children had not attended the nuptials. It was a marriage in name only, a brief service, followed by drinks on the terrace, then a cake and kiss for the cameras...

As the owner of several prestigious hotels, Gian was the keeper of many secrets.

So outrageous were the many scandals that Gian was privy to that the Romanos and their rather reprobate ways barely registered a blip. But it would be a seismic event if Ariana found out the truth about her parents.

Their marriage had been over long before their divorce. Angela Romano had been with her lover for decades.

Prior to the divorce, Angela and Thomas had often enjoyed extended midweek breaks at La Fiordelise.

Rafael would not blink an eye if he knew; in fact, Gian, assumed that he did. For those long business lunches Rafael had enjoyed with Roberto—his lawyer—had, in fact, been rare public outings for a devoted couple who had been together for more than fifteen years.

As for Mia…

Well, Gian to this day did not understand Angela's hatred towards her, when close friends all knew that Mia was Rafael's beard—a prop used to prevent the world from finding out in his declining years that Rafael Romano was gay. Perhaps, if Ariana could have this necessary conversation with her father, it might lead him to reveal his truth before it was too late or, worse, before she inadvertently found out.

'Why don't you tell your father that you regret not being at his wedding?' Gian suggested. 'Talk to him about it…'

'I try to stay upbeat when I visit him.'

'Tell him how you feel,' Gian gently pushed, and saw that she was thinking about it.

'I might.' She nodded and then turned to him with a question no one had ever dared ask. 'Were your parents happy?'

It was just a question, and it flowed from the context perhaps, but he had to think for a long moment, to cast his mind back, to the parties, to the laughter, to the inappropriate mess that had been them, and for once he did not choose silence. 'Yes,' Gian finally answered. 'They were happy because they followed only their hearts and not their heads.' When she frowned, clearly nonplussed, Gian explained further. 'Their happiness was to the exclusion of all else.'

'Including you?'

He did not answer and Ariana knew she had crossed the line, but now they were in this odd standoff.

They looked at each other. His thick black hair was so superbly cut that as she looked up at him she felt the oddest temptation to raise her hand and simply touch it, and to see if it fell back into perfect shape, but of course impulse had no place here, and anyway it was just a thought. But that made it a red button that said *do not touch*, and consequently made her itch to do so. 'Including you?' she persisted.

'This is an interview, Ariana, the purpose of which is to find out more about you, not the other way around.'

Under her breath she muttered, 'Your life is an interview then.'

'Pardon?'

'It just dawned on me, Gian, that you know an awful lot about me, but I know practically nothing about you.'

'Good,' he clipped.

It wasn't good, though. Suddenly there was a whole lot that Ariana wanted to know about him, and her heart suddenly stopped with its ungainly trot and kicked into a gallop.

He angered her.

Only that wasn't quite right, because anger didn't make her thighs suddenly clamp, or her lips ache. And anger didn't make her knickers damp or give her an urge to kiss that haughty, arrogant face. This was something else entirely, though her voice when she spoke was indeed cross. 'Are you going to hire me or not, Gian?'

'I am hesitant to.'

While he wanted to afford her a new start, Ariana working here spelt Trouble.

In more ways than one.

Yes, she was airy and spoilt and brattish, but he could almost feel the prickle of her under his skin and that was an attraction that was safer to deny. 'If it doesn't work out—' he started.

'It *will* work out,' she broke in. 'I shall make it so!'

And I will push all thoughts of fancying you aside, Ariana hurriedly thought.

'You would still have to do the twelve-week induction.' He wasn't asking, he was telling. 'It is mandatory that all my guest services staff have personally worked in every area of the hotel.'

'Yes.' Ariana nodded. 'I'll do the induction.'

'If you are successful in your introductory period then there might be a position as a guest services *assistant*...'

'But—'

'My managers earn their titles, Ariana.' He watched two spots of colour start to burn on her cheeks. 'And there will be no favours and no concessions. From this point on, the trajectory of your career is in your hands. You will report on Monday at seven to Vanda, who deals with staff training, and any issues you have, you take to her, not me.'

'Of course.'

He wasn't sure she got it, though. 'Ariana, this is my hotel, and I separate things, so if you work here you must understand that I don't deal with the grumbles of minor staff. I don't want to hear about your day; I simply do not want to know. I don't want to hear you can't handle vomit or difficult guests. You take it up with Vanda. Not my problem...'

'Of course.'

'And there shall be no stopping by my office for champagne. That stops today! In fact, as of now there will be no need to drop by my office at all.'

She pouted. 'You said I could always come to you.'

He had.

And over the years *she* had.

Not all her confessionals took place in his office, though. They went way further back than that.

Once in Luctano, an eight-year-old Ariana, too scared to confide in her older brother Dante, had admitted to an eighteen-year-old Gian that she had stolen chocolate from the local store. She wouldn't tell him why, just pleaded with him not to tell her father or Dante.

'First, explain to me why you stole,' Gian had persisted. 'You have the money to pay.'

'Stefano dared me to,' Ariana had admitted. 'I haven't eaten it, though. The chocolate is still under my bed, but I feel ill when I try to say my prayers…'

Gian had taken her in to the store and Ariana had duly apologised and paid for the chocolate, and, no, he had not told Dante or Rafael. Instead he'd had a quiet word with Stefano. 'You want to steal,' he had said to the young boy, 'then at least have the guts to do it yourself.'

Another time, some years later, Stefano had been caught smoking and Ariana had arrived here in Gian's office and begged him to impersonate her father when the school in-evitably rang.

'Why would they ring here?' Gian had frowned.

'Because I told Stefano to say that Papà is here at La Fiordelise on business.'

Ariana was a minx and far too skilled at lying. Gian had of course declined to cover for Stefano, and had spo-ken to Rafael himself.

There was *always* drama surrounding Ariana, though it was not always of her own making—just two years ago, in the midst of her parents' scandalous divorce, she had found out that her father was ill and Ariana had sat in Gian's of-fice, being fed tissues but not false promises.

Yes, he had kept his door open to her, but—

'If I hire you,' Gian said, very carefully, 'all that stops.'

And suddenly, if the safety net of Gian was going to be

removed, Ariana didn't know if she wanted her career any more—not that he seemed to notice her dilemma.

'Who the hell orders champagne at a job interview?' Gian mused.

'It was my first ever interview,' Ariana admitted. 'I sensed your irritation and was trying to drag things out.'

'Well done, you, then,' Gian said, and then sighed because he did not need Ariana under his precious roof, and the drama that would undoubtedly entail. 'Why here, Ariana? Why La Fiordelise, Rome?'

'Because I love it,' she admitted. She looked up at the high ceilings and the gilded mirrors and the beauty that never failed to capture her heart. There was a sense of peace and calm that Gian had created, a haven that somehow made her feel safe. 'I am sure your other hotels are stunning—in fact, I have stayed in the London one several times—it is just…' She tried her best to explain it. 'There is so much history here, so much…' She faltered and then pushed on. 'It was your great-great-grandfather's?' she checked.

'You will learn the history in your induction.'

'Can you at least give me the condensed version?' Ariana asked, running a hand along a marble column and frowning at an indentation, a mar in perfection.

'That is a bullet hole,' Gian told her, 'from when the hotel became a fortress in the Second World War.'

She breathed in, shivering at the history and aching, actually aching, to know more. But Gian was glancing beyond her shoulder now, and Ariana sensed she was running out of her allotted time. 'Can I see the penthouse suite? The original one?'

'No.'

'Please.'

God, Gian thought, she was incessant. 'There might be guests.'

'I'm sure you would know.'

He sighed. 'You are most persistent.' He took out his phone and though he knew there were no guests due in the most expensive suite until tomorrow, he double-checked just to be sure, and almost sighed when he saw that indeed it was vacant. 'Very well, but only briefly.'

As they took the elevator up, Ariana had a question. 'Is your apartment on the penthouse floor?'

'No, though it is where I grew up,' Gian told her, 'but when I took over La Fiordelise, I decided I could not afford the luxury of misappropriating the hotel's most valuable asset.'

As well as that, the penthouse floor had been the loneliest place in the world for Gian. He would sometimes glimpse his parents drifting off to some event, or hear first the laughter and merriment of parties, and then lie drenched in dread as the gathering flared and got out of hand.

But as dark as his memories were, the penthouse floor was an asset indeed. This was confirmed by her gasp as she stepped into the main suite.

Rome was spread out before them and from this vantage she looked down at the square and across to Palazzo Pamphili, where her brother's wedding would be held, but that was not all that held her gaze. She wandered the vast space, taking in the ornaments and oil paintings that surely belonged behind a rope in a gallery and yet they were there for the luckiest guests to take in at their leisure.

'This corridor can be closed off,' Gian explained as she peered into the spare bedrooms, each as exquisite as the next; there was even a gorgeous library that had a huge fire, just waiting to be lit.

And then he showed her the master suite and it felt as if she wasn't just in Rome but was at the very centre of it. The bed was draped in gold, the intricately painted ceilings a masterpiece of their own, and it was as if the walls had their own pulse. Ariana was rich, but there was, of course, a pecking order, and the Penthouse Suite was not Ariana's domain. 'Is this where my parents would stay for the Romano Ball?'

Her question went unanswered, for Gian never commented on the sleeping arrangements of his guests and anyway, her eyes would fall out if he told her the truth.

'And now Dante?' she persisted.

Still he said nothing, and it was Ariana who filled the gap. 'I could live here for ever,' she sighed, sinking onto a plump lounge and kicking off her stilettoes.

'Believe me…' Gian started, but did not finish.

Certainly, he would not be sharing with Ariana that he loathed coming up here. There were just too many memories that resided here. Instead, he pointed out another of its disadvantages. 'It takes for ever to clean, which you might soon find out,' Gian said with a wry edge, and he watched as she tucked her slender legs under her. 'A full two days to service properly.'

'Let me dream for a moment,' she sighed. 'So this was built for the Duke's mistress?'

'Incorrect.'

'Correct me then,' Ariana said, her voice dropping to huskiness as, for the first time in her life, she officially flirted. Not that Gian even noticed, for he proceeded to give her a history lesson.

'It was officially built for the Duke and the Duchess,' Gian told her. 'It was actually first called La Duchessa,' Gian said, 'well, officially, but the locals all called it La Fiordelise…'

She watched as he pulled back some ornate panelling to reveal a heavy door and in it a silver key. 'Fiordelise lived through here.'

He turned the key and pushed open the door to reveal

another completely separate penthouse suite, in feminine reds and with a view of the square and a personality of its own. Yet he was somewhat surprised when the rather nosy Ariana did not untangle her long legs and pad over to look at the sumptuous boudoir. Instead she screwed up her nose. 'The poor Duchess.' Her sloe eyes narrowed. 'How awful to live with just a wall between you and your husband's mistress.'

'You don't find the story of La Fiordelise romantic?'

'History makes it *appear* romantic.' Ariana shrugged. 'I find it offensive.'

Of course, given her father's *supposed* affair with Mia, he guessed that infidelity would be one of her hot buttons, but he sensed that her thoughts had been formed long ago. There was a side to Ariana he had never seen: a free thinker was in there, though somewhat suppressed.

'Why do you find it so offensive?' Gian asked. 'Things were very different back then.'

'I doubt *feelings* were different,' Ariana said. 'And I hate it that the Duchess had to vie for his attention. You would hope, once married, all that would stop.'

'All what?'

'Being shut out. It should have been the Duchess on his mind, not Fiordelise.'

Gian looked at her thoughtfully. 'You have a very idealistic view of marriage.'

'Absolutely I do,' Ariana agreed. She stood and padded over to where Fiordelise had once resided and, standing in the doorway with him, peered into the opulent, sensual, feminine suite. Yet she did not set as much as a foot inside, just faced him in the doorway. 'And that is why I am still single.'

His eyes never left her face as she continued to speak. 'My mother has spent the last quarter of a century planning my wedding—any old billionaire will do—but I shall only marry for love.' She smiled at him then and teased him a little. 'Do you even know what that word means, Gian?'

'No,' he replied, 'and I don't care to find out.'

'As is your prerogative, but it is mine to feel sad for the Duchess. What was her name?'

'Violetta,' Gian answered, 'like…' He hesitated, for he had been about to compare the name to Ariana's eyes. For several reasons, that would not be a sensible thing to do. Neither was the way he was looking into them right now.

Yes, he had noticed the huskiness of her voice and the earlier batting of her eyelashes. There was a friction in the Ariana-scented air, and his hand wanted to know for itself the softness of her cheek—so much so that Gian had to focus on not lifting his hand and cupping her face.

Gian, despite his formidable reputation, had scruples, and to kiss her, as he now desired to, while still involved with Svetlana was not something he would do.

And, aside from that, this was Ariana Romano.

The daughter of a man he respected and the little sister of his lifelong friend. And soon to be an employee. A casual affair she could never be, and that was all Gian wanted or knew.

Ariana Romano was completely off limits.

CHAPTER FOUR

'Violetta.' Ariana repeated the name of the forgotten Duchess while gazing into his eyes. 'That's beautiful.'

She practically handed him a response—*and so are you*—except Gian refused to rise to the bait.

Or rather he fought not to rise.

They stood facing each other in the doorway, their bodies almost as close as when they danced their one duty dance each year at the Romano Foundation Ball.

And he was as turned on as he had been while holding her in that dress of silver.

Of course it had been more than an educated guess, for she had looked utterly stunning that night.

Gian was well aware of his past with women.

And he was decided on his future too.

Casual, temporary, fleeting, there were many ways to describe the nature of his relationships, except entering into any of the above with Ariana was an impossible concept. If they were seen out more than a couple of times the press would soon get hold of it and her mother would too. As much as Angela resented Gian for holding Rafael's second wedding here, she would forgive him in an instant to have a title in the family.

No, there could be no kisses, though certainly the moment was ripe for one...

'What?' Ariana said. She could feel a sudden charge

in the air, a slight frisson that had her on her guard. She assumed he was displeased and wondered if perhaps she shouldn't have brought up the Duchess's name, or been so derisive of Fiordelise.

Ariana could not read men.

Well, not real men, which Gian undoubtedly was.

She could read fake men, who wanted to be seen with her just for appearances' sake. And though she tried to convince herself they cared, she could never bring herself to take it beyond anything other than a tasteless kiss.

Despite popular gossip, Ariana was completely untouched.

Her flirting was all for the cameras.

No, she could not read *this* man, who stared into her eyes and gritted his jaw and, in the absence of experience, she assumed he was displeased. 'I've offended you,' Ariana said. Completely misreading the tension, she shrugged, not caring in the least if she had upset him by refusing to rave about the mistress, Fiordelise.

'You haven't offended me,' Gian said, snapping back into business mode. 'I'm just telling you the history of the place—as you asked.'

'Well, I've enjoyed hearing it.'

It was nice to be here with Gian.

Nice to have a conversation that was about more than the latest fashion or who was sleeping with whom.

It was, quite simply, nice.

'Tell me more,' Ariana said, walking back through to the master bedroom and resuming her place on the lounge. Bending over, she pulled on one of her suede stilettoes.

'There's not much more to tell.'

'Liar.' She smiled and caught his eye. 'Go on,' she persisted, 'tell me something that no one else knows.'

'Why would I do that?'

'Why wouldn't you?' she asked, peering up at him through her eyelashes as she wedged the other shoe on.

Usually, Gian could not wait to get out of the Penthouse Suite, yet Ariana was so curious and the company so pleasing that he decided the world could surely wait and he told her a titbit that very few knew. 'The Duke had a ring made for Fiordelise.'

'A ring?' That got her interest and Gian watched as her pupils dilated at the speed of a cat's. 'What was it like?'

'It is the insignia of the hotel,' Gian told her. 'The Duke would only ever let her look at it, though; she never once put it on. He held onto it on the promise that one day he would marry her.'

'I'm liking the Duke less and less,' Ariana said, smiling.

'Then you'll be pleased to know that when the Duchess died and he offered Fiordelise the ring, she declined it.'

'Really?'

'Yes. By then she had fallen in love with a servant. The old Duke was too tired to be angry, and too embarrassed by her rejection to ever admit the truth. Fiordelise saw out her days in her boudoir with her manservant tending to her needs…'

'Good for her.' Ariana smirked.

'Don't tell the guests, though.'

She laughed, and it sounded like a chandelier had caught the wind.

Right there, in the presidential suite of his signature hotel, something shifted for Gian.

Ariana was more than beautiful.

And she was more complex than he had known.

More, he admired her for the mutinous act of trying to shed her pampered existence—with conditions of course. 'Come on,' he said, trying to keep the reluctance from his tone as they left the vast and luxurious cocoon of the suite.

'What's down there?' Ariana asked as they came out

into the corridor and she saw that there was a door on the other side. 'Is there *another* penthouse suite?'

'No, there's a butler's room and kitchen and some storage space…' His expression was grim as she wandered off to explore. What was now the butler's room had been home for his many nannies. 'What's this one for?' she asked, and peered into a dour windowless room, unaware it was where Gian had slept as a child. There were shelves holding spare laptops, computer screens, chargers, adaptors, magnifying mirrors, straightening irons, and anything else a guest might have forgotten or need. 'Miscellaneous items.' Ariana concluded.

'Precisely.'

Oh, that frisson was back, only it felt different this time, and Ariana was quite sure that this time he really was displeased so she closed the door on the windowless room.

They were soon in the elevator. That clinging scent she wore was reaching him again, and he turned rather harshly towards her. 'If you do commence work at La Fiordelise you should know that perfume is banned for staff. It is not pleasant for the guests as some have allergies.'

'*You* wear cologne,' Ariana rather belligerently pointed out, for those citrus and bergamot notes had long been the signature of his greeting and the scent she breathed once a year when they danced.

'Yes, but I am not servicing the rooms. Please remember not to wear perfume for work.'

'I don't wear perfume.'

'Oh, please.'

'But I don't.' Ariana frowned. 'My skin is too sensitive.'

He wanted to debate it, to point out that the small elevator smelt of sunshine and rain and an undernote that he could not define, but the doors opened and he stepped out to the relative neutrality of Reception. He would have a word with Vanda, Gian decided. She could talk to her about perfume and such, because policing Ariana would no doubt be a full-time job! 'Are you sure you aren't just coveting the suit and pearls that my guest services managers wear?' Gian checked, as Bianca, one of his senior staff, smiled a greeting as she passed.

'Of course, not.' Ariana shook her head and flushed at her own lie, because the gorgeous blush tartan outfits were divine. 'I'm not that shallow. I really want this, Gian.'

'Well, I mean it, Ariana. If you blow this, I shall not be giving you another chance. You are to be here at seven on Monday morning,' Gian said. 'If you're late, if you're ill, if your arm is hanging off, I still don't want to hear it. Any problems, any issues, any *excuses* are no longer my concern. Vanda shall deal with you.'

And no doubt Vanda would soon fire her. 'I will say goodbye to you here,' he said.

'I need to collect my bag from your office.'

Of course she did!

He tried not to notice the feeling of the sun stepping into his office again as they walked in. 'Thank you for the tour.' Ariana smiled, 'I absolutely loved hearing about the Duke and Duchess, and Fiordelise, even if I do not approve. I'm glad she never got to wear the ring.'

He should conclude the meeting. They were already running over her unallotted time and Svetlana was waiting impatiently in the Pianoforte Bar, yet such was her enthusiasm, so unexpected the brightness of her company that instead of dismissing her Gian headed to the safe hidden in his wall.

He rarely opened the safe. In it were documents and rolls of plans, and there were also the coroner's and police reports from the deaths of his parents and brother, but there was also one thing of beauty nestled atop them.

'Come here,' Gian told her.

Those words sent an unfamiliar shiver through her, so

unfamiliar that Ariana did not ask why, or what for. Instead, she followed his command and walked over.

He removed a faded velvet box from the safe. It might once have been gold, but it had faded now to a silver beige, yet it was beautiful still. The box was studded with gold tacks and the clasp was so intricate that she wondered how he flicked it open so easily.

'Look,' Gian said.

Fiordelise's ring was the rarest of treasures. It was a swirl of stunning Italian rose gold, and in the centre was a ruby so deep and so vibrant it made her breath hitch.

'I've never seen a ruby of that colour,' Ariana breathed. 'It's the colour of a pomegranate kernel, although it's bigger…'

'It's called pigeon-blood red,' Gian corrected. 'The colour of the first drops after a kill.'

'Don't.' Ariana shuddered. 'I like pomegranate better.'

'Then pomegranate red it is.' Gian smiled and then closed up the box. 'I found this five years after I inherited the place.'

'Where did you find it?'

'Under the very spot you were seated a short while ago,' Gian told her. 'When the suite was being renovated they pulled up the floor. There was a hidden basement and in it was a box. There was a shawl and some sketches of Fiordelise, and also this…'

'What happened to the sketches?' Ariana asked.

'I had them restored and framed.'

'And the shawl?'

'I gave that to an aunt. But this…' He replaced the box in the safe. 'God alone knows it would have been easier to have found this some five years earlier.'

'You'd have sold it?' Ariana frowned. She knew that he had inherited his estate from his family in the direst of conditions, and that La Fiordelise had been on the brink of collapse, yet she could not believe he would have sold something as precious and sentimental as this ring.

But Gian was adamant. 'Absolutely I would have.'

'I don't believe you.'

'Then you don't know me,' Gian said, closing up the safe. He turned to her. 'I shall have Luna bring your coat.'

'Thank you,' Ariana said, trying to quash the thud of disappointment that he hadn't suggested, given the hour, that they have dinner together. Well, she would soon see about that. 'Gosh, it's almost seven!' Ariana exclaimed. 'No wonder I'm so hungry.'

'Indeed,' Gian said. 'I should let you get on.'

She tried to stall him again. 'What about my uniform? Don't I need to be measured?'

'You'll be working as a chambermaid for the first few weeks of your rotation. That uniform comes in small, medium or large, I believe.'

There was the tiniest wrinkle of her pretty nose and then she shrugged. 'I lied,' Ariana admitted. 'I do want the tartan and pearls.'

'I know you do.'

'And I *shall* get them one day. I shall be the best guest services manager you've ever had.' She pictured her pretty pink business cards with her name embossed in rose gold: *Ariana Romano, VIP Guest Services Manager*.

Perhaps she shouldn't be so vocal with her dreams, but when she looked up she was startled by the glimmer of a smile softening his mouth.

It was a smile she had never seen on him before.

Ariana had known him for a long time. If there was trouble in her life—and all too often there was—it was Gian she ran to. And when, inevitably, she thanked him for sorting whatever problem she had placed in his lap, he would nod and give her his grim, somewhat weary smile. There was another smile she knew: each year they sat side by side at the Romano Ball, and each year he performed a duty dance, and so of course she was privy to his duty smile.

Yes, his duty smile, she called it, for that was exactly what it was.

She saw it used on guests, on dignitaries and on herself as recently as this evening when she had first walked in. *This* smile, though, was different. This *off-duty* smile felt as if it was just for her, though it was fading now and his grey eyes returned to guarded.

'I really do need to get on,' Gian said as Luna appeared with her coat.

As she and Gian walked out, Ariana saw the stunning woman from the Pianoforte Bar smile over at him. 'I'll be with you in just a moment.' Gian nodded to her and from the lack of affection in his tone she assumed he had another client.

'I thought I was your last appointment,' Ariana said.

'You were.'

He stalked off then to the waiting woman, who lifted her face to him, clearly expecting a most thorough kiss, but instead Ariana heard his slight rebuke. 'I said I would meet you at the theatre, Svetlana.'

'I thought we might have dinner in the restaurant,' Svetlana purred and needlessly fiddled with the lapel of his jacket. 'You still haven't taken me there.'

Oh!

Ariana's face was on fire, yet she could not look away. It was unsettling to see him with a woman when of course it should not be, given his reputation. It just felt different seeing it first-hand and flicked a little knife toward her heart.

'Maybe after…?' Svetlana persisted.

Gian was not enamoured of women who purred, or those who felt the need to pick an imaginary piece of lint from his lapel, and Svetlana had been doing a lot of both of those of late.

He had already decided they were over, and was about to tell Svetlana, but with Ariana so close, for reasons he did not care—or dare—to examine, he chose not to. 'Come,' he said, 'we'll be late.'

He didn't even glance in Ariana's direction as he headed off. After all, if he stopped to say goodbye to each member of staff, he would never get out of the door.

Ariana Romano as staff?

Ariana in his hotel each and every day…

Instantly, he regretted his decision to take her on.

But then, on Monday morning, an hour after Ariana *should have* commenced her first shift, he received a text.

Gian, I am sorry! There has been an Extraordinary Board Meeting called!!!! Can I start in the afternoon instead?

Very deliberately, Gian didn't respond.

He didn't even scold her for her excessive use of exclamation marks; after all, Ariana personified them. This could never, ever work, and when she came in, hours late, on her very first day, Gian would tell her exactly why.

At lunchtime, rather than text she called him, no doubt with yet more excuses.

'Gian—'

'I don't want to hear it,' Gian cut in abruptly. 'Ariana, I simply do not want to know. Even after I gave explicit instructions not to do so, you still think you can call and text me with excuses for why you're late or not coming in. I don't deal with junior—'

'Gian, please, just listen to me…'

She was starting to cry, but Gian was way too used to her crocodile tears. 'I knew on Friday you were unsuitable for the role and your behaviour today merely confirms it. This could never have worked.'

'Gian…' she sobbed, but though he refused to be moved his mask slipped and he forgot to be polite. 'You sat in this office and pleaded for a start, and I gave you one. The contracts were drawn up and waiting to be signed, but clearly something more enticing has come along. I don't want to hear about extraordinary board meetings. The only extraordinary thing was that I actually thought you had changed your precocious, self-serving ways, but clearly you have not.'

Problem solved, Gian thought as he terminated the call. He was a little breathless, and barely holding onto his temper but he also felt a strange disappointment that, yet again, Ariana had let herself down. She was incapable of seeing things through. She was absolutely devoid of any sense of responsibility. She was always onto the next best thing the second it showed up.

Yet there was a mounting sense of disquiet to have heard her tears, for there had been an unfamiliar rasp to them that had, on reflection, sounded real.

She'd probably been putting it on, Gian told himself. If Ariana really wanted a career then perhaps she should have considered acting.

The ridiculous thing was, as he sat there, he was envisioning her in the blush pink tartan suit and the string of pearls that she had admitted she secretly desired.

Ariana, whether he wanted her to or not, made him smile, and for Gian that was rare indeed.

His private phone was buzzing and he saw that it was Dante who was calling, no doubt hoping to sway Gian from his decision.

'*Pronto,*' Gian said.

There was silence for a moment.

'Dante?' Gian checked. 'Look, if you're calling to excuse Ariana and ask—'

'Gian,' Dante interrupted. 'I don't know what you're referring to. I just wanted to call you before word got out. I'm sorry to have to tell you, but a short while ago my father...' Dante cleared his throat. 'Rafael has passed away.'

CHAPTER FIVE

GIAN DE LUCA MIGHT BE the last Duke of Luctano, but to him Rafael Romano had always been King.

In modern times, Rafael Romano had put Luctano on the map far more than the De Lucas, who had long ago sold off their land and moved to Rome.

This cold grey morning he flew in to bid farewell to a man Gian considered not just a brilliant business mind but a man he had been proud to call a friend.

The landscape beneath his navy helicopter was familiar. A lattice of bare vines weaved across the hills and down into the valley but, deep in winter, the poppy fields were bare and silver with ice. The lake, beside which Rafael was to be buried, was at first a black, uninviting mirror, but now rippled as his helicopter neared its location.

It was to be a private burial, for Rafael's wife and children only, and Gian was there just for the church service.

The family would now all be at the house, and though Dante had invited him to have his pilot land there, without Rafael, Gian felt he would be invading on this solemn day.

A driver had been arranged to meet him and as he took the steps down from the helicopter Gian felt a blast of bitterly cold air: the weather in Luctano was always more extreme than in Rome. He wore a long black wool coat over his tailored black suit. His thick black hair had not quite been due for a trim, but his barber had come to his apartment that morning to ensure a perfect cut and he was particularly close shaven.

With good reason.

As a car took him to the church, he recalled Rafael's words from long ago. 'Look immaculate,' Rafael had once told him. 'You are not a university student any more but the owner-manager of a five-star hotel. Get your hair cut, and for God's sake, shave.' His advice had not ended there. 'See a tailor, buy fine shoes...'

At the age of twenty, Gian had been studying architecture and living in the residences, having turned his back on his family two years previously. His scholarship had covered accommodation and his bar work funded books and food, but barely stretched to a haircut, let alone designer clothes. 'I can't afford to,' a proud Gian had dared to admit.

'You can't afford not to. Now, listen to me, it is imperative that you look the part...'

But Gian had held firm. After the tragic death of his family, he'd discovered the financial chaos his parents had left behind and the many jobs that depended on him. 'No, the accounts are a disaster. Before the fancy suits, first the staff are to be paid.'

'It doesn't work like that.'

Rafael had taken a reluctant Gian to Via dei Condotti— a fashionable street in Rome—where he had met with artisan tailors and been fitted for bespoke Italian shoes in the only true handout that Gian had ever received. But better than the trip had been the glimpse of having if not a father then a mentor to advise him.

The day had ended at a Middle Eastern barbershop, with hot towels and a close shave. Rafael continued with the sage advice: 'You need to attract only the best clients.'

'How, though?' Gian had asked, staring at his groomed reflection and barely recognising himself. 'La Fiordelise's reputation is in tatters and the building is in disrepair.'

Gian loathed the destruction of history—how there were only a few decent areas remaining in the once elegant building. The rest was cordoned off and for the most part the hotel was faded and unkempt.

But Rafael remained upbeat. 'La Fiordelise has survived worse. It has a new owner now and its reputation will recover: all we need is a plan.'

A couple of weeks later they had contrived one.

A plan that, to this day, few knew about.

Yes, Rafael Romano had been far more of a father to Gian than his own, and Gian would miss him very much indeed.

Arriving at the church, he could feel eyes on him as the absent Duke made a rare return. Gian declined the offer of being guided to a pew and instead stood at the back of the small church and did his level best to keep from recalling the last time he'd been here—at his own family's funeral. He pondered his handling of Ariana when she had tried to tell him her father had died. Of course he had tried to call her back and apologise, but had been sent straight to voicemail...

Gian's words, though, had been an unwitting lifeline.

It was Gian's deep, calm voice on this terrible morning that brought Ariana a little solace.

'Ariana,' Dante snapped as they all stood in the entrance hall of their father's home, preparing to head out for the funeral procession. It was exquisitely awkward as of course it was Mia's home too. Her older brother was in a particularly picky mood. 'Surely you can get off your phone for five minutes?'

But Ariana ignored him as she listened again to Gian's message.

I should have let you speak. Ariana, I apologise and I am so deeply sorry for your loss. Call me if you want to, if not...' His deep voice halted for a few seconds. *'You will get through this, Ariana. You are strong. Remember that.'*

Ariana didn't feel very strong, though.

She was weak from having to comfort her mother through the day, and at night, though exhausted, she could barely sleep. She felt as if she were holding a million balls in the air and that at any moment one might drop, for her family, scattered by Mia's presence, had not been under one roof since the divorce, let alone the roof of a church.

Surely her mother would not create a scene?

Or her aunts or uncles...

As well as the worry of that, as she headed out to the waiting cars, the loneliest morning of her life felt even more desolate when Dante decided to take a seat in the front vehicle with Mia, rather than make her travel to the church by herself. That left Ariana with Stefano and Eloa, which lately felt like the equivalent of being alone.

As the cortège moved through the hills to the village, Ariana tried to come to grips with a world without her father while acknowledging a disquieting truth.

Since her father had found Mia, he too had pushed her aside.

For two years, she had felt like a visitor in the family home and later at his hospital bedside. Perhaps she could have accepted Mia more readily if they had accepted her more into their world. Yes, she regretted now not going to the wedding, but the truth was her father hadn't exactly pushed for her to attend.

In fact, he'd seemed a touch relieved when Ariana had declined.

Once she had been the apple of her father's eye and they would talk and laugh. They would fly to the London office together, and she had felt there was a real place for her on the Romano board, but since Dante had taken over all she had felt was supernumerary.

Ariana didn't just miss her father today; she had missed him for the last two years of his life. And now she would miss him for ever, with no time left to put things to rights.

'We're here,' Eloa announced, breaking into her thoughts, and Ariana looked up and saw they were at the church.

The doors were opened and the trio stepped out. Her legs felt as if they had been spun in brittle steel wool, and might snap as she walked over the cobbles and into the church. Her heart felt like a fish flopping in her chest that might jump out of her throat if she let out the wail she held in. The sight of her father's coffin at the front of the church, though expected, was so confronting that she wanted to turn around and flee, unsure whether she was capable of getting through the ceremony.

But then, just as she felt like panic would surely take over, came an unexpected moment of solace.

Gian was here.

Of course he was, but it was the actual *sight* of him, the glimpse of him, that allowed Ariana to draw a deeper breath.

He looked more polished and immaculate than she had ever seen; his black hair was brushed back from his face and she could see both the compassion and authority in his grey eyes.

Yes, authority, for him standing at the back with a full view of proceedings instantly calmed Ariana.

Gian would not let things get out of hand.

He would keep things under control.

And then she knew that it wasn't the hotel, or the haven in Rome that Gian had created, that calmed her.

It was Gian himself who made the world safe.

The look they shared lasted less than a moment—Gian gave her a small, grim smile of sympathy, a nod of his noble head, more by way of understanding than greeting—but time had taken on a different meaning, for the velvet of his eyes and the quiet comfort they gave would sustain her through the service.

You are strong.

He had told her so.

And so she did her best to get through the eulogy and the hymns and the hell.

Gian had been through this before, Ariana reminded herself as she did her level best not to stare at the coffin.

There had been three coffins in this church when his family had died. Pink peonies on his mother's, white lilies on his father's and a huge spray of red poppies on his brother's.

'I don't like this, Papà,' she had whispered, for she'd been ten years old and the chants and scent of incense had made her feel a little ill.

'I know, bella, but we are here today for Gian,' her *papà* had said.

'Shouldn't we sit with him, then?' Ariana had asked, for even beside his aunts and such he had looked so completely alone.

'We are not family,' her *papà* had said. *'Hold my hand.'*

His warm hand had closed around hers and imbued her with strength, but she had looked over at Gian and seen that there was no one holding his.

And there was no one holding Ariana's today.

It was an emotional service, but Gian refused to let it move him and stood dry-eyed even as the coffin was carried out to the haunting strains of his favourite aria—Puccini's 'O Mio Babbino Caro'. *Oh, my dear Papà...*

Ariana looked close to fainting, but her damned mother was too busy beating at her chest to see.

'Hey,' Gian said. To the frowns of the congregation, he broke protocol and joined the family on the way out. 'You are doing so well,' he murmured quietly.

'I am not.'

'You are, you are.' He could feel her tremble. As the family lined up outside the church, instead of guiding her to join them, he took Ariana aside and held her.

She leaned on him for a moment, a blissful moment that smelt of Gian, and she learned something more about him. There were no tears in his eyes, he looked a little pale but unmoved, yet his heart beat rapidly in his chest and she could *feel* his grief as he held her in his arms.

As they held each other.

'You'll miss him too,' she whispered.

'Ever so.'

It was the closest she had ever been to him, this blissful place on a terrible day, and she wanted to cling on, to rest in his arms a while longer, but he was pulling her back and returning to his usual distant form.

'Gian.' It was so cold to stand without him, especially when she wanted the shield of his arms. 'I don't think I can face the burial.'

'Yes, Ariana, you can.'

But hysteria was mounting. 'No. I really don't think so...'

'Would it help if I came with you?'

It would, but... 'You can't.' She gave a black laugh. 'Stefano practically had to put in a written request to Dante to have Eloa attend, and she's his fiancée. Mamma has been denied. God, Gian, I don't...'

'Take this.'

From deep in his coat pocket he handed her a *cornicello*...a small gold amulet. 'Your father gave me this to hold when I buried my family. You *can* do this, Ariana; you will regret it if you don't.'

* * *

It was the most private of burials.

Mia, who could barely stand, held a single lily.

And Dante, who loathed Mia possibly the most of all Rafael's children, was the one who had to take her to the graveside so she could throw the flower in.

Stefano wept and was comforted by Eloa, and that left Ariana standing alone, holding onto the little sliver of gold.

Ariana had never felt so cold as when she returned to the house and stood by a huge fire, grateful for the large cognac someone placed in her hands. Looking up, she saw it was Gian. 'Thank you.'

'How was it?' Gian gently enquired.

'It is done,' Ariana responded, without really answering and then held out the amulet. 'Here, I should give this back to you. Thank you.'

'Keep it.'

'He gave it to you,' Ariana said, suddenly angry at his lack of sentiment. This man who would sell a priceless ring, this man who would let go of a gift from her father. 'Why would you give it away?'

'Did it help?' he asked, and she nodded. 'Then you yourself might pass it on someday when someone else needs your father's strength.'

Never, she thought.

Never, ever.

For it was her first gift from Gian and it almost scared her how much that meant.

'It seems strange to be here without him,' Gian admitted, trying to gauge how she felt, but for once the effusive Ariana was a closed book. She gave a tired shrug and her black lashes closed on violet eyes highlighting the dark shadows beneath them.

'It has felt strange to be here for quite some time.' Her

eyes opened then and came to rest on Rafael's widow, and Gian followed her gaze as she spoke. 'My father and I used to be so close.'

'You were always close,' Gian refuted.

'No.' She shook her head. 'It fell away at the end.'

He would like to take her arm and walk her away from the funeral crowd, to walk in the grounds and gently tell her the difficult truth—the real reason her father had pulled away from his family and from the daughter he had loved so very much.

It was not his place to do so, though.

Oh, today he loathed being the keeper of secrets, for the truth would surely help her to heal.

'How long are you here for?' Ariana asked, determinedly changing the subject, then wishing she hadn't for the answer was not one she liked.

'I'll be leaving shortly. I just wanted to see the house one last time and…' He hesitated but then admitted the deeper truth. 'To see how you were after the burial.'

Stay longer, she wanted to say, yet she dared not.

'And,' he added, 'I wanted to properly apologise for how I spoke to you on the day you called. I was completely out of line.'

'Not completely,' Ariana said, and he watched her strained lips part into a brief glimpse of her impish smile. 'Not to come in because of a board meeting *was* inexcusable on my first day…'

'Oh!' Her burst of honesty and the explanation surprised him. 'I thought you must have had word that your father was ill.'

'No, no,' she said. 'That wasn't till later.'

'Well, even so, I'm very sorry for the way I spoke to you.'

'It's fine,' Ariana said. 'I would have been annoyed with me too.'

He watched the dart of anxiety in her eyes as he looked

around the room, filled with low murmurs of conversation and her veiled *mamma*, sitting weeping on a chair against the wall surrounded by aunts. 'Mamma and Mia have never been under the same roof…'

'Everyone is behaving,' Gian pointed out.

'For now they are,' Ariana said, and let out a nervous breath, unsure how long the civility might last. 'There is the reading of the will soon.'

'It will be fine,' Gian assured her, though he quietly thought Ariana's concerns might be merited and she didn't even know the half of it! Roberto, the family lawyer, had also been Rafael's long-term lover and he was reading the will. With the current wife and widow in the room, one could be forgiven for expecting fireworks.

'Do you want me to stay until afterwards?' he offered.

'I would like that,' Ariana admitted. She looked up at the man she always ran to, always turned to, yet the moment was broken by the sound of her mother's voice.

'Gian, I was hoping that you'd come back to the house…' She placed an overly familiar hand on his arm, and Gian would have liked to shrug it off. He loathed the sudden fake friendliness from Angela, although of course it was for a reason. 'Could I ask you to take me back to Rome with you? I simply cannot stand to be here.'

'It would be my pleasure,' Gian politely agreed, for even if he did not particularly want Angela's company, he would do the right thing.

'I have to stay for the reading of the will,' Angela explained, 'but if we could leave after that? Ariana will be coming with us also…'

'But, Mamma, Stefano and Eloa are heading back to Zio Luigi's…' Ariana started, but clearly her desires had no importance here and Gian watched her shoulders slump as she acquiesced. 'If that is what you want.'

Naturally, Gian did not enter the study for the reading

of the will. Instead, he poured himself a brandy from Rafael's decanter, as his friend had often done for him, and silently toasted his portrait.

What a mess.

He looked at the portrait and wondered if Rafael's truth would be revealed in the will.

Of course Angela had long since known the truth about her husband, and had fought like a cat to prevent it getting out, more than happy to let the blame for the end of their marriage land on Mia.

He looked at the pictures above the fireplace—family shots. There was a surge that felt almost like a sob building when he saw his own image there, for he had never considered he might appear on anyone's mantelpiece. Certainly there had been no images of him at his childhood home.

Yet here he was, fourteen or fifteen years old, on horseback, with Dante.

Good times.

Not great times, of course, because the end of the holidays had always meant it would be time to head back to Rome and his chaotic existence there.

The door of the study opened and the subdued gathering trooped out; Gian quickly realised that Rafael's truth had not been revealed.

'How was it?' he asked Dante, who was the first to approach him.

'Fine. No real surprises.'

And then came Ariana. She looked pale and drained, as if all the exuberance and arrogance that he was coming to adore had simply been leached from her.

'How did it go?' Gian asked.

'I don't even know how to answer,' she admitted. 'I am taken care of. I have an apartment in Paris and I will never have to work.' She gave a tired shrug. 'Does that mean it went well?'

'Ariana,' he cut in, and his hand reached for her arm but she pulled it back.

Not because she didn't want physical contact, more because of how much she did. 'I should go and say my farewells.'

'Are you sure you want to come back to Rome tonight?'

'Not really.'

'Your family are all here,' Gian pointed out. 'Wouldn't it be better to spend time with them?'

'Yes, but I think Mamma needs me. She feels so out of place here.'

It was a subdued little group that flew back to Rome. Gian's car was waiting at the airport and he gave Angela's address to the driver.

'Ariana, darling,' her mother said, 'I have the most terrible headache. I think I might just head home to bed. After I've been dropped off, Gian's driver will take you home.'

'But, Mamma, I thought I was to stay with you tonight.'

Gian heard the strain in Ariana's voice. She was clearly asking to be with her mother, rather than offering to take care of her, although Angela, just as clearly, chose not to hear it as that. 'Ariana, I know you're worried about me but right now all I really need is some peace.'

Gian gritted his jaw because he could see the manipulative behaviour, pulling Ariana away from the rest of the family just because she could when she'd always intended to spend the evening with Thomas, her lover.

He knew now that he loathed Angela because she was as selfish as his own mother had been.

'I'll call you tomorrow,' Angela said to her daughter as she got out of the car. 'Thank you, Gian, for seeing us home.'

Eternally polite, usually he would have wished her well and forced himself to kiss her cheeks, but the best he could manage was a curt nod.

As the driver closed the door, he looked over at Ariana. She was staring straight ahead and there was the sparkle of unshed tears in her eyes that he knew were waiting to fall the very second she was alone. 'Let's get you home,' Gian said as the car pulled away.

'I don't want to go home.' Ariana shook her head and blinked back the tears. 'I might call Nicki.'

Ariana's friend Nicki ran rather wild and she would undoubtedly prescribe a night of drinking and clubbing as a cure for Ariana's troubled heart. 'How come Nicki wasn't at the funeral?' he asked.

'She only got back from skiing this afternoon.' Ariana scrabbled in her purse for her phone. 'She'd have come if she could.'

Gian doubted it.

Nicki liked the galas and balls, and the spoils of being Ariana's friend, but where was she now when her friend needed her most?

Gian did not quite know what to do.

If it were Stefano, or Dante, or even Angela—who he didn't even like—Gian would suggest a drink at the hotel, or a walk perhaps. Conversation or silence, whatever they chose.

But this was Ariana.

He wished he hadn't noticed her beauty, or the colour of her eyes.

Gian wished he could snap his fingers and return them to a time when she had been just the annoying little sister of a friend, the daughter of his beloved mentor... That thought had him stepping up to do the right thing, for he did not want Ariana in questionable company tonight. 'Would you like to come back to La Fiordelise for a drink, or something to eat perhaps?'

'I...' His offer was so unexpected. Gian usually made her feel like an annoying presence, always trying to cut short their time together, and now it was he who was offering to extend it. 'I don't want to impose.'

'It doesn't normally stop you…' Gian teased, but then, seeing her frown, realised that even the lightest joke wasn't registering. 'It would be my pleasure,' he said. 'I just need to make a quick call.'

Ariana pretended not to listen as he cancelled his date for the night. And his date for the night did not take it well.

'Svetlana,' he said, and Ariana blinked at the slight warning edge to his tone as she looked out at the dark streets. 'Not now.'

And that slight warning edge had her stomach clenching and a small flush rising to her cheeks. She looked at Gian, who appeared incredibly bored at the unfolding drama.

Yes, drama, for she could hear the rise in Svetlana's voice, and foolish, foolish Svetlana, Ariana thought, for she literally watched his impassiveness transform to disdain.

'Svetlana, I am unable to see you tonight,' Gian said, and then, when it was clear she had asked why, rather drily he answered, 'Because I am unable to see you tonight.'

His lack of explanation must have infuriated Svetlana for even with the phone to his ear, Ariana heard her angry retort. 'When then?'

'Do I have to spell it out, Svetlana?'

It would appear that he did, and Ariana listened as very coldly and firmly he ended their relationship.

'Gian,' she said as they pulled up at La Fiordelise, 'please, call her back. I can go home. I really didn't want to make trouble for you…'

'Forget it.' He gave a dismissive shrug. 'We were always going to end.'

In fact, he hadn't seen Svetlana all week.

Somehow they had bumped through the concert at Teatro dell'Opera but instead of returning to the sumptuous suite behind his office, Gian had taken her home.

'Why did you break up with her?' Ariana asked as they stood outside the car beneath the bright entrance lights.

'Because she wanted more.'

'More?'

'She had started to drop into the hotel unannounced,' he said. Ariana just frowned. 'And she wanted to come up to my residence...'

Her frown deepened.

'As well as that, she wanted to come with me to your father's funeral.'

'Oh?' Ariana said, but it was more a question, because she didn't really understand.

'As if we were a couple.' Gian attempted to explain his closed-off life, but clearly still bewildered, Ariana gave the tiniest shake of her head and so he elaborated. 'She wanted things to progress and that was not what we had agreed.'

'What did you agree to?'

'Only the best parts.' Gian did not soften his words. 'Dinner in a nice restaurant, a trip to the theatre...'

'I assume sex?'

'Correct.'

'So if not in your residence...'

'Ariana, I am not discussing this with you. Suffice it to say I never want a relationship.' He ended the matter. 'You're cold, let's go in.'

'To the restaurant?' Ariana asked.

'I thought the Pianoforte Bar...'

Her eyes narrowed, recalling Svetlana being denied a seat at his restaurant. Despite his kind invitation to keep her company, she knew she was also being kept at arm's length.

'No, thank you.' She shook her head. 'I don't need the noise of a bar tonight, even one as elegant as yours...' Ariana fished and she fished, but Gian did not take the bait, nor upgrade her to restaurant status, even as she stood there and sulked. 'I think I might go for a walk.'

'In heels?' Gian frowned.

'I have my flats in my bag. I'll be fine on my own,' she said, waving him away as she took off her heels and went to put her flats on, but where was a marble pillar when you needed one?

Gian would not be waved off, though, and neither was he Prince Charming, for he did not go down on his knees to help, instead offering his arm. 'Lean on me.' He took one black stiletto that she handed to him and passed her a flat, and then it was all repeated with the other foot.

'Let's walk,' Gian said.

For Ariana, it felt like the right choice. Piazza Navona, the grand, elegant square overlooked by La Fiordelise, was beautifully lit. Its fountains were hypnotic and a little of the tension of the day left as they strolled.

It felt different at night.

Or rather it felt different being here with Gian.

His presence was a comforting warmth in the chilly night air and his voice felt like a welcome caress, as he enquired how things were with her brothers.

'Dante is…' Ariana let out a long sigh. 'I don't know. He's just been so focused on the funeral. I think it will all hit him afterwards. He and my father were close.'

'Yes,' Gian agreed.

'Well, they were until Mia came along.'

'They grew close again, once your father became ill,' Gian pointed out. 'And Stefano?'

'I wouldn't know,' Ariana said tightly. 'You would have to ask Eloa.' She heard the bitterness in her own voice and screwed her eyes closed, because she had told no one, not even Nicki, how left out she felt. 'Sorry, I didn't mean that.'

'Yes, you did,' Gian said gently. 'I know the two of you are close.'

'*Were* close,' she corrected. 'I know it sounds childish, but we used to speak every day. Now he calls Eloa, and that's correct, of course, and how it should be; they're getting married in May. However…' She didn't know how best to describe the loneliness that had descended almost the moment Eloa had been introduced to her and Ariana had felt shut out.

'You miss him?'

'Yes.' She nodded. 'And especially now.'

'Since your father died?'

'Before that,' Ariana admitted. She looked at the moon lighting up the square. If ever there was a time for honesty it was tonight. 'When our parents broke up it was Stefano I turned to. Papà had eyes only for Mia; he didn't want me around so much…'

Gian stayed silent, for he knew that wasn't quite the case. Rafael had found out he was dying and wanted his final years to be spent in peace with Roberto; Mia had been a front of respectability. Of course he could not reveal that and just listened as she continued. 'But Stefano met Eloa around then,' Ariana said. 'I just felt as if everyone I was close to disappeared. I know I have Dante, but he is so much older…'

'Ancient,' Gian agreed drily, for he and Dante were the same age.

'I have Mamma, of course, but…' She wished he would interrupt, or finish her sentence for her, because it was perhaps not something she should say out loud, yet his continued silence compelled her to speak. 'I have Mamma, though only on her terms, and it can be a little stifling at times.'

Still he remained silent as they walked.

'And a little solitary at others,' Ariana admitted. 'I thought things were different with Stefano. He's my twin; I'm used to him being there and I thought, no matter what, we'd still be in each other's lives. I'm happy for him, I honestly am. I'm just not so happy for me. I'm being selfish, I know. Childish…'

'Ariana.' Gian thought for a moment and then decided he could be honest about this much at least. 'For what it's worth, I think Stefano is wrong to shut you out.'

Her head turned towards him, her eyes wide with surprise. She'd expected to be scolded or told she was being petty or jealous. Instead he seemed like he was on her side. 'Really?'

'From everything I can observe, since Eloa came along he's dropped everyone and everything. I didn't realise until today that that also extended to you. Don't you and Eloa get on?'

'That's the ridiculous part,' Ariana said, relieved to speak about something other than death, and also relieved to share what had been eating at her for months. 'I like Eloa, I really do. They just don't seem to want to spend any real time with me.'

'I'm sorry.'

'It doesn't matter.' She gave a tight shrug, at first closing the conversation but then opening it up in a way he had not anticipated. 'Were you close to your brother…' She had to think for a second to recall his name. 'Eduardo?'

'No,' Gian said. At first his answer was final, but she had shared so much with him that he felt it right to share a little more. 'We were for a while.'

'Oh.'

'For a long while I looked up to him. Admired him…'

'And then?'

'And then I didn't.'

He gave her no more.

'Wait there,' Gian said. She assumed he had to make a call, perhaps to Svetlana… Maybe he was bored already with the company he had chosen tonight.

Alone for the first time that day, Ariana quietly admitted her deep feelings for him.

Ariana wanted more of Gian.

She wanted to know his kiss. She wanted…more.

More than his kiss…

To know his touch…

To sit holding hands at his table…

The more she admitted to herself, the more honest her admissions became…

She wanted Gian to hold her and she wanted to know how it felt to be made love to by him.

For Gian De Luca to be her first…

It was a reckless thought, though, for by his own admission Gian came with a warning.

But since when had Ariana heeded warnings?

She stared up at Fontana dei Quattro Fiumi—the Fountain of Four Rivers, said to be the most complex of the many fountains in Rome. She looked at the four river gods and then up, ever up, to the tall obelisk that topped it. Her feelings were spinning in her mind as the crush she had on Gian transformed into need.

She loathed being twenty-five with barely a kiss to her name.

Yet while kisses did not excite her, the mere thought of Gian's kiss did.

'Here.' His voice startled her and she looked at the paper cone filled with hot chestnuts that he held out. 'You looked cold.'

'You got these for me?' Gian watched as her pale face broke into a smile, and her eyes shone as if he were handing her a purse of gold. 'Thank you.'

Hot chestnuts on a cold night had never tasted so good as they sat at the base of the fountain, biting into the salty treats. 'These are the best I have tasted,' Ariana said, every single time she ate one.

'They're just chestnuts.' Gian did not really get her enthusiasm for such a familiar winter treat. 'I used to come down here at night as a child and buy these.'

'You would sneak out?' she nudged.

'No sneaking required.'

'What do you mean?'

'Just that…' Gian said, and he looked at Ariana, quietly watching the world go by. He knew why he had not left her alone tonight. He knew better than anyone how it felt to be alone in Rome after dark, that frantic search for company, any company, that compelled you to speak to a stranger or hang out with a wayward friend, anything other than return to your room and lie there alone. 'So…' he changed the subject and looked over at the stunning Palazzo Pamphili, where the wedding was to be held '… you arranged the wedding reception.'

'I managed to secure the venue,' Ariana corrected.

'Good for you.' He smiled.

His smile was like being handed the earth.

'Come on,' he suggested, when they had finished eating, 'let's walk.'

They passed the impressive building where a few months from now the wedding would take place. It seemed so wrong that such a celebration would take place and their father would not be there.

'Are you going?' she asked, because the idea of him being there really helped. She was so out of the wedding loop she had no real idea if he'd been invited, let alone responded.

'No,' he admitted. 'It's the weekend of the opening of my Florence hotel so I shall be sending my apologies. I am sure I shan't be missed.'

You shall be missed, she wanted to say, but did not know how. 'I'm kind of dreading it,' she said, hinting a little that his presence might help.

'You'll be just fine,' Gian said assuredly, and gave her hand a squeeze, yet her fingers were cold beneath his so he held onto them as they walked.

Gian did not do hand-holding.

Ever.

Yet tonight he did.

For a second, Ariana felt as if she were walking in the Tuscan fields in the middle of summer, not sad and frozen in Rome. But then she remembered the reason for his kindness this night, and wondered how it had been for him. 'You must miss your parents…' she ventured, though immediately knew she had said the wrong thing for he dropped her hand like a hot coal.

'I didn't know them enough to miss them,' he said, but Ariana refused to be fobbed off.

'What about your brother?' she probed, but he was equally unforthcoming.

'Leave it, Ariana.'

She refused. 'How did you find out about the…?' She hesitated, unsure what to call a raging fire on a yacht in the middle of the ocean. 'The accident?' she settled for.

'Hardly an accident,' Gian retorted, and she heard a trace of bitterness to his tone. 'With the amount of alcohol and class-A drugs my family consumed, I think it could be called inevitable.'

Ariana was stunned.

She had heard whispers, of course, like little jigsaw pieces of scandal that had been gathered together over dinners and parties, but all too soon scooped up and put away. But now it was Gian himself putting the pieces together and giving her a glimpse.

'They were renewing their wedding vows?' Ariana checked.

God, she was persistent. Perhaps it was the emotion of the day, but he found that tonight he didn't mind. 'Yes. It sounds romantic, doesn't it, like the Duke and Fiordelise, but the truth is it was an excuse for a party. They renewed their vows every couple of years,' Gian said drily. 'They would fight, they would make up, they would say never again… I got off the hamster wheel and left before then. I was at university, studying architecture. I was asleep in the residences…'

'You didn't live at La Fiordelise then?'

'God, no.' He gave a hollow laugh. 'I was more than happy to leave it all behind. Luna came with the police and woke me…'

'Luna worked for your parents?'

'She was actually working her notice,' Gian said. 'They had been late again paying her and she had resigned, but after they died Luna said she would stay until things were more stable.' Gian gave her a tight smile. 'Fifteen years later, she still reminds me on occasion that she is working her notice.' He shook his head and closed the subject.

Except Ariana wanted to prise it back open. 'Tell me…'

'Tell you what?'

'How you felt when they died?'

'As I told you, I barely knew them.'

'They were your parents, your brother…'

'Just leave it,' he warned. 'Ariana, I respect your boundaries. Why can't you respect mine?'

'Because I want to know you some more…'

He kept right on walking, though a little faster than before. 'Wait…' Ariana said, and grabbed his coat to slow him down, except her hand found its way back into his. 'I'm sorry for pushing. I just wonder…' she didn't know how best to say it '…when the grief goes?'

'I can't answer that,' Gian admitted. 'I grieved for them long before they died.' He should close it there, but her hand was warm and he sensed she would walk for ever just to hear some more. 'Eduardo and I were both repulsed by their ways. He was older, the one who would look out for me when I was small, make sure my nanny was paid, that sort of thing…'

She stayed silent in the hope he would continue and her reward was great, for he revealed more.

'Then he took up their ways and I ended up looking out for him.'

Still she stayed silent but she felt the grip of his hand tighten and it seemed like the darkness of his truth guided her through her own pain.

'I found Eduardo one morning; I thought he was dead. I couldn't rouse my parents. The hotel doctor came and for all the hell of that morning, by that evening the incident was forgotten.'

Now she spoke. 'Not by you.'

'Never by me,' Gian said. 'It happened several times again. I said to Eduardo one day, "I won't always be there to save you." And it was then that I stopped…'

'Stopped what?' Ariana asked.

'I can't answer that,' Gian admitted. 'And I'm not being evasive, I just…' He shrugged. 'Stopped.'

Ariana stopped asking, which he was grateful for, because revelations like these were hard.

He had stopped…not loving, not caring, just stopped all feelings.

Stopped hoping for change.

Stopped trying to control their chaos.

'I like order,' he admitted, and looked over at her. 'Why do you smile?'

'Because it's hardly a revelation. I know you like order, Gian.'

'You know too much,' he said, and dropped a kiss on the top of her head as they walked.

It was a tiny kiss, but when it came from Gian, it felt as if he had just picked her up and carried her.

It felt so perfect that she actually let out a little laugh and touched her head to feel where his lips had just pressed, for her scalp tingled. 'You're crazy, Ariana,' he told her.

'A bit.'

It was unexpected bliss on the saddest of nights, to be walking on a cold Rome night, hand in hand, along Piazza d'Arecoli, their breaths blowing white in the night air. Ariana had run out of words, and she was terrified that he might drop her hand.

His hand was warm and it was so unexpected and so nice and just everything she needed tonight.

Gian too was pondering the light weight of her fingers that wrapped around his and how, on the near-empty street, when they could easily walk apart, they were strolling like this.

It was Ariana Romano.

She's a friend, he told himself.

He was simply doing what any friend would.

Except he did not have friendships of this type.

And he never confided in anyone, yet he just had.

Still holding hands, they took the stairs and there before them, ever beautiful, was the Altar of the Fatherland. Soldiers stood guarding the tomb of the unknown soldier and Ariana knew she should guard her own heart with the same attention and care.

'Oh,' she gasped as they took in the altar of the goddess of Rome.

His stomach growled and he turned her to face him. There were tired streaks of mascara, like delicate lace, smudged on her cheeks. Her mouth, rarely devoid of lipstick, was swollen from days of tears. She smiled briefly and it lit up her face for a moment. He wanted to capture it, to frame it and hold onto it—and he did so with his hands.

She felt the brush of his fingers on her cheeks and then

the soft pressure as he held her face. Surely the eternal flame flared, because something lit the sky and seared her as his lips made first contact.

Just the gentlest brush at first then soft and slow and exploring.

His kiss made her slightly giddy in a way no other had. His touch was both tender and firm and she felt she could fall right now and be caught, even though his hands barely held her.

Only once did she peek. Ariana opened her eyes, while praying that she wouldn't be caught, for she did not want to break this spell. Gian's eyes were closed, though, as if savouring the most exquisite wine. He continued to hold her cheeks, so firmly now that her head could not move. He kissed her thoroughly and his lips were like velvet, his tongue so shockingly intimate it felt charged as each stroke shot volts of ecstasy to her own. His hand moved into her hair, holding the back of her head and knotting into her scalp as his tongue danced with hers.

A craving for more built in her but he pulled back. Gian looked at her wet lips and dilated pupils and the frantic, somewhat startled look and he tried to rein in his usual common sense. 'I should get you home…'

'Please,' Ariana said, but her voice was low and husky and told them both what she wanted.

Ariana's decision was made.

Gian De Luca would be her first.

Perhaps that was the reason she had held on for so long, because there was no one else who held a candle to him. No one who made her shiver, even without touching her, no one who made her mouth want to know his kiss…

'Ariana.' His voice was gruff. 'When I said home, I meant to your door.' Gian was serious. A kiss was one thing, but bedding her was out of the question. 'If we were so much as seen out together…'

'That would get them talking.' Ariana smiled as Gian clearly hated the thought. 'Mamma would have us married in a moment if she knew her virgin daughter was out with the Duke...' Her voice trailed off, unsure how Gian would receive the news of her inexperience, but he gave a low laugh.

Ariana was not, he knew, dropping in his title; instead she was capturing her mother's thought process and agreeing with exactly how it would be if they were seen. 'Exactly. Though,' he added, 'I'm sure all mothers think their daughters are virgins.'

'But I am one.'

He almost laughed again, and then realised she wasn't laughing. He almost hauled her off him, but decided that reaction might be a bit extreme and so instead he offered her his smile.

His duty smile, which she determinedly ignored.

'Let's get you home...' Gian said.

'Yes,' Ariana agreed. 'Take me to bed.'

'Absolutely not.'

And he meant it, for he was headed down the steps. Ariana did not quite know what she'd done wrong, just that everything had changed.

'Gian.' Now she really did have to practically run to keep up with him. 'Why are you being like this? Didn't you like our kiss?'

'It was a kiss,' Gian snapped, 'not an open invitation.'

But Ariana would not relent. She had made up her mind and was all too used to getting her own way. 'I want my first to be you.'

'Well, it won't be. If we are even as much as seen, people will talk and it will be...' He had to be cruel to be kind. 'They will turn it into something bigger than it is.'

'I know that.'

'Do you?' Gian checked. 'Do you understand that I

don't do relationships? That the very last thing I want is to be involved in someone else's life?'

'You're always dating.'

'Yes.'

'So what's the difference?' Ariana frowned. 'I might be innocent in the bedroom, but I am not stupid, Gian…'

'I never said you were.'

'I'm not asking for love. I don't want lies to appease and promises that you won't keep,' Ariana said. 'I'm all too familiar with them, but I do want you to make love to me.'

'Ariana—'

'No,' she broke in, and they argued in loud Italian all the way home. 'Don't make me ashamed for admitting it. I'm twenty-five and a virgin. I don't want to be married, Gian. Do you not think my mother has endless suitors in mind for me? I can't have a casual relationship or it will be a kiss and tell. You know that…'

He looked at the spoilt, immature Ariana speaking like the woman she was.

'Surely there have been kisses…?'

'Yes,' she admitted, 'plastic kisses from plastic men, but your kiss nearly made me come.'

He laughed because she fascinated him.

Like a stunning portrait, like a song you had to pause just to go back and listen to the lyrics again.

He loved how she stated her case.

They argued all the way to the swish apartment block where she lived. 'I get that I'm not as experienced or as worldly as Svetlana…'

'Stop,' Gian said. 'Just stop right there. Why would you sign up for inevitable hurt, Ariana?' Gian asked. 'You know it'll go public, and you know your family will find out, and I know that I'll end things…'

'How?' Ariana asked. She wasn't begging or persuading, more genuinely perplexed. 'How do you know?'

'Because I never want to get too close. I date women who understand from the get-go that we'll never progress further than we did on the very first night.'

'So I would get no more than a kiss and a cone of hot chestnuts,' she teased. 'Well, rest assured, you wouldn't have to worry about dumping me, Gian. I would grow bored with you very quickly.'

He didn't smile at her joke and he would not relent, but rather than face being alone she turned off the voices in her head and tried to argue with a kiss. She put her arms around his neck and pressed her mouth to his, but there was no longer solace there for his was pressed closed and unyielding, and she sobbed as he pulled his head back.

'Go in!' he warned her.

'Please, Gian, I don't want to be lonely tonight.'

But when he remained silent, Ariana got the message. He did not want her, so she scrabbled around for her dignity. 'Thank you for seeing me to my door.'

'Get some sleep.' Gian said.

'Oh, please,' Ariana scoffed as she huffed off. 'As if that's going to happen.'

He watched her leave, and by honouring Rafael he felt like he'd failed her. 'Ariana…' Gian called out, and it troubled him how quickly she turned and was back at his side.

He would not sleep with her, no matter how much they both wanted it.

He would do the right thing by Rafael *and* Ariana.

'I'll come in, but I'm taking the sofa.' She nodded, both regret and relief flooding through her as he spoke on. 'You don't have to be alone tonight.'

CHAPTER SIX

THEY PASSED THE dozing doorman and took the elevator, although Gian stood like a security guard to the side of her, rather than like a man who had almost kissed her to orgasm.

She was all dishevelled in her head as they stepped into her apartment. 'Thankfully,' Ariana said as she closed the drapes, 'it was serviced while I was away, or we would be knee-deep in…' Her voice trailed off.

Knee-deep in what? Gian wanted to ask, for there was no real evidence of her here. He could be walking into any well-heeled woman's apartment in Rome—and Gian had walked into many—and the décor would be much the same. It was all very tasteful with plump sofas and modern prints, yet it was rather like a show home and there was barely a hint of Ariana. Even her bookshelves offered no real clues, for there were a few classics on the shelves as well as elegant coffee table books. There were at least some photos up, but even they seemed carefully chosen to show, so to speak, only her best side.

'Do you want a drink?' Ariana offered.

'No, thank you.'

Now that she had him here, Ariana didn't quite know what to do with him. It was, she thought, a bit like stealing a bear from the zoo, making it your mission to get him home and then…

'I'll show you around,' she offered, 'where you're sleeping. Given that you'd rather it wasn't with me.'

'I don't need a tour,' Gian responded. 'I will stay here.' He pointed to the sofa.

'I do have a guest room.'

'I'm not here to relax.'

'You are *such* a cold comfort.'

'Better than no comfort at all. I do have some scruples, Ariana. I am not going to make love to you on the night of your father's funeral when you are upset and not thinking straight.'

'Oh, believe me, I am thinking straight. Life is short, Gian, life is for living, for loving.'

'Then you've come to the wrong man because, as I've repeatedly said, I don't do love.'

She wanted to stamp her feet. She knew she was being a bit of a diva but she was beyond caring.

When Ariana wanted something, she wanted it now, and when she'd made up her mind…well, it was made up.

'Can you unzip my dress, please?' Ariana lifted her hair and stood with her back to him, waiting for the teeniest indicator—a run of his finger, a lingering palm, him holding his breath—as he found the little clasp at the top of the velvet dress and undid it. Yet Gian was a master of self-control and without lingering he tugged the zip down so that her back and the lacy straps of her black bra were exposed.

'There,' he said, with all the excitement of an accountant relocating a decimal point.

She turned around and her dress slipped down, exposing her shoulders and décolletage, but he looked straight into her glittering eyes and smothered a yawn. 'It's been a long day,' Gian said. 'Perhaps you should go to bed.'

'So much for the playboy of Rome,' she sneered as she

headed for her room, embarrassed that he clearly did not want her.

No wonder, Ariana thought as she stood in the bathroom and looked at her blotchy tear-streaked face.

She cleansed her skin and then ran a brush listlessly through her hair. She pulled on some shorts and a T-shirt and then climbed into bed. Sulking, she pulled the covers up to her chin.

'Do you want milk or something?' Gian called.

'I'm not ten!' she shouted through the darkness. It was worse having him here like this than being alone. Except, as she lay in the dark, Ariana knew that wasn't strictly true. She loathed the dark and the night, especially since her father died, and now it did not seem quite as dark and the place not quite so lonely.

In fact, there was comfort just knowing that Gian was near.

Finally, whatever it was that had possessed her, that had had her angrily demanding sex, left her.

Oh, Papà!

Gian listened to her cry, and knew that for once it was not for attention. Though it killed him not to go to her, Gian knew they were necessary tears.

He opened the drapes and looked for something to read. Some might call it snooping, but really he was looking for somewhere to charge his phone when a cupboard *fell* open and he could see that this was where *Ariana* had been hiding. It was rather chaotic and piled high with photos, wads and wads of them, and dated boxes too. Ah, so she must have been knee-deep in photos, Gian realised, trying to choose some favourites for the funeral montage. As well as that, there were fashion magazines and blockbusters and recipe books...

An awful lot of them!

Gian selected one and tried to block out her tears by

reading. He just stared at the method for tempering white chocolate until finally she fell into silence.

He was reading how to make cannelloni when he heard her again.

It was almost hourly, like some tragic cuckoo clock, but Gian kept the door between them closed for he would *not* sleep with her on the night of her father's funeral. Surely only foolish decisions were made then…

Gian was completely matter-of-fact about sex. To him it was as necessary as breathing. Perhaps it was an exaggeration, but he felt he would not have lived to the age of twenty-five without the escape of it, and he knew he could give her that, but only when her head was clear.

To know she trusted him was significant, for the thought of her misplacing her trust in someone else left him cold.

He watched the black sky turn to a steel grey and, even though Gian knew his logic was flawed, when the silver mist of a new day dawned and he heard her little cry, Gian went through and sat on the bed.

Ariana was far from a temptress at dawn. She covered her face with one hand as he came in, and little bits of last night played like taunting movies.

'Did I make a complete fool of myself?' she asked in a pained voice.

'Of course not,' he said magnanimously, then teased her with a slow smile. 'You just pleaded with me to make love to you.'

'Perhaps it was the cognac,' she said hopefully, but they both knew it had been a small sip and that had been back in Luctano. There had been a lot of walking and talking since then and she could hardly blame the chestnuts! 'I'm sorry for my behaviour. I don't actually fancy you, Gian.'

'Really?'

'Well, sometimes a bit, but then I remind myself that

you are just a hunk of good-looking...' She liked his slow smile. 'I remind myself how mean you can be...'

'Mean?'

'*One* glass of champagne at my interview!'

He smiled for he thought she hadn't noticed the absence of a bottle.

'Ah, that.'

'A meal at your bar instead of your restaurant...'

'You make it sound like the local dive.'

'Perhaps, but even so I *deserved* five stars last night. Anyway,' she continued, 'when I do find myself fancying you, I remind myself how remote you can be and how humourless you are.'

'Well, it's good you've come to your senses,' Gian said, 'especially as I don't have condoms with me. I tend not to keep them in my funeral suit.'

She stared back and resisted smiling, determined to prove her humourless point.

'Except we wouldn't need them.' He held up a purple foil packet of contraceptive pills. 'What are these for?'

'You've been snooping.'

'Not really, I wanted toothpaste. I just wondered what you were doing on the Pill if you're not sleeping with anyone...'

'Yet!'

His jaw was set in a grim line. He had this vision of Ariana chasing some bastard who sensed her fragility, yet she was not fragile now. Ariana was looking right at him and there was none of last night's desperate need for comfort, just the desire that had always been beneath it.

'So?' he asked. She looked at the purple Pill packet and was about to lie, as she so often did, and say she was on the Pill for her skin, or so that it made her cycle more predictable, or whatever she would say if her mother found them.

But Gian was certainly not her mother.

And with Gian there was no reason she could see to lie.

'I went on it because I feel like the only person in the world without a sex life, and when I go away with friends I don't want them to know I'm the only one...' She shrugged. 'Pathetic, huh...'

'No more pathetic than when I was younger and would have condoms on me, just to have them on me...'

'Really?'

'Yes.'

They shared a smile in the thin dawn light but then hers wavered. 'Look, I'm sorry I've made things even more awkward between us. I should never have foisted myself on you. I was all a jumble.' She looked at his suave good looks and then at his chest. His tie was gone and his shirt unbuttoned, though just at the top—enough to see a glimpse of chest hair—but she reminded herself of how empty a vessel his chest was and again tried to salvage some pride. 'And it's not as if I enjoyed kissing you last night. In fact, it was like kissing a screen. I felt nothing...'

'Really?'

The thin morning light disappeared as his face came closer, but she refused to be moved by the brush of his lips and the softness of his mouth, just as he had refused to be moved by hers.

Except his kiss was more refined, more skilled, more measured and she found she could not quite catch her breath as her mouth fought not to relent.

'Like kissing a screen?' he checked.

'Yes,' she said, and felt the scratch of his chin drag on hers. As his fingers came to her jaw, his tongue slipped in, and she absolutely refused to moan at the bliss. In fact, she held her mouth slack as his tongue moved in and out. He tasted divine, all minty and fresh, but there was nothing clean about his kiss—it was filthy, in fact. Thorough, probing and potent with skill, his tongue felt like it ran a wire straight down between her legs and she bunched her hands into fists rather than reach for his head.

'Still nothing?' he checked, and now his hand was stroking her breast through her top and Ariana was sure that if she hadn't been lying down she might have fainted.

'Nothing,' she lied.

'Do you want me to stop?'

'No.'

'Do you understand it is just this once?'

'Oh, stop with the lectures,' she said, as his fingers slid inside her top. 'I accept the terms and conditions…'

He laughed.

Gian actually laughed. Not that she saw it, for he was pulling her T-shirt over her head, and Ariana was loose limbed and compliant and letting him.

'Please get naked,' she said. 'I want to see you.'

'For a virgin, you certainly know how to provoke me,' Gian commented as he rose from the bed and started to undress.

'Because you provoke me,' Ariana responded. She felt a blush spread across her chest as he removed his shirt and discarded his clothes.

Oh, God. She had always known he was stunning, but he looked so toned, and so male—his chest hair, the thick line on his stomach—and she was holding her breath in nervous, excited anticipation as he unzipped.

He was the most beautiful thing she had seen and she was far from shy, just staring with hungry eyes. It made her blood feel too heavy to move through her heart as he took her hand and closed it around his thick length.

He was warm and hard and he felt like velvet and he let her explore him. Gian kissed her neck, and he kissed down her chest and when his mouth met her breast she wept inside.

'Help me,' she said, because he made her so frantic with

desire and his warm hand was on her stomach, which made her want to lift her knees.

'Does that help?' he said, and she moaned as his hand moved down and he stroked her.

'Not enough,' she gasped. 'God, Gian…' And then she whimpered, for the soft vacuum of his mouth on her breast and the relentless pressure below created a feeling akin to both panic and bliss building inside her.

And though his intention had been to bring Ariana to the edge and then take her, instead he indulged in the pleasure of watching her orgasm build.

Her eyes opened to his for a moment, and she had never felt more bathed in attention, or so in tune with another person.

Then she gave up watching him and shut her eyes, arching her neck as she surrendered to the sumptuous pleasure he so easily gave. He kissed her then so slowly that it felt like a revival but then his thighs were between hers and his mouth was by her temple as her hands held his hips, holding him back, digging him in, both wanting and conflicted. She was desperate for fusion and for the initiation she would allow only Gian to give her.

It hurt, and yet it did not.

He squeezed into her tight space and it was both pleasure and a pain that must surely end. Yet her lungs were expanding and cracks of light returning to the blackout he had brought upon her, and everything multiplied as he moved slowly inside.

'Gian.' She said his name as she had wanted to since her interview. She rolled it on her tongue and tasted it as he moved deep inside her.

She felt crushed, she felt covered, she felt found. 'Gian,' Ariana said again, as he moved faster, but his name was more like a warning now, for he was tipping her towards the edge and she almost did not want to go.

For then they would end.

'Let go,' he told her. He could feel her slight panic and the mounting tension, and then when she shattered he shot into her in relief.

Both breathless, both dizzy, they lay there, catching their breath.

He adored her inexperience, not just because of the honour of being her first but because she could never know that, even while making love, he held back.

CHAPTER SEVEN

THEY LAY THERE together in silence. Ariana examined her conscience and heart for regret and found none.

Not a jot.

For Gian, there was rare peace as he lay there, their limbs knotted together. Only one thing missing. 'We need food.'

'I have none,' Ariana happily admitted. Her world had been turned upside down since the death of her father, and anyway she tended to eat out. 'Well, I have some ice cream.'

'Ice cream?'

'A lot of ice cream!' Making it was her hobby, her absolute guilty pleasure. Wearing a small wrap, she padded to the kitchen. There she defrosted two croissants and filled them with ice-cream in flavours of cardamom and pistachio and a dark chocolate one too while she waited for the mocha pot to boil and wondered how best to take back her heart.

How to accept his terms and conditions and somehow let him go with grace.

Gian lay there breathing in the scent of brewing coffee, trying to pinpoint the moment he had started wanting her.

On the day of her farcical interview, when he'd first noticed the true colour of her eyes? No, a more honest examination told him it had been before that, and even Ariana herself had voiced it: the night of the silver ball.

Or had it been when she'd swept into the planning meeting and said she wanted silver as a theme?

Instead of gritting his teeth, he had found himself smiling, at least on the inside, for Gian rarely showed how he truly felt.

But, no, while *it* might have started then, for Gian things had really changed the night she had worn silver. Rafael had not been there, and Gian had stood by Ariana's side as she played host. He'd been in awe of how long she'd smiled with the guests and carried on with grace.

He'd wanted to take her aside and tell her that he knew how hard this was, and how proud of her he felt. Instead, they had danced their duty dance and he had held her back from him with rigid arms so she would not feel how turned on he was and how he had ached to drop a kiss on her mouth, on her bare shoulder.

And he was hard for her again.

'Colazione!' Ariana announced breakfast as she came into the room and blinked at his obvious arousal. 'Good grief,' she said. 'I'm far too sore for that.'

'Sore?'

She nodded. 'Nicely sore, the best sore ever.' Oh, God, she wanted him again, but then the ice cream would melt and her phone had already pinged in several messages. She had Nicki coming round *and* she had to do this without starting to cry. 'Eat,' she told him. 'You can have the chocolate one.'

It sounded like she was making a concession, but Gian could tell when she was lying. 'I want the other one.'

'No, no,' she said, 'I'll *let* you have the chocolate one.'

'But I want the pistachio.'

'And cardamom.' Ariana sighed and handed the one she really wanted to him. 'I put in extra when I made it.'

Gian, though used to breakfast in bed, was not used to

this—just sitting in bed, eating and tasting food with a woman, and taking bites of each other's.

Bites so big she nearly lost her fingers to his mouth, and they laughed as they fought over food. 'You really made this?' he checked.

'Not the croissant, just the ice cream. I'm going to make salted roast chestnut next, and I shall get them from the same vendor. They were the best I've tasted...'

'They're just chestnuts.'

'No,' she said, and then she gave him the speech she had prepared in her kitchen. 'They kept me warm. *You* kept me warm last night, Gian, even if you did not share my bed. You cared for me last night and then again this morning and I thank you.'

She had surprised him, and then she surprised him further when, with breakfast done, it was Ariana herself who suggested he leave. 'You'd better go. Mamma might drop in.'

'Doesn't she call first?' Gian asked.

'No,' Ariana said. 'I always ask her to but then she reminds me that she's my mother and shouldn't need an appointment...'

'I'll get dressed then.'

'Have a shower,' she offered.

He declined, or he would be trailing a floral boutique all day if he used her scents. 'I'll have one back at the hotel.'

It was odd, Ariana thought as she lay watching him dress, that he did not call La Fiordelise home.

'I like you unshaven,' she admitted. 'You're always so...' she fought to find the right word '...well-presented and groomed.'

'It's my job to be.'

'Perhaps, but...' She shrugged and his eyes narrowed, trying to interpret yet another of her actions, for those slender shoulders could say many things.

'But what?'

'Nothing.' She smiled wickedly. 'There are other sides to you, I'm sure. I guess I won't find out now.'

'You could. Why not tell the doorman to lie and say you're out?'

'He's so lazy he'd forget,' Ariana rolled her eyes and tried to sound casual, when in truth she wanted to cry and cling onto his leg and beg him to never leave.

Not a good look, that much she knew!

'You really ought to go,' she said as he buckled his belt, though she wanted to reach up and unbuckle it so she was only half listening as he spoke.

'So how do you have a private life, with her dropping in and out? How do you have a…?' And then his voice faded. After all, this morning had been her sex life to date. 'You'll be okay?' he checked as he did up the buttons of his shirt and half tucked it in.

'Yes.'

'If you're not…'

'Gian,' Ariana broke in. 'I have my family and I have my friends.' He hovered on the edge of both of her inner circles but was not fully in either. She felt the indent of the mattress as he sat down and bent over to do up his laces, and though she ached to reach out to him, Ariana told him of the practicalities of her day. 'Also, Nicki is dropping by to tell me about her holiday…'

He sat up and looked right at her. 'As opposed to coming by to see how you're faring after the loss of your father?'

'Of course she's coming for that.' Her eyes narrowed as she took in his sulking mouth; she knew he didn't like Nicki. 'It's a bit early in the relationship for you to be dictating who I see. Oh, that's right, it's not a relationship, and even if it were…' she gave him a tight smile '… that still wouldn't give you a right to say who my friends are, Gian.'

'Fine.' He put up two hands to indicate he was dropping it.

And he was!

Ariana was right. It was not his place to call out her friends but, still, that Nicki got his goat.

All of Ariana's hangers-on did.

'Look,' he said, and Ariana could feel him weighing things up before he spoke. 'I think you were right about working. I do think you'd be an asset for the hotel and if we can both...' He reached over and toyed with a thick coil of her black hair that sat on her collarbone as he spoke, but she pushed his hand away and her response was sudden.

'No!'

She could not work for him; far too much had changed.

'I can't work for you, Gian,' she said, and used another inevitable truth to disguise the real reason. 'Mamma's going to need me now more than ever.'

CHAPTER EIGHT

HER MOTHER DID indeed need her more than ever.

In the tumultuous weeks following her father's death, Ariana's mother's demands were relentless.

It was still by appointment only—Angela Romano liked her make-up, jewellery and the day's carefully chosen wig perfectly arranged before even her daughter dropped around.

Yet the lunches were endless.

As she sat there, twirling a shred of prosciutto on a fork, Ariana fought to quell a surge of anger as her mother called over the sommelier to tell him that the champagne was a little flat. She wondered how someone so supposedly bereft with grief would even notice, let alone have the energy to complain!

'I'm fine, thank you,' Ariana said, placing a hand over her glass. 'I really do need to get going, Mamma,' she said, reaching for her bag. 'I'm meeting Dante.'

'Oh, he can wait.'

'Mamma, please, I said I'd be there at three.' She tried to temper her irritation. 'I really do have to go…' Her voice trailed off because she didn't want to worry her mother, but Dante's mood of late was pretty grim and nothing seemed to be getting done for the Romano Ball—the invitations hadn't even gone out and it was just a few weeks away. 'Would you like me to come over this evening?'

'No, no.' Angela shook her head. 'I have the priest coming over tonight.'

'Well, take care.' Ariana kissed her on both cheeks. 'I shall see you soon.'

'Tomorrow,' Angela checked. 'Here? Or perhaps we could go shopping...' She ran a disapproving eye over Ariana's navy shift dress and espadrilles. 'We could get you something a little less last year.'

Ariana had never felt more stifled and wished not for the first time that there was more purpose and structure to her day. She took a taxi to Romano Holdings in the EUR district, craning her neck as they passed La Fiordelise. She wished she was working there.

And then she flushed with sheer pleasure when she recalled the very reason she now could not.

It was her favourite memory, a harbour in troubled times she could return to, yet there was confusion there too—how, from the very moment they had kissed, Gian had started the countdown to the end.

She had stopped having drinks there on a Friday. Well, Paulo had been banned and Nicki said they should no longer go in solidarity with their friend.

Except Ariana had loved going there...

'Signorina?'

The voice of the driver startled her and Ariana realised they had arrived. Time tended to run away whenever she thought of Gian, and so she determinedly put him out of her mind as she walked into the plush office building.

Sarah, Dante's PA, gave her a smile. 'Go through,' she said and then added, 'Good luck.'

'Do I need it?' Ariana joked, but then all joking faded when she saw him. 'Dante!' She could not keep the surprise from her voice when she saw her older brother, looking less than his put-together self, for his complexion was grey and his shirt was crumpled and there was just such a heavy air to him. 'How are you doing?' she asked as she went over and kissed his cheeks and gave him a hug. 'I've barely seen you. Mamma is saying the same.'

'Well, work has been busy.'

'I'm sure it has.' She nodded. 'What's happening about the ball?'

'It's all under control. I'm meeting with Gian at five to finalise the details…' His voice trailed off. There was a strange atmosphere in the office, and for an appalling moment she wondered if Dante had found out about their one illicit night, or rather illicit morning.

'And?' she asked with a nervous laugh. 'What are the final details?'

Dante said nothing.

'How are we addressing Papà's passing?' Ariana pushed.

'I'm sure Gian will take care of that.'

'But in the will Papà asked that his children take care of the ball,' Ariana said, but then stopped and sat chewing the edge of her thumbnail. She was worried about Dante. Though not as close to him as she had always been to Stefano, she knew there was something wrong. He was grieving for their father, but she couldn't help but think there was more to it than that. 'Is everything okay, Dante?' she ventured.

'Of course.'

'You can talk to me. I might just understand.' He closed his eyes, as if she couldn't possibly. 'Look, why don't I meet with Gian?' There was genuinely no ulterior motive, just a need to get the ball right for their father. 'I can take over the ball…'

'Would you?' Dante's relief was evident.

'Of course.' Ariana nodded.

It was only then that her nerves caught up!

Ariana walked by the *laghetto* for a full hour. The cherry blossoms were in full bloom and the park looked stunning, and if there was a little trepidation about coming face to face with Gian it was soon displaced as something else took hold. Excitement. It felt like for ever since her brain had been put to work.

Sitting on a bench, looking at the blossom swirl and float like pink snow, it was the perfect place for her imagination to wander. Scrabbling in her bag, she took out a journal and started to make notes.

It was exhilarating, cathartic, and there were tears in her eyes as memories danced while words formed on the page. It was right that she take over the ball, Ariana knew, for she knew how best to celebrate her father.

Ariana wasn't even nervous about facing Gian.

She had so much to tell him.

'I have Ariana Romano in Reception to see you,' Luna informed him.

'Ariana?' Gian frowned. 'But I thought I was meeting with Dante…'

'Well, Ariana is here instead.'

'Fine.' Gian did his level best to act as if it were of no consequence that it was Ariana who had just arrived. It was an informal meeting, but also a very *necessary* meeting. One that Gian had pushed for, given Dante seemed to have—both figuratively and literally—dropped the ball. 'Send her through.'

Damn.

Gian usually had no qualms about facing an ex-lover, but with Ariana it felt different indeed.

It was because they were family friends, he told himself, steadfastly refusing to examine his feelings further than that.

It had been weeks since the funeral and to his quiet surprise he had heard nothing from Ariana. He had expected the demanding, rather clingy Ariana to drape herself like bindweed around one of the columns in Reception, or at the very least find an *accidental* reason for her to drop by.

And now she was here.

He was curious as to her mood, and very determined to get things back on a more regular footing, as if they had never made love.

As if they had not sat eating ice cream naked in her bed.

She stepped into his office, and brought with her an Italian spring. He had to consciously remind himself to greet her the same way he would have before…

'Ariana…' He stood and went round his desk and of course kissed her cheeks. There were dots of pink blossom in her hair and he had to resist lifting his hand and carefully picking them out. 'This is unexpected…'

'I know.' She gave him an apologetic smile and an eye-roll as she took her seat but she was too excited to be awkward around him. 'Dante and I agreed that I will take over the final preparations for the ball. Believe me, I did not engineer it…'

He knew she spoke the truth.

For Ariana with a secret agenda would be immaculate, rather than bare-legged and a little tousled. Plus, she was more animated than he had ever seen her and dived straight in.

'Firstly, I don't want to go with the forest theme…'

'Thank God,' Gian said. 'What theme do you have in mind?'

'None,' Ariana said. 'I want the ballroom to speak for itself, and I want gardenias on each table. He loved them.'

'Yes.'

'And orchids…' she said, but Gian reacted with a wavering gesture with his hand.

'Not together,' he said.

'Perhaps by his photo?'

Gian nodded.

'And I want to change the menu.' She handed him a sheet of paper she had torn from a pad.

He said nothing as he read through it, for Ariana did all the talking. 'These were my father's favourites,' she said. 'I thought we could use some produce from his estate…'

'One moment,' Gian said. She sat tapping her feet as, suddenly in the midst of this most important meeting, he simply got up and walked out. 'Sorry about that,' he said a moment later when he returned. 'Now, where were we?'

'I don't think it should be a solemn night, but if we can acknowledge him in the food and wine…'

She spoke for almost two hours. There was no champagne brought in, just sparkling water, which she took grateful sips of between pouring out ideas. There was no flirting, no reference to what had happened, no alluding to it, just a determination to get this important night right.

'What about the wording for the invitations?' Gian said. 'Mia is technically the host…'

'No!' Only then did she flare. 'We don't even know if she's coming.'

'I'll work on the wording,' Gian agreed. 'Leave Mia to me. I think your ideas are excellent. There's a lot to do but I agree it has to be perfect. Why don't we try the dinner menu now?'

'Now?' she frowned.

'I asked Luna to give your menu to my head chef. He is preparing a sample menu…'

She had her dinner invitation.

He never took dates to the hotel's restaurant, but Ariana wasn't his date. It was business, Gian told himself as they were shown to his table. It looked out onto the restaurant but was private enough for conversation to take place.

'I wish I was better dressed,' Ariana admitted as a huge napkin was placed in her lap. Her clothes were better suited for lunch, or even a gentle lakeside walk, certainly not fine dining in La Fiordelise.

'You look…' He hesitated, for he did not tell his business dates they looked stunning or beautiful. 'Completely fine.' Gian settled for that, yet it felt as flat as the iced water that was being poured, and as shallow as the bowl in which a waterlily floated. 'You look stunning,' Gian admitted. 'Especially with pink blossom in your hair.'

Ariana laughed and raked a hand through her mane. 'I was walking by the office; the blossom is out and it's so beautiful.'

'And so fleeting.'

Like us, she wanted to say as she dropped a few petals from her hair into the water lily bowl between them. 'Yes, so fleeting,' Ariana agreed, 'but worth it.'

It was the briefest, and the only reference to what they had shared.

The starter was ravioli stuffed with pecorino with a creamy white truffle sauce and it brought a smile to her lips as it was placed on the table and she signalled the waiter to rain pepper upon it.

'Taste it first,' he told her.

'Why?' she said. 'If it is cooked to my father's taste then to my mind it needs more pepper and a little less salt.' She signalled to the waiter for even more.

'You love your pepper.'

'I do! And he loved this pasta so much.'

'I know,' Gian told her. 'It was served on the night La Fiordelise came back to life.' He put down his fork and though he had never told another living soul the details, if ever there was a time to, it was now. 'Your father saved La Fiordelise.'

'Saved it?'

'Yes. It was practically empty of guests and running on a skeleton staff when my family died.'

She looked up.

'Papà gave you a loan?'

'Not as such.'

Ariana frowned.

'I inherited a disaster,' Gian said, 'and, believe me, the banks agreed…' He hesitated at how much to tell her and decided, for this part of Rafael's life at least, there was no need for brevity and so as the main course was served he told her what had happened. 'Your father suggested buying into the business.'

'Really?' Ariana hadn't known that. 'But he didn't?'

'No.' Gian shook his head. 'I refused his offer.'

'Can I ask why?'

'I prefer to rise or fall alone,' Gian said. 'I did not see that the hotel could be saved. Still, not everyone was aware that it was on the brink of going under, and I told your father about a request to host some royalty on their trip to Rome. Top secret, of course…

'I couldn't consider it, but your father said it was a chance to turn things around. The Penthouse Suite was still incredible—my parents always kept the best for themselves—and the dining room was, of course, in good shape. And so word got around…'

'How?' Ariana frowned. 'If it was top secret?'

Gian smiled. 'He told your mother.' There was a tiny feeling of triumph to see Ariana laugh. 'Before we knew it, the hotel was at full quota for a certain weekend in February.'

'Really?'

'The helicopter brought in the best produce from your father's estate and the best wines. And my staff worked like they never had before. That's why now I only hire staff who can work in all areas. I had the chief bartender making up suites. Luna herself got the Penthouse Suite ready…'

'My goodness.'

'It was the biggest charade and it went off superbly and La Fiordelise shuddered back to life.'

'Just like that?'

'Not just like that,' Gian corrected. 'Years of hard work.'

The main course was just as delicious but when it came to dessert, Ariana could not choose from her father's favourites, which were all being served.

'I think we choose the two best, and of course ice cream,' Gian said, 'though not this.' He frowned as his silver spoon sliced through a quenelle of ice cream from her menu and pulled a face as he tasted it. 'Tutti-frutti?'

'It was his favourite,' Ariana said. 'Every summer, in the evening, he would send me to the shop to get a cone for him.'

'Really?' Gian checked, and he watched a little flush of pink spread up her neck. 'Because I seem to remember that you would go to the store for ice cream and when you came back with this flavour your *papà* always declined his cone.'

'No.' She shook her head. 'You have it wrong.'

'And Stefano would complain that he didn't like tutti-frutti either, and so you would end up having to eat all three.'

'You're getting mixed up,' Ariana said haughtily, and she dipped her spoon into the quenelle. He watched as she took a taste and closed her eyes in bliss, then opened them to him and looked right at him. 'He *loved* that ice cream.'

Rafael probably had, Gian conceded. Not so much the sickly-sweet candied ice cream, more the little games Ariana constantly played.

'Well, it's not going on the menu,' Gian said. 'It's…' He dismissed it with a wave of his hand. 'A simple *affogato* is a better way to round off the meal.' He watched her pout. 'Ariana, you are one of the few people in the world who like tutti-frutti ice cream. Trust me on that.'

'I suppose you know best,' she said in her best pained voice.

'There is no suppose about it.'

'It would mean so much to me, though…'

Wearily he took another taste and, as he did so, Ariana did her sneaky best and pulled on all her inner resources so that crocodile tears pooled in her violet eyes.

It did nothing to move that black heart, though.

'No,' Gian said, and put down his spoon and, as if to prove how awful her dessert of choice was, took a drink of water before speaking again. 'Would you like some *amaro* or a cognac?' Gian suggested, but Ariana shook her head.

'No, thank you.'

'Are you sulking?' he asked.

'A little bit,' she admitted, and then smiled despite herself. 'Of course not. I just ought to get home…' She looked away then, because the reason she could not stay was surely there in her eyes.

She wanted her cognac.

But not here.

Ariana wanted to curl up with him elsewhere, to talk, to kiss, but most dangerous of all she actually ached to know him better.

And if she stayed she would cross a line. The business meeting had surely concluded and to keep it at that, she needed to leave. 'Thank you for a lovely dinner.'

'I'll arrange a car—'

'Gian,' she cut in, 'the concierge can do that.'

'Then I'll walk you out.'

They stood at the entrance and tried to pretend that they had never tumbled naked into bed, had never been more than old friends.

'Your ideas are excellent,' Gian said as the doorman blew his whistle to summon a vehicle.

'Except for dessert.'

'Except for dessert,' he agreed.

'And you think it's okay not to have a theme?'

'I think it's better.' Gian nodded. 'It's going to be a tricky night…'

'Yes,' Ariana agreed.

They had been over this already. The car pulled up and it was time to stay or leave.

'Gian—' she started, for she wanted so badly to ask why there was no possible hope for them.

'I'll say goodnight,' Gian cut in, because if he didn't he would break his own rules about separate lives and kiss her beneath the lights and take her to his private apartment where no lover had ever gone. And they would take things further than he'd ever dared, for no one was permitted a place in his closed-off heart.

And so he kissed her on both cheeks, and as he did so a little pink petal that had been hanging temptingly from a strand of her jet-black hair, just waiting for him to pick it off, glided down to his lapel. Her eyes drifted down. 'You're wearing my blossom.'

He glanced down. 'Yes.'

She would not be Svetlana, Ariana decided, and pick it off. Or one of the doubtless many others that had come before her and dared to demand more. She bunched her fist so hard that her nails dug into her palm, and smiled. 'You'd better tidy yourself up then.'

To her everlasting credit, Ariana got into the car and went home alone.

CHAPTER NINE

By AND BY, the Romano Ball drew closer.

Gian had quickly forged a strictly business code.

There were emails and phone calls and even a couple of face-to-face meetings, but there was no low-level flirting or alluding to *them*.

For there was no them.

If anything, it was all so professional that Ariana actually wondered if she'd completely misread the mood that night after dinner, if it really had all been just business to him.

Sometimes she wondered what might have happened if she hadn't asked him to leave her apartment that morning, because she'd been unable to grasp at the time that it really was to be the end of them.

Sometimes she just stared into space for a whole afternoon, blinking as she realised it was getting dark, just wondering about him.

A man who did not want love.

Everyone breathed a private sigh of relief when Angela Romano, unable to bear Rome at the time of the Romano Ball, headed off on a cruise.

Phew!

Ariana lay in bed, so relieved not to have to do lunch and placate her mother as well as focus her attention on both Stefano and Eloa's wedding, which she was now help-ing with a little, and organise the ball.

Even when the final menu cards came, Ariana merely fired back a confirmation, saying that they looked wonder-ful and she was certain her father would approve.

There was not as much as a breath of tutti-frutti be-tween them.

Or references to pink blossom.

Or hints about a moonlit night and a deep kiss by the eternal flame.

It was just:

Gian, regarding the orchids, Roberto will bring them on the day...

Blah, blah, blah...

And in turn Gian, kept to his side of the deal. Or he tried to.

Ariana, regarding the seating plan...

But two days from the big day, he was finally so irri-tated that he picked up the phone and called her. 'I don't understand the problem with Nicki,' Gian said. 'We man-aged to find her a seat...' He chose not to add that Nicki was being accommodated at the exclusion of a potential paying guest and this ball was a very high-end ticket in-deed. 'What is her issue?'

'The table is near the back,' Ariana explained, 'and with Paulo not coming because you banned him—'

'I will ban anyone who is abusive to my staff, which he was.'

'Well, she doesn't know anyone she's seated with. She was hoping to bring a friend.'

'*You're* her friend,' Gian rather tersely pointed out.

'Would you like me to move you to sit with her, because there simply isn't room at the top table.'

'Don't be ridiculous,' Ariana said. 'Has Mia RSVP'd yet?'

He knew, even before she asked, that Nicki must have asked her the same question 'Because, if she doesn't come then there'll be a space.'

'Ariana.' It was the first time they had crossed to anything remotely personal. 'I told both you and Dante that you are to leave Mia to me.'

'Yes, but if she isn't even coming...'

'You cannot give Mia's place to...' *to one of your free-loaders*, he was tempted to add, but refrained and reminded himself that this was a business discussion. In truth, if the Romanos wanted a flock of geese seated at the head table then it was his job to accommodate it. He took a breath. Where Ariana was concerned, it was almost impossible to draw the line and differentiate between personal and professional. 'However,' Gian said, 'if you want Nicki at the top table so desperately then she can have my seat.'

'But where would you sit?' Ariana asked, loathing the thought of him not being next to her. Gian was always seated by her side at the Romano Ball, but now it seemed like he was willing to break that tradition.

'In the seat to which she is currently assigned. I'll be working the room anyway. Nicki can have my seat, if that is what you want.'

'No, no,' Ariana rapidly broke in, blushing as she declined his cold and practical solution to salvage her seat beside Gian. 'Just leave it as it is.'

'Very well,' Gian clipped. 'Anything else?'

'I don't think so. Should there be?'

'No.' Gian was assured. 'Everything is under control.'

Except himself, but he was working on that, determined to erase that forbidden morning from his thoughts.

He did not need the complication of Ariana Romano in his life, he insisted to himself. He just had to get past the ball.

It wasn't just Ariana that was worrying him, though. Trouble loomed in another Romano direction…

'Dante!' Gian shook his friend's hand and invited him to take a seat when he arrived unannounced the day before the ball. 'I just spoke with Ariana this morning…'

'I hear it's all under control.'

'She's done very well,' Gian agreed. 'I expect the ball to be a huge success. Your sister has an eye for detail—'

'Has Mia responded?' Dante cut in.

'Not as yet,' Gian said. 'As I said to Ariana, even if she arrives unannounced, she will be greeted as if she had always been expected and made to feel most welcome.'

'Well, if that's the case, could you ensure she gets this gift just before she heads down to the ball?' He handed Gian a black velvet box and envelope. 'I thought it better to take care of the hostess gift myself, rather than leave it to Ariana.' He gave a black laugh. 'Or it would be a doll full of pins…'

Dante was his close friend, yet Gian found himself smiling his on-duty smile. 'Of course. I'll see to it personally.'

'And perhaps it would be best not to upset Ariana with such details…'

'*Naturalmente,*' Gian said.

Damn, he thought.

By and by, the Romano Ball loomed ever closer.

Gian wanted the ball over and done with; he wanted Ariana gone, instead of her voice, her emails, her thoughts all dancing in his mind.

He wanted his life back to neat order, with sex when he required it and no silent demands for a future.

Gian could feel how much she wanted him, which was usually a turn-off.

He found, though, that he liked it that she craved him and yet kept herself under control. He did his best to ignore it as another damned message pinged into his box, with an attachment.

And there, smiling at him, was his friend Rafael.

It was a slight shock.

Unexpected.

He stared back at Rafael and silently swore that he would stay the hell away from hurting his daughter.

Ariana. Yes, the photo you found of Rafael on Ponte Vecchio was most suitable. Kind regards, Gian

Ariana scoured in between the lines for even the slightest sign, the tiniest clue, that he might linger there in the memory of them, but there was not a single needle she could glean in the haystack.

There were no veiled clues or promises.

His briefly open heart had, it would seem, ever so politely, closed.

By and by, a silver car pulled up outside La Fiordelise in the late afternoon on the day of the Romano Foundation Ball.

And trouble loomed large.

'Ariana Romano is here,' Luna informed him. 'You wanted to see her when she arrived.'

'Yes.'

'Shall I send her through?'

'Of course.'

'Gian!'

She smiled her red-lipped smile and for someone running later than the Mad Hatter, she still looked pretty incredible in a loose top that showed one shoulder and a skirt that showed a lot of leg.

Gian, though, did not look his usual self.

'You look…' she started, but then stopped. It was none of her business that the immaculate Gian was unshaven and that his tie was pulled loose. No doubt he was saving his shave for the evening, but the unrufflable Gian looked, well, ruffled.

She wanted to hold him, to climb onto his knee and kiss that tense face, but instead she stood stock still.

'Ariana…' He got up and they did the kiss-kiss thing.

'Careful,' she warned, so he didn't crush the orchids. 'Damn things,' she added as he re-took his seat but Ariana did not sit down. 'Who knew flowers could cause so much trouble. Roberto is sick and can't come,' Ariana explained, nerves making her mouth run away. 'And these were the orchids he was supposed to bring…' She held up her free hand in an exasperated gesture. 'I've been standing on a platform at Roma Termini, waiting for a courier to deliver them.'

'It's fine.' He tried not to want her; he tried to treat her as he once would have. 'Do you want a drink?'

'I don't have time for a drink,' Ariana pointed out. 'I have to be greeting guests in a couple of hours. What did you want to see me about?'

He was silent for a moment as he poured his own drink while wondering how best to broach things. 'Mia is here.'

'So?' Ariana shrugged and turned to go. 'What do I care? There was no need to drag me to your office. You could have told me that in a text.'

'Yes.' He watched the tension in her jaw and the press of her lips and knew she was struggling to process the news. Aside from that, there was also a whole lot more she didn't know.

Dante and Mia had the adjoining presidential suites.

And Dante had the key.

Yes, Gian De Luca was the keeper of many secrets and at times it was hell. 'I want to speak to you,' he said. 'About tonight.'

'You're going to tell me to behave and be nice. Don't worry. I've already had the lecture from Dante. Poor Mia is struggling to face us all tonight. Poor Mia—'

'Ariana!' He spoke more harshly then, but that was like holding up a red rag to a bull, Gian knew, for nothing tamed her. 'Do you remember how you felt at your father's funeral, as if everything might get out of hand? Well, Mia is surely feeling that way...'

'*Poor* Mia, you mean.' She looked at him then, really looked, and she could see the fan of lines beside his eyes and feel his tension. She assumed he was concerned about Mia; it never entered her head that his concern might be for her. 'Why do you always take her side?' Ariana asked, jealousy rearing its ugly head. 'Don't tell me you have a thing for her too...' She simply could not bear it if that was the case, and spite got the better of her. 'Well, I guess at least she's closer to your age than Papà's.'

'Enough!' Gian cut in. 'Why do you have to be so petty and cruel whenever you speak about her?'

'Because I hate her.' Ariana shrugged. 'And I hate it that my parents divorced. I'll never forgive her.'

'You forgave your father when it was he who had the affair. Mia, at the time, was single.'

'Stop it,' Ariana said, loathing his logic. 'And please stop telling me what to think and how to feel. We slept with each other once—that doesn't give you licence to police my friends and now how I interact with my family.'

'You're insufferable, Ariana.' He strode over and took her bare arms. He wanted to shake some sense into her, but even as he scolded her Gian actually understood her anger more than she knew.

Ariana was only ever given half-truths.

Or a quarter.

Or an eighth.

The Romanos were masters at smoke and mirrors and Ariana had grown up stumbling blind through their labyrinth of lies, and he loathed it that he was only giving her a tiny sliver of the truth now.

'I'm trying…' He held on to his words, because if he said one thing more it might well be too much. 'I'm trying to ensure that this night goes well.'

'Have you delivered Mia this pre-function lecture?' Ariana goaded. 'Have Stefano and Dante been summoned too? No!' She answered for him. 'Because you don't trust me.'

'No, because I—' Gian abruptly halted himself, because he didn't want to admit, even to himself, that he cared about Ariana more than he wanted to. 'Because I know how you feel about Mia, and I also know that you want the night to be a success.'

'Then we want the same thing,' Ariana replied tartly.

They did indeed want the same thing and now they were face to face in no way that could be construed as professional.

She looked up at him through narrowed eyes. She wanted to exit in a huff, but his hands were on her bare arms and she liked the odd comfort of him, of someone, the first person ever, pulling her back before she went too far.

They were both breathing hard, as if they had just kissed.

Ariana looked at his mouth and unshaven jaw and felt his fingers holding the top of her arms. He turned her on so easily that she could feel the heat at the top of her legs, and the ache of her breasts in her flimsy bra. She knew he was hard, she just knew, the same way she did not need to look at the sky to know it was darkening.

'Ariana,' Gian said in a voice that sounded a touch gravelly, 'if there are any issues tonight, then you are to come to me.'

She always did, Ariana realised.

Whether it was stolen chocolate, or her father's widow showing up, she always leaned on Gian, yet she could not when it came to the urgent matter of her heart, for he was the one who was quietly stealing it.

'I need to get on,' Ariana croaked.

'Of course,' Gian politely agreed.

'And you need to shave.'

When she had gone, Gian opened up the safe and took out the black box and envelope.

He would not break his own rules and deliberately did not look inside.

He would go and get ready and then drop off the gift to Mia, and then get through this night and once that was done, hopefully he wouldn't have to see Ariana for some considerable time.

Except that was easier said than done. First he had to dance with her and hold her and for the first time ever he found he wanted someone in his life.

And so he reminded himself of all the reasons why he did not want someone in his life.

When he should have been meeting with the barber in his apartment and then seeing to the final preparations for this important night, instead he took out the official papers he did his level best to avoid.

It was all there.

The drugs, the debauchery, the *findings*… The absolute hell of love.

For he had loved them.

Even if his parents had not wanted him.

And he had loved his brother Eduardo, even if it had been safer to stop caring, to detach and close off his heart.

To refuse all drama.

And Ariana really was pure drama.

'Gian?' Luna knocked on his door a long time later and found him sitting almost in the dark. 'Should you still be here?'

'No,' he admitted, and stood. 'Luna,' he said, 'can you…?' He was about to hand over the papers to shred. 'It doesn't matter,' Gian said, and returned them to the safe in case he ever needed another reminder of why he refused to let someone into his life.

And, by and by, the Romano Foundation Ball was here.

CHAPTER TEN

ARIANA WORE BLACK.

A simple black velvet halter neck and the diamond studs her parents had given her for her eighteenth.

She put on her red lips, though, and lashings of mascara. There was a ridiculous pit of anticipation building at the thought of dancing with Gian, for she was still floating from the encounter in his office and getting her hopes up as she made her way down for the ball.

His warning, however poorly she'd taken it, meant that Ariana was at least slightly prepared when her father's *widow* made her entrance. And what an entrance. Mia was standing at the top of the stairs in crimson! Her blonde hair was piled up, and heavy diamond earrings glittered at her ears as she made her way down. Ariana saw red—as red as the dress that Mia wore.

'So much for the grieving widow,' she hissed to Dante.

She was, in fact, grateful to Gian for the heads-up and even managed a somewhat stilted greeting to the widow in red, but then all rancour drained from her when she saw Gian approach.

He was still unshaven, but sexily so.

His attire was immaculate and his black hair gleaming but it was such a change from his more regular suave appearance at such an event that she felt a pull, down low. He simply hollowed her out with desire.

'Eloa,' he said in that low, throaty drawl. Even the happily engaged, blissfully-in-love Eloa had the hormones to blush when bathed in his attention. 'You look exquisite.' He kissed her cheeks and then shook Stefano's hand. 'Dante.' He nodded to his friend. 'I trust everything is satisfactory.'

'Absolutely.' Dante agreed.

He turned to Ariana, finally acknowledging her. Sort of. His eyes did not as much as dust over her body, and she felt the chill of a snub, even as he spoke politely. 'Ariana, you look beautiful.'

They were the same words he said every year when he greeted her at the ball, and he kissed her on the cheeks as he always did when they met, except he barely whispered past her skin.

As if she were an old aunt, Ariana thought.

'Thank you,' she said. 'Everything looks beautiful.' And then she leaned in and murmured, 'Even the grieving widow.'

He didn't smile, and neither did he return her little in joke.

There was an edge to him that she couldn't quite define, an off-limits sign she could almost read. He was essentially ignoring her.

Damn you, Gian, she thought as she headed into the ballroom. But really she was cross with herself. Somewhere, somehow, she had lost sight of the clear message he had given right at the start and had been foolish enough to get her hopes up.

The ballroom could never be described as understated, but without hanging moons and ivy vines tonight it looked its elegant best, and Ariana caught the sweet scent of gardenias as she took her seat. Mia entered and took her seat at the table too, Gian sitting between them. He was, of course, his usual dignified self and made polite small talk alternately with both Mia and Ariana.

Like a parent wedged between two warring siblings and trying to give both equal attention, Ariana thought.

'I shouldn't have worn red,' Mia said as the pasta was served. 'It was the gown I had for last year...'

'You look stunning,' Gian told her—*again*. And Ariana gritted her teeth.

Gian tried his level best to be his usual self, as Ariana smouldered beside him. The drama of waiting for her to explode was painful, but he told himself she was not his problem. He told himself that the Romanos, the whole lot of them, were each a theatre production in themselves.

The bed-hopping, the scandals—Dante and Mia doing their best not to make eye contact. He was rather certain that the heavy earrings she wore had been in the box that he had earlier delivered to her door. Rafael's lover was too ill to attend but his orchids took pride of place. Eloa and Stefano were desperate for the night to be over so they could be alone.

And don't get me started on Ariana, he thought.

He could feel her, smell her, hear her when she spoke, and of course she was asking for more pepper.

She jangled his nerves and she beguiled him, because for once she behaved.

Almost.

She turned her back when Mia tried to speak, which he did his level best to ignore and gloss over.

And then the appalling Nicki came over between courses and moaned about her seat. 'Ariana, you really have stuck me beside the most boring people and I'll never hear the speeches back there.'

Gian stared ahead, but said in a low voice for Ariana's ears, 'My offer still stands.'

He would move, Ariana knew. Right now, Gian would get up and stalk off and it was the last thing she wanted. She looked at her friend and, for the first time ever, stood up for herself. 'Nicki, the sound engineer is the best in Rome. I'm sure you'll be able to hear.'

Well done, he wanted to tell her. *Well done, Ariana.*

But he stayed silent. It was not his place.

Yet he wanted it to be.

There was just one unkind comment, as dessert was being served, when Eloa spoke of her wedding that was now just a few short weeks away. She told Mia, 'Ariana is helping us organise a few things,' clearly trying to feed her into the conversation.

'Yes.' Ariana flashed a red-lipped smile at Mia. 'It's going to be amazing. Anyone who's anyone has been invited…'

Meaning—*not you!*

Gian caved.

Ariana felt his hand on her thigh, and the grip of his fingers actually halted her words.

'That's not a good idea,' she said to Gian, while looking ahead. 'If you reward me each time I go too far…'

'Would you prefer the discipline method?'

She threw her head back and laughed.

Even with Mia at her table, Ariana found that with Gian beside her she could still have such a wonderful night.

And it was then that she got another reward, for as the desserts were served and shots of coffee were tossed over ice creams, there was a special dish, made just for her. Tutti-frutti.

Ariana gasped.

'Yes.'

It was better than being handed chestnuts on a freezing night; it was better than a sliver of gold when she could not face her father's funeral alone.

'Thank you.'

She wanted to cry as she tasted the sweet candied ice cream and remembered how her father had, over and over, let her get away with buying three cones, just so she could devour them all.

Happy memories reigned as little shots of sugar burst on her tongue and when she finished she had to dab at her eyes with her napkin. 'Ice cream has never made me cry before,' she admitted to Gian as the waiter cleared her very clean plate. 'Happy tears, though. It was beautiful, thank you.'

'Shall we get it over with?' Gian asked as the band struck up.

'Get what over with?' Ariana said, as if she didn't know.

'The duty dance.'

It had been months since she had known the bliss of his arms, and for Gian it had been months with no feminine pleasure.

He'd known he would only be thinking of her and, besides, no one else had her scent.

'Your perfume,' he said, as he held her at a distance and resumed their old wars.

'I've told you,' she said, 'I don't wear any.' She looked right at him. 'You're the only one who complains.'

'I'm not complaining.'

'Why do you always hold me at such a distance?'

'You know why,' he said, and pulled her deep in so she could feel him hard against the softness of her stomach. She flared to the scent of citrus and bergamot and testosterone and the roughness of his skin seemed to burn her rouged cheek. 'You didn't shave...'

'Because you like me unshaven.'

'Gian.' She was trying to breathe and dance and deal with the change all at the same time. She simply didn't understand him. 'You've ignored me most of the night...'

'I tried to,' he admitted.

'You've ignored me for weeks...' He shook his head, but then nodded when she quoted his impersonal sign-offs. '"Kind regards, Gian"?'

'How else could we get the ball done?'

'And after tonight will you ignore me again?'

He didn't answer because he didn't know. He could not afford to think of tomorrow now.

The judgements of the coroner's report should be flicking through his mind, except tonight those violet eyes turned his warning systems off.

He gave her no promises, just told her the card for his private elevator would be in her bag and left her to stumble her way through the rest of the evening.

The speeches were brilliant, the whole night was perfect, but it felt as though she might faint with desire as she said farewell to the guests.

'We should go for a drink in the bar,' Nicki said.

'It will be closed.'

'I meant the bar in your room.' Nicki smiled, but Ariana shook her head. 'I'm exhausted, Nicki.'

It was a lie.

Ariana felt as alive as an exposed wire as she slipped away and took the private elevator to his floor and let herself in.

It was not the view that she craved, or the stunning surroundings; it was the glimpses of him.

There were paintings, the sketches of Fiordelise he had told her about, his history and lineage all there on the walls.

The older Dukes and Duchesses too, and it went right down to his parents, his brother...

But where was Gian?

Her eyes scanned the walls.

Where was the man she adored?

Then she found him, in a suit, at the desk in Reception, and she frowned at the one single image of him, but her thoughts faded as she heard the whir of the elevator.

And her heart moved to her throat as he stepped through the door.

It had been agony not to touch him, but both were relieved of that agony now.

As they reached for each other, almost ran to each other, it was like falling into another dimension.

He was undoing her gown so it fell like a black puddle on the floor. His tongue was cool and his kisses hot as she impatiently pushed down the sleeves of his jacket, and they were so *desperate* for each other, for more than this.

He picked her up, dressed only in her underwear, and deposited her onto a vast gold bed.

His eyes never left her face as Ariana removed her bra and lay on her back, propped up by her elbows and watching him undress.

He threw off the tie as though it was choking him and she gave a satisfied smile when the cufflinks dropped silently to the carpet for he was as desperate as she.

He slowed down to take off her strappy high heels. First the right, and he was so annoyingly slow with the strap that she took her other high heel and pressed it into his toned stomach.

Gian caught her calf.

She could see his erection, the one that had been pressed against her on the dance floor, and she almost writhed in frustration as he took off her left high heel. Now the soles of her feet were on his stomach as he slowly pulled her silk knickers down, revealing her to him. Finally, he buried his face in her.

'Gian!' She was shocked at the delicious roughness of him, at the sounds of him, at her own reaction to him, for she was coming as quickly as that.

Suddenly she was pulsing as he devoured her and then she was falling where she lay, but with him atop her.

'We need condoms…' she said frantically, for she had cursed herself after the last time.

'There's been no one since.'

Those words made her too weak for reason.

He was holding her naked as she tumbled through space, and for all the terrible decisions she had made in her lifetime, this, Ariana knew, was not one of them.

He kissed her mouth and her face, the shells of her ears, and the tender skin of her neck as he took her.

He devoured her and rained kisses and words on her that should not be said to someone you were not prepared to love the next day.

'You make me crazy,' he told her.

And that made her heart sing.

He told her how he had wanted her all night, how he had wanted her for weeks, in fact, all this as he moved within her and stared right into her eyes. The prolonged intensity astounded her, the focus, the climb, the ache of want and the desire to give. Her hips moved involuntarily with his and they were wild for each other, rolling and tumbling across the bed. He took in her flushed features and brushed the damp hair back from her face as he drove into her and gazed at her.

Help, Ariana thought, for she had never seen Gian so tender before.

There was passion and there was desire, but there was something else too.

He was also aware of it, this slip into a deeper caring, this moment, when he rolled her onto her back again, and one lesson in tenderness moved to the next.

He was up on his forearms, his body sliding over hers, each intimate stroke of him winding her tighter and tighter. His pace built and built and she wrapped her legs around his hips and simply clung on as he took her to wherever he chose.

He took her to bliss, pounding her senses, making her more his with each thrust.

For Gian it was a dangerous space. He knew that as he looked down at her, her black hair splayed on his pillow, her body tight around his. He would regret this later, Gian knew, but at that moment he didn't care.

Especially as he swelled that delicious final time and filled her. Completely.

And this time it was Gian shouting out her name.

He dragged her into an orgasm so deep and intense that for a moment she existed there with him.

It was dizzying…too much…never enough, and she was crying as it was fading.

And he kissed her back to consciousness.

'I loved my ice cream,' she told him, and then stopped, because there was another thing that Ariana knew she loved too.

Don't say it, she told herself as he turned off the lights with a single bedside switch and Ariana curled into him, loving the feel of being utterly spent yet curiously awake in her lover's arms.

Ariana usually hated the dark and the night, but not this night. The thud-thud-thud of his heart and the sound of Gian collecting his breath brought Ariana a sense of contentment in the soft thrum of her body as she came down from the high he had taken her to.

'Why are there no paintings or sketches of Violetta?'

'There are a couple but they need to be restored.'

'And why are there no photos of you?' Ariana asked a question that could only be asked in the dark, in that black hole where gravity did not apply, where words floated and drifted in nonsensical patterns, before logic applied.

'There are,' he said. 'There's one in the gallery, taken during the royal visit to La Fiordelise—in the entrance hall.'

'You mean the Employee of the Month photo?' Ariana

said, mocking his formal business photo. For some reason her words made them both laugh.

But then the laughter faded.

'Why are there no photos with your parents?'

'I was not a part of their plans.'

'What were their plans?'

'To party,' Gian said. 'And a late baby nearly put paid to that.'

'But it didn't?'

'No,' he admitted. 'They carried right on.'

'With a baby?'

'Without,' Gian said. 'A lot of nannies, a lot of time in Luctano… It's better this way, though. It taught me independence, so by the time they were gone, there was nothing to miss. They were never a necessary part of my life, or I of theirs.'

She could not imagine it.

Sure, her father had pulled back, but that had been in her twenties, and her mother still called her every day.

And even though she and Stefano were not as close now as they once had been, she would die if he pulled away so completely.

Even Dante, always remote and distant, was still a vital part of her world.

To have no one.

To miss no one.

'I don't believe you,' she admitted. 'I can't believe you don't miss them.'

'Truth?' Gian said, still floating in that void where there were no sides and no barriers hemming you in. 'I have missed them from the day I was born.'

'Gian?' She lifted her head when he fell silent.

'Go to sleep,' he said, but she wanted to ask him how they were supposed to be with each other in the cold light of day.

'What?' he asked her, when her head stayed up and her eyes remained focused on him.

Self-preservation struck—or was it sanity?—and Ariana, even with little experience in the bedroom, knew that pushing the issue with Gian would be something she would live to regret.

'I'm cold,' she said, though she had never felt safer or warmer.

Ariana knew when, and how, to lie.

CHAPTER ELEVEN

GIAN WOKE TO DISORDER.

Not just the knot of limbs and the scent of sex, for that he was used to, but the exposure of thoughts and the deep intimacies of last night had brought disorder into his mind.

He did not want to love her.

Ariana awoke to a cold empty bed and the sound of the shower.

She could almost feel the weight of his regret in the air.

There was no sense of regret from her. In fact, she wanted to stretch like a cat and purr at the memory of their lovemaking.

She had thought nothing could beat the first time, but again Gian had surprised her.

In his arms, as he'd driven her to the very edge and then toppled them, it had felt as if they were one.

Not now, though.

She looked over to the bedside table and the cufflinks he had dropped last night; his tux was hanging over the suit holder.

Order had been brought to the bedroom.

Except for the hot mess that lay in his bed, Ariana thought.

Yes, an utter hot mess, because despite assurances and promises, both to Gian and herself, she had completely fallen for him.

Well, that was a given…

No, this was bigger.

This feeling was almost more than her head could contain.

It was a cocktail of affection and craving and desire and hunger but she refused, even to herself, to call it love.

It was lust, Ariana told herself.

He had turned on her senses, introduced her to her body, and she must not allow herself to believe that the kisses and intimacies shared last night were exclusively known to her.

Except it had felt as if they were.

It had felt, last night, when she had been trapped in his gaze, being kissed, being held, as if this feeling had been new to them both.

She heard the shower being turned off, and she imagined him in there naked, the mirrors all steamed up. She willed him to come out and face the woman who should not be in his bed and she hoped he wasn't wondering how to get rid of her.

Oh, God, this was going to be a million times harder than the first time. Then, it had felt like she had been party to the rules, but this time, naked in his bed, she had to find the armour to brazen out a smile and leave without revealing her heart.

He came out of the bathroom with a distinct lack of conversation and a thick white towel wrapped around his lean hips.

'*Buongiorno,*' Ariana said, and looked at Gian with his black hair dripping and unshaven face.

Unshaven, for Gian had barely been able to bring himself to look in the mirror.

He had got too close, and what had felt like a balm last night now felt like an astringent. He couldn't bear to let anyone in.

More, he couldn't bear that he was about to hurt her.

'I'll call for breakfast,' he said in a voice that attempted normality but failed. She noted that he did not get back into bed.

Ariana gave a half-laugh at his wooden response in comparison to the easy flow of words last night. 'You sound like the butler.'

He said nothing to that and Ariana pulled herself up from the bed. 'I'll have a shower.' It served two purposes: one, she refused to force a conversation on an unwilling participant and appear needy and pleading; and, two, she felt the sudden sting of tears and desperately wanted to hide it.

'Sure.' Gian said, fighting with himself not to dissuade her. He stepped back as she brushed past and he only breathed again when she closed the bathroom door.

Why the hell was he like this?

Gian generally fought introspection, but he sat on the bed and wrestled with his demons.

The panicked part of Gian wanted the maids to come in and service the apartment so he could get back his cold black heart, instead of fighting the urge to go into the bathroom and join her in the shower before spending a lazy Sunday in bed.

The buzz of his phone had him glancing at the bedside table. Luna calling at such an early hour on a Sunday morning would generally cause him to curse, yet now he leapt on the distraction and took the call.

It was not good news, to say the least.

Ariana, he knew, would freak.

When he'd ended the call, he made a couple of his own and by then Ariana had come out.

'Don't worry about breakfast,' Ariana said, her voice a little shaken, though she was clearly doing her best to control it and keep things light. She had given way to a moment of tears in the shower but she'd pulled herself together and let the hot jets of water flow over her. She would serve herself better to wait until she got home so she could weep alone.

'I'm not really hungry. I might head down to my own suite…' She wouldn't even bother putting on her gown. Wearing the robe and with wet hair, anyone who spotted her would assume she had been for a swim in the luxurious pool in the hotel spa. 'If you could just send my things down to my suite, please…'

'Ariana, wait.'

As she headed for the door, she stiffened, fighting the surge of hope that he was calling her back to apologise for the shift in mood and the silent row that had taken place. Slowly she turned around.

'It's better that you hear this from me,' Gian said, and his voice was deadly serious.

'Hear what?'

'There was a photo taken last night at the ball…'

'There were many photos taken.'

'I mean, there has been an image sold to the press. It hasn't got out yet and my team are doing all they can to suppress it, but I fear it is just a matter of time.'

'What sort of photo?'

'One of Dante…'

'Dante?' Ariana frowned. 'What has Dante got to do with anything?' Dante's behaviour had been impeccable last night. He had delivered a speech that had encapsulated the essence of their father and he had worked the room like the professional he was. Though Dante was rather well known for his rakish ways, that had all been put on hold last night.

Or so she'd thought.

'There is an image of Dante and Mia in the atrium.'

'And?' Ariana was instantly defensive. Dante was her brother after all. 'He's allowed to speak to her, for heaven's sake. He told us himself to be polite. She's my father's widow...' Her voice faded as Dante handed her his tablet and there, on an eleven-inch screen, was an image that washed away any further excuses.

Her father's very young widow was locked, groin to groin, with her elder brother, and raw, untamed desire blazed in both their eyes. Oh, she recognised that desire for what it was, because it was exactly what she had shared with Gian last night.

But Dante and Mia?

Her brother and her stepmother?

'No!' Her lungs and head shouted the denial, but the single word caught in her vocal cords and it came out a strained, husky bark. 'He would never,' she implored. 'It's been doctored, cropped...'

'Ariana, the image is real. I called Dante just now and apologised that such an invasion of his privacy took place in my hotel. My legal team are onto it, as are my security team. We are doing all we can to stop the photo getting out and,' he added darkly, 'I shall discover the culprit.'

But Ariana didn't care who had taken the photo, only that this moment in time had ever existed.

Oh, Papà!

She wanted to weep at the insult to his memory. She wanted to hurl a thousand questions at her brother, who went through women like socks. Except surely this woman, the widow of his father, should have been out of bounds?

'How long have they been together...?' Her accusing eyes looked at Gian.

'Ariana, you are asking the wrong person.'

'I'm asking exactly the right person. You're a who's who of all the scandal in Rome!' She wanted to claw the hair from her scalp. 'Did. You. Know?'

'Yes.'

He might as well have stabbed her for she put her hands to her chest and moaned exactly as if he had. 'Traitor!'

'Stop it.' Dante pointed a warning finger and moved swiftly into damage control. But this time he was moving swiftly to protect not his hotel's reputation but Ariana from the fallout that was surely to come. 'Look at me,' he said, and waited till finally she met his eyes. 'It is not so terrible.'

'But it is.'

'Because you make it so! Remember how you accused me last night, how you said Mia and I were closer in age…?'

She blinked as she replayed her own accusation.

'Your brother is my age.'

'She's his stepmother…'

'So will say the headlines, but that's just click bait… Listen to me, Ariana.' He could feel her calming just a touch. 'Think of how Dante will be feeling right now.'

She nodded, and looked down the barrel of recent weeks. 'I knew something was wrong. I thought he was just missing Papà, not just…'

'I know what you mean. Ariana, it must have been hell for him.'

'I need to speak to him.' Though still frantic, he could feel her calm beneath his touch. 'Both of them…'

'Yes,' he agreed, 'but without accusation. He and Mia have taken off to Luctano…'

'You've spoken to him.'

'Just now,' Gian said.

'Can you take me there?'

'Of course. I'll have Luna arrange the pilot. Go down to your suite and get dressed and I'll meet you there.'

She took the elevator down to the spa floor and then stepped out and took the guest elevator back up to her own. There she pulled on some underwear and a pretty dress.

Gian's calm manner was somehow infectious, for she even dried and styled her hair.

But then her phone rang and she saw it was her mother, just back from her cruise.

'How much more can I be shamed?' her *mamma* shouted.

'Mamma, please,' Ariana attempted. 'Maybe there is some explanation.'

'Mia and Dante. My son!'

'Mamma, you should surely hear what Dante has to say. They are closer in age…' Ariana pleaded, repeating Gian's words, but nothing would placate her.

'That woman!' she sobbed. 'She has killed my family, my joy, my life. She takes and she takes and she leaves me with nothing.'

'You have me,' Ariana pleaded. 'Mamma…' But she had run out of excuses for Mia and Dante. 'I'm going now to speak with him.'

'Well, you know what to say from me.'

If Ariana didn't know, she was specifically told.

'Okay?' Gian checked as they headed up to the roof-top, except she barely heard him. All she could hear was her *mamma*'s acidic, angry words.

'I wanted the ball to be perfect for Papà.'

It was all Ariana said.

Sitting in his helicopter, Gian looked from her pale face down to the rolling hills and the familiar lace of vines. Now they were deep into spring and the poppy fields were a blaze of red, and there was foliage on the once bare vines.

He turned back to Ariana, who sat staring ahead with her headphones on, her leg bobbing up and down. He didn't doubt that she was nervous to be facing her brother.

Gian was sure that it would soon be sorted out. He knew how close the Romano siblings were. At least, they had been growing up. And surely even Ariana could understand that grief and comfort were a heady cocktail. Hell, she'd sought comfort herself on the night of the funeral after all.

He spotted the lake and soon they were coming in to land. Only then did Gian wonder how it might look that he was arriving with Ariana.

Would it be obvious they had spent the night together?

Did it announce them as a couple?

Gian was nowhere near ready for that. If anything, a couple of hours ago he'd been ready to end things, as was his usual way.

But, as it turned out, Ariana wasn't expecting anything from Gian, other than the equivalent of a rather luxurious taxi ride.

'Wait there,' she said, as she took her headphones off. 'I shan't be long.'

'What?' Gian checked, unsure what she meant.

She was more than used to entering and exiting a helicopter, and the second it was safe to do so, the door opened and the steps lowered and Ariana ran down.

'Wait…' he called, and then looked in the direction she ran.

Dante, even from this distance, looked seedy and was striding towards her, no doubt surprised by her unannounced arrival.

If Gian had thought for a moment that Ariana Romano had finally grown up, he was about to be proven wrong, for she was back to the spoiled, selfish brat of old. Only, instead of being placed over her father's knee, it was Ariana delivering the slaps.

He watched her land a vicious hit on her brother's cheek and then raise her other hand to do the same, but Dante caught it.

The scene carried echoes of another world, one Gian had loathed—champagne bottles on the floor, fights, chaos, all he had sought to erase, and the scars on his psyche felt inflamed.

Ariana heightened his senses. Gian was more than aware he had let down his steely guard in bed last night and it had shaken him. For a moment he had glimpsed how it felt to need another person, to rely on someone else, and that could never be.

Right now, though, her actions plunged him straight back into a world that had spun out of control—the chaos and fights between his parents, finding his older brother unconscious on the floor and shouting frantically for help, and their smiles and the making up that came after, the promises made that were never, ever kept.

Always they had taken things too far, and it was everything that he now lived to avoid.

'Hey.' He was speaking to the pilot, about to tell him to take off, for he wanted no part in this. Yet some odd sense of duty told him not to leave Ariana stranded, and so he sat, grim-faced, as a tearful Ariana ran her leggy way back to the helicopter and climbed in.

'We can go now,' Ariana said once her headphones and microphone were on. 'I'm done.'

And so too was he.

And he told her so the minute they stood alone back on the roof of La Fiordelise.

'You never cease to disappoint me, Ariana.'

He watched her tear-streaked, defiant face lift and her angry eyes met his as he gave her a well-deserved telling-off. 'I thought you were going there to speak with your brother, to find out how he was…'

'He shamed my mother!' Ariana shouted. 'She went on a cruise to get away from the ball and had to return to this!'

'Ah, so it was your mother talking.' He shook his head as he looked down at her, realising now what had happened between her leaving his suite and boarding the helicopter. 'And there was me thinking you had a mind of your own. How dare you put me in the middle of this? I would never have offered to take you if I'd known your plan was to behave this way.'

She had the gall to shrug. 'You have no idea what she did to us.'

'I have every idea!' Gian retorted.

'Meaning?'

But Gian was not about to explain himself. 'You know what, Ariana? I don't need your drama.'

It felt like a kind of relief that he could finally walk away without the painful struggle with his demons he had faced earlier when considering how to draw a line under all that had happened between them.

Except Ariana Romano ran after him.

He didn't want to hear her sobbing or begging for forgiveness, except Gian received neither. Instead he was tapped smartly on the shoulder and was somewhat surprised by the calm stare that met him when he turned around.

'You should be thanking me, Gian.'

'Thanking you?'

'Absolutely,' she responded. 'You were about to give me my marching orders this morning, and you were fumbling for an excuse. I handed you this on a plate.'

'You don't know that.'

'But I do.' Ariana was certain, for she could clearly recall the heavy atmosphere and the absolute certainty that Gian had been about to end things. Well, she'd given him the perfect reason to now. 'It isn't a relationship you're avoiding, Gian; it's emotion.'

Ariana struck like a cobra, right to the heart of his soul. He looked at her and all he could see was the chaos she left in her wake. He thought of the knife edge he had grown

up on, the eternal threat of disaster that had hung over his
family, and the eternal calm he now sought.

'Don't worry, Gian,' she said to his silence. 'I'm out of
here. You keep your cold black heart and I'll carry right on.'

CHAPTER TWELVE

IT WOULD BE NICE, Ariana thought early the next morning, to pull the covers over her head as she nursed her first ever broken heart.

Officially broken.

She knew that since they had first made love she had been holding onto a dream. The fantasy that Gian would bend his rules for her and decide it was time to give love a chance...

Because it felt like love to Ariana.

Now she had to let go of that dream. Her mother called and then called again, but Ariana ignored it.

But then Stefano called and Ariana could never ignore a call from her twin...

'There's an extraordinary board meeting at nine,' he told her.

'Pass on my apologies,' Ariana mumbled, but Stefano was having none of it. 'We are to meet at the offices at eight,' Stefano told her. 'A driver has been ordered for you; he should be with you soon.'

'Eight?' Ariana checked.

'Mamma wants to speak to the three of us before the board meeting.'

'She's coming to the offices?' Ariana frowned. 'But she hasn't been there since...'

Since the news of her father and Mia's affair had broken.

This was big, Ariana knew as she quickly showered, squeezing in eye drops to erase all evidence of tears. She selected a navy linen suit and ran the straightening iron through her hair, trying to look somewhat put-together while she pondered what was about to take place. Ariana arrived at Romano Holdings and took the elevator up to where her family were waiting for her.

Her *mamma* was as pale as she had ever seen her, and Stefano looked grey. She could barely bring herself to look at Dante, but when she did she saw the bruise beneath his eye and felt sick that it had come from her own hand.

'I'm sorry,' she said to Dante. 'I just…'

'I get it,' Dante said, and gave her a hug. 'Ariana, I know how confusing this has all been, but there's something you need to hear, both you and Stefano…' He turned to their mother. 'It's time, Mamma,' he said.

This *was* big.

Gian knew that, because even as he tried to focus on his weekly planning meeting with Luna, little pings from his computer had him looking over. The press were gathered outside Romano Holdings, where an extraordinary meeting was being held, and in an unprecedented move Angela Romano was seen entering the building.

Gian watched as Ariana duly arrived in a silver car and he scanned the short piece of footage for a clue, a glimpse, as to what lay behind the mask she most certainly wore.

Her parting shot to him yesterday had seriously rattled him and he had spent most of the night simultaneously disregarding and dwelling on her words.

You keep your cold black heart and I'll carry right on.

Yet he was struggling to carry on, knowing that Ariana must be suffering now. For the first time, Gian wanted *more* information on the details of a woman's private life.

He was fighting with himself not to call Ariana to see what was going on, how she was coping, what she knew…

Her brief appearance told him nothing. She was immaculate. Ariana really should be on the stage, for there was no hint of tension in her body language.

She wore a navy linen suit and her hair was smooth and tied back in a slick ponytail. She even paused and smiled her gorgeous red-lipped smile for the cameras.

'This can wait,' he told Luna, and wrapped up their morning meeting so he could focus on the news. 'If you could just bring coffee.'

'Of course.'

Throughout the morning, the little pings became more and more frequent for there was drama aplenty. Dante Romano and Mia were engaged to be married! Gian could not imagine that going down well with a certain hot-headed lady, but there Ariana was, still smiling for the cameras as she left the building and climbed into a car.

Ariana would come to him.

Of that Gian was certain.

Despite their exchange yesterday, Gian was quietly confident that Ariana would arrive in his office, because whenever there was drama in Ariana Romano's life, inevitably Luna announced she was at his door and a mini-tornado would burst in.

'Any messages from Ariana Romano?' he checked with Luna.

'None.'

'If she arrives here,' Gian said, 'please send her straight through.'

Ariana did not arrive, though, for she *refused* to run to him.

The car was mercifully cool and, rather than stare ahead, Ariana looked out of the window and smiled at the cameras as if the drama surrounding Dante and Mia hadn't affected her in the slightest. In fact, their engagement was the merest tip of an iceberg that had just been exposed to her in all its blinding glory. Ariana was having trouble taking it all in.

'Home?' the driver checked.

'No…' She hesitated, not quite ready for the emptiness of her apartment and the noise of her own thoughts. 'Just drive, please.'

She took a gulp of water from a chilled bottle the driver handed to her and tried to come to terms with the fact that her life, her childhood—in fact, all she had ever known—had been built on a lie. Her parents' marriage, of which she'd been so proud, had been a sham. They'd both had other partners and the marriage had been in name only, so much so that she and Stefano had been IVF babies.

It felt as if she was the very last to know.

They drove for ages. It was rush hour in Rome, all the workers spilling out, some rushing for transport, others taking their time for a coffee, or to sit in a bar.

She felt like an alien.

A stranger in her own body.

As they passed La Fiordelise she had never been more tempted to ask the driver to pull in, to push through the brass doors and escape to the cool calmness of Gian's office and unburden herself, as she would usually do. Except, thanks to their argument yesterday, that refuge was denied her now.

Instead, Ariana asked to be dropped off where they had walked that lonely night. She wandered there, too shocked and stunned for tears. It was a sticky late spring day and she drifted a while, ignoring the buzz of her phone.

Finally she glanced at the endless missed calls.

He came first and last.

Gian.

Mamma.

Gian.

Gian.

Mamma.

Gian.

Stefano.

Gian.

She had nothing to say to any of them, at least not until she had gathered her thoughts. Eventually, drained from walking and with a headache creating a pulse of its own, she wandered listlessly home.

'Hey,' she said to the doorman, who was dozing behind his cap. She took the elevator up, jolting when she saw a very familiar face. Gian was leaning against the wall, but came to his full height as she approached.

Her heart did not lurch in hope or relief. In fact, it sank, for right now Gian felt like another problem to deal with, another person to hide her true self from.

For her true self was hurting and dreadfully so—and her emotions were clearly too much for him.

'What are you doing here, Gian?'

'You didn't respond to my calls…'

'No.' She didn't even look at him. 'Because I was not in the mood to speak to anyone. How did you get up here?' She let out a mirthless laugh as she answered her own question. 'I really am going to fire that doorman.'

'I told him we were friends.'

'Friends.' She let out a mirthless laugh at his description of them. 'Well, however you described yourself, the doorman shouldn't have let you up.' She opened her door and her words dripped sarcasm as she invited him in. 'Come through, *friend*.'

She did not rush around making him welcome or offering a drink. Instead, she dropped her bag and headed straight to the kitchen, where she went to a drawer and took out two headache tablets and poured a glass of water.

For herself.

Gian watched as she downed the tablets and wondered how she still managed to look so put-together, even though he was sure her world had just been turned upside down. 'I saw you leaving Romano Holdings…' He tried to open the conversation, but Ariana didn't respond.

She was in no mood for conversation, and for once she didn't fill the silent gaps, offer drinks, or make him welcome. In fact, it was Gian who finally broke the tense silence.

'What happened?'

'We've been having a family catch-up and filling each other in on a few things.' She had been holding it in all day, sitting through revelation after revelation, and then a formal board meeting, always having to find a way to smile. 'Dante and Mia are expecting. That's for family's ears only,' Ariana needlessly warned, for she knew, because of his damned discretion, she might as well be telling it to the wall. 'There is to be a marriage in May, so that makes two Romano weddings.' Her voice rose and she almost let out an incredulous laugh, that both her brothers, who had always been indifferent to marriage, would soon both have all she had ever craved for herself.

But there was far more on her mind than her brothers. 'Gian, there's a reason I didn't take your calls. I have nothing to say to you. Nothing polite anyway.' Her confusion at the unfolding events was starting to morph into anger and she turned accusing eyes on him. 'Did you know?' she asked, her eyes narrowing into two dangerous slits.

'I told you—'

'I'm not talking about Dante and Mia.' She put down the glass with such a bang that he thought it might shatter, but Gian didn't even blink. 'Did you know that my father was gay?'

'Yes.'

'For how long?'

'Since I took over the hotel, I guess.'

'You guess?' she sneered.

'I wasn't taking notes, Ariana.'

'And what about my mother's affair?'

'I knew about that too. Look, your parents didn't sit me down and tell me, but given the nature of my work, they rightfully expected discretion. I would never gossip or break a confidence. I didn't even tell Dante and he is my best friend…'

'We were lovers!' Finally she shouted. Finally a sliver of her anger slipped out. 'I had every right to know.'

'Oh, so in your perfect world the fact we were sleeping together meant we should have started holding hands and gazing into each other's eyes and *sharing*?' He spat the last word with disdain. 'Tell me, Ariana, when was I supposed to tell you? The first time we made love? The second…?'

'If we were ever to have a relationship—' She stopped herself then, her nose tightening as she fought to suppress the tears building in her eyes, because a relationship, a real one, a close one, was the very thing he didn't want. 'You could have at least told me as a friend.'

'I wanted to,' he admitted. 'But it was not my place. They were not my secrets to tell. I tried to get you to speak to your father, that day of the interview—'

'You didn't try hard enough then.' Her anger, however misplaced, she aimed directly at him. 'For two years I felt pushed away by Papà. Now I find out that he just wanted to live out his days in peace with Roberto. My God! I was led to blame Mia. I was goaded and encouraged to hate her by my mother, just because she didn't want the truth getting out.'

'Ariana...' He tried to calm her down. 'Your mother came from a time—'

'I don't care!' She swore viciously in Italian and told him what rubbish he spoke. 'I'm his daughter. I deserved to know...' He crossed over as she swallowed down a scream that felt as if it had been building since her father died. 'If I'd known the truth, I could have spent quality time with him. Had *you* told me...'

She was almost hysterical and for once he was not trying to keep a lid on the drama or stop a commotion. It was not for that reason that he pulled her into his arms, but to comfort her. But she thumped at his chest and then scrunched his perfect shirt in her fist, knowing it wasn't his fault, knowing that the truth could only have come from her father.

'It was all just a farce...' She was starting to cry now in a way she never had before. Angry, bitter tears, and Gian held her as she drowned in his arms. 'I was so proud of their marriage, but it was just a sham. Even Stefano and I were conceived by IVF to keep up the charade...' All she had just learned poured out in an unchecked torrent he allowed to flow. 'They didn't really want us...' It was then Gian intervened.

'No.'

'Yes!' she insisted. 'It was all just a sham.'

'You were wanted,' he insisted, but Ariana would not be mollified.

'You don't know that...'

'But I do.' He was holding her arms and almost shaking her in an effort to loosen her dark thoughts before they took hold. 'I know for a fact you were wanted and loved.'

'Oh, what would you know?' Ariana responded. 'What would a man like you know about love?'

'Nothing!'

She stilled in his arms at the harsh anguish in his voice.

'I know nothing about love!' He hated to tell her, for Gian was loath to share, but he would expose his soul if it saved her from the dark hole she was sinking into. 'I wasn't wanted, Ariana. I was a regretful mistake and they never let me forget that fact. When Eduardo caved to their lifestyle, I brought myself up. I could see my mother's loathing on the rare occasions she actually looked me in the eye. You know how your mother called me a beggar? Well, I was one. I walked the streets at night, just for conversation, for contact...'

Her stomach clenched in fear at the thought of a child out there alone.

'They didn't even notice or care that I was gone. You want the truth, Ariana? I wanted to disappear...'

She couldn't breathe. So passionate was his revelation that there was not even the space to take in the air her lungs craved.

'No!' she refuted. It wasn't that she thought he lied, more that she could not bear his truth.

'Yes,' he said, 'so while I have never known love, I know what it looks like, and I know how much you were wanted and loved...'

They were the words she was desperate to hear, but she wanted to hear them from him. She was so desperate that she managed to twist her mind to pretend that Gian was saying *he* wanted her, that *he* loved her.

'Gian...' His name was a sob, a plea that she could hold onto the dream that those words were for her. Ariana honestly did not know who initiated their kiss but it was as if he read her cry in his name. For a man who knew nothing of love, he knew a lot about numbing pain. The room went dark then as their mouths melded, hot angry kisses to douse the pain. As his mouth bruised hers, as their teeth clashed, Ariana reacted with an urgency she had never known.

She kissed him as if it were vital.

And Gian kissed her to a place where only they remained. His hands were deft, shedding her jacket and lifting her top, pushing his hands up and caressing her breasts through her flimsy bra, his palms making her skin burn, then leaving her smouldering as he tackled her skirt.

He scalded her with desire, his hands hitching up her skirt so impatiently that she heard the lining rip. And Ariana, who had thought desire moved more slowly, could not begin to comprehend that she might simply seize what she craved.

He offered oblivion in the salty taste of his skin as she undid his shirt and buried her face in him. He offered escape as she unbuckled his belt and trousers.

'Ariana,' he warned, for he had not come for this. He had come to offer more, yet it was a poor attempt at a protest for he was lifting her onto the bench and tearing at her knickers as their mouths found each other again.

She had not known that the world could feel empty and soulless one moment and then find herself wrapped in his arms and drowning in the succour he gave.

He spread her thighs and she let out a shout as he pushed inside her. It was not a cry of pain but of relief, for here she could simply escape and be.

'Please,' she sobbed, because she never wanted it to end, yet they were both building rapidly to a frantic peak.

The glass she had slammed down spilled and her bottom was cold and wet, but it barely registered. There was only him, crashing against her senses again and again, a mass exodus of hurt as he touched her deep inside and somehow soothed the pain.

'Gian!' It was Ariana who offered a warning now, for she was trembling on the inside, her thighs so tight it felt like cramp. A sudden rush of electricity shot down her spine and she clenched around him, dizzied by her own pulses, and she was rewarded with his breathless shout.

They were both silent and stunned as their breathing gradually calmed. Ariana was grateful for the empty space between her thoughts. It was the first time she had felt even a semblance of quiet since her phone had shot her awake that morning. Gian too was silent, somewhat reeling at his own lack of control, for he had come here to speak, to talk, to offer Ariana comfort…

Now, though, he lowered her down from the bench and tidied himself. Ariana twisted the waistband on her skirt so the damp patch was at the side, and she even smoothed her hand over her hair, as if order could somehow be resorted.

Except it was chaos, Ariana knew, for she had made love to him again.

She had convinced herself, once again, that Gian might one day change and want her the way she wanted him.

'Ariana.' He cleared his throat. 'I didn't come here—'

'What did you come here for then?' she interrupted. 'A chat?'

'Yes,' Gian said, as the blood crept back to his head. 'A proposal.'

She looked at him with wide, nervous eyes, for this was new territory to Ariana. How one moment they could be locked in an intimate embrace, and the next attempting to speak as if his seed wasn't trickling down between her thighs. 'A proposal?'

He nodded. 'I thought a lot about what you said yesterday, and you're right, Ariana, I do avoid emotion…' He smiled a pale smile. 'Which is impossible around you.'

She swallowed, unsure where this was leading, but hoping…

Hoping!

'What you said about moving…' Gian ventured.

'I meant,' Ariana said, 'I'm not going to live in an apartment my mother feels entitled to use as a second lounge.' Her decision was crystal clear now. 'I want to take the Romano name off for a while. I want to work on myself.' She gave a hollow laugh. 'I want to actually *work*...'

'I get that,' Gian agreed. 'And, as I said, I have a proposal for you. Fiordelise Florence hotel opens at the end of May. What if you do your training here, and then work as Guest Services Manager there?'

'Sorry?' Ariana frowned, though clearly not for the reason he was thinking.

'I know I said you would start as an assistant, but I agree, you have an exceptional skill set and would be an asset.'

'Your *proposal* is a job.'

'More than a job,' Gian said.

'A career then?'

'No!' She was missing the point, Gian thought. Though he could understand why, given his usually direct style of communication. He was not good at this relationship game. 'We could see each other...*more* of each other,' he said. 'Away from your family.'

'Without them knowing?' Ariana frowned.

'Of course,' he agreed. 'We both know that would cause more problems than it would solve so we would have to be discreet. I'll have an executive manager there, so I would not be so hands-on in running the place. There would be no impropriety at the hotel and far less chance of being seen out. I would, of course, get to Florence as often as I was able.'

Oh, she understood then. 'I'd be your mistress, you mean?'

'I never said that.'

'Perhaps not in so many words, but...' Her lips were white but still turned up into the kind of practised smile she flashed for the cameras all the time, all the brighter to disguise how she was breaking down on the inside. 'Tucked away, my family in the dark, no one finding out… that sounds an awful lot like a mistress to me. Well, I won't be your Fiordelise.'

'You're complicating matters.'

'Then I'll make it simple. Where would this lead, Gian?'

'Lead?' Gian frowned. 'Why does it have to lead anywhere?'

'Because that's what my heart does.' Ariana could say it no more honestly than that. 'My heart wants to know where this might go one day.'

'I'm offering you the best parts of me, Ariana.'

'No, you're offering to keep me tucked away, to flit in and out of my life whenever it's convenient. Gian, I want my lover by my side. I want to share my life with him, not live a secret. God knows, my parents did enough of that and look how it turned out.'

'That is so you,' Gian said. 'You have to get your own way. Everything has to be now—'

'I'm not asking for now, Gian,' Ariana interrupted. 'I'm asking if there's a possibility that this might lead to more. You want directness,' she said. 'You tell your lovers up front that it will go no further. Well, I'm being direct too and I'm telling you that I want at the very least the possibility of more.'

'I have no more to give.'

She had known that getting involved with Gian would ultimately hurt her, so why did she feel so unprepared to deal with the pain he so impassively inflicted?

'No, thank you.' Her voice was strangely high.

'Think about it…'

'I already have.' She was staring down at the barrel of a future spent mainly alone. Christmases, weddings, the birth of Dante and Mia's baby, christenings and even funerals… all the things she would have to deal with alone.

Her love unacknowledged and unnamed.

'I won't be your mistress, Gian.' Her response was clearer now, her decision absolutely made. She started to show him the door, but then changed her mind. 'Actually, before you leave, I have something I need to put to you.'

Gian frowned. He was not used to being told no in this way, particularly when he had offered Ariana more than he'd ever offered anyone. 'What?'

'I can't pretend,' Ariana said. 'And I don't want to keep making the same mistake again.'

'You think that was a mistake?' He pointed to the bench where they had both found a slice of heaven just moments ago.

'Not at that time I didn't,' Ariana said. 'Even now, no, I don't think it was, but if we make love again then, yes, that would be a mistake.'

'You make no sense.'

'I want you to stay away,' Ariana said. 'Not for ever, but at least until…' She swallowed down the words, loath to admit how he turned her on merely by his presence, how with one look, one crook of his manicured finger, she would run to him. 'Until I can act as if nothing ever happened between us.'

As if I don't love your soulless heart.

'I can't face you in front of my family until I can look at you as if nothing ever happened between us. I have to get to that place where we can do the kiss-kiss thing and…'

She took a breath to steady herself. Right now it seemed like an impossible dream, that one day she might merely shrug when she heard that Gian had arrived.

'I'd like you to stay away from my brothers' weddings…'

'I'm already not going to Stefano's, but Dante…' He shook his head. 'Dante is my closest friend…'

'Oh, please.' Ariana found a new strength in her voice then, a derisive one, a scorn-filled one. 'What would do you care about that? You've told me relationships are the very thing you don't want.'

He couldn't deny that.

'So, please, Gian.' She said it without derision now. 'If you care about me at all, then do the decent thing and stay away.'

Gian did as she asked.

He stayed away from Dante's wedding, citing an urgent issue at La Fiordelise Azerbaijan, which he had to deal with personally.

That meant Ariana could smile her red smile at the wedding and have fun with her regular posse of friends.

Yet, despite him acquiescing to her request, she missed him so much: the little flurry in her stomach that existed whenever there was the prospect of seeing him; the small shared smiles; the occasional dance; and, most of all, the prospect of a late night alone with him...

Instead, she stood in the grounds of what had once been the family home and tried to push Gian out of her heart and focus on the nuptials. Mia looked utterly gorgeous and Dante looked so proud and happy as his bride walked towards him.

'That didn't take long, did it?' Nicki nudged.

'What?'

'She's showing!' Paulo said.

Ariana pressed her lips together. Only family had been let in on the secret that Mia was pregnant. Dante had assured them all that nothing had taken place before Papà died, although for four months Mia did appear rather, well, large.

'It must have been going on for quite some time,' Nicki whispered. 'Your pa only died in January...'

'Thanks for pointing that out,' Ariana sniped, but Nicki didn't notice for she had moved on. 'Where's Gian? I thought he'd be here.'

'I've no idea,' Ariana said, practising her shrug, as if Gian De Luca was the very last person on her mind.

As the vows were made, and Nicki jostled to take photos on her phone, Ariana asked herself why she hadn't told Nicki about what had happened with Gian. Neither had she told her the truth about her parents...

Paulo she wasn't so close to, but she and Nicki were supposed to be best friends.

It was a question of trust, Ariana realised.

Deep in her soul, Ariana realised that she did not trust the woman who sat by her side and it had nothing to do with Gian's opinion of Nicki...

The answer had arrived in its own time and the conclusion Ariana came to was all hers.

Ariana said nothing, of course. She just smiled through the proceedings and raised a glass when Dante announced in his speech that he and Mia were expecting twins— likely the reason for her showing so much. Not that Nicki corrected her earlier assumption. 'You're going to be an aunty...twice!' Nicki screeched, and called to the waiter for another bottle of champagne.

'Make that two bottles,' Paulo said, and Ariana's eyes actually scanned the room for Gian, as if hope and need might make him somehow appear.

He did not.

Apart from his absence, it was a wonderful wedding, their love so palpable it made Ariana both happy and pensive.

'It will be your turn soon.' Nicki smiled as they took a break from the dancing. 'And I shall be your bridesmaid...'

'You'll be the oldest bridesmaid in Rome if you wait for me,' Ariana said. 'I want a career.'

'Why?' Nicki frowned. 'It's not as if you need to work.
You have Daddy's trust fund. Didn't he leave you an apartment in Paris? We should go there and check it out...'

'It's not enough—'

'Please,' Nicki scoffed. 'Poor little rich girl.' Her narrowed eyes snapped back to wide and friendly and she
pushed out a smile. 'Let's join Paulo.'

'You go,' Ariana encouraged. 'I'll just sit here awhile.'

Her rare absence on the dance floor did not go unno-
ticed. 'Get off your phone, Ariana,' Dante called. 'Come
and dance...'

Except it wasn't her own phone that Ariana was going
through, it was her friend's. Some might call it dishonest,
or an invasion of privacy, a breach of trust...

Except, from where Ariana now sat, those titles belonged to Nicki.

There was a sneaky little shot of Mia in profile as she
made her vows, a definite confirmation of the pregnancy
that had been announced only to family and friends. That
could be excused, though, as lots of people had been taking photos.

What could not be excused was an earlier image of
Mia and Dante, locked in a passionate embrace. It was
the photo that had been taken at the ball, the one that had
caused so much pain.

To a heart that Ariana had thought could not be broken
further, the knowledge that her friend had betrayed her
added another river of pain.

The ridiculous part was that the one person in whom
she would have confided, Ariana had asked not to attend.

She missed him.

Even with his selfish guidelines as to what a relationship with him might entail, she *needed* him tonight.

'Ariana!'

Her name was being shouted by lots of people now.

Maybe she had grown up some, because instead of confronting Nicki and causing a scene at her brother's wedding, she did the right thing.

Ariana put down the phone, topped up her lipstick…
…and danced.

CHAPTER THIRTEEN

ARIANA WASN'T AVOIDING sorting out her life.

If that had been the case, then she would have said yes to Gian's offer to be his mistress. She would have left her chaotic family and Janus friend and headed for Florence to be wined and dined and made love to over and over.

Instead, she faced the mountain that at first had looked far too high to climb. Yet, bit by bit, she found the tools to tackle it, some of which had been given to her by Gian.

The doorman received a stern warning that from now on Ariana's whereabouts were to remain private and heaven help him if an unannounced guest arrived at her door. She declined nights out with Paulo, *to be seen*, for she had felt Gian's exasperation and knew he was right.

It wasn't just Gian's suggestions she followed, though. She also took Dante's perpetual advice and finally turned off her phone.

Apart from Eloa's hen night, where red lips were certainly required, most were spent sitting on her apartment floor, eating ice cream and finally sorting out her photos into albums.

Ariana chose to withdraw from the endless vacuous socialising and learned to rely on her own company, arranging her past into a more honest shape as she prepared for a new future. Finally, she was ready for a couple of nights in

Luctano, where she spoke at length with Roberto and got to know her father, a little too late, but a whole lot more.

'He loved you,' Roberto said.

'I know.'

She did.

On the Thursday before she headed for home, ready now to visit his grave, Ariana spread an armful of gorgeous hand-picked daffodils, which meant truth, rebirth and new beginnings, and a little sprig of violets, for peace in the afterlife, and told him about Stefano and Eloa's wedding, which was just two days away.

'I am his wedding *padrihnos*, or wedding bridesmaid,' Ariana told her father. 'It basically means I am Stefano's best man.' She knew that would make him smile, wherever he was now. 'And Nicki is coming over tomorrow and I shall be telling her she is not welcome at the wedding and I don't want to see her any more.' Ariana swallowed. 'I still haven't told Dante about the photo.'

It wasn't her brother's wrath that worried her, more that he would, of course, tell Gian. She couldn't bear the thought of him rolling his eyes, for he had warned her about Nicki more than once.

There was something else too, something she hadn't told anyone yet, not even herself, but she admitted it out loud now. 'I am in love with Gian, Papà.'

She wouldn't be the first in her family to act in her own interests and keep it secret, were she to become his mistress, but despite how she felt about Gian, she could not reconcile herself to it. Not now she was finally becoming someone she could be proud of.

'You're not ready!' Nicki frowned, when she saw Ariana dressed in a pale grey dress and flat sandals and with her hair wild and her eyes all puffy and swollen.

'Actually, I am ready,' Ariana corrected. She had been

up all night, completing the finishing touches to gifts for her loved ones, and she had worked through the day, only stopping to refuel with coffee, thinking about what must be done. 'Come in, Nicki.'

It was up there with the hardest things she had ever done, because Ariana had truly thought of Nicki as a forever friend. Confronted with the evidence of what she had done, Nicki attacked her friend, and Ariana didn't have the energy to muster a defence against the tirade of abuse she was subjected to. Instead she listened and then said, 'I think you should leave now.'

'But we have the wedding tomorrow,' Nicki flailed. 'It'll look odd if I'm not there and we have our trip to Paris—'

'*I* have a wedding tomorrow,' Ariana interrupted. 'You're no longer welcome at Romano family events.'

It hurt and it hurt and it hurt, and once Nicki had gone, she cried for a while. But Ariana wanted this chapter of her life firmly closed, which meant that she had to tell Dante and Mia that it had been her friend who had invaded their privacy and outed them to the press.

And in turn they would tell Gian.

Only that wasn't right, Ariana knew. It wasn't up to Dante to tidy up after her. It was *her* friend who had caused this, and it was Ariana's mess to clean up. With that thought in mind, she grabbed a wrapped parcel from her bed. She had intended to mail it, but that was a cop-out and so she walked, or rather marched, her way down cobbled lanes and packed streets then pushed through the gorgeous brass door of La Fiordelise and towards his office, where she was met by his gatekeeper, Luna.

'Gian is in a meeting at the moment,' Luna said.

'It's my fault for arriving unannounced...' Ariana shook her dizzy head '...but if he can spare me a moment when he's done it would be very much appreciated.'

'Of course.' Luna nodded. 'Would you like some refreshments while you wait?'

Ariana guessed she was being sent to the Pianoforte
Bar, or, as his lovers should name it, the Relegation Bar,
and her braveness evaporated. 'It's fine.' Ariana had
changed her mind. 'I'll catch up with him another time.'

'No, no…' Luna said, and it dawned on her that she was
not being sent to the Pianoforte Bar. Instead, Luna gently
suggested that she freshen up and pointed her towards a
powder room. 'Still or sparkling?' she asked.

'Sorry?' Ariana frowned.

'Acqua,' Luna said patiently. 'Would you like still or
sparkling?'

She must thank Luna one day, Ariana thought as she
splashed her face with water and ran a comb through her
hair, because she still had a morsel of pride left, enough
to know she had been saved from facing him looking so
terrible.

Terrible.

Ariana hadn't so much as glanced in a mirror since her
confrontation with Nicki. It looked as if she'd rolled out of
bed this morning and just pulled a dress on.

She had.

As if she hadn't brushed her hair.

She hadn't.

Her skin was all pale and blotchy, and her lips were
swollen from crying so there was no point painting her
usual red lipstick on. Still, she was grateful for the re-
prieve and the chance to freshen up somewhat, as Luna
would no doubt have told him that yet another of his exes
had shown up in a state of distress…

No, not she!

'I have Ariana Romano in Reception, asking to see you.'

Gian was just packing up his laptop, about to head to

Florence. He had no time for theatrics. And yet, with each day that passed, he found that he missed the colour she had brought to his world, the drama and emotion she always brought to his table, to his bed…

He wanted them.

It had been hell missing his friend's wedding because, despite his supposed lack in the heart department, under any other circumstances he would have moved heaven and earth to have been there.

'I can tell her that you are due to fly out—'

'It's fine,' Gian cut in.

'I should warn you then, Gian, she seems distressed…'

'Was she short with you?' Gian asked, almost hopefully, because if Ariana was throwing her weight around with his staff, he could at least be aggrieved, but Luna shook her head.

'Of course not. Ariana is always polite with me.' Luna suddenly laughed.

'What's so funny?'

'Ariana always makes me smile,' Luna said. 'Anyway, I'm just letting you know that it looks as if she's been crying.'

He nodded and nudged a leather-covered box of tissues to her side of the desk in preparation for her arrival. 'Send her through.'

Gian was certain he knew what this would be about. It had been a few months since the funeral, and there had been the ball, and of course what had taken place in her kitchen. Whatever way he looked at it, Gian was sure he was about to be told he was to be a father.

Yes, there were always consequences, and not once, but on three separate occasions he had not taken the level of care he usually would, relying on her to take the Pill. It was his own fault entirely and he would handle this with grace, even if a pregnancy was everything he had always dreaded.

Gian did not know how he felt.

When she arrived in his office, she was most un-Ariana-like.

Her dress was crumpled, her espadrilles tied haphazardly, her hair, dared he say it, a day past needing a wash, and her make-up but a distant memory. And yet, to his eyes, this was the real Ariana, the one who shot straight to his heart. To see her so fragile and clearly distraught had him fighting not to go straight over and take her in his arms.

Instead, for now, he kept his arms to himself.

'Ariana.' He rose to greet her and they did the kiss-kiss routine she had referred to so painfully in their last conversation. He gestured for her to take a seat as they both tried to go back to a world where they hadn't done more. 'Can I offer you some refreshments?'

'No, no…' She shook her head. 'Thank you, though.'

'Some champagne?' Gian suggested. 'A bottle this time.'

But she did not smile at his little reference and instead shook her head. 'No, thank you.' She took a breath. It wasn't just La Fiordelise and the oasis he made that calmed her; it was Gian himself.

Despite there being so much on her mind, there was a chance to pause, to just sit in the calming low light of his office and take a moment.

That was what he gave her.

Always.

This tiny chance to pause, and it was in that moment Ariana knew that she really did want things resolved between them. No matter her blushes, it was time to face things head on.

'Before I say what I came to say—' before he got angry

about Nicki '—I just want to clear the air. I'm sorry for asking you to miss Dante's wedding. It wasn't fair of me to do that.'

'There were extenuating circumstances and it was right that you did,' Gian said. 'I'm sure we'll get to managing steely politeness at family gatherings soon.'

'Yes!' She shot out a laugh and tried to glimpse a time when she wouldn't want him, but it was such an impossible thought that her smile slid away.

'Dante understood,' Gian said. 'The wedding was at such short notice. He dropped by the other day, we had lunch, and he told me about the twins. So we're all good...' He was so certain that Ariana was here to tell him she was pregnant that he kindly gave her an opening. His eyes never left her face as he watched carefully for her reaction. 'Twins must run in the family...'

'Oh, please.' Ariana gave a mirthless laugh. 'Twins don't run in my family, Gian. I assume my mother had more than one egg put back. Anything to keep up the charade!'

'It wasn't all a charade, Ariana.'

'I know that now.' She gave him a thin smile.

'Are you talking?'

'Of course we are,' Ariana said. 'I am hurt, yes, but I love her.'

Lucky Angela, Gian thought, to have her Ariana's unconditional love.

A love he himself had discarded.

'I have something for you,' Ariana told him. 'I've been sorting out some of my father's things...' She handed him a leather-bound book as she explained what she had done in recent days. 'I've made one each for my brothers and one for my mother. The contents are different in each, of course...' She was talking a little too fast, as she did when she was embarrassed, unsure if he would even want her gift.

'An album?'

'Yes, there were a lot of photos, and I thought you might like the ones you were in. But please don't look at it now: that's not what I'm here for...' She took a breath. 'Gian, there's something I have to tell you. I wasn't going to; I've tried to deal with it myself, but you do deserve to know...'

Gian braced himself to hear the inevitable.

'I've had my suspicions for a couple of weeks.' Ariana's voice was barely above a whisper, and she cleared her throat. 'I should perhaps have come to you sooner but I wanted to be sure myself...'

'You could have come to me,' Gian said. 'You can always come to me. You know that.'

'Yes.' She nodded. 'I just wanted to be very sure before I said anything, and so this afternoon I confronted her.'

Gian frowned, not sure what Ariana meant by that. 'Confronted...who?' he asked, surprised. 'What do you mean?'

'I've just come from speaking with Nicki.' Ariana ran a shaking hand through her thick dark hair and then forced herself to look at Gian and simply say it. 'It was Nicki who took the photo of Mia and Dante at the Romano Ball...'

That was it?

Ariana wasn't here to tell him she was pregnant! Instead, she had found out who had sold the photos to the press! Gian waited to catch the smile of relief that should surely be spreading over his face.

Except the smile didn't come, and the anticipated relief didn't course through his veins, as he looked at Ariana sitting tense and hurt, let down by a friend she had trusted.

'You're sure it was her?' Gian checked.

Ariana nodded. 'At Dante's wedding she was acting

strangely, and when I got a chance I looked through her phone. I'm so sorry, Gian.'

'*You're* sorry?'

'Nicki was my guest on the night of the ball. I know the photo caused problems for you—'

'It's fine,' Gian cut in. 'Well, it's not, of course, but don't worry about me.' He wanted to go over and take her hands, which still twisted in her lap. 'I'm sorry she let you down.'

Ariana nodded.

'Does Dante know?'

'Not yet. It's taken me a couple of weeks to get my head around it all, and I decided I would tell you first.' She looked at the man she had always run to with troubles that seemed too big for this world. 'I might leave it until after Stefano's wedding. Really, I don't think Dante will be too upset. After all, the photo forced things out into the open. I know it angered you, though, and that it was damaging for the reputation of the hotel.'

'The only reputation that has been damaged is Nicki's,' Gian said kindly. 'What did she say when you confronted her?'

Ariana let out a pained, mirthless laugh. 'Plenty.'

He saw a fresh batch of tears flash in her eyes and knew that the confrontation hadn't been pleasant and so he asked again. 'What did Nicki say?'

'That it was my fault. That I treated her poorly and always made her feel second best…'

'No.'

But his words couldn't comfort her now. She was still shaking from the recent encounter with someone she had considered to be her friend, someone she had defended so often to this man.

'I'm sorry,' Gian said.

'I know you never liked her.'

'I mean, I'm sorry you had to go through that.'

'I should have listened to you in the first place. In fact, I'm starting to think you might be right…about the value of not letting people get too close.'

'Never take relationship advice from me,' Gian said. 'As you have undoubtedly seen, I am not particularly good at them.'

'I don't know about that.' Ariana smiled. 'You made me feel pretty wonderful, at least for a while.' But she hadn't come here to discuss her time with Gian. She'd said what she'd come to say. 'Anyway, thank you for being so gracious. I just thought it was something you should know. I don't know if Nicki will have the audacity to come here again…'

'It'll be fine. I'll let my security team know.' He looked at her swollen eyes and knew Nicki had said plenty more. 'What else did she say?' Gian asked.

Ariana was rarely silent.

'Tell me,' he pushed.

'That I'm spoiled…'

'You deserve to be spoiled.'

'You do too, Gian.'

'What do you mean? I have everything I could possibly want or need.'

'You really don't get it, do you?' He was so self-assured and yet so remote, just so impossible to reach. She ached, literally ached, to shower him with kisses, to bring him ice cream in bed, to be there at the beginning and the end of his day… 'It's not about the best bits, Gian.' He just stared back at her, nonplussed.

It was time to let go of her fantasy that he would change his mind, that he would see her as anything more. It was time to go.

She stood to leave, but it was Gian who delayed her. 'Are you ready for the wedding tomorrow?'

'Yes.'

He wanted her to elaborate, as she usually did. Gian wanted to know if she was dreading tomorrow, if she was speaking with Mia, and lots more besides, but it would seem he had lost his front row seat to her thoughts.

'Good luck with the opening,' Ariana said.

'Thank you. Enjoy the wedding.'

'I intend to.'

This really was it, Gian realised.

The tears she had shed and her sudden appearance hadn't been about him. It had been about Nicki and a friendship lost.

There was no baby, no emotional issues to deal with, it really was just time to move on.

Gian was usually very good at that. So why did he feel this way?

The opening of La Fiordelise Florence was a tremendous success and on the Saturday night esteemed guests mingled and celebrated. While he should be quietly congratulating himself, he had never felt more alone in a crowded room.

The best food, the best champagne, and if it was sex he wanted, well, there would be no shortage there, for there were beautiful women vying for his attention.

The problem was him, because instead of enjoying the spoils of his own success Gian found himself slipping away not long after dinner, sitting in his impressive suite leafing through a leather-bound book… There were several pictures of him fishing or riding with Dante and later with the twins. There was one of a teenage Gian rolling his eyes while Dante kicked a stone to Stefano as a very spoiled Ariana sat on a fat little pony, the absolute apple of her parents' eyes.

But then Ariana faded from the images as life took its twists and turns and he had headed to university. There were a couple of years without any images while the disasters that had unfolded back then had played out.

He had never really liked Angela Romano, but there was a picture of him smiling at her the night La Fiordelise had been saved. Angela was dripping jewels and being her usual affected self, as she stood with her husband and Gian.

This really was a gift without an agenda, Gian knew, for there was even a picture of Gian standing with the Romano family on the night Ariana had attended her first ball. He knew Ariana had made this album purely for his benefit because she would prefer that this picture of herself be relegated to burn in a fire for she looked scowling and awkward.

It was a slice of time he had forgotten.

Even now, as he looked at the photo, there was no flash of memory.

He would have been in his mid-twenties then, and Ariana at that awkward age of fifteen, her hair done in a way that now looked very much of its time, and she had been wearing too much make-up.

They had all been there for him throughout his life, and he couldn't help but wonder what each of the Romanos was doing now.

How Ariana was coping with the nuptials.

He turned back the pages and looked again at a podgy little Ariana sitting on a podgy little pony, only he saw it differently this time... Not the pony, or the pampered heiress, just the absolute adoration on her face as she smiled at her parents and pleaded with them, with her eyes, to be loved, loved, loved...

It could have been a cone full of chestnuts they had given her; it wasn't the pony she had craved, it had been attention and love.

Gian went out onto the balcony and gazed on the Ponte

Vecchio, the gorgeous old bridge that was the soul of Florence, and sung about in 'O Mio Babbino Caro'.

Yet it was not the music that filled his soul tonight, for he would never look at this bridge and not think of her.

Ariana.

Yes, he was proud of his new hotel, but tonight his heart was in Rome.

CHAPTER FOURTEEN

'COLOUR,' ELOA HAD SAID.

A Brazilian wedding was a colourful affair, and that was evident even before the nuptials had started. Even though Gian was not in Rome this weekend, he had ensured La Fiordelise was at their disposal. The reception area was a blaze of colour and forbidden perfume, Ariana noticed as she walked through Reception and headed up to her suite to get changed.

Ariana would have preferred to wear black, as she had to the Romano Ball, to denote that she was in mourning. For her father, of course, but the end of a relationship also felt a whole lot like grief. She awoke with a weight of sadness in her chest that never quite left, and she felt Gian's presence beside each and every thought. Yet she must push it all aside today, so she chose a dress as red as her signature lipstick. She wore her jet-black hair up, teased, with a few stray curls snaking down, meaning that she looked far more vibrant than she felt.

As Stefano fiddled with his tie, Ariana stepped out for a moment onto the balcony and looked down at the square beneath and remembered the night of her father's funeral, that desperately lonely night made so much better by Gian.

Why had she insisted that he stay away, when the truth was that she missed him already?

Half the congregation were clipping their way across

the square to the venue and Ariana watched the colourful display from the balcony of Stefano's suite. The sun seemed at odds with the greyness of her world, and the flowers looked like placards from angry protesters to her tired eyes, yet they waved their petals and demanded she sparkle.

And so Ariana put on her best smile and stepped back inside. 'We should head over soon,' she told him.

'Before we do, there's something I want to say,' Stefano said. 'Ariana, I'm sorry for shutting you out.'

'Stefano, we don't need to do this now. It's your wedding day…'

'And I want it to be perfect,' he said. 'I want the air to be cleared between us. Gian suggested—'

'Gian?' Ariana frowned.

'He called me this morning to wish me well and apologise for not being here. We got to talking…' He took a breath.

Even though he wasn't physically here, Gian was still looking out for her, Ariana realised. He was still fixing the pieces of her life that he could, and she was so grateful to him as Stefano spoke on and finally gave her his reasons for keeping his distance. 'You see, I knew Mamma was having an affair, and I was having suspicions about Pa and Roberto. I was worried I might let things slip when I spoke to you and so I stayed away as much as I could. I was wrong…'

'No,' Ariana corrected. 'You did what you thought best at the time, and the air is clear now.' Clear, if a little thick with unshed tears when she thought of Gian and this moment he had created to bring her and her twin back together.

'We have some catching up to do,' Stefano prompted.

'We do…' Ariana smiled '…though it can wait till after your honeymoon.' But certain things would wait for ever.

They were close again, but it would never be like it was before. Gian had changed her, she realised. She was far more independent now and did not need to run and tell Stefano everything, certainly not about herself and Gian.

It was her secret to keep.

'Do you have the rings?' Stefano asked for maybe the twentieth time.

'I have the rings.' Ariana smiled as she checked again for maybe the thirtieth time! 'Are you nervous?'

'Very,' Stefano admitted, and looked at his sister. 'I miss him.'

'I know you do.'

'It's the bride who should be crying…' Stefano said as he took a deep breath. 'I'm so happy yet I miss him so much today.'

'Hey,' Ariana soothed, and then she did something she never thought she would do. She reached into her purse and took out a tiny sliver of gold she had sworn she would never give away, but that Gian had told her she might. 'Papà gave Gian this for strength when his family died…'

'Really?'

'And he gave it to me when I felt weak at Papà's funeral, but I don't need it any more.' She put it in his top pocket. 'Papà is with you today.'

Ariana got on with her designated job: getting her brother to the embassy on time and remembering the rings.

Eloa was a stunning bride and the day brimmed with happiness. Well, that was what Ariana determinedly showed, even if there was a squad of elves holding down the cork on a vat of tears she would later shed.

'No Nicki?' Dante checked after the service as he handed her a glass of cachaça—a rather smoky Brazilian rum that made her eyes water. Ariana shook her head, deciding that she would tell him another time about the photo.

Tonight was a celebration after all.

And then Mia had a question for her new husband. 'No Gian again?'

'His new hotel,' Dante said. 'The opening was booked before the wedding date was decided and couldn't be changed...'

It was a throwaway sentence as he took his gorgeous wife off to dance and Ariana stood there, wondering how she would get through not just tonight but every future Romano family event at which Gian should be present.

Because Mia was right, Gian should be here.

The Romanos loved him like their own and he belonged here amongst them.

And when the next one happened, and the next, Ariana had to somehow work out how *not* to tumble into bed with him afterwards.

For. The. Rest. Of. Her. Life.

Oh, those elves were working overtime, yet she refused to cry and so she danced with Pedro, who was a cousin of the bride, and she danced with Francisco, who was a friend of an aunt, and Ariana laughed and danced and determinedly refused to give in to a heart that was breaking.

'Come on, Ariana...' They were all dragging her to the centre, where it would seem it was a Brazilian tradition to dance around Eloa's gold shoes. Really, Ariana had no idea what she was doing, but she swayed her hips and laughed and did a sort of Spanish flamenco around the shoe, tapping her feet and swishing the ruffles on her dress.

He had almost missed this, Gian thought when he saw her.

He had almost missed another Romano wedding and another night with people he could only now admit to himself were family.

The usually unruffled Luna had nearly thrown a fit when Gian had declared that he was flying back to Rome and asked if she could arrange it urgently, as well as a couple of other small assignments he wanted her to swiftly organise. 'I need to be there tonight.'

Fortunately, Ariana had arranged the reception just across from La Fiordelise so, with his helicopter landing late into the night, it was a simple matter of checking everything was in place and feeding some official documents through the shredder.

Gian didn't need reminders of the past.

It was a future he wanted now.

And with the past shredded, he walked across the square to Palazzo Pamphili and found, to his pleasant surprise, he was still on the guest list.

Walking through the grand building with its intricate ceilings and formal galleries, there was a moment to gather himself in such esteemed surroundings. It felt deserted, yet finally he could hear the laughter and merriment as if calling for him to join in. And even without his feelings for Ariana, it was right that he was there tonight for, perfect or not, these people had been more of a family to him than his own.

'Gian!' Dante caught up with him as he congratulated the bride and groom and apologised for arriving so late. 'It is good that you made it.'

It was said completely without implication or malice that he had missed theirs, Gian knew; Dante and Mia were simply pleased to see him.

Gian was back in the fold, as easily as that, and he stood watching the celebrations for a moment, taking it all in. He did not have to strain to locate Ariana; she was completely unmissable, of course.

Dressed in red, she was the belle of the ball, dancing and laughing and having the time of her life, so much so that even Gian could not see the hurt he was certain resided within.

He wasn't vain enough to believe it was all to do with

him. There was the loss of her father, her relationship with her mother, Nicki, Stefano…

He was proud of his diva and her acting skills, proud of her resilience, and also aware of an unfamiliar sensation tightening his chest as she danced happily in another man's arms.

And another!

Damn it, Ariana, Gian thought, *I get it. Your life will go on without me, but please tone it down!*

He had never cared about anyone enough to know jealousy before, yet he learned there and then to breathe through it, even smiling as she kicked up her heels.

No longer able to resist, he caught Ariana's arm as she stamped past him, and saw how startled she was in her violet eyes when they locked with his.

Gian was here.

Damn!

Just as she did her best to move on and prove to herself she could party without him, the best-looking spanner in the world was suddenly thrown into the works.

'I'm busy dancing,' she told him, and reclaimed her arm.

'It's a Brazilian wedding, Ariana,' he told her. 'Not a Spanish one.'

'I know that.'

'Yet you're doing the flamenco.'

'So I am…' Her heart was hammering because she could not quite believe that he was here. 'These cachaças are very strong.' She was trying to act normally, or rather how she would have acted a year ago at a family event when Gian De Luca suddenly showed up. 'I thought you had to be at the La Fiordelise Florence, opening—'

'I left early and gave myself the rest of the night off…'

'Why are they all called La Fiordelise?' she snapped. It had always annoyed her and she let him know tonight. 'It's hardly original.'

'Your father said the same.'

'Well, you should have listened to him. La Fiordelise, London. La Fiordelise, Azerbaijan...' *Gosh those cachaças must be strong*, she thought, because she allowed a little of her resentment to seep out. 'Perhaps you could send me there...'

He just smiled.

But it was a smile she had never seen before. Not his on-duty smile, or his off-duty one; it was just a smile that let her be, that simply accepted her as she was and, she felt, suddenly adored.

'Hey, Ariana...' Pedro was waving her to join in another odd-looking dance.

'Your boyfriend is calling you to dance with him again,' Gian said, and with those words let her know he'd been watching her for a while. 'You're very popular tonight.'

'Yes, I am,' Ariana said, and she'd never been happier to be caught dancing and smiling and laughing, even if she was bleeding inside. 'I am in demand!'

'Have you time to dance with me?'

No.

She had to practise saying no to him, had to have that tiny word fall readily from her tongue.

For. The. Rest. Of. Her. Life.

Except that tiny word felt far too big when she looked into those beautiful slate-grey eyes. She would start tomorrow, Ariana decided, and allow herself just one tiny dance tonight. 'One dance,' Ariana said, and found herself back in his arms. 'For the sake of duty.'

Yet this was no duty dance, for his arms were no longer wooden and his hands ran down her ribs and came to rest on her hips and there was slight pressure there to pull her against him. He moved like silk and this time it was Ariana who was the one holding back.

'Dance with me,' he moaned.

'I am.'

'Like we did.'

'No,' she said. 'My mother is looking.'

'Let her look.'

'You know what she can be like.'

'Tell her that your sex life is none of her business.'

'I have.' Ariana laughed. 'But we no longer have a sex life, so there's nothing to tell.'

She felt the heat of his palm low on her hips and heat somewhere else as he pulled her hard up against him. His voice was low in her ear and made her shiver. 'You're sure about that?'

This wasn't fair, Ariana thought as they danced cheek to cheek with their bodies meshed together. He wasn't being fair after all that had passed between them.

'They will guess…' Ariana started.

'Stop worrying about them,' Gian said, and for a little while she did. Her family all danced with their various partners and she danced with a man who was always there for her. There was something so freeing about Gian's acceptance of her, and the way he lived life on his terms. It was something she was starting to embrace herself and so she wrapped her arms around his neck and told him a little of her new world. 'I've told my lazy doorman that he's not allowed to let guests up without my permission, not even my mother, and I shall petition the other residents to have him removed if he doesn't improve.'

'Good for you.'

'And I have an interview next week with your rival company. I used my mother's maiden name, so I know I got the interview on my own merit.'

'Very good,' Gian said.

'And I will never give up on love.'

'I'm pleased to hear it.' He was serious suddenly. 'Can we go outside?'

'It will cause too much gossip and rumour...'

'I don't care.'

'Well, I do,' Ariana said. 'I'm not leaving Stefano's wedding to make out with you.'

'That is a revolting term,' Gian told her, 'but fair enough.' For though he was desperate to speak with her, she was right not to leave during her brother's wedding reception. 'Will you come over to La Fiordelise afterwards?' Gian asked.

'No...' she said slowly. Her reply was tentative, but with practice she would perfect it, Ariana decided. 'No.' She said it more clearly this time.

No. No. No.

Easy as pie.

'Come to me tonight.'

They were still cheek to cheek, though the music had ended, yet they carried on dancing. She could feel herself weakening at his touch. 'No,' she told him as he reached into his inner pocket and slipped a cold thin card where the ruffle of her dress parted. It was all discreetly done, yet Ariana knew she should have slapped him there and then, but lust moved faster than anger where Gian De Luca was concerned. It took a moment for her to form the proper reply. 'Leave me alone, Gian.'

'I can't.'

'Ariana!' Her *mamma* was laughing and calling her over. 'Gian!' In fact, she was calling them both, for the music had restarted and upped its tempo and the bride and groom were about to be waved off into the night.

It was loud, it was fun, and it was over.

Stefano and Eloa were officially married and it was kisses and final drinks and then they all spilled out of the venue into the square. She was so happy for Stefano and Eloa, especially now the air had been cleared between her and her twin.

And happy for Mia and Dante too, Ariana thought as she watched them walk hand in hand into the night.

If it was possible to be lonely and happy at the same time, then she was lonely and happy for herself too, for Gian had already gone.

She wanted not just to be part of a couple, but she wanted to be part of that couple with Gian.

Walking hand in hand in public, kissing without secrets, in love for all to see.

The square had never looked more beautiful. There was a carousel all lit up and the stunning fountains were gushing and spouting. It was a special place indeed, where they had eaten hot chestnuts on the night she'd said farewell to her father, and where she now stood so confused and so wanting to go into La Fiordelise if it meant another night with the man she loved.

She would always want him.

That was a given.

If, somehow, forty years from now, they were here at Stefano and Eloa's ruby wedding celebration, there would still be a longing and an ache for what could have been. If learning the truth about her family had taught her anything, it was that regrets were such a waste of a life. She didn't want to have any regrets when it came to Gian.

She would start saying no on Monday.

Not caring if she was found out, Ariana slipped away and found herself in the reception area of La Fiordelise, heading straight for his bed and the bliss he would temporarily give.

Life was better with Gian in it than not.

Yes, she was turning into Fiordelise, Ariana decided as she took the elevator up.

He opened the door and, before she fell into his arms, she stated her case. 'There will be rules,' Ariana said.

If she was to be his mistress then there would be rules and *she* would be the one making them.

'We shall discuss them,' Gian agreed.

'If you cheat on me, you die.'

He laughed. 'I'm saving you from prison then. I never cheat.'

'Liar.'

'Never. Even at your interview when I wanted to kiss you but Svetlana—'

'Stop!' She halted him. 'Don't ever try to redeem yourself with another woman's name.' She was way too needy to ignore it though. 'You wanted to kiss me then?'

'All over,' he told her. 'Come, there's something I want to show you…'

Down his hallway they went and she smiled when she saw there were pictures of Gian. 'When did you do this?' she asked.

'Tonight. The maintenance man has been busy.'

'Oh, Gian.' Her eyes were shining and happy to see his childhood finally featured on the wall, but then her smile died. 'What the hell is this doing here?' It was the most appalling, awkward photo of her at her first Romano Ball. She had been tempted to tear it up, but had decided it wasn't just her memory to delete.

'No!' She was appalled. 'That photo was for your eyes only, I look terrible!'

'You do and, believe me, your mother had nothing to worry about then… It was here that things started to change for me…'

Her breath stopped, as there she was, in a silver dress, standing next to Gian, in an informal shot of a night that had been more difficult than the picture revealed.

It was the first Romano Ball without her *papà*. He had been a last-minute withdrawal due to a deterioration in his health. On the one hand, she had been relieved that she wouldn't have to see him with Mia.

On the other hand, it had meant her *papà* was getting worse.

Gian had steered her through it, though. He always did.

He had held her in those wooden arms and told her that she was doing well, and it had meant the world.

'I think,' Gian said, 'well, I know, that for me things changed that night…' She swallowed as he went on. 'You were right. I easily remembered what you were wearing, for my eyes barely left you that night, and I think things changed for you too, Ariana. You didn't come by my office so much after that…'

'No…' She flushed as she admitted to herself something that for so long she had denied. 'I have liked you for a lot longer than you realise, than even I dared admit.'

'Come,' he said, 'I have something for you.'

Of course that something was in the direction of the bedroom, and as they walked there, she said, 'I'll make a terrible mistress, Gian. I talk too much, I'm not very discreet…' But then her voice trailed off for there on the bed lay everything she had once thought she wanted: a blush tartan suit, a silk cowl-necked cami, a string of pearls and even a little wallet for her business cards.

'Gian…' She wanted to weep, for he made her so weak.

This time when he unzipped the back of her dress, his fingers lingered and she closed her eyes as he peeled it off and slowly kissed her shoulder.

'Turn around,' he said in that voice that made her shiver. She was a little bewildered and a lot in lust as she complied.

He undressed and then dressed her.

She lifted her arms as he slid on the silk cami, and she lifted her feet as he negotiated the little kilt. The only resistance was in her jaw as he put on the jacket, for it was everything she had wanted, and yet Ariana knew she deserved more.

He dressed her neck in a string of pearls and she closed her eyes as he secured the clasp, then turned her around and knelt as he dressed her feet in the gorgeous neutral stilettoes that his guest managers wore. 'We can't work together, Gian.'

'We can.'

'No, because I'm not going to spend my career worrying about when my time will be up...'

'It will never be up.'

But Ariana had too much to say to stop and listen. 'I don't want to be hidden away, and I don't want hide my love.'

'You won't be hidden away,' Gian said. 'And you don't have to hide a single thing.'

'It would be unprofessional,' Ariana insisted, 'to be sleeping with a member of your staff.'

'I think it would be perfectly reasonable for the owner to love his wife, who just happens to be a guest services manager.'

She swallowed and then corrected him. 'VIP Guest Services Manager.'

'Absolutely.' He smiled. 'Ariana, Duchess of Luctano, VIP Guest Services Manager...'

'Stop.'

'Well, we might leave off the title on your business card...' He looked at her frowning face. 'I'm asking you to marry me.'

'Please, stop,' Ariana said, for she did not want him playing games with her heart.

'No,' Gian said, and from the bedside drawer he took out a box she recognised. 'I don't want to stop, and I don't want my lineage to end. I want ours to be a different legacy...'

She looked at the most beautiful ring, in shades of

pomegranate, and it was so unexpected, but not as unexpected as what he said next. 'When you walked into my office yesterday, I thought it was to tell me you were pregnant…'

'Gosh, no.'

'I think I wanted you to be.'

Her world went still as that black heart cracked open and revealed all the shining hope for their future inside.

'I don't want to be like that old fool who left it too late,' Gian said. 'I want the woman I love by my side. I love you,' Gian clarified, and she felt the blood pump in every chamber of her heart as it filled with his words. 'You are the most important person in my day.'

It was the one thing Ariana had wanted her whole life— to be the centre of someone's world, to be wanted, to be cherished, for exactly who she was.

'Ariana,' Gian said, 'you are the love of my life. Will you be my wife?'

Her answer was a sequence of squeaks, a 'Yes,' followed by 'Please,' as an ancient ring slid onto a slender finger, and because it was Ariana, she took a generous moment to properly admire it. 'I love it,' she said, and he watched massive pupils crowd the violet in her eyes. He adored her absolute passion for his ring. 'You would never have sold it…' She scolded the very thought.

'No,' he said, 'it belongs with me, as do you.' He was silenced by her kiss, a kiss that held nothing back but showered him in frantic love. Another 'I do, I do,' she said, and then followed that with another needy, necessary question. 'When?' she asked. 'When can we marry?'

'Soon,' Gian said, and got back to kissing her, but Ariana had something else on her mind.

'And can we have…?'

'You can have the Basilica, if you want it,' Gian said.

'No,' Ariana said, 'can we have tutti-frutti and salted chestnut ice cream for dessert…?'

He laughed. 'Trust you to have chosen the dessert by the end of the proposal.' And then he kissed her to oblivion, and behind closed doors he took his newly appointed guest services manager and made love to her as the Very Important Person she was.

To him.

For life.

Was the writing that meant that was all you ... was known about ... she would get itself ... of course ... that she could help you would now before she would be said ... entitled not her in ... while it ... knew and ... entitled her not.

... you do.

It's ... but well known there ... so where ... it is either ... for her in that he had I know ... set not me ... shortly she is ... and know ... he you out her ... so good I know she serves ...

EPILOGUE

'YOU HAVE ANOTHER phone call.' Gian gently shook a sleeping Ariana's shoulder. 'Stefano,' Gian added, watching her eyes force themselves open, knowing she could never not take a call from her twin.

And certainly not on an important day such as this.

'*Stai bene?*' Stefano urgently asked if she was okay.

'Of course.' Ariana smiled sleepily as she sat herself up in bed. 'We are doing wonderfully.'

'Have you decided on a name for her?' Stefano asked.

'We are waiting until you arrive to announce the name,' Ariana said. 'I want us all to be together when we do.'

Eloa and Stefano and little George were in Brazil and soon to board a flight to Florence. Dante, Mia and the twins would fly in with their mother and Thomas tomorrow, and all would meet the newest member of the family. But, tired from an exhausting day, Ariana was grateful that for now it was just the three of them.

'How is Stefano?' Gian asked when she ended the call.

'Excited to meet her,' Ariana said, gazing over to the little crib that held their sleeping daughter.

She was so beautiful, with dark hair and a little red face, and tiny hands with long delicate fingers.

They were both aching for her to wake up just to look into those gorgeous blue eyes again and hear her tiny cry.

'I wish Papà had got to see her,' Ariana said. Her father

was the only part of her heart that was missing. 'I wish he had known about us.' She would get used to it, of course, but she couldn't help but think how happy he would be today. 'I am glad we had her in Florence,' Ariana said. 'I feel closer to him here.'

'I know you do.'

La Fiordelise Rome was no longer where Gian resided. For the first time he had a home—a real one—a luxurious villa just a little way out of Florence, with a gorgeous view of the river.

This morning, as labour had started, Ariana had stood on the terrace, taking in the morning, the pink sky, and the lights starting to go off in the city they both loved and thinking what a beautiful day this was for their baby to be born.

And now she was here and it was right to have a little cry and to miss her *papà*.

'I have something for you,' Gian said, and he went into his pocket and pulled out a long, slim box. But instead of handing it to her, he opened it and took the slender chain out and held up the pendant for her to see.

She smiled as he brought it closer, but she didn't immediately recognise what it was.

'Gian?' she questioned as she examined the swirl of rose gold and saw that instead of an F for Fiordelise, there was an A, sparkling in diamonds. 'It's beautiful, but...'

'Take a look,' Gian said, and he pulled back the heavy drapes that blocked out the world and the city skyline. Her eyes were instantly drawn to the sight of La Fiordelise Florence, for it was lit up in the softest pink.

And there was something else different.

The elegant signage had been changed. Oh, there was still the familiar rose gold swirl, but like her pendant the letter in the centre was now an A.

'The hotel has had a name change,' Gian said. 'It is now Duchessa Ariana.'

'But…' She was overwhelmed, stunned actually, that this private man would share their love with the world.

'I've been planning it for months,' Gian said. 'Even the letterhead has all changed. The last time I saw your father, like you, he told me I could do better with the hotel names and, like me, he thought your name should be in lights. I think he knew the way the wind was blowing, perhaps even before we did.'

She liked that thought so very much, and then, better than any insignia, came the sweetest sight of all: their daughter stretching her little arms out of the swaddle of linen. They both smiled at the little squeaking noise she made.

Gian clearly wasn't going to wait for her to cry.

'Hey, Violetta,' he said, and gently lifted her from the crib.

They had named her after her great-great-grandmother, the forgotten Duchess, somehow lost in all the tales of Fiordelise.

Well, she was forgotten no more.

Violetta's restored picture was mounted on the gallery wall of their home in Rome, and soon it would be joined by her namesake's first photo.

Ariana buried her face in her daughter's and breathed in that sweet baby scent, and then lifted her head and gazed down at her.

'I cannot believe how much I know her already,' Ariana said, playing with her tiny fingers, 'and at the very same time I cannot wait to get to know her more…'

That was, Gian thought as he looked at his wife, a rather perfect description of his love.

* * * * *

THE SECRET THAT CAN'T BE HIDDEN

CAITLIN CREWS

CHAPTER ONE

IF SHE CONCENTRATED on how outrageous the situation was, how humiliating and impossible, Kendra Connolly knew she would never do what needed to be done.

Yet there was no way around it. She had to do this.

Her family was depending on her—for the first time. Ever.

She'd been sitting in her car for far too long already in the parking structure deep beneath Skalas Tower in the hectic bustle of Midtown Manhattan. She'd been given a certain amount of time to appear on the cameras in the elevators before the security officials who'd checked her in would investigate her whereabouts, here beneath the North American power center of one of the world's wealthiest men. The clock was ticking, yet here she was, gripping the steering wheel while staring at her knuckles as they turned white. Psyching herself up for the unpleasant task ahead.

And failing.

"There must be some other solution," she had said to her father.

So many times, in fact, that it had really been a lot more like begging.

Kendra was desperate to avoid…this. But Thomas Pierpont Connolly had been unmoved, as ever.

"For God's sakes, Kendra," he had boomed at her earlier today, when she'd tried one last time to change his mind. He'd been leaning back in his monstrously oversized leather chair, his hands laced over his straining golf shirt because nothing kept him from a few holes at Wee Burn when he was in the family home on the Connecticut island his Gilded Age forebears had claimed long ago. "Think about someone other than yourself, for a change. Your brother needs your help. That should be the beginning and the end of it, girl."

Kendra hadn't dared say that she disagreed with that assessment of the situation. Not directly.

Tommy Junior had always been a problem, but their father refused to see it. To him, Tommy had always been made of spun gold. When he'd been expelled from every boarding school on the East Coast, Thomas had called him *high-spirited.* When he'd been kicked out of college—despite the library Thomas had built to get him in—it had been excused as *that Connolly bullheadedness.* His failed gestures toward entrepreneurial independence that cost his father several fortunes were seen as admirable attempts to follow in the family footsteps. His lackadaisical carrying-on as vice president of the family business—all expense account and very little actual work—was lauded by Thomas as *playing the game.*

Tommy Junior could literally do no wrong, though he'd certainly tried his best.

Kendra, meanwhile, had been an afterthought in her parents' polite, yet frosty marriage. Born when

Tommy was fourteen and already on his fifth boarding school, her well-to-do parents had never known what to do with her. She'd been shunted off to nannies, which had suited her fine. The old Connolly fortune that consumed her father's and brother's lives had been meaningful to her only in that it provided the sprawling house on Connecticut's Gold Coast, where she could curl up in a forgotten corner and escape into her books.

Her mother was the more approachable of her parents, but only if Kendra conformed to her precise specifications of what a debutante should be in the time-honored fashion of most of *her* family, who proudly traced their lineage to the *Mayflower*. To please her, Kendra had attended Mount Holyoke like every other woman in her family since the college was founded, but as she grew older she'd come to understand that the only way to gain her father's attention was to try to take part in the only thing that mattered to him, his business.

She wished she hadn't now.

The clock kept ticking, and Kendra had no desire to explain why she was dragging her feet to the Skalas security team, who had already thoroughly searched her car and her person and had sent her photograph up to the executive floor. Where, she had been told coldly, she was expected. Within ten minutes or she would be deemed a security risk.

Kendra forced herself to get out of the car and shivered, though it wasn't cold. She didn't like New York City, that was all. It was too loud, too chaotic, *too much*. Even here, several stories beneath ground with the famous Skalas Tower slicing into the sky above her, an architectural marvel of steel and glass, she was certain she could feel the weight of so many *lives* streaming about on the streets. On top of her.

Or, possibly, that was her trepidation talking.

Because she'd been so sure she would never, ever have to come face-to-face with Balthazar Skalas again.

She smoothed down her pencil skirt, but didn't give in to the urge to jump back in the car and check her carefully minimal makeup for the nineteenth time. There was no point. This was happening, and she *would* face him and the truth was, she was likely flattering herself to think that he would even recognize her.

The flutter low in her belly suggested that it was not so simple as mere *flattery,* but Kendra ignored that as she marched across the concrete toward the bank of elevators, clearly marked and unavoidable.

It had been years, after all. And this was an office building, however exquisite, not one of her family's self-conscious parties packed full of the rich and the powerful, where Kendra was expected to present herself as her mother's pride and her father's indulgence. Such gatherings were the only reason she'd ever met or mingled with the kinds of people her father and brother admired so much, like Balthazar Skalas himself—feared and worshipped in turn by all and sundry.

Because Thomas certainly had no interest in letting Kendra work alongside him in the company.

Tommy had always laughed at her ambitions. She'd love to think, now, that he'd wanted to keep her at bay because she'd have discovered what he was up to sooner. But she knew the truth of that, too. Tommy didn't think of her at all. And was certainly not threatened by anything she might or might not do, as he'd made clear today in no uncertain terms.

A reasonable person might ask herself why, when her father and brother had always acted as if she was an interloper as well as an afterthought—and her mother cared about her but only in between her garden parties and charity events—Kendra was carrying out this unpleasant task for them.

That was the trouble.

It was the *only* task she'd ever been asked to perform for them.

She couldn't help thinking it was therefore her only chance to prove herself. To prove that she was worthy of being a Connolly. That she was more than an afterthought. That she deserved to take her place in the company, be more than her mother's occasional dress up doll, and who knew? Maybe get treated, at last, like she was one of them.

And maybe if that happened she wouldn't feel so lonely, for once. Maybe if she showed them how useful she was, she wouldn't feel so excluded by her family, the way she always had.

No matter how many times she told herself it was simply because she was so much younger than her brother, or because she represented a strange moment in her parents' otherwise distant marriage, it stung that she was always so easily dismissed. So easily ignored, left out, or simply not told about the various issues that affected all of them.

Maybe this time she could show them that she belonged.

So even though the very idea of what she might

have to do made her stomach a heavy lead ball, and even though she thought Tommy would be better off accepting whatever punishment came his way for his behavior—for once—she marched herself to the elevator marked *Executive Level*, put in the code she'd been given, and stepped briskly inside when the doors slid soundlessly open before her.

That her heart began to catapult around inside her chest was neither here nor there.

"I don't understand why you think a man as powerful and ruthless as Balthazar Skalas will listen to me," she'd told her father, sitting there in the uncomfortable chair on the other side of his desk. She had not said, *My own father doesn't listen to me, why should he?* "Surely he'd be more likely to listen to you."

Thomas had given a bitter laugh. He'd actually looked at her directly, without that patronizing glaze that usually took him over in her presence. "Balthazar Skalas has washed his hands of the Connolly Company. As far as he's concerned, I am as guilty as Tommy."

A traitorous part of Kendra had almost cheered at that, because surely that would encourage her father to finally face the truth about his son. But she knew better.

"All the more reason to want nothing to do with me, I would have thought," she'd said instead. "As I, too, am a Connolly."

"Kendra. Please. You have nothing to do with the company." Thomas Connolly had waved one of his hands in a dismissive sort of way, as if Kendra's dreams were that silly. "You must appeal to him as…a family man."

Her head had been alive with those too-bright, too-hot images of Balthazar Skalas she carried around inside and tried to hide, even from herself. Especially from herself. Because he was… Excessive. Too dangerous. Too imperious. Too arrogantly beautiful. Even his name conjured up the kind of devil he was.

But it didn't do any justice to the reality of him, that cruel mouth and eyes like the darkest hellfire. And oh, how he could make the unwary burn…

She'd flushed, but luckily her father paid little attention to such inconsequential things as his only daughter's demeanor or emotional state. This was the first time he'd ever wanted more from her than a pretty smile, usually aimed at his lecherous business associates at a party.

"What does he know of family?" Kendra had been proud of herself for sounding much calmer than she felt, though it had taken an act of will to keep from pressing her palms to her hot cheeks. "I thought he and that brother of his were engaged in some kind of civil war."

"*He* can be at war with his brother, but I do not suggest anyone else attempt it. They are still running the same company."

"I'm sure I read an article that claimed they'd balkanized the corporation so that each one of them need not—"

"Then you must appeal to him as a man, Kendra," her father had said, very distinctly.

And they'd stared at each other, across the width of that grand desk of his that he claimed some ancestor or another had won from Andrew Carnegie in a wager. Kendra told herself she must have misheard him. Or misunderstood it. Her heart had been pounding so hard that she felt it everywhere. Her temples. Her wrists. Beneath her collarbone.

Somehow she had kept her composure.

But in case she'd had any doubt about what her father might have meant by that, Tommy had waylaid her moments after she'd left her father's study. She'd rounded the corner and he'd been there, flashing that grin of his that always meant he thought he was being charming.

Kendra knew better. She hadn't found him charming in as long as she could remember. Ever, even. A side effect of knowing him, she would have said.

Not that anyone had ever asked her.

"Don't tell me you're wearing that," he'd growled at her, a contemptuous glare raking her from head to toe. "You look like a secretary. Not really what we're going for here."

"No need to thank me for running off to rescue you," Kendra had replied tartly. "The sacrifice is its own reward."

Tommy had grabbed her arm, hard. Deliberately hard, she'd assumed, but she'd learned a long time ago never to show him any weakness.

"I don't know what Dad told you," he snarled at her. "But there's only one way out of this. We have to make sure that Skalas won't try to press charges against me. And that's not going to happen with you in this dowdy, forgettable outfit."

"I'm going to appeal to his sense of family, Tommy." She'd ignored his comments about her outfit because there was no point arguing with him. He always went low and mean. Always.

Tommy had laughed. In a way that had sent cold

water rushing down her spine in a torrent. "Baltha-zar Skalas hates his family. He's not looking for a trip down memory lane, sis. But rumor is, he's always look-ing for a new mistress."

"You can't mean…"

Her brother had shaken his head. Then her, too, because he was still gripping her arm. "You have one chance to prove you're not useless, Kendra. If I were you, I wouldn't waste it."

Hours later, she was still numb. The inside of the executive elevator was sleek and mirrored, and Ken-dra could *see* the panic on her own face, mixed right in with the smattering of freckles her mother abhorred. She wanted, more than anything, to pretend her father had meant something different. That Tommy was just being Tommy.

But she knew better.

That sinking feeling inside told her so.

What's the difference, really? she asked herself as the elevator shot up. *A mistress or a loveless marriage?*

Because Tommy might have asked her to make her-self a mistress, but her mother had been trying to marry Kendra off for years. Emily Cabot Connelly hadn't un-derstood why Kendra hadn't graduated from college with an engagement ring. And she'd taken a dim view of Kendra's attempts over the past three years to con-vince Thomas to give her a job at the company when that was no way to find an appropriate husband.

"I don't want *to get married,"* Kendra had protested the last time the topic had come up, a few weeks ago on the way to a dreary tea party for some or other pet charity of Emily's.

"Darling, no one wants *to get married. You have*

certain responsibilities due to your station in life. And certain compensations for the choices that must result." Her mother had laughed. *"What does* want *have to do with anything?"*

Kendra knew her mother expected her to do as she had done. Marry to consolidate assets, then live a life of leisure as a reward that she could make meaningful in whatever way suited her. Charities. Foundations. If she wanted, she could even hare off to the Continent like her black sheep of a great-aunt and "forget" to come home again.

If she thought about it that way, Kendra supposed becoming a mistress to a man like Balthazar Skalas would be much the same thing, if of shorter duration.

The reward was the point, not the relationship.

No one seemed to care that Kendra wanted to make her own reward.

The elevator rose so fast the leaden ball that was her stomach stayed behind, buried beneath the ground. She saw a security camera with its red light blinking at her from one corner and was happy that it was there. It reminded her to remain composed. She was here for a business meeting, in sensible heels with her pencil skirt and a dark, silky blouse that made her feel like the vice president of the family business that she intended to become one day.

I do not look like a secretary, she told herself, eyeing her reflection.

But she also did not look like a woman auditioning to be the mistress of a man like Balthazar Skalas.

A man she kept assuring herself would not remember her. He must attend a thousand parties, and if that flash of heat that sometimes woke her in the night was any guide, affected at least a thousand women in precisely the same way.

As she watched, her cheeks grew red.

It didn't matter what her father or Tommy said, because she was the one who had to do this thing. And she had to believe that a cool, measured approach, neither denying Tommy's transgressions nor attempting to find a better side to a man who she already knew had only hard edges, was a reasonable course of action.

Unless he remembers you, a treacherous voice inside her whispered.

When the elevator doors opened again, she walked out briskly. And if she'd been in any doubt as to where she was, the lobby she found herself in reminded her. It was all sleek marble with the company name etched into stone. *Skalas & Sons*. Almost as if theirs was a quaint little family enterprise, when, in fact, the late Demetrius Skalas had been the richest man on earth at one time.

When he died, his two sons had taken the reins of the multinational corporation that sprawled about into different industries. Everyone had predicted they would run the business into the ground. Instead, the two of them had doubled their father's wealth within the first two years of their ownership. Each one of them was now far richer than their father had ever been.

Something no article she'd ever read about the Skalas family—and she'd read them all—failed to trumpet.

Balthazar was the eldest son. He split his time between the company's headquarters in Athens and important satellite offices like this one and was considered the more serious of the two brothers. Constantine was the flashier of the two, thanks to his penchant for race cars and models, and he spent more time in the London office.

The rumor was they detested each other.

But neither Skalas brother ever responded to rumors about their personal lives.

Kendra had expected the office to be empty as it was coming up on eight o'clock that night—the only time the great Balthazar had found in his tightly packed schedule. Instead, she could hear the hum of activity, and as she walked toward the reception area, could see people hurrying back and forth as if it was eight in the morning.

The woman waiting behind the reception desk offered a perfunctory smile. "Ms. Connolly, I trust?" When Kendra nodded, because she seemed to have lost her voice somewhere on the trip from her car, the woman pressed a few buttons. "Mr. Skalas is on a call, but will be with you shortly."

She stood and led Kendra through the great glass doors behind her desk into the rest of the office. Then walked briskly on heels that were not the least bit sensible, making it look as if she was gliding on air.

It made Kendra instantly feel inadequate.

Still, there was nothing to do but follow the woman where she led. Instead of turning toward the noise and people, the receptionist took her in the other direction. Where there was only a long, gleaming, marble hallway with one side dedicated to an art collection so fine it made Kendra's head spin. On the other side, floor-to-ceiling windows showed Manhattan laid out at her feet. She couldn't help but feel as if she was walking along the ramparts of an ancient castle, forced to sacrifice herself before a terrible king for the good of her village—

But imagining that she was in the Dark Ages didn't make this any better.

At the end of the hall the receptionist led her into another room, this one clearly also a waiting area, but far more elegant. And hushed.

"This is Mr. Skalas's private waiting area," the woman told her. "Please make yourself comfortable. If you require assistance, you may step across the hall, where the secretarial staff will be happy to help in any way they can."

Then she was gone.

Leaving Kendra alone with her mounting panic.

She couldn't bear to sit, afraid she might come out of her own skin. She stood and stared out the windows instead.

"There's nothing to fear," she told herself firmly, if under her breath. "He won't remember anything about you."

The real trouble was that *she* remembered all too well.

She didn't recall what charity event her mother had used as an excuse that summer. Kendra had only just graduated from Mount Holyoke, certain it would be a matter of months before she could take her rightful place in the family company. She'd figured it was her job, then, to act the part of the businessperson she intended to become. She might not have taken naturally to the world of business—far preferring a good book and a quiet place to read it to the endless rounds of deals and drinks and men in their golf togs—but who ever said life was about what *felt* good? Surely it was about what a person did, not what they dreamed about. Accordingly, she'd been putting herself out there. She might not have *felt* sparkling and effervescent, the way her mother always told her she ought to, but she could pretend.

And so she had, waving a cocktail around as she'd laughed and mingled and exhausted herself so thoroughly that after dinner, she'd sneaked off for a few moments' break. The dancing was about to begin beneath the grand tent that sprawled over the part of her parents' lawn that offered the best views of Long Island Sound.

She paid no mind to the distraught woman who passed her in a rush of tears and silk on the trellis path that led to her favorite gazebo, set up above the rocky shoreline. It was a pretty evening and the air was warm with scents of salt, grass, and flowers. She could hear the band playing behind her as she walked, and she welcomed the dim light of the evenly spaced lanterns along her way because they were far less intrusive than the brightness inside the tent. She could drop her smile. She could breathe.

It was only when she climbed the steps to the gazebo that she saw him standing against the far rail, almost lost in the shadows.

And then wondered how she could possibly not have *felt* his presence, so intense was he. The *punch* of him.

Kendra had felt winded.

He wore a dark suit that should have made him indistinguishable from every other man at that party. But instead she found herself stunned by the width of his shoulders, his offhanded athletic grace. His mouth was a stern line, his eyes deep set and thunderous. His hair was thick and dark and looked as if he had been running his fingers through it—though it occurred to her, with a jolt, that it had probably not been *his* fingers.

It had been a clear, bright evening, but she suddenly felt as if a summer storm had rolled in off the Sound. As if the clouds were thick and low. Threatening.

And all he did was lift a brow, arrogant and ruthless at once. "I don't believe I sent for a replacement."

It had made no sense. Later, she would tell herself it was something about the way he'd gazed at her as if he'd brought her into being. She'd never seen anything like it before. All that fire. All that warning. And other things she couldn't define.

He'd lifted two fingers and beckoned her near.

It hadn't occurred to her to disobey. Kendra drifted closer, aware of herself in a way she never had been before. Her breasts felt thick and heavy in the bodice of her dress when she usually forgot they were there. Her thighs seemed to brush against each other, rich whispers. And between her legs, she felt herself heat, then melt.

But this spellbinding man gazed at her in stark command, and she could do nothing at all but go to him.

"So eager," he murmured when she drew near.

Kendra hadn't known what that meant, either. His words didn't make any sense, and yet the sound of them soared inside of her. She felt as if she was a fluttering, desperate, small thing that he could easily hold in the palm of his hand—

Then he did.

He wrapped a hand around the nape of her neck

and hauled her those last few, thrilling inches toward
him. She found her hands on his chest and the sheer
heat of him seemed to wallop her, making her knees
go weak.

"Very well," he'd said. "You'll do."

Then he'd set his mouth to her neck.

And Kendra had died.

There was no other explanation for what happened
to her. His mouth against her skin, toying with her,
tasting her. She felt her mouth open wide as if on a silent scream, but all she did was let her head fall back
in delicious, delirious surrender.

The hand that gripped her neck dropped like a
band of steel around her hips, drawing her even harder
against him.

It was too much. She could hear the sound of the
party in the distance, laughter and the clinking of
glasses, but she was *on fire*.

And then she felt his hand move beneath the hem
of her dress, volcanic and impossible.

She didn't like to remember any of this. It had been
three years and it was as if it had only just happened.
She could feel everything as if it was happening now,
high above Manhattan with her hands pressed to the
glass that was all that separated her from stepping out
into air.

A fall that seemed tame in comparison to Balthazar Skalas in a darkened gazebo on a summer night.

She had opened her mouth again, that time to stop
the madness—or so she liked to tell herself now—but
nothing came out. His mouth continued to toy with her
skin, chasing fire along her clavicle and sucking gently
on the pulse at the base of her neck.

And meanwhile, his hand, huge and utterly without hesitation, skimmed its way up the inside of one thigh to the edge of her panties. Then, before she could even find the words to protest—or encourage him, more like—he stroked his way beneath.

Her whole life, Kendra had considered herself remarkably self-possessed. It came from being raised like an only child, so much younger was she than her brother. Always in the company of adults. Always expected to act far older than she was. Her friends in boarding school and college had always allowed impetuousness to lead them down questionable roads, but never Kendra. Never.

But that night, none of that mattered.

Because Balthazar stroked his way into her melting heat, and Kendra…disappeared.

There was only that strong arm at her back, his mouth on her neck, his fingers between her legs as he played with her. He murmured something she didn't understand, rough and low against the tender skin in the crook of her neck, that only later it would occur to her was likely Greek.

But she didn't have to understand the words to know that whatever he said, it was filthy.

It had shot through her like a lightning bolt.

She'd made a noise then, a sob, and he'd growled something in reply. And then he'd pinched her. Not hard, but not gently, either. That proud little peak that already throbbed—

Kendra had bucked against him, lost and wild and heaving out another kind of sob, high-pitched and keening.

How had the whole of the East Coast not heard her?

When she finally stopped shaking, she'd found him staring down at her, a kind of thunder on that face of his, so harsh that it was almost sensual. Brutally masculine and connected, somehow, to all the places where she'd still quivered. To where his hand still cupped her, so that all her molten heat was flooding his hand.

A notion that made another shudder rip through her.

"You are surprising," he'd said, rough and low. "I am not usually surprised. Come."

He'd pulled his hand from her panties, and she'd thought that harsh line of his mouth almost curved when she'd swayed, unable to stand on her own once he released her.

"Come?" she repeated.

"You're more of a meal than a snack," he had told her then, too much heat in his dark gaze. "And I prefer to savor my meals. I have a house not far from here."

Reality had reasserted itself with a sickening thud. What on earth did she think she was doing?

A question she still couldn't answer, three years later.

The back of her neck prickled then. She sucked in a breath as she turned, then froze.

It was as if she'd summoned him. He stood in a door she hadn't known was there, that must have opened soundlessly, because she had no idea how long he had been watching her.

He was just as she remembered. Balthazar Skalas, the devil himself, his deep dark eyes alive with mockery and that cruel twist to his mouth.

And she could tell, instantly, that he remembered her perfectly.

"Kendra Connolly," he said, as if he was tasting her name. His dark eyes glittered and she felt it. Everywhere. "Your brazenness is astonishing, truly. Have you finally come to finish what you started?"

CHAPTER TWO

BALTHAZAR SKALAS DETESTED the Connolly family.

He had long despised Thomas Connolly, who considered himself far more charismatic than he was and acted as if that supposed charisma made him a force to be reckoned with. When the only thing it had truly made him was appealing to the vulnerable and therefore a sworn enemy to Balthazar and his brother. His son had always been useless at best and otherwise wholly laughable.

Balthazar had been waiting for the time to deal with the elder Connolly for years. He might have forgiven the younger's nonsense—or at least ignored it, the way he did all things beneath his notice—had foolish Tommy Connolly not believed he could steal from Balthazar with impunity.

In the grand scheme of things, overcharging Skalas & Sons and pocketing the difference mattered little to Balthazar. It was the principle that offended him. It was the noxious Tommy Connolly's clear belief that he *could* cheat Balthazar that he could not allow.

Still, he could admit that sending the daughter to handle her family's sins was an inspired choice. He would have refused to see the father or the son.

"I was certain my secretarial staff was mistaken when they told me you kept calling." He watched her closely as she stood there, framed by the gleaming city behind her, yet seeming to glow the brighter. "Begging for an appointment when, last I saw you, you were far more interested in running away."

Kendra had fooled him back then, when no one fooled him. *Him.* And in the privacy of his own mind, he could admit that it had been more than her brother's theft that had made him detest her family. That her brother's behavior had merely confirmed what he had already concluded. Because of that night long ago, with her.

Balthazar was not accustomed to wanting things he could not have.

Instantly.

"I'm here on behalf of my family," Kendra Connolly said, her voice cool. Something like professional, when he could see the heat he remembered on her cheeks and in her gleaming, golden eyes.

A liar, then. He should not have felt even the faintest inkling of surprise.

Much less something that veered a little too close to disappointment for his taste.

"They consider you the most appropriate weapon, do they?" he asked smoothly. "I think your family is misreading this situation."

She blinked at that, but didn't collapse. Or shrink in on herself. Both reactions he'd seen in puffed-up male CEOs who stood before him and risked his displeasure.

Unlike them, Kendra...bothered him. Balthazar could remember too well the heat of her in his hand—though he still couldn't understand why she should affect him so. When women blurred in his recollection, becoming one grand and glorious smear of sensation and release. Yet he could recall her taste in his mouth. The silk of her skin.

The way she'd come fully in his grip.

To say that Balthazar resented that was a vast understatement.

"I appreciate you seeing me," Kendra said in the same collected way, folding her hands before her in a manner that might have seemed polite and calm had he not also seen the evidence that she was gripping her own fingers much too hard. Why did he find that... soothing? "I'm not here to excuse my brother's actions."

"I should hope not. He stole. From *me*. And worse still, believed that he could get away with it." He smiled. Thinly. "It is the arrogance I cannot abide."

He had tasted that pulse in her neck. Perhaps that was why he could not seem to look away from it now. Particularly not when he could see how hard and wild it beat.

He blamed her for that, too.

"I don't expect you to forgive him. Or even think kindly on him. Why would you?"

"Why, indeed?"

"What I'm hoping is that you and I can come to some kind of agreement. If there's a way that I might convince you that notifying the authorities isn't necessary, I would love to find it."

Balthazar laughed at that, though there was little mirth in it. He pushed himself away from the doorjamb and made his way into his actual office, a sprawling affair that shouted out his wealth and consequence from every possible angle. There were walls of glass on two sides, making it seem as if they floated over Manhattan. Steel and granite everywhere, gleaming as much with quiet menace as with wealth.

He liked to announce who he was. So there could be no mistake.

When he rounded the great slab that served as his desk, he was not surprised to find that Kendra had trailed after him and now stood uncertainly just inside the door.

"What on earth makes you think that I would do such a thing?" he asked her, genuinely interested in her answer. "The sheer hubris of it. The unmitigated gall. You must rate yourself highly indeed if you imagine you can convince me of…anything."

She spread her hands out in front of her, a gesture of surrender. It should not have made him so greedy for a taste of her, surely. "I'm not going to pretend to you that my brother Tommy isn't problematic."

"You are here anyway. Sent to defend him. Yet what defense can you possibly mount for a creature so reckless and self-destructive?"

"None."

That surprised him, when he prided himself on never allowing business machinations to surprise him. He stood behind his desk, one finger on the granite surface, and it was only when he realized he was tapping it that he understood he was more agitated than he allowed himself to appear in public.

Balthazar added that to the long list of things he blamed on this woman.

"You did not come here to mount a defense for his sins?"

"What defense could there be?" Kendra asked quietly. "I know my brother's weaknesses better than you, I assure you. While I cannot imagine why he should find it necessary to fudge the books when he already has more than enough money of his own, it's clear to me that he did. Even my father, always Tommy's greatest defender, had nothing to say to help this make any sense. Tommy himself offered no explanation."

"Of course not. Greed is really quite simple, *kopéla*. He wanted more. So he took it."

"I'm not going to pretend to you that I understand every detail of the accounting here." She lifted her chin, but kept her gaze steady on his, when men twice her size would quail before him. "I understand stealing, however. I'm prepared to pay you back, with interest. Today."

"And again, you misunderstand." He smiled then, noting the way she flinched, then tried to hide it. "I don't want your money. I want your ruin."

Or her father's shame, but that would come. Her cheeks had been bright since she'd followed him into the room, but she paled then.

"My understanding is that it added up to two and a half million, give or take. A good chunk of change, I grant you. My father intends to pay it back from his personal account. In cash, if necessary. And there should be no cause for financial ruin."

Balthazar had spent some time imagining this moment. He relished it.

"You mistake me," he said quietly. Distinctly. "I am not speaking of money. It is your family I wish to see ruined, Kendra. Your father and his arrogance in particular. You and I both know perfectly well that your family would be tarnished forever if I dragged your brother through the courts. No one would be surprised, mind you, only distinctly horrified in that particular old money way that your Tommy was caught. And I believe the rest of your family might find themselves... less welcome in the circles you all currently enjoy."

And he would count that a decent start.

She looked distressed for the first time since she'd appeared in his waiting room, and he'd expected that to feel like more of a triumph than it did. "There must be some way I can convince you that you don't need to do that."

Balthazar studied her. "What do you have that you think I might want?"

Something in him swelled then, bitter and almost furious, as Kendra swallowed. Hard. Then started toward him with determination stamped all over her face.

If she'd put up a sign advertising her wares on a street corner, she could not have been more obvious.

And he'd expected this, hadn't he? It confirmed what he'd already suspected. That three years ago, she'd been sent out to that gazebo to see how far she could get with him.

To tempt, then tease.

It had Thomas Connolly's hands all over it. And damn the man, damn his unforgivable arrogance, but he had succeeded.

Balthazar would rather die where he stood than admit *how* successful Thomas Connolly had actually been.

Because at first he hadn't known who she was. He had stood there longer than he cared to remember after she'd left, trying to understand what had occurred. He could not recall the last time a woman had *fled* from him. Because it had never happened.

Women tend to run toward him, not away.

He had been irritated, courtesy of Isabella, the mistress he'd finished with only moments before Kendra had found him there in the gazebo. And not because any of the insults or accusations Isabella had flung at him had landed. Much less held any weight. He had never cared for her emotional outbursts and had paid them little mind throughout the six months of their arrangement.

But he liked his sex regular and often. Knowing that, Isabella had deliberately forced their conversation that night, well aware that he'd been aching for release.

Isabella might have cried as she'd stormed away from him, but he knew the tears were more for the loss of her access to her allowance than any true emotion. Just as he knew that the moment she stepped back into the light of the party, the tears would miraculously dry up, she would take deep pleasure in having left him unsatisfied and she would begin scouting for a new benefactor.

He had sent an abrupt message to his assistant to cut Isabella off and then had stood there, annoyed.

But then Kendra had appeared.

He hadn't known who she was and so to him, Kendra had seemed like a breath of fresh air after Isabella's sultry, cloying, obviousness.

Those soft, rosy cheeks. The hint of freckles across her nose, when he would have sworn no imperfections were permitted in these hallowed halls of the so-called American elite. Her hair had been swept up into something elegant, though tendrils fell down, and the red in it had shone like flame in the soft light from the lanterns outside the gazebo.

She had stopped before him like a startled fawn, her gleaming eyes wide, her sensual lips parted.

Balthazar did not believe in innocence. And yet that night, he had been tempted to imagine she might be the exception that proved the rule.

She had proved him wrong in short order.

No innocent could possibly melt like that, arching back beneath the onslaught of his need, his longing, both pounding through him like a storm. No innocent would open herself up to him so eagerly, then come apart in his palm so readily.

He'd been so hard he'd ached, another new sensation. He'd wanted to peel her out of the dress she wore, lay her out beneath him on a wide bed in a room with a locked door and sate himself fully.

Instead she had turned away, then run.

And when he'd finally made his way back into the tedious party, astounded at what had happened to him, everything had made a sickening kind of sense.

Thomas Connolly, the pompous git, had been making a speech with his family arrayed behind him. Smirking Tommy, the sort of vicious alcoholic heir who thought his money would protect him from his sins. The overtly medicated wife, looking blank and distant even up close.

And Kendra, the daughter, Balthazar understood in that instant was as corrupt as the rest of them, for all she had stood beside her mother, reeking of the innocence he knew she did not possess.

Eighteen months later, when the first discrepancies in Skalas & Sons' accounts with the Connolly family's shipping concern appeared, Balthazar could have made his move. But he had remembered that night, the sheer heat of Kendra in his hand, and had waited.

He had not merely allowed Tommy his rope. He had spooled it out himself so there could be no doubt whatsoever when Tommy hung himself with it.

Balthazar told himself it was triumph, not disappointment, that pounded in him as Kendra came to stand just there on the other side of his desk.

Because he should have known that night three years ago that she was like the rest of her family, whether he'd known who she was or not. That he'd been fooled for even a moment gnawed at him.

There was no such thing as innocence. Not in his world and certainly not in her morally bankrupt family. For his part, Balthazar had been raised a Skalas, which was akin to walking forth with a golden target on his back. He had never had a single friend—or woman, or colleague—who had not betrayed him, or could be prevailed upon to betray him, for the right price.

A lesson he had learned young.

His own brother would cheerfully stab him in the back if it benefited him. Balthazar had no doubt about that. It was why he and Constantine had split things up neatly between them. Better not to offer each other the temptation, they'd decided.

The threat of mutually assured destruction kept them friendly enough, no matter what the tabloids said. They were the only thing they had, after all.

Something that was certainly not true of Kendra Connolly.

"What exactly are you offering me?" he asked her, trying to keep his tone even when inside, he raged.

She was close enough now that he could read her expression. Or try. He could have sworn what he saw there was something like misery. Or apprehension.

Or, a cynical voice inside him chimed in, *she's merely good at what she does.*

Too good.

Because he was certain, for a moment, that he could detect a faint tremor in her lips. Before she firmed them into a straight line and he became equally certain he'd imagined it.

"Name your price," she invited him.

"I am more interested in what it is you think I want." He eyed her as he would any conquest, business or personal. Assessing profit and loss. Looking for weaknesses to exploit to his benefit. "What can you imagine you have to offer that I do not already have?"

She spread out her hands again, though this time it read as less of a surrender.

"Me," she said.

Balthazar watched that pulse in her neck react. If he didn't know better, he would think that she was desperate when he felt certain that she was not. That this, like that night three years ago, was nothing but more deception.

"I think you overestimate your charms," he said with cruel deliberation. "Do you really imagine you are worth more than two million dollars?"

She blanched at that, but stood her ground. "Of course."

"I do not wish to insult you," he murmured. Though that was a lie. "But I would not pay a single dollar for something I could get for free. In abundance. And do."

"And here I thought you preferred to keep mistresses," she shot back at him, to his great surprise. "Hardly free, is it?"

"You should be less opaque." Balthazar shrugged. "One night to clear your brother's debt? That is not so appealing. But a mistress? Mine for as long as I am interested? That is a different proposition altogether. Though far more…strenuous."

Her lips were pressed tight together. If he was not mistaken, her hands had started to curl into fists before she dropped them to her sides.

"Marvelous," she said with a certain brightness he could see was false. As she, herself, was false, no matter his body's response. "Is that what you want?"

"Normally I am the one who makes this offer." He smirked. "It is not pressed upon me by a woman desperate to clear the name of a brother she would be better off disowning."

"Families are complicated."

"I thought my family was complicated. I am forever reading fables the media has created to explain things between my brother or myself. Or tales of my late father." He studied her, then affected a measure of outraged astonishment. "But I will confess, when I granted you this appointment, I never expected *this*."

Her chin lifted higher. "What did you expect?"

"Excuses." He eyed her until she flushed. "What a martyr you are, Kendra."

Her eyes, that intriguing shade of amber that sometimes looked like gold, glittered. "I would never call myself a martyr."

"Oh, no? And yet here you are. Sacrificing yourself." He laughed when all she did was glare at him. "You do not understand how this works, do you? You're supposed to at least *act* as if you're motivated by un-controllable lust, whatever your true motivations."

"Tell me what you need," Kendra implored him, her voice tight. "There's no need to play all these games, is there?"

"But perhaps what I want from you is the game."

She looked away then, her throat working. "Very well then."

"But how will we come to terms?" Balthazar mused, and stopped pretending he wasn't fully enjoying himself. "There are so many considerations. You will not need my financial support, clearly, as you will be paying off a debt. I will require full access, of course, but that is easy enough. I have any number of properties that will suit."

"Access," she echoed. "Full access."

He laughed. "What is it you think a mistress does?"

She cleared her throat, still looking away. "To be honest, I thought it was a silly, archaic word to describe a rich man's relationships."

"You can call it a relationship if you like. In truth, it is a business arrangement. I find it is better to spell out any and all expectations in advance, the better to avoid unpleasant misunderstandings." He shrugged again, expansively. "I want what I want. When I want it."

To her credit, she turned back and met his gaze. "By which, you mean sex."

"Sex, yes. And anything else I desire." He laughed at the expression on her face. The one she tried to hide. "That could mean accompaniment. The ability to charm business associates at tedious dinners. Clever conversation, sparkling repartee, and all while looking like a bauble most men cannot afford. But if I were you, Kendra, I would focus more on the sex. I require rather a lot."

He was fascinated by the way her expression changed, then. By the way the color on her face matched. If he didn't know better—if he didn't know to his detriment that she was a loaded, aimed weapon—he might have been tempted to think she was doing this against her will. Or if not precisely against her will, without the level of enthusiasm he would have anticipated from an operator like her. Like all the members of her family.

Because surely she had done things like this before or why would they have sent her?

You know she's done things like this before, he reminded himself sharply. *She's done it to you.*

"Are you prepared?" she asked him after a moment, and though her voice was slightly husky, there was no hint of uncertainty about her. She was hiding it well—another indication this was a role she was playing. "If you take me as your mistress, you will be linked with my family. In a way I'm guessing you will not like."

"I do not think that I am the one who will dislike it most."

"You and I can stand here and speak of a business arrangement, but I think you know the tabloids will assume that it's a more conventional relationship."

"If the tabloids did not make assumptions, they would not exist." He made a dismissive gesture. "This is of no interest to me."

"All right then." She squared her shoulders as if prepared to march forth into battle. "How do these things normally begin?"

He might have admired her bravado had it not been

predicated on how little she actually wanted him. And how little she was attempting to hide that fact from him.

"I have not invited you to be my mistress, Kendra," he rebuked her. Mildly enough. "This discussion, while illuminating, is nothing more than academic."

"What do you mean, academic?" Color flooded her cheeks again, and he found himself far more interested than he ought to have been. Fascinated, even, despite himself. "I'm offering myself to you."

"But you cannot be trusted." He shook his head sadly. "You are a Connolly, first of all, and by definition a liar. More importantly, you have already attempted to lure me in once."

"You thought I was attempting to…" When Kendra shook her head it was as if she couldn't quite get her balance. She blinked. "My mistake. You're apparently playing strange games. If you did not wish to do business, you should have said so."

"I admire a woman who can barter. Particularly when what she is bartering is herself. No coy games. No fluttering about like all the rest, never quite getting to the mercenary point."

Her eyes flashed. "If you're not interested in the business arrangement you suggested, tell me what would interest you instead."

Balthazar was intrigued, and that should have worried him when he knew her to be an empty, grasping liar, like all the rest of her family. She was treacherous and as dirty as the rest of them. But he could not deny that he was hard. That he ached for her.

There was only one way to soothe that kind of ache, no matter what manner of woman inspired it.

"This particular kind of business arrangement requires, shall we say, a down payment," he told her. Matter-of-factly.

"A down payment. On sex."

"But of course. I prefer my sex—"

"Abundant," she clipped out. "I heard you."

"Abundant, yes. But I also require a certain level of excellence, or what would be the point?" He smiled at her, edgily. "All I know about you is that you are selfish. And a tease. And entirely too willing to do your family's bidding. None of that, I must say, suggests to me that you would be any good at all in the bedroom."

He thought he heard a sharp sound, like an intake of breath.

"Am I to understand, then…?" Her eyes had gone a brilliant shade of bright amber, but her voice was precise. Crisp and to the point. "That is to say, I assume what you're asking for is an audition?"

"We're talking about more than two million dollars, Kendra," he said with no little dark amusement. "I need to be certain I am getting my money's worth. You understand."

He expected her to turn and run from the room, screaming perhaps. No matter how many times she'd attempted to vamp her way out of trouble—a notion he could not say he enjoyed entertaining, though he shoved it aside—he doubted very much that anyone had ever spoken to her quite like this.

All those preppy, pastel-wearing country club scions of this or that supposedly elite family, as if there was such a thing in this adolescent country. All those Ivy League boys. All this American nonsense so many millennia after his own country had taken shape and changed the world.

It was something, all these pretensions to aristocracy. It really was. Balthazar could never tell if he admired these brash people or pitied them.

Still, he didn't like imagining any of them with Kendra.

And if there was something in him that regretted what he planned to do here—what he should have been *delighted* to do here—he shoved it aside.

But to his surprise, she only shrugged in return. "That sounds fair." Her voice was so nonchalant it poked at him. She arched an elegant brow. "Right here?"

He felt that like a shot of electricity, straight to his sex. When he should have felt nothing of the kind. When he had anticipated feeling only the sweetness of his long overdue revenge. And had perhaps imagined she would run from him again.

Still, he did not back down. He was Balthazar Skalas. Backing down was not in his blood—his father had seen to that by spilling it himself, long ago. More, he had vowed that he would wipe the Connolly family off the map, one by one.

And so he would, starting now.

"Right here is fine, Kendra." He inclined his head. "You can begin by stripping."

CHAPTER THREE

KENDRA KEPT WAITING for the floor to open up and swallow her whole. But it did not.

The situation had gone from terrible to outrageous to something far worse, and she wanted nothing more than to run away. But she couldn't.

Because this was Tommy's only chance. She might not think much of Tommy and his endless messes, but she knew that Balthazar was right. If he dragged her brother through court, it would kill her parents.

And Kendra might think that her father could use a little humbling, sure. It certainly wouldn't do him any harm. But she didn't think her mother deserved the same. After all, what had Emily ever done but what she was expected to do? Did she truly deserve the scorn of all the women who'd made the same choices she had—because that was what she would get, in spades.

It didn't seem fair that Emily should bear the brunt of Tommy's poor decisions.

Honestly, it didn't seem fair that Kendra should, either.

But she'd wanted to do this, hadn't she? Wanted to help, anyway, even if she hadn't wanted *this*, precisely…

Liar, a voice inside chided her. *You want whatever you can get.*

Because what little she'd gotten from him had been haunting her for years.

Why was that so hard to admit?

She told herself to calm down. To get a hold of herself. Yes, Balthazar was every bit as awful—and if she dared admit it to herself, as exciting—as she remembered. He was like a force of nature. Overwhelming and electric and impossible to look away from. The idea of actually *having sex* with this man made her feel hollowed out with the heat of it.

Kendra wasn't sure she'd survive.

Oh, come on, she chided herself. *How hard can it really be to do what he's asking you to do? People do it all the time. The world is filled with people doing it* right this minute.

Maybe not bargaining to be the mistress of a man who was essentially a stranger, but the sex part, certainly. Kendra bet if she went and looked out the vast windows at the other lit up buildings, she would see people doing all kinds of things in those anonymous squares of light. That was what big cities were for, surely.

She cleared her throat and wished she could clear her head as easily. "To clarify, you want me to get naked, right here in your office. Now."

"Stalling is probably not a good way to begin this arrangement. Or any arrangement, but particularly not one that relies on your naked obedience. Literally."

He sounded amused. More than amused. Those dark eyes of his were glittering, and that cruel mouth of his was set into something not quite a curve. As if he was taking pleasure in this.

In what he was asking her to do.

More, in how desperate she must be if she was really considering *doing* it.

He was a horrible man. The way he spoke about sex and *mistresses* and even her family said absolutely nothing good about his character—

But that wasn't the point, was it? This wasn't about his character.

You don't care about his character, something in her asserted, with a low sort of heat that shook around inside her and made her bones ache.

Because if she wasn't mistaken, what this was really about was how far she was willing to go. Something inside her seemed to soar at that notion.

You don't have to care about what he thinks of you, or what anyone else thinks of you, either, that same voice whispered, hot and deep, making her ache all the more. *You were sent here to do these things.*

In a way, she felt free.

Kendra had always been so afraid of putting a foot wrong, of embarrassing her parents, of causing trouble... But that all seemed to her now to be the dim concerns of a girl she hardly remembered.

Because she was standing before Balthazar Skalas, who wanted her naked.

His dark eyes blazed with how much he wanted it.

She understood, then. He hated her family. She couldn't really blame him for that, of course, given what Tommy had done. But she was a part of that family. Kendra had to assume that he hated her, too.

And she told herself she didn't care about that, but

she knew that wasn't true when something in her... hitched.

It didn't matter. She still had to do this.

If only because it was something she alone could do. Neither her father nor Tommy could solve this problem, but she could.

All it took was this.

Free, something within her whispered.

The way she never had been.

"All right, then," she said with as much dignity as she could muster. "If that's what you want."

"Something else you should know about me," Balthazar said mildly, though that fire in his gaze did not diminish in the slightest, "is that I do not like to repeat myself."

Kendra had the slightly hysterical urge to say something inappropriate. Or perhaps...salute. She bit her tongue. And then, telling herself it was no different from stripping in a doctor's office, started removing her clothes.

Except she didn't.

She ordered herself to move, but her body did not obey. For one jarring thud of her heart. Then another.

All while he stared at her, ruthless and darkly entertained.

Everything seemed to fuse inside of her until she couldn't have said, in that moment, if she was doing this for her family or if she was doing this because Balthazar clearly didn't think she would.

If she stepped back even an inch, she knew it didn't make sense. Getting naked proved nothing at all.

But suddenly it felt as if Kendra's entire life had

been leading her to this very moment. As if she needed to prove herself in this bizarre way, or die.

That did it.

She kicked off her shoes. Then, holding his gaze, unfastened the zipper at the back of her skirt, letting it fall to her feet. She stepped out of the circle of fabric and felt that hitch again inside her, because his gaze changed.

The way he looked at her made her think of wild things. Birds of prey, fast and dangerously large cats, predators of every description. There was something impossibly masculine in the way he gazed at her, and it made that place between her legs throb as if his hand was already there, cupping her.

That hard, decidedly male grip, that she'd dreamed about since. Too many times to count.

She pulled off her dark silk blouse, then dropped it to the side. She still held his gaze because that was all heat and demand, and better, somehow, than accepting the fact that she was standing before Balthazar Skalas wearing nothing but her bra and some panties.

She realized he'd gone still. As if he'd turned to stone, though there was absolutely no doubt that he was a real, live man. Even if made of flesh, she suspected he would scald her if she leaned across the desk and touched him.

Why did she want to do it anyway?

Kendra didn't wait for him to egg her on further. She reached around and unhooked her bra, then shrugged it off.

He made a sound then, perhaps nothing more than a breath, but it was like fireworks going off inside of her—bright and hot and uncontrollable.

She fought it, but her own breath came faster, then.

It was as if there was an electrical charge between them, too intense. Almost painful.

But she wasn't done. She couldn't dwell on what was happening inside of her, because she still felt a kind of drumming in her chest, threatening her ribs, that made her feel as if she *needed* to show him exactly how wrong he was about her.

So Kendra finished the job, stripping off her panties and dropping them on top of the pile of her clothes.

Leaving her…standing there. Stark naked.

And though her cheeks were hot and she felt certain that the flush extended all over the rest of her body, though she was *aware* that she had so many competing emotions it actually hurt, she couldn't access the things she was feeling. Not quite.

Because his gaze was all over her.

And then, to her horror—*no, no*, a voice in her chided, *that's not* horror *and you know it*—Balthazar moved out from behind the desk.

He hadn't said he would touch her, and she assured herself that if he did, if he dared, she would—

But that was a lie. It wasn't even a fully formed thought and it was a lie.

Because the thought of Balthazar touching her made her shiver. That low heat bloomed.

And once again, she was as slippery and hot, as if he'd just finished stroking his way deep into her core.

Maybe she wanted him to.

But all he did was come to stand before her, that cruel face of his unreadable.

If it weren't for that blazing heat in his dark gaze,

she might have crumpled into the pile of her discarded clothes.

He let her stand there as he regarded her for what felt to Kendra like a lifetime. Three lifetimes.

Then he walked in a circle around her.

As if she was a horse.

"Do you need to inspect my teeth?" she asked. Acidly.

"Not yet."

She had to bite her tongue again, particularly as he took his sweet time. She could *feel* him and his dark perusal. His gaze was like a touch, running all over her, tracing over her body and making her pulse get faster and faster by the second.

When he finally made his way around the front again, it was almost worse. Her breasts felt heavy once more, the way she remembered they had in that gazebo years ago. Beneath his commanding gaze, her nipples puckered and shamed her. Because she could tell herself that it was the chill from his air-conditioning units, but she knew better. And so, she could see, did he.

He let his gaze drop, coming to rest between her thighs. And Kendra was absurdly grateful that he couldn't see what was happening there. He couldn't see how much she truly wanted him.

Even though something in her whispered that he could.

"How extraordinary," Balthazar murmured after a while. "I was sure that color had to be fake."

She had no idea what he meant. But then, when he lifted his gaze to hers again, she got it.

And hated the fact that her cheeks burst into a brighter flame. She could feel it roll all the way over her body, like a flash flood of heat, so that she likely matched the hair on her head and between her legs that he'd apparently found so hard to believe was real. She felt *red* and *obvious,* and had to grit her teeth to keep from diving for cover.

"There are so many things I find surprising about you, *kopéla*," Balthazar continued on, as if this was a deeply boring dinner party and he was sharing his views on something distressingly civil and dry. As if she wasn't *naked* before him. Why did that make it even harder to pull in a full breath? "This shocking show of obedience, for example. I would have said a girl of your station would find it impossible."

She made herself breathe, somehow. "I told you I was here to make amends, if possible."

"Naked amends." As if she might have missed that. He considered her for a moment, that face of his stern. "What a good daughter you are, Kendra. Far more of a sister than your brother deserves, don't you think?"

She didn't answer that.

"How far does this obedience extend, I wonder?" He stood before her, the devil in a dark suit that fit him much too well, fully aware of his power. Exultant in it, even. "If I asked you to drop to your knees and take me in your mouth, would you? If I bent you over this desk and took my release without bothering to see to your pleasure, would you allow it? There are so many options available to us, are there not? So many ways to audition, after all."

And somehow, it was only then that it occurred to Kendra to take stock of the precariousness of her position.

It was only then that she really thought about what she was doing here.

Because her head was filled with new images now. Balthazar doing exactly what he'd just told her he might. She could see it too clearly—too vividly—and she couldn't decide if it seemed like peril or passion. To sink to her knees, tilt her head back, and taste the most male part of him. Or to be tossed across the vast expanse of his desk as if she'd been put on this earth with no other thought but to please him, when and how he wished…

She couldn't decide if those things terrified her. Or if they didn't.

"Look at you," he mused, his voice a dark, rough abrasion. She felt her skin prickle, breaking out into goose bumps. "So eager to please."

She was breathing too hard, after failing to breathe at all for a while. She couldn't seem to speak.

And then he made it worse by reaching out and fitting his hand to her cheek.

It was not a soft, caring sort of gesture.

He might as well have slid it straight between her legs. Again.

Kendra shook so hard she thought her bones might have flown apart. She had to check a moan, but it still made her teeth rattle.

Balthazar laughed, dark and terrible. "You're not a martyr at all, are you, Kendra?" he asked quietly. Cruelly. "You're just a little whore."

It took her too long to register those words. Even longer to understand them.

And when she did, when that blow landed the way it was clearly meant to, she actually staggered back.

But by then, he had already walked out and left her there.

Naked, in his office, alone and sick with shame.

It was as if all the blood that had been pumping inside of her drained away, and suddenly she was freezing cold. Her teeth began to chatter. Her hands felt thick and unwieldy, but she did the best she could to hurriedly climb back into the clothes she'd discarded.

What was she thinking? How had she let this happen?

How had she actually *wanted*—

But none of that mattered, she told herself sternly, shutting it down. This was no time to spiral. There would be all the time in the world for that.

What mattered now was that he hadn't agreed to anything.

He could have left his office to call the authorities *right now*, and all of this would have been for nothing.

Kendra didn't think she could survive it.

When she was finally dressed again, she took an extra moment with her reflection in the mirror on the far wall. Because her skin might have been several shades too red for comfort, but she thought she really might die if she marched back out into all that corporate luxury…disheveled. So clearly a fool.

Her breasts were still too sensitive. She was horrifyingly damp between her legs. But none of that mattered, not yet. Kendra imagined she'd have the rest of her life to regret, deeply, what had happened here. But right now she needed to figure out how not to disappoint her father.

She headed toward the door, her mind racing. She should have expected that Balthazar would want to humiliate her. Clearly he wanted to humiliate the entire Connolly family—which, if she was honest, she couldn't really blame him for. Two million dollars wasn't exactly pocket change.

Okay, maybe it was for Balthazar Skalas.

Kendra couldn't blame him for wanting to punish someone who'd stolen from him, so she focused on the real culprit in all this. Her brother. If she allowed herself, she would get so furious with Tommy that it might take her to her knees—

And she really didn't want to think about being on her knees. Not after Balthazar had introduced an entirely new way of thinking about kneeling to her today.

She strode out, still trying to come up with a new game plan, and then stopped dead.

Because Balthazar was there, leaning against the long, white wall that served as his gallery, waiting. And the way his gaze found hers, she understood that this interaction had gone exactly as he'd intended it to.

That helped. It reminded her why she was here— what was at stake.

And how little it had to do with those maddening sensations he stirred up in her.

This is your chance to prove you're valuable, she reminded herself sternly. *Don't waste it.*

"I'm disappointed," she said briskly as she walked toward him, ordering her knees not to buckle beneath her. Because there could be no *kneeling,* God help her. "I expected better of you than cheap, juvenile namecalling."

"Did you? I can't think why."

"Not to mention, I would have thought that a man who trafficked in mistresses would prefer an experienced practitioner. Or are you under the impression that a woman who accepts a mercenary position as your mistress somehow… isn't?"

"Don't be silly," Balthazar said, a kind of dark humor in his voice. "A good mistress always pretends that she would never, ever succumb to anyone else."

"Surely, once again, what you mean is an accomplished proficient. Isn't the expectation that she'll always make the client feel as if, were it only up to her, she'd be doing it for free?"

He let out a bark of laughter. Real laughter, Kendra thought, when she nearly missed a step. Her heart didn't know how to process it.

All kinds of parts of her didn't know how to process it.

She stood there a few feet away from him, stricken, too aware of the way that laughter licked its way through her. And equally aware that despite her best attempts here—despite actually removing her clothing and standing there naked before this man—she had failed.

He was laughing at her. He had already rejected her. What else did she have to offer him?

"You must go back to your father and your brother and tell them about these offers you have made me," Balthazar said, when his laughter finally stopped. He straightened from the wall, and she was struck anew by the *physicality* of this man. Unlike the rest of her father's associates that she'd met over the years, there wasn't the faintest hint of dissipation stamped on his skin. No paunch, no alcoholic redness about his cheeks. Just that glare of his, like smoke and condemnation— and all else a pageant of lean muscle and tightly leashed power. "How proud the two of them will be, I am certain, that you are prepared to go to these lengths for them. The obvious next question is, how often have you done exactly this on their command?"

"That's more of a philosophical question, really," she made herself say, trying to sound witty and urbane. Or something other than shattered. "Are fallen women born or made, do you think?"

It was only as his expression changed, shifting to something far more heated and intent, that she realized that she'd been backing up. That he was advancing on her. And she really ought to have stood there, stood her ground—

But she didn't have it in her. She was still trembling, from the inside out, and he was bearing down on her.

She could either kneel or back away, and she didn't dare kneel.

Kendra was terrified that she might not want to do anything else once she did.

"The philosophy of fallen women," Balthazar said in a musing sort of voice, though there was nothing *musing* in the way he looked at her, then. "I confess I have never given it any thought."

"Of course not. Why think of such things when all that is necessary is using and discarding them on a whim?"

She threw the words at him as if she thought they might hurt him. As if she thought anything might hurt him.

His mouth moved into something even more cruel. Her breath caught. Then Kendra had the confusing sensation of moving through something—only belatedly realizing that he'd backed her straight through the door of his office again.

"Shall we test your theory?" he asked, his voice a growl.

She was something like bewitched. She could only watch as he reached out a hand again, sliding it along her jaw, his fingers over her lips, then hooking the nape of her neck as he had long ago.

Her breath was a wild, flickering flame between them—

Then Balthazar's mouth was on hers, obliterating everything else but need.

CHAPTER FOUR

HE SHOULD HAVE let her go.

That had been Balthazar's plan. Humiliate her, then dismiss her.

A neat revenge for how she'd left him in that gazebo three years ago. Also a slap at her father and brother, who kept aiming their tawdry secret weapon at him. He'd been looking forward to aiming it right back in their direction, without giving them even a shred of what they'd wanted from him in return.

Only a small taste of what he had in store for Thomas Connolly and his spawn.

He had been congratulating himself on a job well done while he waited for her to slink out, her proverbial tail between her legs.

But she'd come out of his office tucked neatly back into the sleek skirt and blouse she'd worn. There hadn't been the faintest hint of any slinking. It was as if nothing happened in there. There was only some turbulence in her gaze.

And that husky note in her voice.

Balthazar honestly didn't know what had come over him. Maybe it was when she hadn't wilted away into nothing when he'd used the word *whore*.

When she'd debated the point instead.

He had been unable to control himself. Or more precisely, perfectly able to control himself, a skill that had been beaten into him by his merciless father—but wholly uninterested in doing so.

And now his mouth was on hers, at last.

At last.

The half-formed notion he might have had that he'd mistaken things three years ago, along with any story he might have been tempted to tell himself about the ways he'd convinced himself it had been more than it was, disappeared as if they'd never been.

Because the taste of Kendra was far better than any memory.

It was the richness of her mouth, the way her lips met his. It was the slickness. The heat. It was better than anything he could have imagined. *She* was better.

Worth the wait, a voice inside whispered.

He tried to shove it aside, but something in him... snapped.

As if he truly had been waiting for her all this time, instead of merely interested that an opportunity to pay her back had arisen.

As if this was what he'd wanted all along.

This. Her.

He reached out blindly with his free hand and slammed his office door shut. That was the last thought he planned to give to the outside world. He moved her across his floor, every cell in his body focused on the same thing.

More.

Kendra had as much as told him she was precisely who and what he'd thought she was all along. She'd

offered herself to him. Attempted to barter the terms
of selling herself to her family's enemy. Despite what
he'd imagined in those first moments in that long-ago
gazebo, she was no innocent.

He told himself that was a gift.

Because it turned out that Balthazar was in no way
above taking what she'd made it clear was his to take.

Surely he'd initially meant to aim for the sofa that sat
across the room, but it was suddenly too far. He made
it to his desk and laid her down across the vast granite
surface, making her its only adornment.

Like a sacrificial lamb, something in him thought,
though that was a reach. This was no sacrifice.

This was a reckoning.

Balthazar couldn't seem to get enough of her mouth.
He braced himself over her, his palm near her head,
and lost himself for far too long in the simple act of
kissing her.

Again and again.

But there was nothing simple about it.

It was carnal. It was a rush. The taste of her coursed
through him, storming through his veins and pooling
in his sex.

More than worth the wait, that voice in him said,
more definitively this time.

Like a kick to the side of his head. Balthazar tore his
mouth away from hers, outraged that he felt as close to
shaky in the presence of a woman as he'd ever become.

Shaky, of all things. When his father had made him
pay hefty prices for weakness. Until now, Balthazar
had been certain he'd stamped any hint of his out.

And it was only when he set his mouth to Kendra's
neck, finding that raucous pulse again, that it finally

dawned on him that he hadn't kissed her three years ago. No wonder a simple taste of her had set his head to ringing.

He wanted to strip her naked again, but he wasn't certain he could handle it.

That truth was humbling.

He, Balthazar Skalas, who had proven himself again and again in the course of his lifetime whether he wished to or not. Against his father's heavy hand, his mother's defection. Against fair-weather friends and false intimates. The trials of handling both the Skalas's wealth and business concerns with all the questionable, obsequious grifters both attracted.

He had always assumed that his ruthlessness was bone-deep.

But this mercenary little liar, an emissary from a man he despised, who wanted her to trade her body for her thieving waste of a brother—

Why on earth should it be this girl who got to him like this?

He could see her body still, as if she hadn't put her clothes back on. He could see how she'd stood before him, not unaffected by her nudity, but not cringing or cowering, either.

He thought of his beloved Greece and all the great statues of goddesses, breasts bared, bodies more weapons of awe than shame.

And he thought that for the rest of his life when he looked at such pieces of art he would see Kendra instead. Small yet plump breasts with rosy crests. The tempting slope of her belly. The auburn tangle of curls at the apex of her thighs.

Somehow, with the taste of her in his mouth, he thought that if he stripped her again it might kill him.

That was absurd, of course.

But even so, he reached down and began to tug her skirt up instead of removing it. She made a wordless sort of noise, then lifted her hips, helping him clear the fabric from around her hips.

He could smell her arousal.

It made him think of gardens before a summer storm, heavy with scent. Flowers and a raw bloom.

It almost made him lose himself completely.

Balthazar didn't understand what was happening inside of him.

She was spread out before him, his entirely for the taking if the blissed-out look on her face was any clue, and he should have felt cynical and triumphant at once.

He'd had any number of beautiful women below him before, but this was different. This was Kendra Connolly. And much as he might like to imagine otherwise, he had been imagining something like this for very long time indeed.

There was a part of him that had been thrilled to discover that her vile brother had been foolish enough to get himself into such trouble.

Had he hoped that this would happen? He had expected her to offer, but had he hoped all along that he would accept that offer—even though he'd assured himself that he was only taking this meeting for the chance to humiliate a Connolly?

He had to face the fact that this was exactly what he'd wanted.

Balthazar felt something like drunk, when he never allowed himself such indulgences.

But her legs were free of the constriction of her skirt then, so he stepped between them, pulling her bottom to the edge of the granite desk.

Her arms seem to move of their own accord, rising over her head. She arched back with a kind of inbred grace that poured through him, a new kind of storm. Looking at her made his chest feel tight.

But he shoved all of that aside and concentrated on the part of him that ached for her the most.

Balthazar reached down to unzip himself, then pull his own throbbing length free. Finally.

He heard an indrawn breath and when he looked up again, Kendra's eyes seemed even wider and brighter, and she was biting down on her bottom lip.

And he felt something sharp move in him then, like fragments of broken glass, embedding themselves in his flesh.

She was the very picture of innocence on the verge of surrender, wasn't she? Balthazar could admit, deep inside himself where he would never discuss it with another living soul or admit it out loud, that there was no small part of him that wished the picture she presented was real.

That had been the issue three years ago. It was worse now.

He reached between her legs and pulled her panties to one side. Then, giving in to the brute in him, he tore them off her and tossed them aside. He could see goose bumps rise on the smooth flesh of her inner thighs and wasn't surprised when she covered her face with her arms, because they both knew the truth, didn't they?

She wanted him. This was the game. And better she should hide now that he was winning it.

If he had been more in control of himself, he wouldn't have allowed it. He'd have pinned her hands above her head, bent close, and studied her face as he thrust deep into the very center of her molten heat.

He'd have enjoyed every moment of this victory.

But this was far wilder than he'd anticipated. Whatever it was that beat in him, it made him feel savage. Something like mad with it.

She was too hot, too wet.

He felt himself growl, like the beast only she brought out in him, and then he simply slammed himself home.

She arched up against him and he gripped her hips, because she felt so good. She was impossibly tight and hot around him, and for a heady beat or two of his heart he thought he might finish there and then.

Surely not.

Balthazar braced himself against the desk, fighting for control. And as he did, he became aware that she was breathing rapidly. Her chest was moving, and there was a deep red flush all over her neck.

"Show me your face," he ordered her.

He felt her clench down hard, internally, and swore as that tight grip nearly threw him over the edge. She moved her hips almost tentatively and held her arms in place, tighter, for a few more moments before she let her arms fall.

Her face looked even more flushed than her neck, her eyes so bright it made him freeze. Almost as if she was on the verge of tears—but that made no sense.

"I don't understand why we're stopping," she threw at him. Reminding him that this was a fight, and no matter if there was a strange note in her voice as she spoke. He could see the echo of it reflected in her too-bright gaze, burning like the sweet, hot center of an open fire. "This is what you wanted, surely. Do it."

A kind of alarm rang in him at that, but she made a greedy sort of sound and then locked her ankles in the small of his back.

And then, her eyes fastened fiercely to his, she began to move her hips.

It was crude and inelegant and, oddly, the most erotic thing he could ever recall happening to him.

There was something about the determination on her flushed face. The way she moved, taking all of him, then retreating, over and over, her teeth almost bared as if she was determined to get this right.

He'd expected practiced moves, soft laughter.

What he got instead was…this fierce attack of pleasure that should have put him off.

Balthazar thought it might be the hottest thing he'd ever seen.

And it felt like magic.

He slid his hands beneath her and lifted her up, gripping the soft curves of her bottom and holding her before him so he could take control.

He started slow, matching her deliberateness. Her intensity.

Stroke after stroke, deep and hard, so there could be no mistake about who he was. Who she was. What was happening here.

And something extraordinary happened as he kept going, communicating the truth of things the only way he could. That sheen of ferocity seemed to mellow, as if the heat between them was doing the same work in her as it was in him. The sharpness in her gaze became something else, something molten.

He kept on, maintaining a deliberate rhythm even as he watched a different kind of heat wash over her.

And when she stiffened again, her head fell back in that same beautiful surrender he recalled years ago.

Once again, Kendra cried out heedlessly as she shattered all around him.

He wanted more. He wanted everything. He *wanted*.

Balthazar dropped down and set his mouth against her neck. His hips pounded into her, faster and faster. He reached between them and found the proud center of her need, then worked it with his fingers as he finally, greedily, cast off what few chains of control remained.

And let himself go wild.

This time, when she screamed she bucked against him, hurtling straight off that edge and taking him with her.

But the noise he made felt torn from deep inside him as he followed her over.

Ruined, that voice in him whispered.

And Balthazar could do nothing about it. He was… broken into pieces, sprawled over her without breath.

For a long while there was only the way their hearts thundered, almost as if to the same beat.

He wanted to gather her to him. He wanted to do things that made no sense, like press kisses against the line of her jaw. When it finally penetrated that he felt the urge to do these mad things, it was like dousing himself in a cold plunge.

Balthazar pulled out, though it caused him something almost like pain to leave behind that silken grip.

He told himself to turn away abruptly, but he didn't. He took his time, fully aware that it was likely to be burned into him forever, the sight of her like this. Sprawled out on his desk, her skirt rucked up to her waist, thoroughly debauched and thoroughly his.

You're a fool, he growled at himself. *That was revenge and nothing more.*

But that felt very much like a lie, when he had long considered himself allergic to dishonesty in any form.

When he finished putting himself to rights, he focused on her and found her doing the same. Her eyes were downcast as she slid from the desk. And though she tugged her skirt back into place competently enough, her hair told a different story.

Balthazar did not advise her to smooth it down. A clear indication that no matter how smooth an exterior she tried to present, the reality remained.

He liked that more than he should have.

"Shall we consider that a down payment?" she asked, her voice so crisp and cold that it took him a moment to realize she hadn't actually hauled off and slapped him.

And he chose not to question why it felt like a betrayal. When he knew it shouldn't. When he knew who she was.

Who she always had been. Why did he insist on wishing it could be otherwise?

"Don't be ridiculous, Kendra," he replied in kind. "That was merely finishing what we started three years ago."

He watched the column of her throat move. He was suddenly, deeply furious that she wouldn't raise her head and look at him directly. "Surely it can be both."

Balthazar made himself laugh and took some pride in how she stiffened at the sound.

"I wouldn't pay two dollars for something I could get so easily, *kopéla*. Much less two million."

Her gaze snapped to his then, bright and hot.

And worse, a kind of knowledge flickering there in the depths that made everything in him tighten. Sending him into a spiral of something perilously close to shame.

Especially when she didn't crumple before him.

She held herself almost regally. "Shall I tell my brother to expect to see you in court?"

"You can tell your brother to go to hell," he growled at her, because he didn't care for the sensation still curling around and around inside of him. He didn't acknowledge shame. But he could still feel her, clenched tight around him. And the taste of her was in his mouth. And all of it was part of the same game. He would never forgive it. "You can go right along with him, for all I care."

He saw her gaze grow brighter and he thought once again that she might sob. He didn't know what he would do if she did—

But instead, she only nodded, once.

"Understood," she said icily.

Then Balthazar watched as Kendra Connolly marched over to his door, threw it open, and left as if she'd never been here.

As if she'd never screamed his name while he was buried deep inside her. Twice.

Leaving behind nothing but a torn bit of lace that had once been her panties.

Balthazar stood there a long, long while. His phone rang. His mobile buzzed. He heard one of his secretaries come to the door and say his name, then retreat when he failed to respond.

Outside the walls of windows, New York was a mess of color and noise.

Like her.

While inside, Balthazar was nothing but cold.

So cold that it took him much, much longer than it should have to realize that for the first time in his life, he had not only failed to use protection with a woman—and not just any woman, the daughter of the man who Balthazar had long ago vowed to destroy if it took him his whole life—it had not so much as crossed his mind.

CHAPTER FIVE

THREE MONTHS LATER, Kendra had succeeded in convincing herself that what had happened at Skalas Tower was some kind of bad dream.

Well. She called it a bad dream in the light of day. What a nightmare! What a horror!

But the more unpalatable truth was that sometimes she woke in the night, convinced that she could feel all that thick, hot masculinity moving inside her again. Sure that if she blinked away the sleep from her eyes she would see his face, so stern and sensual at once, right there above her as he blocked out the world...

The way she felt in the dark had nothing to do with horror. She was wise enough to keep that to herself.

Because she had better things to think about than one evening of pure insanity three months ago. Such as finding herself a new life because, like it or not, she'd left the old one in tatters on the floor of Balthazar's office that night, and there was no pretending otherwise.

Her father and brother had not been impressed when Kendra had returned that night without any good news to report. She had been similarly unimpressed to find them both waiting up for her, since the drive back out from New York City had in no way allowed her to settle down after…him.

"Well?" Tommy had demanded.

Angrily, as if waiting for his baby sister to return from this vile errand was beneath him.

When it was *for* him.

He had been swilling his gin and looking at her in disgust, neither of which was new. But after her intense, provoking experience earlier, something inside of her had… Not *snapped*, exactly. But she'd stripped naked in front of Balthazar Skalas. She'd argued for leniency and she'd bartered herself, all for the brother who was making no secret of how little he cared for her.

Why are you trying to help this person? an unfamiliar voice asked from deep down inside her. *When he would quite clearly never, ever so much as consider doing the same for you?*

Kendra had never thought about it quite like that before. Once she had, she couldn't think of anything else. Why was she trying to prove herself to him? Or her father?

Why do you feel you have anything to prove?

She couldn't answer that question, either.

It was as if letting Balthazar inside her body had changed her, profoundly.

Not simply the act itself, which she couldn't quite let herself think about at that point—too overwhelming and raw, painful and then transcendent, all mixed in together—but the *fact* of it.

She didn't feel like the same naive creature who had set off in her sensible shoes, so determined to fight off a dragon and save her family. She wasn't the same. The dragon had eaten her alive and there was no pretending otherwise.

That had been the first evidence of how different she was after her encounter with Balthazar. The fact that she could see her selfish, petulant brother for who he was and feel no matching surge of need to prove herself any further.

"What exactly did you think would happen?" she'd asked as she stood in the door of her father's study. And after matching wits with Balthazar Skalas, she'd rather thought her brother unequal to the task. "Did you really think that a man like that could be tempted into forgetting what you did to him?"

"I hope you're not saying that you struck out, girl," her father had grumbled from his favorite armchair. "That's not what you're saying, is it?"

Even then, Kendra had wanted badly to tell herself that he'd wanted her to succeed because he believed in her. And not because he'd wanted her to sort out Tommy's mess.

But she'd lost her ability to fool herself that night.

"I tried my best," she had said, because what else was there to say? Even if she'd told them what she'd done, they wouldn't understand. They hadn't been there. They wouldn't get the weight of her surrender. That exquisite tension that had flared between her and Balthazar that she'd still been able to feel tight around her, like his hands around her throat. Or his palm between her legs. She'd shrugged instead. "I tried and I failed. I don't know what he's going to do now."

"You frigid bitch," Tommy had snarled at her. And even though their father had made a tutting sort of noise, Tommy hadn't retracted it. He hadn't backed down. Instead, he'd taken the tumbler he was holding and threw it so that it exploded against the stone of the fireplace. "I told you not to go dressed like that. Of course you failed. Just *look* at you! You look like a dowdy, frumpy, boring secretary. Who would want that?"

She'd stared back at her brother, seeing his sulky expression and remembering Balthazar's beautiful, brutal masculinity. His grace and ferocity. Tommy had not done well by comparison.

"I can only wonder why you were pinning all your hopes on me if I'm so deficient," she'd said calmly. Almost coldly. "There's nothing more that I can do. And if I'm honest, I think I've already done too much— particularly if this is the thanks I get."

Kendra had turned and marched from the room, paying no attention when she heard her brother's voice raised in fury behind her. She had not glanced at her father again. She'd had the revolutionary thought, after everything, that what happened next to the pair of them had nothing to do with her.

Instead, she'd run up the stairs to her childhood bedroom, locked the door behind her, and then crumpled down on the other side of it. She'd hugged her knees to her chest, held herself tight, and tried to figure out what to do with herself now everything had changed.

Now that she had changed.

Now that she knew the things she knew. Now that she'd finally faced the truth.

Kendra had wanted to dissolve into sobs, but hadn't. She'd breathed a little too heavily for a while, ragged and overwhelmed, and had eventually found her way into the shower. There she'd done her best to use up all the hot water on the eastern seaboard as she'd done her best to scrub off the evening she'd had.

She'd failed at that, too.

It was only later, when she'd tucked herself up in her childish canopy bed as if that could make her the girl she'd been again, that she'd finally allowed herself to go through the whole thing, step by step.

He'd braced himself above her, so fierce, almost furious.

And he'd called her a whore, so Kendra had been determined that he never suspect that she was anything but. She'd told herself that she was a modern woman, after all. She'd ridden horses her whole life. Surely, if she didn't tell him, he would never know that she'd never let anyone close to her before. That she'd been too busy trying to be perfect in one way or another, and had never seen how a boyfriend fit into that.

It won't hurt, she'd told herself. *If it hurt as much as people claimed it did, no one would do it again.*

Then Balthazar had slammed his way inside her, and it was as if he'd plugged her into an electrical outlet, the most fragile part of her first.

Her first reaction had been shock.

Her body had reacted without her permission, arching up in a way that could as easily have been surrender as a scream. She hadn't known herself.

She'd hidden her face, bitten down on her own arm, and it was only when her teeth dug into her own flesh that she'd begun to sort through the storm of it all.

Pain wasn't the right word. She'd felt *everything*, that was the trouble. The shock of his intrusion. The shape of him, lodged deep inside of her. Big, hot, long.

There was *a person inside her*, and that notion made her want to cry even as it sent spirals of a different sensation dancing through her.

He'd told her to drop her arms, she'd obeyed, and again she'd been swept up in the certainty that if she let him see that this was her first time, if she let him know that this was anything but what she wanted it to be, she would die.

Die.

So instead, she'd dared him to do it faster. Harder. Deeper.

But when he did, everything had changed again.

And by the time they were finished, Kendra had learned a great many things about herself.

In the three months since that night, she'd had a lot of time to think about those things.

That she was not at all who she'd always thought she was if she could be so easily taken. Not just taken, but possessed, fully. A man who hated her could do those things to her body, and more astonishingly, her body could respond to him with pure jubilation.

No matter what *she* might have thought about the situation.

If that was true, and Kendra knew it was, then she didn't know herself at all. And if she didn't know herself at all, if she even now found herself something like hungry, constantly going over that night in Balthazar's office in her head—

She'd concluded mere days after that fateful night that she needed to change her life entirely.

And so she had.

Her Great-Aunt Rosemary, the despair of Kendra's haughty Grandmother Patricia, had taken herself off to the French countryside rather than settle down into marriage the way her parents would have preferred. She had never bothered to return to the family, but she'd left Kendra her cottage when she'd died the previous year.

On the off chance you are not like your mother or hers, Great-Aunt Rosemary's will had read, *I offer you a place to land.*

Kendra had always meant to make it over to inspect her inheritance…someday.

Someday had turned out to be a lot sooner than she'd imagined.

"Don't be ridiculous," her father had thundered at her when she'd announced her plans to remove herself to the French countryside. At once. "What on earth do you plan to do in *France*, of all places?"

"Whatever I like," she'd replied. "Would you like me to stay? That will only happen if you give me a job in the company."

"Kendra. Sweetheart." The unusual endearment had shocked them both, and her father had looked away. "I don't see the company as a part of your future."

She'd braced herself for the pain of that to swipe at her, but there had been nothing. As if she'd finally moved past it. "Then what does it matter where I choose to live?"

And that was how she'd found her way to her great-aunt's lovely little cottage, suspended between the mountains and the sea. Nestled amid rolling vineyards on country roads, the cottage itself was a bookish girl's dream. A few bright, happy rooms filled with books and art, paths through the fields to walk on, and more than a few trees with abundant shade if she wanted a break from the glorious Côte d'Azur sunshine.

She went down into Nice to do her shopping, and it was easy enough to drive down into Italy, or take the long train ride to Paris. She told herself it was the best few months of her life.

She wanted it to be. Desperately.

And if sometimes Kendra felt so melancholy that she almost got sick with it, she dismissed it as growing pains. She was lucky enough to be in the position to take a time-out to figure out what her life ought to be. Accordingly, she tried to imagine what her life would look like now if she took the family company off the table. If she stopped pushing so hard.

Maybe it was a good thing that she wasn't working with her father and brother now that she'd lost a huge amount of her respect for them. But Kendra had always wanted to work. She had no interest in the kind of highly charged, gossip-soaked idleness her mother preferred—and no aptitude for it, if she was honest.

All the sorts of play jobs other women in her position had, she dismissed. Virtuous charities with flashy balls, prized internships only those with trust funds could afford to take, silly publicity positions that were usually about getting on the guest lists to highly photographed parties. None of that appealed to her. Kendra tried to encourage herself to think outside the box. She'd been so focused on getting into her father's good graces that she'd never spent any time imagining what would happen if that…stopped mattering to her.

Because it didn't. The further away she got from that night with Balthazar, the more angry she found herself.

Not at Tommy, who had never made a secret of who he was or pretended to be anything else. Not Balthazar, who was wholly and completely himself, always.

But at her father.

Her father, who had preferred that his daughter give herself to a man he considered an enemy than deal with Tommy's behavior himself. Tommy had put the company, the family, and his own sister into peril—but that hadn't inspired her father to handle him, once and for all. And at no time had Thomas Connolly thought, *Maybe it would be smart to try out the one child who hasn't caused me problems.*

Kendra was humiliated she hadn't seen all of this before. It wasn't as if anyone had hidden it. She'd simply seen what she'd wanted to see. She'd believed that if she worked hard enough, there was a way for her to take her rightful place at her father's side. All she had to do was prove it.

Now she thought that if given the chance, she'd burn the whole Connolly family down. Great-Aunt Rosemary had clearly had the right idea.

A darling little cottage tucked away in the south of France was the perfect opportunity for Kendra to uncover her heretofore unknown artistic leanings, she'd figured. She kept a journal. She tried a bit of creative writing. She took a painting class. A pottery class. She tried to learn how to play piano.

But by the end of her second month in France, neck deep in all things Provençal, it was clear that Kendra had no aptitude whatsoever for anything creative.

Not even the faintest shred of it.

And that was how she'd found herself at one of the local wineries nestled away in a glorious, sweeping vineyard down the road from her cottage. The owners thought it would be helpful to have an American on hand for the summer to help with tourists, and Kendra quickly found that her real aptitude was in customer service, of all things.

Because she was fantastic at it. And more, enjoyed it.

It was a beautiful summer afternoon. The breeze was scented with lavender and the hint of earth. Groups of tasters and merrymakers had come to enjoy the vineyard and its offerings, some coming up from the crowded beaches along this magical stretch of coastline, some engaged in winery tours, and some on self-guided explorations of the area. They sat in merry little clusters at the tiled tables out beneath bright blue umbrellas and graceful trellises wrapped in jasmine and wisteria vines.

Kendra moved from table to table, making sure everyone had the food they'd ordered from the small kitchen or the sommelier's attention. She got to use the French she'd taken in boarding school and college or her English, depending on the group. And maybe there was something wrong with her, she thought when she ducked back inside to see if the kitchen was ready with the charcuterie platters one of her groups had ordered. There had to be, because most people surely didn't find it easier to know themselves while they were interacting with strangers. Or not know herself, perhaps. But feel at ease with herself all the same.

Because to all the customers sitting at these tables, she was nothing but an American girl on a lark. Enjoying herself abroad, perfectly carefree.

And the more they treated her that way, the more she believed it was the truth.

No Connolly family power struggles. No demands she marry a member of her mother's yacht club, the red-shorts-wearing hedge fund brigade. No contending with Tommy and his latest fiasco.

Carefree felt *good*.

Kendra had her back to the door when it opened again. She sang out a greeting in French as she picked up the two heavy plates of charcuterie that the chef arranged in glorious piles of the finest meats and cheeses, all arranged on their own private stones.

"Please take a menu and find a seat outside," she said over her shoulder. "I'll be with you in a moment."

She turned as she spoke, her happy carefree smile on her face.

But it was not a new group of tourists.

It was Balthazar.

He did not speak. But then, he didn't have to speak when all he did was reach up and remove the mirrored sunglasses from his face, letting that blazing dark gaze slam straight into her.

He was Balthazar Skalas.

That harsh look on his face was as good as another man's shout.

Kendra would never know how she managed to keep holding those heavy platters aloft. Possibly it was that she was frozen solid. Turned to stone.

Incapable of anything but staring at the apparition before her.

One ice age passed. Then another.

"Excuse me," she said in totally unnecessary French. "I must deliver these."

She hardly knew what she was doing, only that it was critical she do it. She set off across the floor, then ducked out the door to the patio while he stood there beside it like a smoldering ember.

Outside, she smiled and laughed on cue. She set down the platter and then spent a long, long time telling the group at the table the involved history of every cheese, cured meat, and olive. Only when she'd exhausted that topic did she turn back and head inside.

Slowly, having half convinced herself that Balthazar was a figment of her imagination.

But no.

He was still there, in the exact same place where she'd left him. The devil himself, so incongruous in a French winery's tasting kitchen that she almost laughed at the absurdity.

Almost. Because there was very little about Balthazar in his considerably mouthwatering flesh that made her feel like laughing.

Another eon or two dragged by as she stared at him. As he returned the favor with the full force of his stern regard.

It took everything Kendra had to fight off all the images that threatened to flood her then. The memories of what had happened between them.

"You must connect these dots for me," Balthazar said. Eventually. His voice was as she remembered it. Dark. Stirring. Dangerous. "Tell me how a Connecticut heiress finds herself a waitress half a world away."

"As it happens, I have an innate talent for customer service," she replied, using her brightest, happiest tone, as if he was really interested in her answer. "That's not something I knew before I came to France."

"How can it surprise you?" His voice only got more lethal. More than that, it was a whole storm inside her, so that not only was she forced to remember every single thing that had happened that night in Manhattan, she could *feel* it. Her body was reliving it, one sensation after the next. "Look what you were willing to do for your brother. How could you doubt that it was a... talent, as you say?"

"I'm delighted you haven't changed a bit." She forced her usual happy smile. "Have you come for a tasting? I handle the food, but if you take a seat on the terrace, the sommelier will be with you shortly and can lead you on the journey of your choice through our wines. Today we're featuring—"

"If I wished to sample wine, Kendra, I would not come here. I have my own vineyards."

She rolled her eyes. "As one does."

His face tightened. "I still do not understand. Are you hiding?" If possible, his gaze darkened. "Do you have some reason to hide?"

"This is the south of France," Kendra said, frowning at him. "People do not *hide* here. They spend their entire lives concocting reasons to come visit. Then come back. Then find a picturesque cottage surrounded by sunflowers and lavender to grow old in. It's paradise, Balthazar. Who wouldn't want to live in paradise?"

"You surprise me. I would have expected you to stay tethered to the family apron strings, running errands for your father and brother. That is your role, is it not?"

She pulled in a breath, surprised at how much that hurt. When really, Kendra had been expecting something like that the moment she'd seen him.

"Don't beat around the bush," she said softly. "If you want to call me names, call me names."

One of his dark brows rose. "Did I not do so?"

"I'm afraid I've stepped away from my former profession." She managed to use her usual bright and shiny voice, and took some pride in the fact she could when he'd left her bleeding. If she didn't show it, that was almost as good as not bleeding at all. "If that's why you've come, you're going to be deeply disappointed."

Balthazar pushed away from the wall, then prowled around the small shop with its souvenirs and keepsakes along one wall, the refrigerated case filled with takeaway options, and the menu stand for table service.

Somehow, Kendra had never realized how small the place was before. How…close.

But then, Balthazar took all the air from the room.

"If you have business with my family, you know how to find them," she said after a moment, though her pulse was drumming loudly in her ears. "I have nothing to do with this."

"Perhaps."

His back was to her then. His gaze was directed out the windows, down over the gentle slope of the vineyard before them. The view she'd loved, until now. Would she ever be able to look at it again without seeing him?

"Tell me this, if you please," he was saying, low and commanding. "It has been some time since I saw you in New York."

"Since you saw me," she echoed, and even laughed. "How sanitized that sounds."

Balthazar turned to her. She thought the way his gaze cut through her was stark. Brooding, even. But he didn't speak.

"It was three months ago." Kendra tried to summon her smile, but gave up when it didn't materialize. She repressed the urge to rub at the nape of her neck, where she was certain every single fine hair was standing at attention. "But I feel certain you know that."

"Indeed."

And something in the way he studied her then made her feel as if she was trembling again, from the inside out. As if her own bones had betrayed her. She had the wild notion that she should leap across the room, slap her hands over his mouth if necessary, do anything she could to keep him from saying whatever it was he'd come here to say... But she didn't.

"Three months," he repeated, as if for emphasis. "And in that time, have you bled?"

She felt all the color and sensation drain from her. "What?"

"It is a simple question, if indelicate. Because we did not use protection, Kendra. And if you have not bled—"

Her pulse was taking over her body, beating *at* her. "Why are we talking about this? How is it your business? And anyway, I moved to a different country. It's not unusual to miss one or two—"

She cut herself off, horrified.

The reality of what she was saying slammed into her anyway, flattening her. And then it was as if she was swallowed up in the ferocious blaze of his glare.

Balthazar did not move. He did not close the space between them.

And still Kendra felt as if he'd lunged at her. Or did she only wish he had?

Did she really long for his touch so much? But she knew the answer to that. She lived it every night.

"Is this your family's latest attempt to force my

hand?" Balthazar asked idly, though his gaze was afire with the darkest, harshest condemnation. With a bitter hatred that made her breath hitch. "This will not end for you the way you imagine, Kendra. I promise you that."

CHAPTER SIX

BALTHAZAR'S WORST FEARS had come true.

And he still couldn't quite believe it.

He followed the remote road to the cottage Kendra had said was hers. Which could mean she was letting it, or could mean it was her father's, or could mean, well, anything. He didn't believe a word she said. He didn't believe *her*.

He certainly hadn't believed her flustered response to his appearance earlier. That he would come for her was the point of all this, surely. It was the final move in her game.

Balthazar had been well and truly played. He still couldn't quite accept it, but facts did not wait for his acceptance to be true.

He certainly did not believe that Kendra Connolly wasn't fully aware that they hadn't used protection that night. He imagined she'd been counting down the days, same as him. The fact that she'd taken herself off to a foreign country was evidence enough of her guilt, to his mind.

And he'd been waiting all this time for her to show her hand.

Instead, she'd appeared to first take on the life of a

middle-aged expatriate. Pottery and painting and God only knew what other pointless things, the province of the entitled and bored. Then she'd begun waiting tables, of all things, which might have been more age appropriate, but made no sense for the Connolly heiress.

It had to be another part of her game, though he couldn't imagine how it fit.

The road opened up and a cottage came into view. Balthazar gritted his teeth. Because it looked like...a cozy, pastoral scene of Provence. Yellows, blues, and purples. Fields of wildflowers on either side with a humble dwelling on a soft rise, lit up against the darkening summer sky.

He had been anticipating the kind of "cottage" people like Thomas Connolly like to call the gaudy, massive mansions in places like Newport, Rhode Island.

This was not that.

And Balthazar didn't quite know what to do with this unpretentious house. Much less the woman who stood in the open doorway, the buttery light from within making her glow.

Damn her.

Balthazar came to a stop in a cloud of his own bad temper. He slammed out of the car, unfolding his body from the low-slung leather seats and taking longer than necessary to smooth his shirt into place when it did not require smoothing. His clothing did not defy him. It was only this creature before him, standing there like an innocent again, who dared.

"I hope you didn't have any trouble finding this place," she said in that bright, chirpy voice he'd heard earlier at the winery.

He detested it.

"I am capable of using navigation technology, thank you," he growled at her.

Kendra did not back down. She only sighed, slightly. "I see this is going to be contentious. What a lovely change."

Balthazar did not appreciate her ironic tone of voice.

Because it had been three months of worrying about this very thing. Three months of assuring himself that nothing would come of the one and only time he'd failed to protect himself, his family, and his wealth.

And with a Connolly, to add insult to injury.

Still, his self-delusion might have illuminated his darker moments, but he was a practical man. That, too, had been impressed upon him by his father's heavy hand, whether he liked it or not. He had therefore enlisted a special security detail to track her movements. To see if she would give herself away.

To make sure that whatever happened, he was on hand to intervene if it went in a direction he didn't like.

He'd expected her to head to a clinic in an attempt to draw him out. Her relocation to France had confused him. But perhaps it, too, had been as good as waving a flag—because here he was.

Still, he hadn't been sure.

Not until that performance she'd put on earlier in the kitchen of the winery.

"Perhaps you can explain to me what exactly it is you think you are doing, pretending to be a plucky waitress?" He moved around the front of the sports car and then stayed there, not quite trusting himself to venture any closer to her, which was another personal betrayal. They were adding up. "It does not suit you, *kopéla*. I think you must know this."

She might have seemed happy, but Balthazar could not accept that it was real. It was a role she was playing, nothing more. It was a way to hide from what she'd done, who she was, and what must come next.

Surely she had to know this.

He certainly knew it.

As she was almost certainly carrying his child, this rustic life she'd arranged around her this summer was unacceptable, as she must surely have been aware. The mother of a Skalas heir could not be *in service*, God forbid.

He told himself this supposed happiness of hers had to be fake. It had to be part of the bait in her trap.

There was no other explanation.

She only looked at him for a moment as if *he* was the one who made no sense. It meant there was nothing to do but gaze back at her.

Damn her, but she looked…angelic.

It made him want to break things.

The light from inside the cottage made her hair look strawberry blonde and drenched in gold. That heart-shaped face had haunted him for months now—years, if he was honest—and it was far prettier in person than it had been in his memory.

That infuriated him all the more.

If he didn't know any better, if he chose to rely on all his usual instincts, Balthazar would have been tempted to swear that there wasn't a shred of deceit in this woman.

She was the best manipulator he'd ever seen, he reflected in that moment, as the light exalted her and made her look something like beatific. The apple did not fall far from its gnarled, ugly tree.

He ordered himself to unclench his fists.

"I have to do something with myself," Kendra said quietly. *Thoughtfully*, he would have said, if she was someone else. "It turns out a life of leisure doesn't suit me at all."

"Yet three months ago I could have sworn you were attempting to be some kind of businesswoman. Wasn't that your game?" He could remember that night entirely too well. "That outfit. The bartering."

A kind of shadow moved over her face, and she shrugged. It forced him to pay attention to the fact that she was not dressed like any kind of businesswoman now. She had changed out of the summery shift dress she'd been wearing at the winery and was now dressed simply in a pair of denim jeans and a deep blue tank top with wide shoulder straps that only drew more attention to the elegance of her neck and that clavicle that made his mouth water.

He did not understand how he could want her like this.

Even now.

"My services were not required in the family business," Kendra said.

"Were they not? That sounds like a remarkably antiseptic version of family drama."

Another shadow crossed her pretty face, but this one looked like temper. "What does it matter if it's antiseptic or not? I don't work for the family company. And if I'm not working for the family company, why stay with the family?"

"So your father and your brother, those paragons of virtue—"

"There's no need to overdo it, Balthazar." Her tone

was dry. Almost amused, though not quite. "At a certain level, being that sardonic might actually hurt you, don't you think?"

He almost laughed, but caught himself. "They were happy to send you out like a pair of pimps, is that it? But couldn't find it in them to offer you a cubicle tucked away in their offices?"

The color in her cheeks bloomed. "That is…an absolutely revolting way to put it."

"Is it incorrect?"

She made a sound as if she was clearing her throat, then swung around and walked into the cottage.

"I think," she said as she moved, "that this conversation is going to require wine."

Balthazar prowled in behind her, expecting to see…he didn't know what. Something that shouted out her guilt. Something that penetrated this front she put on.

But instead he found himself in an open, bright room that sprawled from the front door into an open kitchen at the back that looked out over a small terrace. There was real art on the walls, placed in a haphazard way that suggested they were there because the owner enjoyed them, not because she was showing off a collection. There were bookshelves and stacks of books and magazines everywhere, but the cottage didn't feel fussy or overstuffed. The overall effect was of a kind of bohemian joy in art and literature.

It didn't fit with his impression of this woman. He found himself frowning at the wide, cozy couches that still held the imprint of her body.

Then he remembered what she'd said as she'd walked inside.

"No wine for you, *kopéla*," he growled.

He closed the front door behind him and watched her closely as she turned, halfway across the airy room. He noticed that her feet were bare, and could not have explained why that poked at him if his life had depended upon it.

Nor could he understand why it very much felt as if it did.

"No wine for me?" She looked baffled. "If you're some kind of teetotaler—"

"Hardly." He waited for her to get his meaning and when she didn't, another surge of fury swept through him. "Have you forgotten you might be pregnant?"

He didn't quite know what to do when she paled, as if she truly had forgotten. When that couldn't be true.

How could that be true?

And because she seemed frozen there, staring at him with her eyes wide and horrified, he moved toward her and tossed the small package he'd brought with him onto an accent table beside her.

She cleared her throat. "Why do I doubt you brought me gifts?"

Balthazar didn't trust himself to speak. But he must have communicated himself all the same, because Kendra moved to the table and picked up the small carrier bag, then blew out a loud breath when she looked inside.

"Wow." She laughed, though he could see from the color on her face and the sudden sheen in her eyes that she didn't find any of this particularly amusing. *Good*, he thought.

"Pregnancy tests. You thought I needed pregnancy tests. Five of them, no less."

"It will do for a start."

She raised her gaze to his and actually had the gall to look shocked. "You can't possibly imagine that I'm going to…"

"Now, please."

His voice was soft, but a command. He saw it move in her, a kind of jolt.

"No." She dropped the carrier bag on the table as if it had fangs. "I will not—"

"Allow me to explain to you what is going to happen, Kendra." Balthazar didn't move closer to her. He didn't trust himself. Nor did he raise his voice. Even so, she jolted again, harder this time. Her eyes snapped to his and he approved. Maybe now she would take this—*him*—seriously. "I do not know how you intended to play this game. But you chose the wrong man to play it with. I do not believe the innocent act because, lest we forget, I know the truth about you. And even if I did not, I know exactly what your family is capable of."

"I'm not acting. I'm not an actor, and even if I was, I certainly wouldn't bother to put on a performance for a man I never planned to lay eyes on again."

"Silence."

That command sliced straight across the room, and if he wasn't mistaken, straight through her.

Kendra's breathing sounded a little heavy, almost as if she was having an emotional response…

Or, the appropriately cynical part of him chimed in, *she knows she's caught.*

"Your intentions do not matter to me," he told her, harsh and precise so there could be no mistake. "I would prefer to determine, here and now, if you are pregnant. If this nightmare is truly happening."

"I vote no, it's not." She jerked her head toward the door. "Feel free to leave. Now."

"But of course, I do not trust you, Kendra." Balthazar wanted to reach for her and lectured himself, sternly, to keep his hands to himself. This situation could hardly be improved by repeating the same mistake. And besides, he needed to interrogate himself as to why and how he could possibly want this woman the way he did, when he knew what she was. When he knew exactly what she'd done. "Therefore, tomorrow—regardless of what we discovered tonight—we will fly to Athens for an appointment with my personal physician."

He stood there, feeling like an avenging angel, as she gaped at him.

The way an innocent he was railroading might—

But Balthazar dismissed that.

"There is not one part of what you said that's going to happen." Kendra crossed her arms and held herself stiffly. "Not one single part."

"This is nonnegotiable."

"Are you under the impression that I...work for you?" This time, her laugh bordered on the hysterical, and he had to fight—again—the urge to put his hands on her. "The only interest I ever had in you was as an emissary from my family on behalf of my brother. Who, I can't help but notice, you have yet to report to the authorities."

"Was this not the entire point of your little gambit?"

Against his will, against his own orders, he found himself moving closer to her. When he noticed that he'd placed himself within arm's reach, he stopped, but it didn't help.

Nothing helped. This woman was the only addiction Balthazar had ever had, and he would not succumb to it. To her.

He refused.

"There is no gambit," she was saying, her voice hot and her eyes dark. "This is my life. A life I put together to suit *me*, not anyone else. I don't care what you think of it and I certainly don't appreciate you storming in here like you have some claim—"

"I have every claim."

Balthazar's voice was pure ice.

Kendra made a soft sound that might have been a gasp, as if he'd punctured her straight through. He rather hoped he had.

"Whatever life you think you might have had here, you forfeited your right to it when you involved me," he told her. Ferociously. "You must realize that there exists absolutely no possibility that I will allow you to give birth to my child anywhere that is not under my direct supervision."

"If I'm pregnant," she said, and on some distant level he noticed that she almost stuttered over that word, "I will handle it. My way. It has nothing to do with you."

"I will require genetic testing to determine paternity, obviously. Because oddly, Kendra, I do not trust you."

"Genetic testing..." She blinked, then lifted a hand as if warding him off. "I understand that you take great pride in crashing about the planet, ordering everyone around and taking your revenge when they don't do what you want. But I have already spent a lifetime putting up with that from my actual relatives. I have no intention of allowing you to take up where they left off."

"How will you stop it?" he asked with genuine curiosity, though there was a kind of silken threat in his voice.

He did nothing to hide it.

And he expected her to cower. To look away, keep her eyes downcast, make herself small, the way most of his subordinates and rivals did in his presence.

Instead, Kendra Connolly charged across the few feet remaining between them and actually brandished her finger in his face.

It was...astonishing, not alarming.

Such a thing had never happened before. Not with anyone other than his father, that was.

"You can go straight to hell," Kendra threw at him. "And you can start by getting out of my house."

Balthazar shrugged. "Whether I am in this house or out of it, that will make no difference. The outcome will be the same."

"You have absolutely no authority over me. I don't even *like* you. And even if I did, the state of my womb is none of your business."

"Think again, Kendra."

He saw sheer murder on her face, and something about it...delighted him.

Balthazar had now seen a number of different versions of this woman. The fluttery, overcome, supposed innocent that night in the gazebo. The cool, controlled businesswoman who had sold herself so matter-of-factly and then kissed him like the culmination of a lifetime of his most erotic fantasies. The sunny, happy little waitress at the winery.

And even the woman who had greeted him at the door tonight, seemingly angelic. Bathed in light and not nearly as intimidated by him she ought to have been.

Now there was this version. Unafraid, uncowed, and somehow even more beautiful because of it.

He had come here wanting to do absolutely nothing but crush her, and instead he found himself hard again. That longing, that impossible need, stormed through him as if it intended to tear him apart.

She had no idea how close he came to simply sweeping her into his arms and tasting her mouth again. To lose himself that completely, that quickly.

No matter what she'd done to him.

This weakness will soon rule you, a voice inside that sounded far too much like his harsh father lashed out at him. *Then you will be no better than she is. Is that what you want?*

His trouble was he knew exactly what he wanted.

Kendra dropped that finger, but only so she could prop her hands on her hips. "You make a lot of threats but I think we both know they're empty. Because this is the modern world, not whatever medieval daydream you have going on."

Balthazar laughed, then. "I would advise you not to make yourself comfortable with that fantasy." He laughed again when she scowled at him. "I would prefer it if you agreed to my terms. I would prefer it if you took those tests now, to spare us both the suspense. But I don't require your agreement or cooperation, *kopéla*. Either way, I will have my answers in the end."

"*Either way?* What are you going to do?" Kendra scoffed at him. "Kidnap me?"

But Balthazar only smiled.

CHAPTER SEVEN

THEY LANDED IN Athens the next morning.

And while Balthazar had not, technically, kidnapped her, he hadn't exactly left her any choice.

Kendra hated herself for not finding a way out of the situation, but she hadn't.

She hadn't—and she wasn't sure she really wanted to ask herself why that was.

Balthazar hadn't bothered to continue arguing with her last night. He'd left her after flashing that enigmatic smile, the one that had made her shiver with foreboding. But before he'd driven off in that absurd sports car of his that she was fairly certain was as bespoke as the clothes he wore, he'd made a quick call in emphatic Greek.

Within moments, two glossy black SUVs had pulled up.

"You called the cavalry?" she'd asked.

He'd smiled again, and it wasn't any better that time. "Insurance, that is all."

"Weird." Kendra had eyed the men who poured out of the SUVs. Balefully. "They look a great deal like your own private army."

"You may call them whatever you like, Kendra," Balthazar had said. "They are not here for you."

"Excellent news. I'll have them make themselves comfortable in the lavender fields while I take myself off to Monaco for the weekend."

"Do as you like." Another, third version of that smile of his made her bones feel cold. "My men will protect my potential heir."

And then he'd taken himself off in that obnoxious car, leaving *his men* behind.

Men who would protect the baby she refused to believe she was carrying, not her.

Kendra had retreated back into the cottage and barricaded herself inside. She'd pulled all the curtains and then had sat there on one of Great-Aunt Rosemary's cozy little couches, very deliberately *not* staring across the room at the sack of pregnancy tests Balthazar had left behind.

She had done nothing but obsessively count days since he'd showed up at the winery. She'd gone over it again and again. The truth was, she hadn't spared a single thought about whether or not her monthly cycle was showing up as it should have been…because she'd never had any reason to think about such things. Not only had Kendra never been late, as far as she knew— she'd never had any reason to worry about it if for some reason she had been.

Why hadn't it occurred to her to worry about it now that there was a reason?

But she knew the answer to that. She might wake in the night, suffused with heat and with Balthazar's name on her lips, but by day she never, ever allowed herself to think about that night. To think about *him*. Part of that was also not thinking about her own body—from the things he'd made her feel to its biological functions.

As she'd sat there in her cottage, barricaded in against truths she didn't want to face, Kendra honestly hadn't known if she'd been motivated by denial… or survival.

Either way, the longer she'd stared at that bag full of pregnancy tests, the more it seemed to overtake the room, crowding out the books and the art Great-Aunt Rosemary had left behind. And the more it seemed directly connected to the panic inside of her, pounding at her, filling her up like a wicked flood.

Until she couldn't breathe.

And so it was that Kendra discovered that she really was pregnant with Balthazar Skalas's child while hiding in the small bathroom of her great-aunt's cottage after midnight, hiding from the men he'd sent to make sure she stayed there, *after* making implicit kidnapping threats.

She'd taken all five tests, sure that they had to be defective. That the next one would prove that she wasn't actually living through…this.

But they all showed her the exact same thing.

Kendra was pregnant.

And when she finally stopped chugging water so she could make a new test happen, when she finally accepted that no new test was going to change the truth… the whole world shifted.

With such a dramatic, irrevocable jolt that she'd found herself on the floor of the bathroom, her back against the wall, staring at the incontrovertible evidence before her.

Five times over.

She'd remembered that night in his office vividly.

Too vividly, really, when she now knew what would become of it.

Had she been so quick to pretend nothing had happened because it had been so…raw? She was an educated, sophisticated woman who not only had not inquired about protection, she'd never given it a moment's thought, afterward. It had never occurred to her that anything like this could happen.

And as she'd huddled there on the cool bathroom floor, she'd had to face a number of realities. Including the fact that she'd tried her hardest to blank out what had happened in New York because it hadn't been anything like the fantasies of him she'd carried around in her head after encountering him in that gazebo. It had been so much more…*physical.* Each and every sensation so intense she still wasn't sure if it had been pain or pleasure—only that she wanted more. She didn't have a single memory or feeling about Balthazar Skalas that wasn't complicated. Complex.

When she'd been taught again and again that sex was no place for tangled emotions and overwhelming memories. It was meant to be a lovely, celebratory thing, that was all. Not an experience so darkly erotic that she could only face it fast asleep.

"Daylight is no place for unpleasant things, dear," her mother had always said.

Kendra had only realized then, curled up on the floor, that she'd taken that to heart. Maybe a bit too much to heart. Because she'd been living her whole life like this, hadn't she? Her head so far in the sand she was surprised she could breathe through it.

The last few months had been nothing more or less than the inevitable conclusion of a lifetime of her own ostrich impression. She'd ignored the obvious indicators that her father was always the kind of man who would send his own daughter off to *appeal to Balthazar as a man.* She'd ignored the unpleasant reality that he supported Tommy, who was by no definition a good man. She'd ignored everything that didn't suit her.

Maybe it wasn't a surprise that she'd ignored what was happening in her own body, too.

She'd sat there, her knees pulled beneath her chin, too stunned by her own stupidity to even bother crying about it.

That would come later, Kendra had suspected. She could almost feel an emotional breakdown hovering there like a storm, just out of reach over the horizon.

But first she could do nothing but marvel at her own naivete.

Balthazar was upsettingly correct. Her own family had pimped her out.

And it wasn't as if *he* was much better. She could feel the hatred in him. He seethed with it. He hated her brother. He detested her father.

Much as some part of her didn't wish to think about it, he was no fan of hers, either.

And still she had marched herself into that office building, a lamb to the slaughter—though in her case, she'd actually believed she was some kind of wolf, not a lamb at all.

But now it was all worse.

So much worse, Kendra didn't truly understand how she was going to live through whatever came next.

She'd spent her whole life trying to be perfect, and instead, she'd gone and gotten herself knocked up the first time she'd so much as touched a man. It was her parents' worst nightmare, as they'd made clear a thousand times while she was growing up. Her mother might very well slip off into a coma, so appalled was Emily Connolly sure to be at this news.

That was bad enough. Far worse was the trepidation she could feel churn about inside her as she tried to imagine how on earth she was going to navigate *sharing a child* with a man like Balthazar when she wasn't sure she could survive sharing a car ride with him.

She'd actually laughed out loud, there in her bathroom, then winced at how unhinged she sounded.

"I'm sorry," she'd whispered, sneaking her hands over her belly, though it still seemed impossible to her that there could be a life inside. A *life*. A baby. *My baby*, something in her whispered. "I'll find a way, don't worry."

Because Balthazar Skalas might be his own level of impossible, but Kendra had no intention of hiding from reality any longer. She was going to be a mother. She was not going to be *her* mother.

She'd never been any good at fighting for herself, but she would fight for this child.

"No matter what," she'd promised the tiny life growing inside her, there on the bathroom floor and a few more times in her bed, too, for good measure.

But the next morning, far too early for someone who'd stayed up as late as she had, Balthazar had been pounding at her door, and Kendra had made a decision on the spot that there was no point fighting him. Probably because she knew he would win. And she really didn't want to see how, exactly, he would go about physically removing her from France.

She'd seen no reason to share the news with him. He

could wait for the ill-gotten gains of his kidnapping attempt to learn what she already knew. If he marinated in his temper while he waited, all the better.

He'd stood there in the cottage's main room, a thundercloud of fury as she'd moved about collecting items like her passport and her great-aunt's oversize scarf that she could fling about her neck and pretend was a fashion accessory when really, it was more like a portable blanket she planned to use to soothe herself.

Because if the look on Balthazar's face had been any guide, Kendra was going to need some soothing.

He'd driven her to a private airfield outside of Nice without a word. The flight had been short and equally silent.

The tension between them was so thick it seemed to settle on Kendra like smog.

Once in Athens, Balthazar herded her off the plane and into yet another astonishingly glossy and aspirational sports car, then drove her into the center of the ancient city itself.

"I'm astonished," she managed to say when he stopped before what looked like an indistinguishable block of flats. "I would have thought that the mighty Balthazar lived on his own mountaintop. In an appropriate castle. With *several* moats."

"This is a medical facility," he clipped out, sounding bored and impatient. "And this is a private entrance."

He parked the car at the behest of a set of overawed attendants, then marched her into an elevator. She was whisked up to a series of private rooms, a waiting area and then an exam room, and Balthazar only glared stonily at her when she dared to suggest she might like some privacy.

"Really," she tried. "I would prefer it."

His mouth curved into that hard line. "This is no time for fantasies, Kendra."

When it was done, both pregnancy and paternity had been determined.

Kendra felt the truth like a stone, heavy and unwieldy, crushing her even when she stood upright. Balthazar, meanwhile, had transformed from a mere thunderstorm to the threat of a far more terrifying tornado, evident in the blazing fury she could see in his dark eyes.

The trip back to that offensively bright car of his was so tense that she found herself shaking.

"Balthazar," she began as he roared his way out of the parking area and back into the crowded streets of Athens, "I really think—"

"If you have any sense of self-preservation whatsoever," he growled, an imposing fury beside her as he drove, "you will be quiet."

The ferocity in his words left her winded.

Kendra decided self-preservation was an excellent idea and stayed silent for the rest of the drive. It was a short one, ending at another private entrance to a corporate parking area and another gleaming elevator. Where he ushered her, in that same grim silence, up to the roof of an office building she only belatedly realized was the corporate headquarters of Skalas & Sons. Where a helicopter waited to carry them off.

She could have argued, she supposed. Thrown a fit on the rooftop, where there were no witnesses but Balthazar's men and the ancient city spread out beneath them. She could at least have *tried*.

But she didn't see how fighting a losing battle with a tornado was going to help either her or her baby.

Her baby.

Kendra might hate herself for her weaknesses when this was all said and done, but for the moment, she wrapped her arms around the middle she'd thought was expanding thanks to eating her way through Provence and sat with that. She was having a baby.

His baby.

And when they landed on a small island surrounded by a gleaming blue sea, she didn't have it in her to make smart remarks about castles or moats. Because the island was not large. There was no sign of anything like a village. There was one sprawling house on the higher end of the island, a collection of outbuildings, and beaches.

She supposed most people would consider it paradise, but she knew better.

It was a prison.

Balthazar marched off into the sprawling villa, a celebration of Greek architecture with wide-open spaces that flowed in and out of the outdoors. Letting in the sea and sky from every angle.

Kendra followed him because what else was she to do? Attempt to fly herself back to the mainland?

"There is a skeleton staff on the island," he informed her when he led her to a bedroom that sat above the sea and then stood there, glowering at her, as if she'd impregnated herself purely to spite him. It occurred to her that he thought she had. "They'll operate according to the orders of the housekeeper, Panagiota, who has been with my family since my father was young and is deeply loyal to me. You may assume that anything she says comes directly from me."

"You're leaving me here?" Kendra should have assumed that was what he was doing, she knew. She had the absurd thought that if she'd known she wouldn't be returning to the cottage, she would have packed more of her things. As if *her things* were what mattered at the moment. "For how long?"

He took a long while to simply *look* at her, as if he was trying to see beneath her skin. As if he was looking for something. "For as long as it takes."

She tried to gather herself. "You are aware, I hope, that there's a specific timeline? And we're in the second trimester. Leaving only one remaining."

"I can count." His tone was withering.

"Are you really planning to leave me here for *six months?*"

But even as she asked the question, she knew the answer. She was glad she'd wrapped her great-aunt's gauzy scarf around her on the helicopter ride. It felt like a hug.

"Consider this a kindness," Balthazar bit off. "There's nothing I have to say to you right now that you would like to hear, I promise you."

"Right," she managed to say, trying to find her feet beneath her. Trying to remind herself that no matter how intimidating she found him, and no matter how beautiful, this wasn't only about the two of them any longer. "Because when we had sex with each other and were both present and accounted for *in your office*, only I was scheming. You were nothing but a naive maiden, lost in the woods."

"Do not test me, Kendra." His voice was something

like a whisper, though lethal. She could feel it pierce her like a blade. She gripped the scarf around her even more tightly. "You will not like how I handle you. How I address what you have done to me. Let me promise you this."

"You can't really think I'm going to quietly remain here." She shook her head at him. "I have a life, Balthazar. One I made all for myself, no matter what you might think of it. I have—"

"If you wished to have a life, you should not have irrevocably changed mine."

He moved closer then, towering over her, and she could see a stark ferocity in his gaze that should have terrified her. Instead, something in her longed to meet it. Rise up on her toes, tilt her head, and—

Well. It wasn't as if she was unaware of her own issues. There was that.

"Perhaps it's escaped your notice," she said, hoping the things she longed for so foolishly weren't written all over her face, but mine is the life that is already changed. Mine is the life you decided to alter in more ways than one. I'm the one carrying this baby. I'm the one you've carted all over Europe today, and apparently plan to leave behind on this island."

"The life you knew is over." She watched as a muscle clenched in his jaw. "I suspect this was your plan from the start. I must congratulate you. I did not see it coming."

"Yes," she snapped at him, "I decided that I would miraculously become pregnant, the way all women do. That's why there is no such thing as fertility issues. All women *decide*, and then do it."

He made a sound she could only describe as a growl,

but she didn't slink away. Something in her *thrilled* to the sound. She kept her gaze steady and forced her knees to remain strong beneath her.

"You may have saved your brother after all," Balthazar said in that quiet way of his that made the world shake around him. "But I promise you, Kendra. You will live to regret this."

For a moment she thought—*wished?*—that those big, hard hands of his were going to reach out to her. Take hold of her.

Touch her the way he did in her dreams, night after night—

But instead, Balthazar turned on his heel and stalked away from her.

Kendra stayed where she was, shaken so deeply by her own longing, even now, that she was surprised she didn't sink to the floor. Was it self-hatred that made her tremble? Or was it that impossible yearning that she couldn't stamp out?

And then she had to force herself not to panic, somehow, when she heard the helicopter's rotors. When Balthazar disappeared into the sky, leaving her behind with these things she knew about herself now.

The worst of them being that no matter what he did, she still wanted him.

It took Kendra a solid ten days to investigate every single nook and cranny of the house and each of the outbuildings, desperate to find something she could use to make her escape.

There had been nothing. Panagiota was kind enough, but firm. She apologized repeatedly, but changed nothing. There was no cell service. Certainly no internet. At least, not any that Kendra was permitted to access.

Though she had to face the fact that even if there was, she had no idea who she would call. Her family would be delighted that she was in a position to bargain further with Balthazar. They would do nothing to help her.

Kendra took it as a mark of her personal growth that she knew this now.

The same way she knew, when she'd finished marching around the small island looking for boats to the mainland, that the real truth was worse.

She didn't want to leave.

She wanted Balthazar to come back.

The way she knew he would, because no matter how angry he might have been, she was carrying his child.

Maybe what she did looked like surrender, but Kendra rather thought she was conserving her strength for the real fight—which certainly wasn't the quietly insistent Panagiota, who was, after all, only doing Balthazar's bidding.

She ate what he wanted her to eat, according to the nutritional guide he'd apparently left with the housekeeper. There was no way off the island—and she'd looked—so she took long, rambling walks on the beaches, over the fields, and through the groves of olive trees.

She slept in the bed he'd told her was hers, and even though he wasn't there, she felt the imprint of him as if he truly was holding her where he wanted her.

"By the neck," she muttered to herself one morning.

But she knew that wasn't quite right. She knew it was quite a bit lower.

One week passed, then another. Summer began to

wane, though on a Greek island in the Aegean it was hard to note the difference.

Balthazar did not contact her. His messages were sent through Panagiota. They were always terse and to the point, and still, Kendra was sure she could feel the gathering storm of his temper from across the sea.

She heard the rotors first on an afternoon six weeks after he'd left her. She was curled up in her favorite spot, a swinging chair out on one of the terraces, the sun in her face and a book in her lap from the library she'd been reading her way through.

Kendra felt a kind of electricity shoot through her at the sound. She sat up, aware that if she squinted, this prison of hers bore a distinct resemblance to what she might have considered paradise when she was younger. Nothing to do but take long walks on a secluded beach and lie about reading books? She should have been delirious with joy.

Sometimes she forgot that she wasn't. That she'd been imprisoned here, no matter how pretty it was.

That she was pregnant with the child of a man who detested her.

A man whose memory woke her in the night, still, on fire with need.

Kendra stayed where she was. She kept on gazing down at her book, even when she heard the faint sound of footsteps against the stones behind her.

And she would have known it was Balthazar even if he hadn't made a sound. She could feel the leading edge of the storm. She could feel the wind snapping at her, the temperature drop, and far off, she was certain, the warning rumble of thunder.

She should have been scared. Instead, what charged around inside her felt a lot more like exhilaration.

"What a pretty picture you make," came his sardonic, insulting voice. Darker than she recalled, maybe. But still, it arrowed straight to her core, making her melt. That easily. "What a shame that I know it is all lies."

Kendra wanted to hurl the book she was reading at his head.

Somehow, she refrained.

"How nice of you to stop in, Balthazar," she said calmly instead. "You do know, don't you, that pregnancies keep going even if you'd prefer to pretend that they don't? I mention this because eventually, when you deign to make an appearance, I won't be the only one here."

"The doctor is even now setting up an exam room in one of the guest bedrooms. He will perform a full examination."

"A prison infirmary," she replied gaily. "What a treat."

Kendra looked at him then and she wished she hadn't.

Because looking at Balthazar...hurt.

He looked like exactly who and what he was. The devil, one of the richest men alive, and her enemy.

All wrapped up in that brooding, near brutal intensity and a dark, bespoke suit that proclaimed his power to the whole of the Mediterranean.

If he was less beautiful, would she be less...thrown?

It shouldn't matter how beautiful he is, she snapped at herself. *It should only matter that he's locked you away on this island.*

"I don't know why you bothered to come," she continued, keeping her voice brighter than it should have been. "At this point, wouldn't it be easier if you just stayed away? I can raise your child in shame and solitude all by myself."

"I doubt you feel anything approaching shame," he said, with one of those hard laughs that nearly made her shiver, though she sat in the sunshine. "And it is of no matter, anyway. I have no intention of leaving you here forever, no matter how tempting the prospect. Like it or not, you will be the mother of my child. And I am Balthazar Skalas. There are certain conventions that need to be followed."

"I can't imagine what you mean. More kidnaps? More insults and accusations? I can hardly wait."

His smile then was wintry. It made something cold and bright flash over her, worse than before.

"Why, Kendra. I thought you knew."

That he seemed to be enjoying himself made her shudder, and she knew he saw it.

He thinks he's beaten me, Kendra thought, and found she was holding her breath.

"I've come to congratulate you, of course," Balthazar told her. His dark eyes gleamed with satisfaction. Worse, with triumph. "As we are to be married tomorrow."

CHAPTER EIGHT

IT WAS ALMOST worth the fact that Balthazar was marrying her against his will, if at his command, to see that stunned look on Kendra's face.

Better still, a flash of temper besides, proving she wasn't nearly as calm or collected as she sometimes acted.

Balthazar almost slipped and showed her how much her reaction pleased him, but caught himself just in time. She didn't deserve to see his own responses, but why should he be the only person dreading the inevitable? She was a Connolly, she had conspired against him from the start with her vile father and brother, and this was her fault.

He ignored the voice inside him that reminded him that her conspiracies could not have gained any ground had he not lost his head completely and sampled her without protecting himself. The way he'd been ignoring that voice for weeks.

But he didn't like to think about that. He was appalled that he'd lost control of himself so utterly, when his father had spent long years teaching him how to strip any and all emotions out of every last moment and situation. Even sex was meant to be a release, nothing more.

Nothing…overwhelming.

He wrestled himself back under control. As he should have done from the start.

"I will not be marrying you," she shot back at him, predictably. She bristled in her hanging chair and he watched dispassionately as she struggled to pull herself out of its embrace, then stood. Rather rounder than the last time he'd seen her, though he refused to focus on that. On what her fuller figure meant. "Not tomorrow. Not ever."

"You're beginning to bore me," he replied, almost idly, and knew he sounded sterner than perhaps he'd intended when she stiffened. "You will not do this, you will not do that. I suggest you come up with a new song. In the meantime, the doctor is waiting."

"What magical powers I must possess that I can bore you in six seconds after your absence of six *weeks*. Maybe the problem is your attention span."

Balthazar did not lower himself to sniping with her, especially because he wanted to do just that. He gestured toward the archway that led into the house and waited for her to obey him.

For a moment, he wasn't sure what she would do. Refuse? Fight him? Worse, he wasn't entirely sure what *he* planned to do if she did either of those things. Nor could he read the expressions that chased each other across her lovely, flushed face when she swept past him, though he got the overall impression of feminine fury.

She would be his wife come the morning. She was carrying his child.

She was his enemy.

All good reasons not to want her with that greedy,

driving need that had gotten him into this mess in the first place. And yet Balthazar had to order himself to stand down. To keep his hands to himself. To stop himself before he made this unfortunate situation worse.

He, who could stare down the most powerful men alive and make them regret catching his eye, could barely control himself in the presence of a woman who should have disgusted him.

It was an outrage and it never eased. Three years hadn't dulled his reaction. Why had he assured himself six weeks would do the trick this time?

Balthazar had no answer. Instead, once inside, he led her down the long, bright hallway, across an interior courtyard covered in pink bougainvillea, then ushered her into the set of rooms his staff had rearranged so they could stand in for a medical suite.

And because he knew his doctor would report to him in full, he left her there.

Though he would have died before admitting it, and by his own hand, he was happy for the breathing room.

Because the truth was that Balthazar had been utterly unprepared for the sight of her.

The glow he'd seen in France and had attributed to the lighting at her cottage—or the glory of the Côte d'Azur itself—was worse now. Or better, more like. She was a gleaming, bright and shining thing, and he had no idea how he was meant to cope.

He stood out in the courtyard, surrounded by flowers and the pitiless Aegean sky, and thought of her new *roundness*. The widening of her hips, the swell of her belly. He found he was wholly moved by the knowledge that she carried his child. *His child* tucked inside that beautiful, gently rounded body of hers.

He hadn't expected that. This… insane response to her. A tenderness he abhorred mixed in with too much pounding, bone-rattling *need*.

Tenderness was anathema to him. Softness of any kind led to desperate places—didn't he know that already?

But he refused to think about his own family. Of the things sentimentality had wrought.

There was no need to think of it when he knew who to blame.

Balthazar had convinced himself that his response to Kendra had been nothing more than two strange moments in time, bookending three years. But it was over now, surely. He'd spent the past month handling the details of what needed to happen next, now that his heir's birth was imminent. Up to and including a meeting with his brother to lay out the changes he would be making in his will and various trusts. For dynastic purposes.

"Kendra… *Connolly*?" Constantine had asked lazily. He had gazed at his brother as he'd lounged about in his typical state of seeming dishevelment all over Balthazar's sleek, modern furniture. Then he'd waved a languid hand at Athens outside the windows as if he expected the whole of Greece to rise up to support his astonishment. "You cannot be serious."

"I would hardly make such announcements in jest."

"She is a Connolly."

"A fact that does not become less appalling the more you repeat it, brother."

Constantine had shaken his head. "What can you possibly be thinking? After everything—" He'd stopped then. The canny look that Balthazar sometimes thought only he had ever seen changed his brother's face. Constantine suddenly looked every inch the shark he was. "Let me guess. You got her pregnant. Good god, Balthazar. How could you be so careless?"

"A simple *congratulations* would do. As you will shortly become an uncle."

Constantine had let out a bark of laughter. "Never let it be said you are not prepared to think outside the box when it comes to taking revenge on our enemies. I am inspired, truly."

And he'd smiled in a way that had distracted Balthazar for a moment, wondering who his brother considered worthy of enemy status—and a revenge scenario to match. He did not fancy that person's chances against the wolf-in-playboy's-clothing Constantine played up for public consumption.

"Prepare yourself," Balthazar had advised his brother that night. "You will be the *koumbaro*."

If Constantine had any further feelings about taking his place at his brother's side in the traditional role of *koumbaro*, combining best man, future godparent, and witness in one, he had wisely kept that to himself.

Possibly too busy concocting his own form of revenge, Balthazar had thought then.

Now Balthazar waited in a riot of blooms and his body's greedy responses to the enemy he planned to take as his wife, forced to remind himself that revenge was the point of this. Revenge had always been the point.

It was simply taking rather a different form than he'd expected it would when Kendra had asked for that appointment with him months back.

He had never imagined how close a Connolly would come to ruining *him*.

Do not allow temptation to change your path, he told himself dourly, despite the sunshine and the bright explosion of pink flowers all around him. *Stay the course.*

And later—after the doctor had announced that Kendra and the baby she carried could not have been in better health, then left them to an evening meal out on one of the terraces over the sea—Balthazar did not bother to wait for the good food or a full belly to dull her temper. He shouldn't have cared what mood she was in. He slid the folder he'd brought for her across the table.

"What is this?" Her voice was clipped. It was at odds with that glow she had about her, and Balthazar disliked it, but he tapped his finger against the thick file anyway.

"These are the agreements that require your signature."

She sniffed, poking at the food on her plate with rather more violence than strictly necessary, to his mind. "I will not be signing anything."

"That does not sound like the new song I suggested you sing," he said, mildly enough. He studied her mutinous expression. "Was I unclear?"

Balthazar expected her to argue with him. If he was honest, he was looking forward to it. Though he wasn't certain he truly wished to acknowledge that what kicked around inside of him was more of that anticipation and hunger than the righteous fury he would have said was guiding his every word and deed.

There was something about this woman that got under his skin. That was the sad truth, no matter how he fought against it. Any hope he might have had that she had released her grip on him in the time he'd spent away from her had disappeared the moment he'd seen her curled up in a chair with the sunlight in her hair, turning it to flame.

Maybe it was time to admit it to himself.

But Kendra didn't make it easy on him. She didn't leap into the fray. Instead, she looked away, her gaze off toward the blue line of the horizon, far in the distance. He imagined she was dreaming of ways to escape him, to avoid the consequences he had been forced to accept.

He resented it.

"I have no interest in your money," she said after a moment, as if studying the inevitable way the sun dipped toward the edge of the world. "You know full well I have my own. There is no need whatsoever to sign agreements to that effect."

"You mean you have your father's money," Balthazar corrected her, sitting back in his chair and absolutely not giving in to his temper. Just because she got to him, it didn't mean he had to lose his grip. He was furious it was even in question. "That is not quite the same thing, is it?"

Her gaze shifted back to him, glittering hot and gold. "Remind me, whose money is it that you were given?"

He found himself smiling. Almost. "Fair point. Though, unlike me, I am unaware of any great financial ventures you've been involved in on your own since you came of age. Please enlighten me."

"I was happily working in a winery in Provence until six weeks ago."

Balthazar lifted a brow. "Are you so divorced from reality that you imagine waiting tables is a wealth-building exercise? Unless, of course, you went about getting your tips in the same way you approached your business meeting with me?"

Kendra didn't rise to the bait and surely he should not have felt a vague sense of disappointment at that.

She sighed as if *he* was the trial. "Surely the man who has spirited me away to his very own private island is not really speaking to me about *reality*."

And he, who had a cutting response for everything, found he had nothing.

Worse, he found himself sitting there, seething, while Kendra returned her attention to the grilled chicken on her plate, helping herself to more fresh greens from the bowl at her elbow. Ignoring him, he was forced to conclude.

Ignoring him.

Ignoring *him*.

He ordered himself to stop gritting his teeth.

"If I am brutally honest—"

"That would be a bracing shift, I'm sure," she murmured aridly.

Balthazar ignored that. And continued, with great magnanimity. "I am not worried about you, *kopéla*. Obviously it is your father and brother and their grasping, deceitful behavior who concern me more."

"Are you marrying all three of us?"

He couldn't quite read that tone she'd used, but he could see the look on her face all too well. He couldn't say he liked it.

"Oh, I see," she said when he didn't reply. "I forgot that I am no more than a tool my father and brother alike use for their own nefarious ends. You think you're taking their little toy away and making it yours instead.

Naturally you want me to sign documents to enshrine these playground antics into contract law. After all, what could be the harm? This was never my life in the first place."

It was the bitterness in her tone, the harsh slap of it, that got to him then. Balthazar felt as if he'd lost something when she reached out, grabbed the folder, and pulled it toward her.

A feeling that only worsened as she rifled through the pages, signing her name with dramatic flourish.

"You do not appear to be reading the documents, Kendra."

"Does it matter?" She didn't look up at him. "Surely the object of this humiliation is the mere fact of it. Not what the papers actually *say*."

She capped the pen, closed the folder again, and then shoved it all back across the table toward him. "Here you go, Balthazar. Congratulations, you have dominion over me and legal documents to prove it. What a glorious environment this will be for your child."

Balthazar told himself it was the mention of the child that got to him then, that was all. Imagining that child torn between warring parents the way he and his brother had been. He told himself that was all it was.

He had been so focused on the fact of Kendra's pregnancy. What it meant in financial and practical terms. What he was going to have to do to contain the damage and attempt to repair this mistake of his own making.

Somehow, he hadn't thought about the fact his child would be an individual, a whole human being who would grow and laugh—and want his parents to be better, as he had—until now.

It felt a great deal like a kick to the gut.

For a moment, he almost dared imagine what things might have been like if his parents had been different. If they had actually gotten better instead of worse. If they had somehow managed not to poison everything they touched—

But that felt uncomfortably disloyal.

He shoved it aside—aware that it seemed harder to do than it should have.

"Why are you staring at me?" Kendra asked after a while, and he wondered if she found the silence between them oppressive. Or if that was only him, again. "It is not going to change anything."

"Nothing needs to change." He shrugged, no longer feeling oppressed. Not when she was aiming that baleful glare of hers his way. "We will marry in the morning. Though as a Connolly you certainly do not deserve such consideration, you will become my wife. You may thank me."

"I would be happier with less consideration, actually. No thanks required."

"Too bad." His mouth curved into something hard. "The child you carry will be my heir, and I insist any child of mine be legitimate. If you had read the documents you signed, you would know that I have made generous accommodation for you *because* you are the mother of this child, no matter what our future holds."

Somehow, he knew she was not likely to thank him for that, either.

"Do we have a future?" she asked instead. Then frowned. "Or, wait. Do you mean a succession of creative imprisonments for me to enjoy?"

"That is up to you, Kendra."

"Why do I find that very hard to believe?"

Balthazar studied her. "This role you keep attempting to play, that of the wronged innocent, does not suit you."

"Whereas the role of overly controlling bastard seems to fit you perfectly. Almost as if you've had practice. I'm betting you have."

"You have only a few months left." It was a warning, not that Balthazar expected her to take it on board. "Indulge your bitterness as you wish. Once the child is born, it stops. Or I will make certain you see as a little of him as possible."

"I don't know what makes you think it's going to be a boy, aside from wishful thinking," she said, when he'd thought she would have reacted more dramatically to his other threat. She lifted a brow. "And you can try to separate me from this baby. But I wouldn't advise it."

The sun had dropped almost to the sea then. The sky was bathed in golds and reds, a commotion of flame and fury, just like Kendra.

He hated that he'd made that connection.

"Perhaps you are laboring under some misapprehension," he said softly. "I am Balthazar Skalas and we are in Greece. There is no court in the land that would concern itself with your position should I make mine clear."

To his surprise, all she did was laugh. "All these threats. Is this how you're used to interacting with the world? Is this what it's like to be your mistress? No wonder you go through them like tissues."

"This is nothing like being one of my mistresses," he replied silkily, because this was steadier ground. "As that role is far more...active."

Kendra leaned forward and propped her elbows on

the table, very much as if she thought she was in a classroom of some kind. "Tell me more about this active mistress lifestyle of yours. Is this going to be a part of my humiliation at your hands? Will I sit, tucked away in this or that luxurious prison, while you prance around with your various women in public places?"

She did not look particularly upset at that possibility, which Balthazar found he disliked. Intensely. "What business is that of yours?"

"I don't ask for myself," Kendra said, aiming that cool smile at him that he remembered too well from his office. "It's your child who concerns me. Then again, perhaps you are not concerned that she will grow up loathing you. Detesting the way you treat her mother and worse, how you humiliate your family in public. But then, wasn't your father that kind of man? Perhaps your child can hope for no better."

It was such a kill shot, aimed so perfectly and with such lethal accuracy, that Balthazar almost laughed. He hadn't seen it coming. In truth, he hadn't imagined she'd had it in her. That was what he got for assuming she was nothing but a pawn.

He found himself sitting back in his chair, tempted to check to see if he was bleeding.

And as he did, she carried on eating, as if she hadn't a single care in the world.

As if she hadn't lacerated him like that.

"Both of my parents had affairs," he said, eventually.

It was true enough, though it was not an accurate summation of his parents' marriage. Much less what had become of it.

"Demetrius Skalas did not have affairs." Kendra

sounded almost placid. Matter-of-fact. "An affair suggests that there were some attempts to keep the behavior undercover. Your father preferred to parade around with a new woman on his arm whenever possible, publicly and horribly. When your mother responded in kind, he divorced her."

"Thank you for reciting facts about which you know nothing," Balthazar managed to grit out, while his pulse pounded at him.

"These are not my facts." She smiled at him, a little more edgily that her calm tone would suggest. "Panagiota may have banned me from the internet, but it turns out that the family housekeeper has a great many facts at her disposal. And is only too happy to share them."

Balthazar shook his head. And tamped down on the urge in him to lash out. Because she wasn't any old adversary. She wasn't her own father, that despicable man. She was the mother of his child, whether he liked it or not. And he was still trying to decide how best to come to terms with that.

"My father was a man of absolutes," he said when the silence between them grew too heavy again. "I do not expect you to understand, but he had strict expectations. And should anyone fall short of those expectations, the consequences were severe. Anyone who knew him knew this."

"Are you saying that your mother earned her humiliation?" Kendra made a face. "I suppose I'd better watch my step."

"I am not my father."

And Balthazar was surprised at how...raw that sounded.

"Are you not?" Kendra sat back, one hand moving to cover her belly. He wanted to decry the theatrics, but he had the strangest notion that it was an unconscious gesture.

Again, he was struck by the fact that *his son* was in there. That *his son* would be out in this same world in a matter of months, calling Balthazar father. Maybe that was why he did not reply to Kendra in the thunderous manner he could have.

The way he should have.

"My brother and I were born in quick succession," he told her instead, because that was also true. "And my mother... After my brother came, I am told, she disappeared. She left us in the care of our nannies and never left her rooms. After that had gone on for some time, my father had her admitted to a private hospital in Austria, where she was better cared for. But she did not return to us for several years."

"And you think that is...evidence against her?"

"It is simply what happened."

"It sounds like you're describing postpartum depression, Balthazar. It wasn't her choice." Kendra studied his face for a moment. "You know that, don't you?"

"What I know is that my father could not abide weakness," Balthazar told her, his voice rough. "In anyone."

Kendra was sitting much too still, that hand still resting on her belly. "So what you're telling me is that your poor mother suffered from a terrible depression and your father took it upon himself to punish her for a chemical and hormonal imbalance that wasn't her fault."

"He was an unforgiving man."

"And what about you?" Kendra asked quietly. "Are you forgiving?"

This was the right time to tell her the rest of it, to see once and for all what she knew and what game she was playing. But somehow, Balthazar couldn't bring himself to do it.

He couldn't stop thinking of a small boy with his eyes, looking at him the way he'd tried to implore his father. Before he'd learned the folly of such things.

Kendra reached over and tapped the folder that still sat there between them. "It would appear that no, you are not particularly forgiving."

"Do you deserve forgiveness, Kendra?" he growled at her, keeping himself still in his chair when he wanted nothing more than to rage. To break things. To hurl the table between them into the sea far below.

Because that was easier than confronting what was happening in him. He thought of his mother, messier and messier throughout his childhood until his father had divorced her. She had gone off to lick her wounds—in horribly public ways. Balthazar had always considered it a defection. He had always judged her, harshly, as much for her particular extramarital affair neither his father nor he could overlook as for her departure.

What he had never done was question how and why she had lost his father's respect in the first place. Much less whether or not that had been fair to her. And he didn't much care for the heavy ball of something like dread that sat in him now he was doing just that.

Thinking about forgiveness didn't help.

"By your reckoning, no," Kendra replied, but she

didn't look particularly broken up about whether or not he might forgive her. As if a lifetime of his father's brand of consequences was right up her alley, when he knew better. He knew what it did to soft creatures like her, didn't he? "But then, I don't need to prove myself to you, Balthazar. I don't care what you believe. I'm going to marry you, not because you've demanded it, but because I'm a rational person who can see that marrying you will afford my child her best possible life. You keep talking about the past if it makes you feel better. I'm focused on the future."

She stood up then, still outrageously graceful despite her fuller figure and her new, big bump. He told himself it was sheer temper that pounded through him. Sheer, unmitigated fury—because what else could it be? What else would he allow it to be?

He was rising before he meant to move, blocking her path.

She stared up at him, her chin lifted as her copper-burnished hair flowed around her, backlit by the setting sun.

"You have no moral high ground here," he gritted out at her. He wanted to put his hands on her, so he did, gripping her shoulders as he held her before him. "You've achieved what you wanted, but I assure you, the price you pay will be steep."

"What I *wanted*," she threw right back at him, "was peace. Quiet. A cottage all my own filled with books and a fire and as many buttery croissants as I could eat. Which, it turns out, is a great many croissants. Instead you stormed in and carried me off to this place. And I'm not an idiot, Balthazar. I'm not *divorced from reality*. I'm perfectly aware that as prisons go, this one is charming. Beautiful. Some people would dream of coming here and staying here forever. But I'm not one of them."

"If I was interested in what you wanted, Kendra, I would have asked you."

He expected her to recoil at that. To react as if he'd slapped her. Instead, she surged up onto her toes, bringing herself even closer to him.

Exhibiting, he couldn't help but notice, absolutely no fear.

He couldn't think of a single reason that should have made him want her so desperately.

"You can issue all the orders you like," she told him in a rush. "You will never control me. If I happen to go along with your wishes, you can be sure it's because I want to. Not because you told me to."

He managed—just—not to sneer. "From a girl who was willing to prostitute herself at her father's command."

"You don't know anything about my family," she threw right back at him. "Or about me. And I don't want you to know. You don't deserve it."

She was so bright with her own outrage. Alight with self-righteous indignation, and Balthazar should have found that laughable. He told himself he did.

But he didn't laugh.

Instead, he jerked her toward him and set his mouth to hers.

At last.

And it was that same wild, impossible fire. That same electric explosion, as if he'd been struck by lightning—yet he wanted more. Always and ever more.

He angled his head to one side, taking the kiss

deeper and growling his appreciation when she met him, all slick heat and greed.

And he was amazed, again, to find his head spinning when she pushed herself away.

"Kissing me changes nothing," she managed to say, though he took perhaps too much pride in the fact her voice shook. "Do you really think that a kiss like that is any kind of punishment at all? Here's a news flash. It's not. If I didn't like it, I would bite you."

"Yes, yes, *kopéla*," he drawled, suddenly enjoying himself when she scowled at him. "You're very fierce. You have fangs, and I promise you, I cannot wait to feel them on my skin."

Kendra bared her teeth at him and he laughed, he wanted her so intensely. So comprehensively it was like pain. But he knew pain. He knew how to live with it. In a dark way, how to crave it.

"Remember you said that, Balthazar," she hissed at him.

It was meant as a dire warning, he was sure. Still, he took her chin in his hand and held her there, smiling hard when temper flooded her bright gaze.

"But one way or another, all this posturing or no, in the morning, you will be my wife," he told her, like an ancient omen. Like a curse. "And that will be an end to it."

CHAPTER NINE

KENDRA WASN'T THE sort of woman who had dedicated years of her life to fantasizing about her wedding one day. Not that there was anything wrong with such fantasies, but she'd always spent her time daydreaming about winning over her father's boardroom, and sitting behind suitably impressive desks in the family offices.

And she'd found herself fantasizing about far different things these days.

Still, if she'd thrown together a few wedding ideas off the top of her head, it would not have been…this.

It was a small affair on a particular stretch of the island that Panagiota informed her, with great seriousness, had been sanctified.

"Is that…good?" she asked.

"It is more than good," the other woman had replied. "It is necessary."

She'd woken the morning of her *sanctified* wedding her mouth feeling swollen and bruised from Balthazar's kiss the night before, though her inspection of her lips had indicated that sensation was rather more emotional than physical. Panagiota had come in, smiling merrily, her arms filled with a flowing white gown. Kendra was tempted to tear it up. Or demand something more suitable for the occasion, like a black shroud.

Maybe she would have done both of those things, but she made the mistake of running her hand over the filmy, flowy material of the gown when Panagiota carefully laid it out. And the next thing she knew, she was slipping it on.

Her body was changing, thickening by the day. She already had a significant belly. She was aware of her body in different ways these days. Clothes never quite fit the way she expected them to, and stranger still, her center of gravity had shifted.

But when she slipped the dress on, it was like a caress. It made her feel sensual and beautiful.

When she looked in the mirror, her heart constricted. Then it began to beat at her, hard.

Kendra told herself that she could make this forced wedding anything she wanted it to be.

She'd said a lot of things to Balthazar last night and then had stayed awake the rest of the night, wondering if any of them were true—because all he had to do was look at her and she trembled.

And after six weeks of solitude, she'd found she enjoyed that trembling. Maybe more than she should have.

"I want what I said to be true," she said out loud now as she stared at the vision in flowing white before her in the glass, her hand over her belly. Her baby grew by the day. Time was moving right along no matter what she said or didn't say to the man as caught in this as she was. "That will have to be enough."

She would make it enough.

Kendra did her own hair, bundling it up on the top

of her head into a messy bun, then pinning it into place so it looked artistic rather than sloppy. She slicked on some lip gloss and decided against any blusher, as she could see she didn't need it. She didn't hide her freckles. She didn't bother to accentuate her eyes.

And strangely enough, she almost felt…free.

Because she knew that if one of those florid-cheeked boys her mother had forever been pushing on her was waiting for her today, her wedding would look nothing like this. She would have been sitting in her parents' house in Connecticut in a far more traditional gown, looking out at a huge tent on the lawn above the water. There would have been veils and churches and brigades of attendants. Guest lists filled with people she didn't know and didn't wish to know.

Maybe, Kendra thought, she'd never bothered to fantasize about her wedding day because it had always been a foregone conclusion. She certainly wouldn't have looked *happy* the way her reflection did.

Her heart did a cartwheel in her chest as she told herself, hurriedly, that was merely the pregnancy talking. The baby was giving her this glow. It wasn't *happiness.* It was hormones.

Either that, she thought when Panagiota came to collect her, or she'd taken leave of her senses entirely. Because as much as she might have shot her mouth off to Balthazar last night, she'd done what he wanted. She'd signed his agreements. She'd put on this dress.

For a woman who had claimed she had no intention of marrying him, Kendra was doing a terrific impression of a blushing, eager bride.

She waited for reality to slap her awake, but it didn't.

Because this was reality. The baby inside her and the man waiting for her.

And both were better than anything involving the life she'd left behind in Connecticut.

That was the truth that slapped her.

Hard.

Kendra tried to catch her breath from the wallop of it as the housekeeper led her through the sprawling villa, whitewashed walls and raucous flowers on all sides, then outside. Past all the terraces, past the ruins of a long-ago chapel, to a small altar on the side of a cliff.

There were three people waiting for her, seemingly suspended between the wide blue sky and the sun-drenched sea. Balthazar in his usual black, severe and unsmiling. The unfathomable priest. And another man she did not know, yet recognized instantly all the same.

Constantine Skalas, looking faintly rumpled and amused, as if he'd just that moment rolled off a supermodel and slouched his way to the ceremony.

As she drew closer, clutching the white gardenias Panagiota had handed her as they walked, Balthazar and the priest stared at her in varying degrees of condemnation. Constantine only smirked.

Kendra reminded herself that she was choosing to be as happy as she liked because she'd escaped the life her family wanted for her, which had to be worth a celebration, and beamed at all of them in turn.

"A white wedding," Balthazar murmured darkly as he took her arm. He did not *quite* scowl. "Let us hope God does not smite us down where we stand."

"This is the day our child becomes legitimate, Balthazar," she replied, smiling at him. Then more wildly when he actually did scowl at her. "Let us give thanks and be glad."

The ceremony was conducted in Greek and English. There were three rounds of blessings. Constantine exchanged their rings three times. There were candles and crowns, the joining of hands, and a ceremonial procession three times around the altar.

Kendra couldn't help being moved by the ancient words, the traditions, the press of Balthazar's hands against her own.

Like the baby inside her, *her* baby, the wedding felt bigger than her. It connected her to something far larger than herself or this man she was marrying or all the dark little squabbles that had brought them here.

Somehow, this wedding she hadn't wanted gave her hope.

She clung to that when it was over. Balthazar and his brother went off somewhere. Panagiota pressed a small bag of what she called *koufeta* into her hands—the word for sugared almonds, it seemed—then left with the priest.

Kendra spent her first moments as a married woman—as the wife of Balthazar Skalas—in a beautiful dress with gardenias and sugared almonds in her hands, alone at an altar. Unwilling to let go of that undeserved hope that ran through her as surely as the breeze.

She moved over to the railing and looked out at the deep blue Aegean Sea, because that felt like the same thing.

And she couldn't have said how long she stood there, but she was all too aware of it when Balthazar returned. She could *feel* him. That brooding, crackling energy, whipping all around her as if he brought his own storm with him wherever he went.

Kendra already knew he did.

"I'll admit it," she said, without looking over at him as he came to stand beside her, a dark and brooding cloud. "I expected to feel different."

"You should feel different. You are no longer a Connolly." He said that as if *Connolly* was a synonym for *rat*. The way he always did. "You are a Skalas."

"Oh, happy day."

They both stood there as the helicopter rose into the air from the pad on the other side of the villa, presumably taking Constantine and the unamused priest back to the mainland. Long after the sound of the propellers died away, they stayed there at the wedding altar.

Silent except for the beat of that same, familiar tension between them and the waves against the rocks below.

Until Kendra could take it no more and turned toward him, gazing up at the forbidding face of this man who was now her husband.

Her husband.

She had a heavy set of rings on her finger to prove it. More, she carried his baby inside of her—and felt the baby move, then. As if in agreement.

And Kendra tried to hold on to her sense of hope. To the beauty of the ceremony that had bound them together. She did. But she didn't understand how she could feel connected to this man in all these different ways, yet see no hint of that intimacy on his stern, remote face.

"What now?" she asked quietly. "Do the humiliations and punishments begin today? Or are we easing into them?"

"Such bravado. I wonder, would you retain it if I called your bluff?"

Kendra shrugged carelessly, though she did not feel careless in the least. Last night she had. Last night she'd felt powerful, because she'd grown comfortable here. The reality of this—of them—grew bigger within her all the time. *She* hadn't been hiding from it as he had.

She didn't know when that had changed. Was it the vows they'd spoken, in two languages? Had that made something shift inside of her?

"Go right ahead and call my bluff," she invited him. "But I intend to eat first. No one likes to be humiliated on an empty stomach."

She took her meal, still dressed in her full wedding regalia, on a different terrace with a different view of the enduring sea. *Teach me how to endure like that*, she thought, though she knew better than to say it aloud.

And then she applied herself to her wedding feast. There was a seafood salad of mussels and scallops, crab and calamari, all heaped together and marinated in lemon and the oil from the island's olives. There was a platter of tender lamb with tomato and orzo, topped with cheese. And when she was finished, heavenly baklava drenched in honey.

Kendra was not wholly surprised that Balthazar joined her, though he did not eat. Instead, he sat across from her. Brooding, clearly. She wondered if he meant to put her off her food, so she viewed it as a kind of rebellion that she ate her fill anyway.

Hope took many forms, she assured herself.

Then they both sat there, in more fraught silence,

as their brand-new forced marriage entered its second hour.

"Well," she said after that went on for some time. "I will say that so far, I'm finding marriage a delight. But I didn't realize that we took a vow of silence. Was that the Greek part?"

A muscle in his jaw twitched. "We have yet to agree to terms."

"And here I thought I signed all kinds of papers last night. What was that, if not terms?"

"That was about money," Balthazar said in a certain, silken way. "But now you and I must decide the rest of it."

Her pulse picked up, kicking its way through her. And there was an answering surge of heat between her legs. But Kendra didn't want to show him her reaction, so all she did was lean back, smile, and wait.

"You have options, of course," he said, his dark eyes glittering and blocking out all the sun and sky. "But these choices have ramifications."

"Are we talking about consequences? Already?"

"I told you. I require a great deal of sex." And he said it so coldly. So devoid of passion that if she hadn't been looking directly at him she might have thought this was a clinical discussion. But she could see the way his eyes blazed. More, she could feel it, sharp and hot, in the softest part of her. Almost better than a touch. "Do you wish to provide it?"

"Why, Balthazar," she said softly. "Are you asking me to be your mistress as well as your wife? My cup runneth over."

It occurred to her to wonder as she said that, why, when he seemed to get grimmer by the moment, she was…moving in the opposite direction. Maybe it was because he'd married her. Maybe it was because she already loved, deeply, the child she carried—and somehow that splashed over on him, too.

Kendra shied away from that word. It came with deep, painful spikes.

All she knew was that she couldn't hate him the way she wanted to. God knew, she'd tried. She'd never quite gotten there, and now? She couldn't.

There had been crowns and rings and vows besides. She *couldn't*.

"If you would prefer that this marriage remain in name only, I'm happy to oblige," Balthazar said with a certain dark inevitability. "I will find other means to meet my needs."

"An open marriage," Kendra said, nodding as if she discussed such things all the time. As if she didn't feel that strange hollow space yawn open inside of her. "I'm told many people in our tax bracket rely on these arrangements."

"We will not have an open marriage," Balthazar told her. It was a stern rebuke. "I do not share what is mine."

Her heart actually *hurt*, there beneath her too-tight ribs. But she made herself smile as if this was nothing more than idle talk over cocktails. "But you assume I do?"

"I told you that you have a choice. I do not recall telling you that you would enjoy the choice." He shrugged in that way of his, so supremely arrogant it should have left marks. "Either way, it is what it is."

Kendra opened her mouth to say something flippant, but something stopped her. Her breath caught in her throat, and she realized in the next second it was because he was holding himself so carefully. All of that leashed power, yes, but a certain glitter in those dark eyes made her wonder...

Something seemed to swell in her then. A kind of optimism, maybe. That same foolish hope.

If what you want is connection, intimacy, a voice in her said with a kind of calm practicality she associated with the great-aunt she'd hardly known, but who she felt she'd come to know over the months she'd spent living in that cottage, *you can't* fight *your way there. You can't demand vulnerability wearing battle armor and imagine it will come to you.*

And it was suddenly as if Kendra could see her whole life spinning around in front of her. As if it was contained in some kind of snow globe she held in her hands, already shaken hard. She'd wanted her father's attention. She'd wanted her brother's companionship. She'd wanted her mother's approval.

All of those were careful ways of saying she'd wanted their love.

That word with all its pain, its sharp edges and deep spikes.

She held her belly in her palms, and she looked at this man who had wrecked her in a thousand ways already. That night on the gazebo. That night in his office. That kiss right here in this villa the night before. All that plus sacred vows and the sea as witness, and Kendra couldn't help thinking that, like it or not, she'd shown him more of herself than she had ever shown anyone else.

On the one hand, she thought maybe that was a sad thing, because she'd spent so long trying to shape herself according to other people's molds. But on the other hand, there was something about Balthazar—something so overwhelming and intense that she felt she could show him anything at all. That there was nothing she could reveal or do that would ruin it. He wasn't her father or brother, who would cut her off so easily if she didn't perform as they wished.

Oh, he said he was.

But she was sitting across from him now in a wedding dress. She wore his rings on her finger. Best of all, she could see the expression on his face.

And somehow, some way, she was sure she knew better.

Kendra didn't know much about sex. But she knew that this man had asked her to strip herself naked and she'd done it. She knew that this man had touched her and changed her forever. He'd moved inside her, and her life had no longer made any sense.

She'd changed it completely after that night, months before she would discover she was pregnant.

Maybe it was sex itself that was that powerful. But she didn't think so. Kendra had expected sex to be fun and maybe a little silly, because that was the way people spoke of it. That was what the movies showed her, dressing it up with a suggestive soundtrack and lighting it all up so it looked like art.

When instead, it was a haunting thing. It came to her still, woke her in the night, and infused her dreams with a dark, erotic need.

Not for sex.

For him.

And if Balthazar could have that kind of power, that meant she could, too.

She smiled, letting it widen as his eyes narrowed. That felt like a power all its own.

"I can't possibly make this choice with so little information," she told him. She waved a hand at him. Regally. "I will require an audition, of course. Isn't that how these things go?"

And then she nearly had to bite her tongue off to keep herself from laughing at the thunderstruck look of sheer, masculine astonishment on his arrogant face.

"I beg your pardon?"

"Don't be coy, Balthazar." She let out a laugh, then. She couldn't help it. "It's so unbecoming in a brand-new husband."

He bared his teeth at her. "I'm not following you."

"You are. You're just pretending not to." Kendra inclined her head at him. "Strip, please."

CHAPTER TEN

BALTHAZAR HAD NO intention of doing anything of the kind.

He gave the orders. He did not follow them.

But Kendra sat before him, a vision in flowing white and her hair pinned up to catch the kiss of the sun. Her cheeks were flushed, her freckles a tempting spray across her nose and over her bared shoulders. It made him want to do nothing but eat her like a dessert far sweeter than Panagiota's baklava.

Kendra was sugar and flame and all his now. His wife.

His *wife*.

Balthazar had not expected that word, common as it was, to get to him like this. Its meaning rocked through him, almost too hot to bear. He blamed that age-old ceremony and the words the old priest had spoken over them. He blamed the rings he'd slid onto her finger, the platinum catching the light and the diamonds so bright they nearly dimmed the sun.

But he could blame anything and everything. What he didn't understand was how she seemed to grow more beautiful by the moment, especially when this should have been a festival arranged around his revenge, not…

whatever it was she imagined she was doing. He glared at her, but she only smiled, looking happy enough to wait forever for him to do as she'd demanded.

He could not imagine what made her imagine she had any power here.

Just as he could not imagine why he wasn't claiming his by right. And claiming her while he was at it.

"What's the matter?" she asked almost offhandedly, a gleam in those golden eyes of hers. "Don't tell me that the mighty Balthazar Skalas is afraid to do something here, on his own private island, that I did without blinking in the middle of a busy office? How funny. I thought you were meant to be the powerful one."

"Do you think goading me will work?"

She only smiled.

It turned that heat inside him...volcanic.

Before he knew it, Balthazar found himself rising from his seat. As he did, he took great pleasure in watching her eyes widen.

Not quite so sure of herself, then. No matter what she said.

And that made everything inside him run molten.

He made short work of his clothing. He shrugged out of the dark suit he'd worn for the ceremony, stripping down until he stood before her wholly naked. The sun poured all over him. The sea air was like a caress.

But best of all was that expression on Kendra's face.

It looked a great deal like *awe*.

He watched her flush. He watched that same giddy heat move its way down her neck. The dress she wore left her arms bare and he could see that same flush there, then goose bumps to match as she gazed up at him.

Balthazar felt everything shift. As if the world had spun about on its axis, then flattened him as it stopped still.

But he liked it.

Because he was the one standing naked before her, but he felt not a shred of supplication. No hint of weakness.

He had never felt more powerful in his life.

Had he called her names because he had sensed this, somehow? That a display of vulnerability led straight to something far more powerful? Had he wanted to diminish this very same light in her?

The notion sat uneasily in him. It pricked at him, reminding him of the reasons they were here, and married, and the revenge he had long ago vowed to rain down upon her father and the rest of her family...

But then he forgot it all. Because her eyes moved, almost convulsively, down over his chest. He was sure he could feel it like a touch over every ridge of his abdomen, every line of muscle. And she kept going until she found the hardest part of him, ready for her where he stood.

More than ready.

"If this is a proper audition," he managed to say, in a voice made harsh with need, "will you require the complete demonstration?"

When she lifted her gaze to his again, the wildfire he saw there made him want to roar like the beast he had always feared he was.

Though he didn't fear it now. Not when she looked at him as if the beast was precisely what she wanted.

God help him.

"Of course." Kendra's voice sounded husky now,

though no less of a taunt. "Or how could I possibly make an informed decision?"

"How indeed."

Balthazar crossed to her then, bent down, and lifted her into his arms.

He spared no thought for his plans. The promises he'd made himself about how he would handle this marriage, how he would treat the wife he'd never wanted, how all of this would become part of what was owed Thomas Connolly. It all seemed inconsequential when he held her like this, her flowing dress wrapping around them as he moved, like tendrils of that same dream he always seemed to have when she was near.

He knew it wasn't true. It could never be true. And yet it haunted him.

Balthazar had intended to make it through his wedding secure in the purity of his fury. Secure in his hatred, his bitterness.

But when he'd looked up from the altar at the edge of the cliff to see Kendra coming toward him—in flowing white as she made her way through the ruins of the old chapel, flowers in hands and sunshine all over her face—the same dream that had woken him up in the night too many times to count now had walloped him all over again.

Constantine had murmured something that sounded suspiciously like *steady*.

Balthazar had been forced to ignore it, because the only other option was acknowledging that he had made some sound, or some face that allowed his brother to think he was ever anything but steady. That had proclaimed his weakness to the whole of the watching Aegean Sea.

And also because his bride was coming to him in the island breeze.

And for the time it took her to walk to his side, he tortured himself with fantasies of her innocence. He had never cared about such things before. It was only her. It was only this woman he could not bear to imagine with anyone else. Only this woman who he could not seem to imagine with anyone but him.

It should not have felt like torture, but she disturbed his sleep. The fantasy that she could come to him like that, bearing his child and no hand upon her but his… The dream that she might truly be his, without any bitterness coloring their days…

He knew better. He'd known better. Nothing had changed when he'd put a ring on her finger. No blessings, however sanctified, could change who they were.

And yet.

He carried her into the villa and took her straight to his private suite. It was a Greek daydream of archways to welcome in the sea and the sky. Everything was white and blue and then, there in the middle, his wife with her hair like flame and eyes of the brightest gold.

Like a treasure.

By the time he set her down gently at the foot of the wide, low bed, Balthazar was so hard, so greedy for her, that he was surprised she hadn't already burst into a thousand pieces with the force of it.

"Let me tell you how I want you to audition," she said, though she had to reach out to him to keep her balance and better still, she sounded breathless.

He found he liked that more than he should have. That no matter what—no matter the truth of things and the dark reality he would return to as soon as he did something about the hunger that was tearing him apart—he got to her, too.

"I find I have a particular take on the role," he told her, his voice dark. The greed in him like its own, beating pulse. "Why don't you tell me how you feel about it once I'm done."

This time, when he set his mouth to hers, he had no intention of stopping.

He kissed her, deep and long. He got his hands in her hair, scattering the pins she'd used to secure it to the top of her head. It wasn't enough. No matter how he angled his head, no matter how close he held her, he wanted more.

He wanted everything.

Balthazar didn't understand this drive in him. This need. The dream and the greed, the *feelings* that battered at him, over and over, when he had been so certain for so long that he had none—

He felt as if something in him had broken. Yet as he held Kendra in his arms, he had the strangest notion that he had never been more whole.

That wasn't something he could take on board then, so Balthazar spun her around instead. He watched the deep, jarring breath she took as he worked to pull that dress up the length of her newly voluptuous body, then off.

Then she was before him in only a bra that wrapped around her back, holding her breasts as if on a shelf, and a skimpy pair of lace panties that made his mouth water. Her back was to him, so he indulged himself without worrying how his face might have been betraying him.

He put his mouth on the nape of her neck, then made

his way down the tempting line of her spine. He removed that bra as he went, his hands trailing behind his mouth to graze her sides but not quite making it around to the particular temptation of those perfect breasts, now much larger than before. Not yet.

He found the small of her back and hooked his fingers in the lace he found high on her hips, then tugged it down as he bared the whole of her to his view.

Crouched there behind her, he turned her around so he could inhale the scent of her arousal. Sugar and heat. Then he indulged himself completely by licking his way directly into all of her soft, wet heat.

She jolted against him, making a shocked sort of sound that only made the greed in him worse. He was sure there was another lightning strike. He felt it go through her, and him.

Beneath his tongue, she quivered, but that was not enough. Not nearly enough.

Could anything be enough? something in him asked.

He wrapped one arm around her hips and pulled one of her legs over the width of his shoulder, opening her to him. Completely.

And then he devoured her.

She was sweet and he was savage. And the noises she made as she arched back, offering herself to him, pulsed in him like light. Like heat.

Like that greed he thought might never leave him.

He felt her convulse against his mouth, her body jerking as she sobbed out something incoherent that he thought might be his name.

And even as she shook, Balthazar was moving. He hauled her up into his arms again and then tumbled the both of them down into the embrace of that wide mattress.

She was still shaking, still making sobbing sounds, and for a moment he lost himself all over again in the slide of her flesh against his.

Skin to skin, head to toe, at last.

Balthazar felt as if he'd never had a woman before. As if he never would again. As if she was the beginning and the end of everything—and all he wanted to do was get closer.

Everything was heat and delight, a dark and encompassing glory.

All he wanted was that everything, even if it killed them both.

He rolled to his back and pulled her astride him. He watched, breathing hard already, as she braced herself against his chest, looking something like intoxicated when he knew she hadn't touched a drop of alcohol.

For that matter, neither had he—and that meant the spinning in his head was entirely due to Kendra.

He waited for her to shift herself into better position, to sheath him on a downward stroke he could almost feel already, but she didn't.

It was as if she was trying to focus on him. Her hair tumbled around her shoulders like another lick of flame. Balthazar wanted to taste each individual freckle he could see in that sweet spray across her nose, and more across her shoulders.

She was busy breathing, so he held her for a moment. This woman who had come to him twice, both times at the bidding of men he despised. This woman he had taken from that cottage in France. This woman he had married and would call his wife, and who would be, no matter what else she was or became in time, the mother of his child.

For the first time, Balthazar let his gaze drop to her swollen belly, even more beautiful now that she wasn't wearing clothes to conceal it.

His heart beat at him in a new way, then. More intense. More wild and dangerous.

A different kind of greed.

Balthazar slid his hands over her belly. He heard her breath catch, and though he ordered himself not to do it, he looked up and caught her gaze.

And for a moment he forgot who they were.

For moment he was nothing more and nothing less than a man holding the pregnant belly of a woman, both of them fully aware that the child they'd made was just there, just inside.

She sat astride him and a different kind of electricity moved between them. He could feel it. It was part of him, part of her. Not a lightning strike from elsewhere, but made from this. From the heat they sparked between them, and had from the moment she'd stepped into that gazebo.

He was unsurprised and something like furious and deeply glad all at once when she moved her hands to cover his.

And for a long while there was only breath. There was only this.

Only *this*.

There was creation and revelation. Wonder and hope. Sex and need and a baby woven into the middle of that.

Woven so tightly it only then occurred to Balthazar that he'd been kidding himself all this time to imagine that this wasn't the very point of…everything.

This was life. Kendra had brought him *life*.

And in that moment, Balthazar could not bring himself to care what her reasons might have been. What her agenda was, then or now.

In that moment, he forgave her anything and everything, because there was this. The two of them, skin to skin. Their hands tangled up together to hold the new life they'd created.

The two of them breathing new life into him. Into her.

There was a *them*.

A family, something in him whispered.

It hit him like an explosion. A burst of near-incapacitating sensation.

It burned him alive.

"I need you," Balthazar gritted out. "Now."

And for a moment, he could have sworn that she was baffled. She blinked at him as if the words he used made no sense.

He shifted his hands to her hips, to grip her and move her into place. As he shifted her it seemed to dawn on her what she could do. She blew out a breath, then leaned forward, bracing herself on his chest.

Then he watched, somehow thrown and charmed at once, as she awkwardly tried to lift herself to take him within her.

And failed.

"Surely we are past this now," he said, his voice gravelly with need. He reached between them to grab his own length and guide himself to her softness. God help him, to her *heat*. It nearly undid him. "I have already married you, Kendra. What is the point of continuing to play these games?"

"What games?" she asked, panting a bit as she wriggled against him, as if attempting to slot him into place.

As if she'd never done something like this before.

But that was not possible.

"I do not require you to pretend to be innocent," he managed to say as she was poised there above him, her hair falling down to cocoon the both of them in all that fire.

His dreams could go to hell. This was better.

"Of course I'm not innocent," Kendra replied with a laugh, holding herself up with her thighs splayed wide. "You took care of that in New York."

"What does that mean?"

She blew out another breath as if gearing herself up. Then she took him into her body with a sudden thrust, sheathing him fully.

Finally.

Sensation punched through him. He almost lost his control, but wrenched back, barely.

Barely.

And she couldn't have meant what he thought she'd meant. He was half-mad with wanting her, that was all.

"What do you mean about New York, Kendra?" he demanded, ordering himself to wait. To hold on.

To hear her answer before he lost his head.

"Oh," Kendra said, sounding flustered and breathless. Sure enough, that telltale flush rolled down the length of her body, lighting her up as surely as a billboard in Times Square. "I thought you knew already. I was a virgin that night."

And then she began to move.

CHAPTER ELEVEN

HER BODY WAS different now. Kendra felt awkward in her clothes and sometimes couldn't figure out how to move the way she'd used to. There were new aches and strange pains in all kinds of surprising places, but this—

This was the same.

Better.

Balthazar was deep inside her again. At last. And this time, she was fully aware of every inch of his flesh and the fact that there was nothing between them.

This time, there was no pain.

There was only the reality of him, hard and thick, filling her so completely that it was almost too much. Almost. She had to keep moving so that the sensation grew, but never quite tipped over into pain again.

The more she moved, the better it felt.

And there was something about the look on his face as he gazed up at her. An intensity so close to a scowl that if she'd been doing anything else, she might have frozen in place—

But there wasn't a single part of her that wanted to stay still. Much less freeze.

Instead, she braced herself against him, leaned into all that glorious heat, and let her hips do as they wished.

She took him inside her, then lifted herself away. She was fully aware of the moment he took over that rhythm, moving her instead of letting her rock herself against him, and that was better.

Everything he did was better.

Sitting up like this, different sensations buffeted her with every thrust. Her breasts bounced gently. There was a stretch in her thighs that seemed to arrow straight to the place they were joined. And that new belly of hers changed how she fit against him.

Or maybe it was as simple as the position. How would she know?

Balthazar muttered something she didn't understand, a rough scrape of Greek. Then he tugged her lower so he could take one of her nipples deep into his mouth.

And just like that, shockingly *quickly*, Kendra shattered all over again.

But he didn't stop. He took his time with her oversensitive breasts and she kept falling apart. Again and again.

He switched his attention from one breast to the other, his hand taking over when his mouth abandoned the job. Back and forth, back and forth, and all the while he maintained that steady, even pounding rhythm deep inside her.

At first Kendra counted the times he made her dissolve.

Three times. Four.

Then she lost count. There were too many flames, setting her alight, making her scream. Making her forget there was anything but this.

But him.

Then Balthazar was rolling her over and stretching her out below him as he propped himself up on his arms. And suddenly he was even deeper, so much a part of her that she thought she could die like this, connected in ways she had never known were possible—

He was saying Greek words as he gazed down at her, as hot as his mouth against her pulse. And he lost that steady rhythm, pounding into her as he took her to that edge once more.

And this time when she bucked against him, fragments of her flying all around and shattering so completely she was sure she would never put herself back together again, he came with her.

For a long, long while, Kendra thought maybe they had died, after all. There was no other explanation for how she felt, floating and perfect and beautiful. Or the rawness of her despair when he moved, withdrawing from her body and rolling over to his back.

It took her some time to realize that her heart was still beating like a drum, but her breath was starting to even out.

And that he had moved to sit with his back to her, there on the edge of the wide bed.

Kendra thought she ought to do something about that, but found when she tried that she lacked the strength. Her whole body appeared to be made of wet clay.

"I will need you to explain yourself," Balthazar said, his voice grim. "Now."

It was a lot like a bucket of ice water in the face, if she was honest.

But even that felt like a pageant of sensation, mixed in with all the rest, so all Kendra did was turn over to her side. She propped herself up on her elbow and wished, with a passionate sort of fervency that might have alarmed her in any other circumstances, that she dared reach out and trace her fingers over the proud line of his strong back.

She hated that she did not dare. That she had married him, was having his baby, and had discovered that they could do these marvelous things to each other... but she did not quite dare a touch.

But he had married her. He had promised her many things at that altar above the sea, but he had not told her it would be easy. "What must I explain?"

Balthazar did not look at her, and still she could sense his scowl. She could feel it. He wasn't the thundercloud, Kendra realized. He was the storm.

And what did it say about her that she wanted nothing more than to dance in it?

She saw him tense. "You came to my office. Your bargaining chip was your body. You stripped down immediately... There's no possible way you could have been innocent that night. None."

"If you say so."

He turned then, twisting around so that she could see a kind of anguish in his face. And worse, a different, searing condemnation in his thunderclap gaze. "You had already tried the game once before, in that gazebo. We both knew the truth of it."

"In the gazebo?" Kendra's heart beat as if she ought to be upset by this, but she was still having trouble following what was happening. How could he be so grim and growly when she wanted nothing more than to start all over again? "I had no idea you were there. I was trying to take a breather in the middle of one of my parents' tedious parties, that was all. And then you were there and your mouth was on me, and I didn't know what to do."

"No. *No.* This is impossible."

A laugh escaped before she could stop it. "Would you prefer that I was the tramp you've always thought I was?"

But then something in her turned over. Because she recognized the expression that moved over his face. He did wish that.

And in the next moment, she understood.

"I thought this was simply how you treat women," she breathed.

Suddenly Kendra felt exposed. Ugly. She sat up and looked around in a bit of a panic for something to cover herself with, but there was only the frothy heap of her wedding gown at the foot of the bed. She pulled it to her, holding it against her like a shield.

Waiting, she knew, for him to say something. To deny it.

But he didn't.

"This isn't how you treat *most women*, is it?" she asked softly, though she wanted to scream. "This is how you treat me. It's not that you think women are whores. It's that you think *I* am. That I always have been."

"Why would your father or your brother send me a virgin sacrifice?" Balthazar thundered. "Don't they know—"

But he cut himself off. Kendra pulled the dress tighter against her chest.

"And, of course, a whore deserves to be stripped naked and humiliated," she said quietly, because she

understood too many things now. His fury. His cold-
ness. He'd used the word—maybe it was her fault for
thinking he didn't mean it. Maybe if she'd had more experience, she would have. "Dispatched by her equally
repellent family to do their calculated work, she deserves zero consideration. A quick tumble on a desktop
and nothing but cruel words. What I don't understand
is why, if that is what you think of me, you didn't
wrap your entire body in latex to avoid the situation
we find ourselves in now. To say nothing of other…
contaminants."

"I lost my head," he growled at her. "I could not understand why I kept imagining your innocence when
it was so plainly long gone. Now I know."

And she could have sworn that sounded like…grief.

"Which is it, husband?" she asked. "Are you angry
that I'm not as free with my favors as you thought I
was? Are you angry that I didn't tell you when I think
we both know you wouldn't have believed me? Or is
it the uncomfortable notion that if I'm not who you
thought I was…neither are you?"

"Is this the true game?" he demanded. "Is this what
you've wanted all along, Kendra? To tie me in knots,
crowd my head, make me into a madman? What does
your father think will be gained by this kind of deception?"

She blinked at that, still holding the dress close. "My
father? What does my father have to do with this?"

"Did he not send you to me in the first place?"

"He didn't send me to the gazebo. He did send me
to New York. What he did not do, ever, was even so
much as hint that he was interested in whether or not
I was in possession of my virginity."

The very idea of discussing virginity with her father made her stomach turn.

Balthazar looked as if he might reach for her then, and Kendra wanted that so much she could feel moisture collect in the corners of her eyes.

But instead he pushed himself off the bed and moved across the bedroom. He stopped in one of the grand archways that opened over a graceful terrace and stood there, staring out toward the sea.

The sun poured in, making him seem like some kind of stone carving, polished to shine. Not a man at all.

Because he was no longer looking at her, she indulged herself and pressed the heel of her hand against the place where her heart beat so hard it hurt.

"You should have told me," he said a long while later, his voice thick. Dark.

"What would have been the point?" she asked simply.

Even from across the room, she could hear the way he drew in a breath at that, and it made her heart hurt even more.

Kendra gathered the dress around her, like a security blanket. She remembered how she'd felt earlier, walking to him where he stood on the edge of that cliff.

As if together they might fly off into all that blue and stay there, as limitless as the horizon.

"Balthazar," she said softly now. "What if we made a different kind of bargain altogether?"

The hand he'd propped up against the side of the open arch clenched into a fist.

Kendra decided to take that as encouragement. Or as a sign, anyway, that she was on the right track. Since he could so easily have shot her down already.

She slid one hand to her belly. She thought about her father and brother, even her mother, and the lives they'd all chosen. Then she thought about Great-Aunt Rosemary, who had walked away from that very same life and done as she pleased.

We can make our lives whatever we wish them to be, her great-aunt had written in loopy cursive on the first page of one of the journals she'd left for Kendra to read.

Kendra could start right now.

"What if we removed everybody else from the table?" she asked softly. "What if all we thought about was you and me and our child? You're going to be a father, Balthazar. I'm going to be a mother. We'll both be the parents of this baby, and that means something. To the baby, I have to think it will mean the world."

The words were pouring from her mouth, though she couldn't have said where they were coming from. They seem to be connected to the blood that pumped through her veins. The soft, hot core of her that was already hungry for him again. The heaviness in her breasts. And the rounded belly he had caressed so gently, making her feel like a fertility goddess. More beautiful than she'd ever been.

She had taken so few chances in her life. She had dared so little—except when it came to him.

But she thought of the crowns they'd worn today and the rings on their hands. She thought of that look of wonder on his face when he'd gazed up at her, both of them holding tight to the future they'd made.

It had to mean something. She would *make it* mean something.

She took a breath. "What if we decided, you and me, to be a family?"

He turned back to her then, though he didn't come closer. He stood there with the light all around him and his gaze bleak.

Kendra fought off a shiver.

"Families like yours?" he asked with a certain, quiet menace. "An overly medicated mother. A morally corrupt father, who would prostitute his virgin daughter to protect his son from the consequences of his own deceitful actions. A man who knows no boundaries, who respects no limitations, who always and ever does only what pleases. What an enticing prospect."

Kendra would have listed any number of reasons she was not thrilled with her family at the moment, but she didn't like him doing it. "Families are complicated. Yours certainly is—you told me so yourself."

He moved toward her then, something terrible on his face.

It didn't make him any less beautiful.

"And would you like to know *why* my family is as complicated as it is?" he asked, his voice stark.

Kendra admitted to herself that in that moment, she really didn't.

"When my mother came back from her stay in her private hospital, she tried to make amends. With my brother and me, it was easy. We loved her." Balthazar's eyes had gone cold. "With my father, on the other hand, she had much less success."

"The poor woman," Kendra breathed.

"My father hated my mother for her weakness," Balthazar told her. "Whether that was just or not is beside the point. It happened. After a while, I found myself following suit." Kendra let out a ragged sort of sound, but that only made his mouth curve into something grim. "He beat me into his image, Kendra. Constantine was permitted his little rebellions but I never was. It was easy to take everything my father said as gospel. My mother was weak. She deserved no loyalty from my father. He believed this and so did I. He acted it out and so did I. *I believed it*."

"Beliefs do not live in your bones, they live in your head and your heart," Kendra threw right back at him. "They're not facts, Balthazar. They're feelings. You can change them. All you have to do is want to."

"If only it were that simple."

"What in life is simple?" She found herself moving to her knees, still clasping the wedding gown before her, like an offering now. "Do you think that I wanted to find myself pregnant with the child of a man who made it clear he hated me?"

"Yes," he said, the simple syllable cutting deep into her. "Until today I assumed that was exactly what you wanted."

Kendra was terrified she might break down into tears. And she couldn't bear it. She crawled over to the edge of the bed and stood, pulling the dress up and over her head once more.

And the irony wasn't lost on her that she stood there, wedded and bedded and discarded at dizzying speed. Barefoot and pregnant. A collection of worst nightmares, really.

She almost thought she should laugh at the absurdity. But the laughter wouldn't quite come.

"You really thought I got pregnant on purpose?"

The look on his face made her hug herself. "My father believed in consequences," Balthazar told her in that same grim tone. "When I was a small boy, he beat me himself. As I grew older and bigger, he used other means of punishment. Sometimes he would beat my brother for my infractions. Other times, he would do things he knew hurt my mother. In time, he promised me, I would stop caring about either, and he was right."

"He sounds like a broken, horrible man, and what does that have to do with us? Or this baby?"

"He raised me to care about the business alone, as he did," Balthazar continued, as if he had no choice. As if these things were being dragged out of him whether he liked it or not. "And I thought it made sense that he should have his other women if he wished, because he was the one who worked so hard to build the Skalas empire. What did my mother do but waft around the house, haggard and pathetic?"

His voice was hard, like bullets, but somehow Kendra thought he was aiming the gun at himself.

"A friend of his started to spend more time with the family," Balthazar continued, a stark, ferocious thing on his face. He stood there, much too still, and though all Kendra wanted to do was go to him, she knew better. She knew he wouldn't allow it. "He flattered my father. He took an interest in what Constantine and I were doing. And then, because he could, he started an affair with my mother. Right under my father's nose."

"But your father was already having his own affairs, wasn't he?"

Balthazar shrugged. "He was not a rational man when it came to the things he considered his. When my father discovered this affair, he confronted the two of them. He made my brother and me witness it, because he said it affected the family. I was sixteen."

"Balthazar..." she whispered.

"My mother was regretful, but she said they were in love. That he was kind to her, which was more than my father had been. That she would sign whatever he liked if he let her go." His grim expression did not alter in the slightest. "But his friend only laughed. He called my mother names and told my father it was no more than he deserved for some or other business deal. He left my mother sobbing on the floor."

"You shouldn't have seen that," Kendra said fiercely. "Your father should have protected you from that."

"He was too busy throwing my mother out," Balthazar said icily. "And when she went, she fell apart."

He ran a hand over his face, then. Maybe she only thought she saw it shake.

"You don't have to tell me the rest of this," she said, even as she racked her brain to remember what had become of his mother. Why did she think it was something sad?

"But I do," he replied. He started toward her then, slow and deliberate. "My mother descended into a squalid little life of men who took advantage of her. She turned to drink. Then to drugs. One night she took too much and slipped into a coma. She has never awoken. She lies there still, slowly wasting away, trapped in her despair."

Kendra's pulse rocketed around inside her. Her stomach twisted. But still he drew closer in that same, terrible way. She wanted to run, but she wanted to stay where she was even more. As if she was proving something.

"My brother and I vowed that we would take our revenge on the man who targeted her," Balthazar said, the ring of something heavy in his voice. And stamped all over his face. If she didn't know better, knowing this man as she did, she might have imagined it was guilt. "No matter how long it took. No matter what it entailed."

"Do you mean your father?"

His smile was thin. "My father did not help, I grant you. But it was not he who pushed my mother over the side of that cliff. It was not he who used her, then discarded her, and laughed about what he'd done."

"You said he was unkind to her."

"He was unkind," Balthazar snapped. "Had she never met this friend of his, she would have survived it like the rest of us."

"I don't blame you for hating him," Kendra said softly.

Balthazar's eyes blazed. He stopped moving, though he was still more than an arm's length away from her.

"I am delighted to hear you say that, Kendra," he said. "Because the man I am speaking of is your father."

It was like the world dimmed, or she slid off the side of it. She stared back at him, convinced her ears were ringing. Convinced her heart had stopped. Convinced she must have misheard him.

But none of those things were true.

"Your father," he said again, so there could be no mistake, "drove my mother to her current state. And has never looked back. He prefers to dance around me in business situations as if I don't know what he did. What he is."

"But…. But you…"

"I assumed you were nothing but another knife he thought to plunge in the side of my family," Balthazar said. "Some men deal with their guilt in extravagant ways. Of course he sent you to me. I have no doubt his greatest hope was that history would repeat itself."

"All along," Kendra whispered. "All along you've…" She felt as if she might collapse, but she didn't. "You don't just hate me, do you, Balthazar? You want to use me to hurt him. You didn't take your revenge—you made me become it."

He bared his teeth as if the pain was too great. As if the villa they stood in was nothing but ash and ruins at their feet.

But she couldn't tell if he wanted it that way, and it broke her heart.

"And I might have dreamed of your innocence, Kendra," he managed to grit out, turned once again to a storm. She could feel the rain on her face. She could hear the thunder in his voice. "I might have imagined what it would be like if you are not as tarnished as the people you come from. But that is not who we are. And this marriage is nothing more than a weapon I will use to cut down a monster."

"Balthazar…" she whispered, agonized. "You can't mean that. You can't."

His mouth was a merciless lash. "You should have run when you had a chance, Kendra. I regret that you are not the woman I thought you were. But you will pay all the same."

And then he left her there, in her wedding gown with his scent all over her like a curse, to let her tears fall at last.

Alone.

CHAPTER TWELVE

BALTHAZAR MEANT TO leave the island entirely.

He stormed from the bedchamber and pulled on the first clothing he could find in the attached dressing room. He would go to Athens, he decided. He would do what he had always done and lose himself in work. In the business. In the things that made him who he was and more, who he wished to remain.

The things that mattered, he thought.

And thinking of what mattered, perhaps heading back to New York made even more sense. He headed for the office suite he kept in the villa, finding all of his devices charged and ready for him, but he didn't pick up his mobile. He didn't give the order to have the helicopter readied for the flight to the mainland. Instead, he found himself staring at the desk before him, seeing nothing.

Nothing but the choices that had brought him here.

And wrapped around everything, shot through it all, he saw Kendra's face. Her beautiful face and her lovely eyes filled with tears.

Tears he had put there, Balthazar knew.

He saw the way she'd stared at him, clutching that dress to her chest as if he was nothing more than a rampaging beast. A soulless monster, as he'd often been accused.

As if he'd finally become his father.

All the way through, at last.

Balthazar pushed away from the desk, moving without thought, almost as if he was trying to get away from that realization when it should have been cause for celebration. He should have been thrilled that he'd finally achieved what had long been the goal of his entire existence on this earth.

Demetrius Skalas had prided himself on his single-minded, emotionless pursuit of the bottom line. He had eradicated weakness, he had claimed. He felt nothing and took pride in it. He acted only in the interests of the company. Even the succession of beautiful women he sported on his arm, each one a blow to his despised wife, Demetrius claimed elevated his profile in the eyes of the world—and more importantly, in the eyes of the other titans of industry he considered his peers. All of whom preferred to do business with men they admired.

They had all admired Demetrius.

Balthazar had taken his beatings as a child, and had come to believe that his father was right—they made him stronger. And as he grew, he had dedicated himself, in word and deed, to following his father's example. To locating and removing every hint of weakness he could find.

In place of any stray emotions, he had tended his thirst for revenge.

And in place of the pesky feelings that plagued other men, he had plotted the downfall of Thomas Connolly and his pathetic son.

Then she had come along and turned everything on its ear.

He found himself outside, the island drenched in the beauty of the setting sun, though all he saw was the past.

A past that was threaded through with the same driving goal, always. Balthazar had told himself that he was giving Tommy Connolly rope to hang himself with while, over the course of years, he'd sat back and watched his enemy's son steal from him. In the months since Kendra had given herself to him in New York, he had continued to wait.

Now, standing outside as the breeze picked up as the sun made its lazy descent, he had to question that choice.

He had told himself it was because he was waiting. To see if Kendra was with child. To see if it was time to flip the script on his revenge and approach it a different way—one that would involve his in-laws. Surely that required a different tack, he'd assured himself. He'd felt perfectly prepared to handle whatever came of Kendra's potential pregnancy. First and foremost, he'd been thinking of the child's legitimacy and the wedding he'd never imagined for himself.

What he hadn't thought to reckon with were emotions.

Balthazar had congratulated himself on feeling nothing for Kendra—because surely, his abiding, distracting hunger for her didn't count. Surely his obsession with her, with what she was doing and where she was going and every expression that crossed her pretty face, was about that same physical hunger.

It was nothing more, he'd told himself, time and again. Nothing but sex, lust and need.

He might not have liked those things in him, making him as basic as any other man, but they were understandable.

What he had not been prepared for was her pregnancy. Not the fact of it, which he'd seen coming or he wouldn't have tracked her. But that wave of emotion that had struck him earlier. It had felt something like sacred when, together, they had held their hands over her belly and the life that grew within.

How could he possibly have prepared for that?

But even as he asked himself that question, he knew that there was another, more pointed query he needed to make. Just as he knew everything in him wanted to avoid it.

He walked until he reached the edge of one of the cliffs, then stood there, bracing himself. His hands were in fists at his side while the sun seemed to pause in its fall toward the sea to hit him full in the face.

A bit too much like clarity for his tastes.

And all he could see was the golden shimmer of Kendra's eyes, as if she was here before him, watching him.

Waiting for him, something in him whispered.

"Beliefs do not live in your bones, they live in your head and your heart," she had told him. *"You can change your feelings, Balthazar. All you have to do is* want *to."*

He had never wanted to do anything of the kind. He had never wanted to feel a thing.

And now he felt ravaged by these *feelings*.

Enemies he could fight. He was good at that. It only took waiting, watching, and then striking their weaknesses when they presented themselves.

But how could he fight this?

Kendra had used the word *family*. That damned word.

Worse, she had suggested that the two of them could make their own, and he had seen the hope in her gaze when she'd said it.

God help him, but he had no defense against *hope*.

He wanted to reject it the way he had rejected her. He wanted to already be far away from here, winging his way back to the only life he knew.

But he couldn't make himself turn around. He couldn't make himself leave.

Because her hope was infectious.

And if he accepted that, he accepted that he was far, far weaker than he'd ever imagined.

Because he'd dreamed all of this, hadn't he? Balthazar had tortured himself, not simply with fantasies of availing himself of her beautiful body and slaking that hunger for her that had haunted him across the years. But more, he'd dreamed of her innocence. And not because he had ever put any great stock in virginity, as it was simply one more thing men liked to use for barter, whether women wished it or not.

But because innocence felt like a shortcut to a different life.

He thought of his poor mother, wrecked so many years ago. Long before she'd been tossed out by his father, she'd been left to fend for herself while Demetrius had cheated on her. After they'd divorced, Demetrius had repeated his behavior with any number of subsequent wives—but none of *them* could claim they hadn't known what they were getting into.

His first wife, the mother of his sons, had been

blindsided. And what had been the sin that Demetrius had believed *deserved* the way he'd responded? Balthazar had stopped asking himself that when he was still a boy.

But he knew the answer now.

His mother had felt far too much and Demetrius had despised her for it.

Balthazar had learned to do the same.

He looked down at his hands, uncurling his fingers so he could see the flat of his palms.

He could still feel the warmth of Kendra's belly, the life she carried within. And then, finally, asked himself the question he'd been avoiding since the night he'd realized that he'd had sex with Kendra Connolly without using any protection.

Did he truly wish to do to his child what his father had done to him?

He thought about taking his own hands, the ones he gazed at there on that cliffside, and raising them against his own child. He thought of carrying out this second phase of his revenge as he'd planned when the child was no more than a possibility instead of a fact, taking it to its logical extreme.

Did he plan to make *his baby* hate its mother?

Was that who he was?

His heart kicked at him, too hard and too loud. And Balthazar tried to tell himself that there was no other way. That he had committed himself to this path and that was the end of it. But the dreams he'd had told him differently.

So had Kendra.

And if Balthazar could decide to be any man he

chose, there was only one real question left. Would he choose to be this one?

Because suddenly, as the sun painted the sky the bright, brilliant shades of gold that reminded him only of Kendra, he looked back and saw the life he'd been living in a very different light than he would have if he'd considered it six months ago.

He had become his father after all. Cold. Unfeeling. Half monster, half machine, and proud of the worst parts of both. Dedicated entirely to a business that already had made him more money than he could ever spend in his own lifetime. Or ten successive lifetimes.

As if that mattered.

It seemed to him here, now, that it was stark. Empty.

A lifeless existence.

Until Kendra had come in and infused the prison he hadn't even realized he lived in with all of her bright color.

How could he sentence his child to that same cell?

And it took him a moment to realize that what walloped him then was grief.

For the mother he had lost when he was young, then had pushed away when she returned because he'd thought that might please his father. Only accepting the guilt and shame he'd felt over her treatment when it was too late for her. No amount of revenge in her name was ever going to change the fact that he was the one who had abandoned her.

And another kind of grief seized him, because while he had seen his father for who he was, Balthazar had always imagined himself immune. He'd been expected to be immune. He'd known Demetrius was a cruel man, certainly. A viciously cold one. A father who could not love and refused to allow such soft sentiments in anyone near him. A man who had raised two sons with enough violence that they felt that they dared not attempt it themselves.

Balthazar could do the same, of course. That had been his plan.

But for the first time he understood, not only how much damage had been done to him, but what he had lost.

How much he had lost.

That he had such darkness in him made him despair of himself. But the greater punch of grief was that, had it not been for Kendra and this baby he would have sworn he did not want, he might never have seen the truth about himself so clearly.

If it weren't for Kendra, he would never have known.

He tried to fight it, but it was no use. Night was coming, bringing with it the heartless stars, each and every one of which seemed to punch their way inside of him.

And he could call it what he liked.

But Balthazar understood that the emotion he'd been avoiding the whole of his life had come for him, at last.

And it was no mystery to him why his father had abhorred them so. Emotions were messy. They tore through him now, storm after storm, never ceasing and always changing, making a mockery of the anger he tried to throw up as a shield.

He took it, one hurricane after the next turning him inside out and then slapping him back together as if he could ever be the same.

When he knew better. Because he'd seen colors now, and there was no way to go back from that. There was no way to make himself willfully blind.

Even if he had tried, he knew that he didn't have it in him to sentence his child to that same stark and lifeless fate.

He was Balthazar Skalas. He surrendered to no man.

Lucky for him, then, that the only person on earth he intended to surrender to was a woman. His wife.

Assuming she would have him now that she knew the truth about her family and his, and the great, ugly weight of the revenge he'd tried so hard to take out on her.

He turned, surprised to find that he'd made his way to the altar where he had married her a lifetime ago on this very same, endless day. The ruins of the old chapel gleamed in the starlight and for moment, when he saw movement, he thought it was an apparition.

Or better still, that dream of his, come to comfort him once more.

But as she moved closer, he saw that it really was Kendra.

His heart skipped a beat.

She still wore her wedding gown, that flowing, frothy gown that gleamed an unearthly white in the starlight. And she looked wilder than she had this morning, as if the daylight had required compliance, but here in the dark, there was only her.

Her hair was a tousled flame, and he longed to run his hands through it all over again. He could see traces of the tears she'd cried, there on her cheeks as she drew closer, but she was not weeping now. If anything, she looked determined.

His own little warrior, who could not stop fighting, no matter what.

Balthazar had a vision of her in his New York office so long ago and felt his heart lurch all over again. In those moments before she'd seen him she'd stood at the window, staring out at the glittering sprawl of Manhattan. Her face had been so soft, suffused with that sweet heat that had entranced him, even then.

He had told himself he was unmoved, but that had been a lie.

And he'd waited longer than he should have, drinking her in. Something he would have denied to the death if she'd called him on it.

Something he couldn't have admitted then, especially to himself.

Kendra stopped before him, the breeze making her seem half ghost, though he knew better. She was made of warmth and sunlight, even in the dark.

Maybe especially in the dark.

"I was sure that you would be halfway to New York by now," she said.

There was a roaring thing in him, but he ignored it. "I intended to be."

"And yet here you are."

"Here I am," he agreed.

And it felt…portentous. Huge. The roaring in him and that white gown in the breeze and the stars all around them, as if they knew.

Her gaze searched his. Balthazar wished that he could understand what he saw there. And he wished even more that he could find the words to tell her what had happened to him. *In* him. What she'd done to him.

But it all seemed inadequate when there was Kendra, staring up at him with that same openness as if he had not hurt her. Again and again.

"You should run from me, little one," he said then. "Screaming, and in the opposite direction."

"What would be the point of that?" she asked. Her lips curved. "This is a very small island. And I have no interest in drowning myself."

He frowned at that, and that hint of levity when he wished to take responsibility, at last, for who and what he had become—

Kendra swayed closer to him, placing her hands on his chest.

And Balthazar…was unarmed.

He stared down at her hands, one of them bedecked in the rings he'd put there this morning. As he did, he became vaguely aware that he'd thrown on trousers and a haphazardly buttoned shirt, so that both of them were in white.

As if that made up for anything.

But it was her touch that astonished him. That would have broken him, he thought, had there been anything in him left to break.

"I told you that I'm your enemy," he said then, his voice severe. "Since the moment I knew who you were, I have thought of nothing but crushing you, Kendra. You must know this."

"I know it." And though her lips were still curved, there was a certain steel in those golden eyes of hers. "But you are also my husband. And the father of my child. And I do not choose to be crushed, Balthazar."

"Is it your choice?" he asked, though even as he did, he found himself moving to trap her hands there against his chest. To hold her, despite himself.

When he knew he should not tempt himself. That he did not deserve it. Or her.

"I want to be outraged, but I'm not," she told him, almost solemnly. "I want to defend my father's behavior, but I can't. I tried to come up with excuses, but I don't have any. The truth of the matter is that I'm not surprised to hear what he did to your mother. To you. Disappointed, maybe. But not, I'm afraid, surprised."

"Do not forgive me, Kendra," Balthazar gritted out. "Not so easily. You have no idea the kind of darkness that lives in me."

"But I do know it," she replied, to his astonishment. And that gaze of hers was steady on him, the sun to the earth. "I know your darkness, Balthazar. I know your fury, your retaliation. I know your absence and I know your touch. And I can tell you, with every part of my soul, that there is nothing you can do that would make me abandon you. Or I would already be swimming for the mainland."

All the broken parts of him seemed to vibrate with the same ferocity, then. And still all he could see was her gaze, as if the sun had not yet set. As if she lit up the world.

She did it effortlessly.

"I don't know how to do anything but plot revenge," he threw at her. "I could stand here and tell you all the things I think I feel, but how would I know? Feelings were my first enemy and I vanquished them long ago. You deserve more than a broken man."

"I deserve you," she countered. Then she leaned in, to underscore the intensity on her face. "Because you have haunted me, Balthazar, since the moment I looked up and found you in that gazebo. My brother and my father might have had their own reasons for sending me to see you in New York, but I didn't have to go. I wanted to. I wanted to see you. And let's be very clear. I wanted to strip for you. I wanted your touch. I wanted everything that's happened between us, because if I hadn't, I could have walked away at any time."

He wanted to believe that. Which was why he couldn't. "I kidnapped you, Kendra. You can't hand-wave that away."

"I'm not the hapless maiden sent off to sacrifice herself to the village dragon, despite appearances," Kendra said, with laughter in her voice. Actual laughter. "I could have ducked away from you when we went to your doctor in Athens. Failing that, Panagiota might have restricted access to the internet here but if I'd really, truly wanted to get online I could have found a way. I didn't want to."

"Kendra…" He managed to breathe. Barely. "Kendra, I can't…"

The stars were upon them and around them, the sea whispered their names, and Balthazar felt caught somewhere between that light from up above and all the sunlight in her gaze. As if all that brightness could make of him a better man.

"I want to promise you that I will change," he told her, though his heart hurt and he wanted things he could hardly identify. But that wanting never eased, not where she was concerned. Maybe it never would. "But I can only hope I will. I want to promise you the world, the stars above us now and the ground beneath our feet. I want to promise you that I will learn to be the kind of man who can love, and hope, and raise our child with those things instead of the back of my hand or the sting in my words. I have done a great many things in this life, Kendra. I was given a fortune and

I made five more. I have feared no man I've ever met. I have faced every challenge set to me. All this, yet I have never loved. I…"

He wasn't sure he could continue. But her eyes had gone bright again, gleaming with emotion.

All that emotion, like color, changing the world around them.

"Do you want to love, Balthazar?" She pulled in a ragged breath. "Do you want to love me?"

"I do," he said, without pausing to consider it. Without worrying over the angles, the ramifications. And it all made sense then. All his broken pieces, all those feelings. The cacophony of the things that howled in him, louder by the second. And the fact that she was there in the middle of it all. The reason for everything. "I do."

And when she smiled, it was like daybreak. But better, because it was all his.

"Then don't worry," she told him. "Concentrate on what you're good at."

He brought her hands to his mouth and placed a kiss there. "If you mean passion, I do not think that will be a problem."

Her smile widened. "I believe you. But I don't mean passion. That's almost assured, I would think. No, Balthazar. I mean revenge."

"I will renounce it," he told her at once.

"But I don't want you to."

Kendra moved even closer, tipping her face back, so it was as if the whole world was her gaze. The press of her round belly into his body. Her hands he held in his.

Here on this altar where he had made her his wife.

"I want you to take your revenge, Balthazar," Kendra told him, solemn and sure. "The most perfect way possible. I want you to let me love you. I want you to love me in return. I want us to raise this child with joy."

"Joy," he repeated, like vows etched in stone.

"Not the way we were raised, always made to feel that we were never enough." She shook her head and her tears spilled over, but she was smiling. God help him, but he could watch that smile forever. He intended to do just that. "I want us to live life, big and bright and happy."

"Then that is what we will do," Balthazar promised her. "No matter what."

"That will be the ultimate revenge," Kendra said as she melted against him. "A life well lived, together."

And as he swept her up into his arms, the stars shone down, like a blessing. A promise.

Their true vows had finally been spoken.

And their real life began.

CHAPTER THIRTEEN

REVENGE CERTAINLY WAS SWEET, Kendra thought ten years later.

She sat in her favorite spot on the cozy sofa in Great-Aunt Rosemary's cottage in France. Outside it was a golden, glorious summer, which reminded her of her first months here. She smiled, remembering it. Pregnant without knowing it and so focused on choosing a new path in life. Treating strangers she waited on with kindness when she hardly knew how to offer the same to herself.

All without the slightest bit of knowledge of how profoundly her life was about to change, like it or not.

"I wish I'd known you better," she murmured to the room at large.

But she would have to settle for knowing herself. And she thought her prickly great-aunt would have approved.

Outside, she could hear the approach of excited voices, and smiled even wider. She could pick them all out from each other, each voice like a new song in her heart. Serious, delightfully odd Irene, who had made Kendra a mother and made her laugh, daily. She was almost a decade old now, when Kendra could still remember the shock and miracle of her arrival. She had been born straight into her father's hands, and as if it were yesterday, Kendra recalled gazing at Balthazar over Irene's tiny, fragile head, the wonder almost too bright to bear.

It was still that bright.

"If we're going to have a family," Balthazar had said when Irene was still new, "then we might as well do it right."

"Is that a proclamation?" Kendra had asked, rolling her eyes at him, so dramatically she thought half of Athens must have seen.

But Balthazar only smiled.

Baz had been born in the following year, and Kendra grinned as she heard her oldest son shouting outside. Never one to pay attention to his older sister's proclamations, far too much like his father, and currently making noise simply because he could.

Because unlike his father, Baz would not be beaten. He would not be cut into pieces and shoved into a cold, iron box.

Kendra stood from the sofa and went to the door, throwing it open so she could see her family come toward her across the fields. The two oldest ones bickering, as they did. And behind them, the most beautiful man she'd ever seen or ever would, holding the youngest two. One in each arm. Five-year-old Kassandra, all stubborn cheeks and a pouty lip. And the sunny, giggly baby, Thaddeus, who was eighteen months old and had the rest of them—and the world—wrapped around his chubby little fingers.

They could have been a painting, Kendra thought.

Walking across golden fields studded with lavender and sunflowers, and the Alps in the distance.

But this was the life that she and Balthazar had made, and it was far better than any painting. It was complicated. Sometimes painful. And most of all, theirs.

They had taught each other how to love, and while there was no part of that Kendra did not find rewarding, that didn't mean it hadn't hurt along the way.

"I love you," he had said the morning after their fateful wedding day, scowling at her as if the words caused him pain.

"I love you too," she had replied, frowning right back at him. "And note that I didn't say it like there was a gun in my back."

Slowly but surely, they learned.

They had stayed on the island for the rest of Kendra's pregnancy, because neither one of them wished to share their fledgling happiness with the world.

The world could wait. And it did.

"I love you," he had said, over and over, every single day, so that by the time Irene was born, there was no more scowling.

And it only got better from there.

Though soon, too soon, it was time to let the world in again.

It had not always been easy.

Kendra had seen her father and brother only once. She and Balthazar had gone back to Connecticut, where it had all begun. There had been one unpleasant conversation, after which Kendra washed her hands of them both.

Balthazar had pressed charges against Tommy. Her

father had not been ruined financially, but the ensuing scandal had made him persona non grata in all the places that meant anything to him.

They both found there was a solace in that. Kendra accompanied Balthazar to the long-term care facility where his mother lived out her days, and sat with him as he told her that it was done. At long last, it was done.

And she felt certain that if the other woman could have forgiven her son, she would have.

But the true surprise was when Emily Cabot Connelly had put down her Valium, contacted her attorneys, and divorced her husband. As part of her settlement she claimed, among a great many other things, that gracious old house on its own point on Long Island Sound that she had brought to her marriage in the first place.

The first thing she did was invite her daughter and grandchildren to visit her there.

And it made Kendra glad that she and her mother had found a way to build bridges in these last ten years. They might not always understand each other, but they tried. No matter what, they tried.

In the end, Kendra thought as she stood in the doorway of her cottage and watched the love of her life and the four children they both adored beyond the telling of it draw close, that was happiness.

True happiness wasn't one thing. It wasn't static. It was layered and deep, forever changing in the light. It was all the colors, feelings and frustrations of each moment and the broader life around it, wound together into the same tight knot.

The secret to life wasn't holding that knot in one place. It was learning how to do the knotting in the first place and then keep doing it, day after day. Year after year. To get up when knocked down, brush herself off, and do it all over again.

Happiness was in the details. Joy was all around.

Balthazar smiled at her as he approached, because gone was that grim, cold, intimidating man she'd met long ago. This Balthazar smiled. He even laughed. He was still fierce in business, demanding in bed, but best of all, he was happy.

They were happy.

They had built on to the cottage over time, adding space for their family, but still maintaining Great-Aunt Rosemary's cozy aesthetic. Tonight, they ate together out beneath a trellis wrapped in wisteria, breathing in the glory of the Provence summer. Just as Kendra's favorite great-aunt must have done herself.

And after the children had gone to sleep, Kendra and Balthazar sat out there together. Beneath the quiet stars, Kendra took her favorite seat. His lap.

"You seem particularly pleased with yourself, *agápi mou*," Balthazar murmured, though his attention was on the line of her neck as he tasted his way down the length of it. "It makes me wonder what you can possibly be thinking about."

Kendra was thinking about that gazebo, long ago. How overwhelmed she'd been. How thunderstruck.

She was thinking of the night she'd surrendered her innocence on that desk in New York that they had returned to again and again over time. Christening it repeatedly, because they could. Because the heat between them only grew.

God, how it grew.

She was thinking of the island, where they spent as

much time as they could, grounding themselves in the quiet. In the peace.

And using the altar where they'd made their vows, first to a priest and then to each other, as a touchstone. A talisman. A way to remind themselves who they were. Who they wanted to be, come what may.

"Tell me," Balthazar urged her, his voice dark and hot, and she could feel his smile against her skin.

"What am I always thinking about?" When he lifted his head, she smiled at him, more in love now that she'd ever known a person could be. And she could see the same reflected back at her, always. "Revenge, Balthazar. Sweet, sweet revenge."

"I love you," he told her.

"I love you, too," she whispered.

And then he showed her exactly how much he loved her, the way he always did, muffling her cries against his chest.

Just as Kendra showed him the same in return. The way she always would, until he groaned into the crook of her neck.

Because, as always, love was the best revenge of all.

* * * * *

MILLS & BOON

Coming next month

CINDERELLA'S NIGHT IN VENICE
Clare Connelly

As the car slowed to go over a speed hump, his fingers briefly fell to her shoulder. An accident of transit, nothing intentional about it. The reason didn't matter though; the spark of electricity was the same regardless. She gasped and quickly turned her face away, looking beyond the window.

It was then that she realized they had driven through the gates of City Airport.

Bea turned back to face Ares, a question in her eyes.

'There's a ball at the airport?'

'No.'

'Then why…?' Comprehension was a blinding light. 'We're flying somewhere.'

'To the ball.'

'But…you didn't say…'

'I thought you were good at reading between the lines?'

She pouted her lips. 'Yes, you're right.' She clicked her fingers in the air. 'I should have miraculously intuited that when you invited me to a ball you meant for us to fly there. Where, exactly?'

'Venice.'

'Venice?' She stared at him, aghast. 'I don't have a passport.'

'I had your assistant arrange it.'

'You—what? When?'

'When I left this morning.'

'My assistant just handed over my passport?'

'You have a problem with that?'

'Well, gee, let me think about that a moment,' she said, tapping a finger to the side of her lip. 'You're a man I'd never clapped eyes on until yesterday and now you have in your possession a document that's of reasonably significant personal importance. You could say I find that a little invasive, yes.'

He dropped his hand from the back of the seat, inadvertently brushing her arm as he moved, lifting a familiar burgundy document from his pocket. 'Now you have it in your possession. It was no conspiracy to kidnap you, Beatrice, simply a means to an end.'

Clutching the passport in her hand, she stared down at it. No longer bothered by the fact he'd managed to convince her assistant to commandeer a document of such personal importance from her top drawer, she was knocked off-kilter by his use of her full name. Nobody called her Beatrice any more. She'd been Bea for as long as she could remember. But her full name on his lips momentarily shoved the air from her lungs.

'Why didn't you just tell me?'

He lifted his shoulders. 'I thought you might say no.'

It was an important clue as to how he operated. This was a man who would do what he needed to achieve whatever he wanted. He'd chosen to invite her to this event, and so he'd done what he deemed necessary to have her there.

'Your business is too important to our company, remember?' She was grateful for the opportunity to remind them both of the reason she'd agreed to this. It had nothing to do with the fact she found him attractive, and everything to do with how much she loved her friends and wanted the company to continue to succeed.

'And that's the only reason you agreed to this,' he said in a deep voice, perfectly calling her bluff. Was she that obvious? Undoubtedly.

Continue reading
CINDERELLA'S NIGHT IN VENICE
Clare Connelly

Available next month
www.millsandboon.co.uk

COMING SOON!

We really hope you enjoyed reading this book.
If you're looking for more romance, be sure to
head to the shops when new books are
available on

Thursday 15th April

To see which titles are coming soon, please visit
millsandboon.co.uk/nextmonth

MILLS & BOON

THE HEART OF ROMANCE

A ROMANCE FOR EVERY READER

MODERN

Prepare to be swept off your feet by sophisticated, sexy and seductive heroes, in some of the world's most glamourous and romantic locations, where power and passion collide.

HISTORICAL

Escape with historical heroes from time gone by. Whether your passion is for wicked Regency Rakes, muscled Vikings or rugged Highlanders, awaken the romance of the past.

MEDICAL

Set your pulse racing with dedicated, delectable doctors in the high-pressure world of medicine, where emotions run high and passion, comfort and love are the best medicine.

True Love

Celebrate true love with tender stories of heartfelt romance, from the rush of falling in love to the joy a new baby can bring, and a focus on the emotional heart of a relationship.

Desire

Indulge in secrets and scandal, intense drama and plenty of sizzling hot action with powerful and passionate heroes who have it all: wealth, status, good looks…everything but the right woman.

HEROES

Experience all the excitement of a gripping thriller, with an intense romance at its heart. Resourceful, true-to-life women and strong, fearless men face danger and desire - a killer combination!

To see which titles are coming soon, please visit

millsandboon.co.uk/nextmonth